You Know It's True

By J.R. Hamantaschen

INTRODUCTION

Thank you so much for choosing to read my newest collection, "The Insufferable and Unendurable Agony of Existence That I Cannot Wait to Escape." I first of course need to thank my doting partner, my children (without whom I'd be lost), my supportive parents, the university where I work that allowed me to complete this collection while on my months-long sabbatical, and . . .

Oh enough of that shit, of course I'm just fucking with you all, having a bit of fun at the cushy sinecures and contented family lives some of my contemporaries return to when they aren't misery LARPing. Let's move on from that and wonder why we find ourselves here, at the introduction to a book that should not be. But not in the fun Lovecraftian way, but an actual book that I'd previously indicated should not actually exist.

Eagle-eyed readers of mine may remember that in the introduction to my previous collection, I wrote [checks notes] "this will likely be my last for the foreseeable future, as I move onto longer works" and called the collection a "fitting end point." So, what happened?

A good question that I don't have an answer to, although I have some theories. I suppose those "longer works" are still out there somewhere, being perfect, in the sense that all things are perfect before their final actualization. The answer for why there is a fourth collection may be mundane. I had some more stories to tell. More interesting is comparing the last collection and this one, my actual, definite, 100% last collection.

My previous collection, *A Deep Horror That Was Very Nearly Awe*, had some hopeful aspects: maybe that's just natural in what was intended to be my last collection, you know, send my long-time readers out with some hope for growth, possibility, a brighter tomorrow.[1] All that shit. Well, things haven't worked out too well for humble ole J.R., so forgive me if some of that latent and oh so natural and comforting mean-spiritedness came back in spades. Enough so for a fourth story collection, at least.

---

[1] I don't want to overstate it, though, I mean the collection was still called "A Deep Horror That Was Very Nearly Awe" and had some dark stories, although maybe they were not as vicious or despairing as the first two collections.

Well, again I don't want to sway you in any such way or create any expectations I might not be able to meet. I should let the stories speak for themselves, for better or worse. But since this is actually my last collection, I'll have a little bit more fun with it, and I've added short postscripts to each story to let you know where it came from or just report any old thing that popped into my head.

As always, I can be reached at Jrtaschen@gmail.com. I'm always just an email away. In addition to my previous three collections, *You Shall Never Know Security*, *With a Voice that is Often Still Confused But is Becoming Ever Louder and Clearer*, and *A Deep Horror That Was Very Nearly Awe*, I also host a weekly podcast called *The Horror of Nachos and Hamantaschen*, where I bloviate about horror movies, horror fiction, and general horror "culture" with my trusty co-host Derek Sotak.

And I've never understood the point of an Acknowledgements Page (who the fuck cares where these stories were previously published?), but I would like to thank those magazines and institutions that have published some of these stories and supported my work: The NoSleep Podcast, Drabblecast, PseudoPod, Signal Horizon, Soteria Press, Chthonic Matter, Novel Noctule, and The H.P. Lovecraft Literary Podcast, and all the people who have emailed me, rated or reviewed any work of mine, or hung out with me at a convention. That's literally it: everyone else is against me.

See you in the postscripts.

Sincerely,
J.R. Hamantaschen
Jrtaschen@gmail.com

Promoting my work hasn't worked for years, but what do they say about the definition of insanity? Who has time to look that up!

"You may 'never know security' on an existential level, but don't let that stop you from buying an Express VPN to protect your internet searches from hackers! That's some kind of security, right?" – Hey, I gotta sell out a just a little bit to make those boffo bucks, after all.

psyche...[the] stories are the kind that tend to stick with readers after the reading is over." - HP Lovecraft eZine

"I have never read anything like this, and I don't know if I ever will. A very high recommendation." - 30 Second Sci-Fi Book Review

"J.R. Hamantaschen's 'You Shall Never Know Security' is one of the best dark fiction collections ever published. It contains fascinating, disturbing and beautifully written stories that range all the way from dark fantasy to horror." - Rising Shadow Magazine

"In all of the above, the author delivers powerful, ugly images, using a battery of verbal pyrotechnics that make the stories demand to be read carefully. Buried in the razzle-dazzle language are clues to the intended meaning. If horror is your poison of choice, these will definitely fill the bill." - Innsmouth Free Press

"J.R. Hamantaschen's 'You Shall Never Know Security' hit me almost immediately with that frisson; the first few pages, the first few stories, crackling with a kind of morbid energy ... the reader will know from the first page whether this collection will enrapture or repel, those in the former camp having found something they have no doubt been starved of and scavenging after for some time." - Ginger Nuts of Horror

"Many regard [this book] as a gem of horror lit. We're inclined to agree." - Space Squid

"J.R. Hamantaschen won't be underground for long." - HorrorWorld (this review gets more and more bittersweet with the passage of time)

"I would urge you to keep on writing. You clearly have a nucleus of talent." - S.T. Joshi, in an email after he said he had mixed feelings about two of my stories. I consider this high praise.

PRAISE FOR MY SECOND COLLECTION "WITH A VOICE THAT IS OFTEN STILL CONFUSED BUT IS BECOMING EVER LOUDER AND CLEARER"

"A brilliant and vital addition to the landscape of dark fiction…It's not often a collection of this caliber comes around." - HellNotes

"Perturbing, anomalous stories that will bore into readers' minds." - Kirkus

"True, great horror. I love this book." - Chris Lackey, HP Lovecraft Literary Podcast

"9 out of 10 ... there are nine tales in this collection, each of satisfying length and immediately striking, from first page to last… stories that will grip you for their humanity and soul." - Starburst Magazine

"Hamantaschen has a knack for crafting what seems to be an unwieldy tale, but plies it with enough realism and logic to make it work. The ridiculous even seems at home next to the cynical and down-to-earth. His tales are peopled by real and richly crafted characters." - Shock Totem Magazine

"An excellent follow-up to the author's debut collection ... It's one of the most impressive dark fiction collections of the year, because it's fascinatingly different from other collections and contains beautifully written stories ... an exceptionally good and original dark fiction collection that deserves to be read by fans of the darker side of speculative fiction. It's a perfect marriage of literary fiction and dark fiction." - Rising Shadow Magazine

"4 out of 5 stars ... Overall, I enjoyed this collection of short stories ... [t]he stories certainly stayed with me for a few days after reading it." - Literary Titan (pretty lukewarm-sounding for 4 out of 5 stars but whatever).

"4 out of 5 stars." - Scream Magazine

"Eclectic, poignant, thought provoking ... too awesome to pass up." - HorrorTalk

"Those who an artistic approach, psychological depth and small details are going to read through this collection and remember it for days to come." - HorrorPalace

"This book is filled with many horrors and some pretty deep and disturbing stories. It may not be for everyone, as any book may or may not, but I found it intriguing and enjoyable." - The Scary Reviews

"Resonating, delectably weird and spooky collection, thoroughly enjoyable." - IndieReader (received Official IndieReader Stamp of Approval)

"Readers would benefit greatly by taking a gander at Hamantaschen's mix of stories that lead from one cold dank corner to another." - HorrorNews Network

PRAISE FOR MY THIRD COLLECTION "A DEEP HORROR THAT WAS VERY NEARLY AWE"

"It discomforts, challenges and refuses to mollycoddle the reader, instead unleashing a torrent of brilliantly-written, intensely imaginative stories that are embedded in the vagaries and horrors to be found in the human condition. Not only is this a fantastic collection of weird horror short stories, it is a gut-punch to the brain and the emotions that leaves you disturbed and uncertain, yet sincerely glad to have read it." - The Sci-Fi and Fantasy Reviewer

"The King of Autistic Horror" - Telling It Like It Is Magazine / AKA Have You Ever Met The Guy?

"They're very hard to categorize, exceptionally strange, make unpredictable plot jumps, are often very nasty, funny, and usually have unpleasant endings. All the necessary ingredients for high quality dark fiction short story writing." - Ink Heist Magazine

"If you love dark fiction and modern weird fiction, J.R. Hamantaschen's A Deep Horror That Was Very Nearly Awe should be at the top of your reading list. This collection is one of the best collections available for quality-oriented readers who want to read good stories, so please, don't hesitate to read it." - Rising Shadow Magazine

"J.R. do I have to sneak into your praise section to get you to return my calls? I'm worried about you, I don't understand why you've discontinued our sessions, is it because I've diagnosed you as on the spectrum or because all the advice I've offered is complete dogshit? Why not tell me about your childhood again I bet that's the ticket! Please, answer me, my kids' college tuition depends upon your sweet, sweet insurance money!" - Every Therapist I've Ever Had

"All the stories in A Deep Horror That Was Very Nearly Awe are highly engaging. Hamantaschen has a way of writing that completely draws you in and makes you feel something–anything–for all his characters." - <u>Monster Librarian</u>

"Its 11 stories bring out a range of emotions from sadness to laughter and anger to glee. If you've never read anything by Hamantaschen, this is a great place to get introduced to his work before you'll want to buy what comes from him next." - <u>HorrorDNA</u>

"Another rock solid collection from J.R. Hamantaschen...J.R. has a way of making the normal seem horrific and frightening and really nails it . . disturbing and scary." - <u>H.P. Lovecraft Literary Podcast</u>

"Without a doubt my favorite read of 2018 . . . [n]ot every book I read is good. And not every good book I read becomes a favorite. But sometimes, you get lucky. Sometimes, you find something that makes you wanna talk. A Deep Horror That Was Very Near Awe is the start of a conversation—and I have a feeling that as the readers grow, the chatter will roar." - <u>Signal Horizon Magazine</u>

"We disclaim J.R. because he unnecessarily allowed a hanging sentence from his Praise section to bleed onto the next page, thereby inefficiently requiring another page to be wasted." -<u>The Union of Uptight Manuscript Formatters</u>

You Know It's True

By J.R. Hamantaschen

"I believe!" Margarita whispered solemnly. "I believe! Something will happen! It cannot not happen, because for what, indeed, has lifelong torment been sent to me? I admit that I lied and deceived and lived a secret life, hidden from people, but all the same the punishment for it cannot be so cruel . . . Something is bound to happen, because it cannot be that anything will go on forever." – The Master and Margarita

CONTENTS

I Should Have Been A Pair Of Ragged Claws / Scuttling Across The Floors Of Silent Seas

Evelyn knew that her son Jerry always liked birds. They were his first fixation – every parent remembers each of their child's first fixation – so at a young age he would prattle on, almost mechanically, about the capacity of a crow to remember a human face, how ravens could mimic human speech, how owls ate their prey whole. He hadn't used such sophisticated language, of course; the precise way he expressed his love for the creatures was lost to time.

When he turned twelve, she bought him a parakeet. (Or a budgie, as Jerry insisted they were properly called in their native Australia; how smart he was, so said the teenage girl behind the counter.) Of course they had to buy a parakeet for Andrea, their nine-year-old daughter, because fair is fair, and pledge to get one for Kyle, then six, when he got old enough to take care of it (an offer he never redeemed).

Was Jerry happy with the blue and green "budgie" that his parents, after some resistance, allowed him to name Bruno? Hard to tell; maybe for a bit. He admired Bruno, enjoyed taking him out to fly around the bathroom, giving him food sticks and watching the bird peck. When Andrea was going to have her bird fly around the bathroom, that's when Jerry needed to let Bruno out, too, and he liked to play Bruno's bodyguard, saying "hey hey hey!" and separating Bruno with an oven mitt if Bruno and Andrea's bird, a bright yellow thing she named Oskar, nipped at each other. Jerry seemed most engaged when the opportunity came to intervene.

But Bruno would peck at Jerry sometimes, and Jerry reciprocated with inanition, letting the bird go too long without food or water or cage-cleaning to the point that he became the "family bird" until Jerry promised his mother he'd be more responsible. Jerry from then on fulfilled his obligations dutifully, by all appearances, although the frequency with which he'd take the bird out lessened each year. How to account for why Jerry remained so abstractly interested in birds, and less-so with the real article; as if he'd been found out in something, he expressed his interest in birds less-and-less, although the same could be said, as he got older, about all topics.

So imagine Bruno broke free from his cage and flew around the household right now, if the poor wheezy bird could still fly for so long. What would he see, as he went from room to room? Evelyn bawling, screaming and nashing, her husband Patrick holding her, so frustratingly stoic. Bruno would see Andrea, now fourteen, and Kyle, too, now eleven, and what would he see of them in their unguarded moments? Relief, indifference? The bird would notice, perhaps with some pleasure, that Jerry was nowhere to be seen.

Would the bird intuit what it saw? If so, would it feel a satisfaction at the calamity, at the grief, payback for his lonely nights shivering in Jerry's room, payback for his inapposite name? No, sweet Bruno, of course not. Why would it enjoy Evelyn's despondency, the woman who oft-cleaned him and would give him a food stick; or Andrea's anguish, the girl who let Bruno flutter about with another of his kind; or Patrick's brittle attempts at maintaining some semblance of composure. Would Kyle have any evident emotion that required deciphering?

Is it worth discussing the other members of the family, their passions, their pursuits, the trajectory their life was taking up to this point?

No, not now. Bruno would fly out, leave this family to their grieving, much as we will now, it's too grueling.

Because Jerry, at the age of seventeen, on the cusp of graduating high school, is dead.

He killed himself, without even whatever quantum of closure might be provided with a suicide note.

*

Let's check back, it's been a month.

When she'd found him, Evelyn had made sure to knock several times. You always had to knock several times because Jerry relished privacy, and expected that preference honored. Evelyn would give languorous, patient knocks, enough time for Jerry to stop whatever he was doing, assemble himself; Patrick would give one or two solid knocks that doubled as

2

commands; Andrea, hers were rapid-fire, impatient knocks in quick succession, the knocks of someone never eager to approach; Kyle's, respectful if unnatural knocks, timid, with deferential pauses.

Evelyn had knocked enough. Opening the door and finding him hanging there was the equivalent of watching him kill himself; it all came in a rush, she could see it, in the afterimages:

The plummet, the tensile arc of his swing, his tongue squirting out in an almost comical grimace, so strange to see that enigmatic face of his so definite, now so unchanging. In some versions of the imagining there was an exaggerated crunch-crash of his neck snapping, instant death; better than some alternatives she saw, his desperate, futile kicks to right himself back on the stepladder. To deepen the wound, she thought despite herself, that to witness those kicks would have been perhaps the first and only time she'd ever seen him zealously *try* to do anything. And what a Jerry outcome, wasn't it: hopeless failure.

Who would have thought you could tie bed sheets to the motor housing of a ceiling fan? Jerry was a skinny boy, but certainly he weighed too much for the fan to withstand; but, grimly, guess not, you can't argue with results. She had never imagined him capable of displaying such physical ingenuity to tie such a stable knot, execute such a plan. He was never a Boy Scout, had worn Velcro sneakers until he was ten.

This is too much. We need to come back after some scabs have formed over these wounds.

*

"My problem is, if I had to sum it up in one issue, is I know I have problems, but I don't value myself enough to do anything about them, I guess. So I continue to suffer but won't do anything about it to lessen my suffering because I always feel like, what's the point?" Jerry said, months before his eventual suicide, as he leaned on his elbows while sitting atop a wooden table in the park, staring into the dreary, cloudy middle distance that lay beyond his outstretched feet.

Graham nodded solemnly, standing behind the table. "That makes sense, and isn't uncommon, unfortunately. This sounds terribly clichéd – and I know how you hate clichés – but some clichés are clichés because truth bears so much repeating. No one hates us as much as we hate ourselves."

Jerry blinked, and then, realizing he was being looked at, nodded. "But some people truly deserve to feel the way they feel. Maybe the suffering, the self-hatred I feel, I deserve it."

Graham looked thoughtful, a slight bob to his head, as if he had to let the speaker know that every sentence uttered in his direction was independently analyzed and computed. "If someone was truly disliked by many, many people, essentially a type of pariah in their community, it would behoove them to better understand why that was. There is great wisdom in a crowd, especially as it comes to why a community of people reject someone, which, to a healthy-minded person, should indicate that there very well may be something about themselves they need to change. We know all about the wisdom of a community, after all."

Jerry signaled his agreement.

"But for you Jerry, the hatred is internal. Your trouble is a self-imposed isolation and loneliness, of pushing people away, not of being actively rejected. You know that, we've talked about that. The reason you do that is because you think you are better than other people, smarter than them. You value intelligence, you recognize your own intelligence and find the mass of others lacking, and that causes you to devalue them."

Jerry bobbed his head again in agreement, the movement helping to conceal his involuntary eye roll. He'd heard all this before, although he recognized its truth. But there was something to be said about novelty.

"Let me ask you Jerry, why are you sitting on top of the picnic table instead of standing here with me?"

Jerry looked back over his shoulder at Graham, then looked again toward the chilly, unused playground.

Before he could ready a response, Graham placed the tips of the fingers of this left hand to his temple and prognosticated: "let me fancy a guess."

"Ok, you do that." Good, this would save Jerry the effort of having to think of something snappy to say.

"First, sitting on top of a picnic table in a park, that's something you aren't supposed to be doing, and there's something you like about distinguishing yourself, even if there's no one else here, because you are still doing something you aren't supposed to be doing. Second, your stance, I see you adjusted yourself to be leaning on your elbows, a kind of cliché casual bad-boy stance, which reinforces your own perception of yourself as outside the ordinary, and from your elevated position it's almost like you are looking down in disdain. And third, or maybe more like as an added bonus, instead of facing me you are facing that playground that's not being used, which I am sure reminds you of the ticky-tack, dreadfully boring suburban environment you can't wait to escape."

Waiting a beat, Jerry asked, "done?"

"So how'd I do?"

"It was more that I just didn't want to be seen walking around with a middle-aged man. For your own protection, you know, doesn't look good."

Graham laughed. Jerry adjusted his position, first sitting up, then descending from the table altogether. He was perceptive, this Graham. Jerry didn't like that feeling of being summed up and explained. It made him feel diminutive, reduced. Even if it wasn't entirely accurate, it *appeared* accurate, and that perception of accuracy made him feel self-conscious. Especially not when there was an undeniable grain of truth – more than a grain, really, more like a half a bushel of truth – but there was much that Graham was missing, and Jerry didn't want to invite continued probing.

Now that Jerry was off the table, Graham came over to him and, with his typical brio of homey, comfortable atavism, shook Jerry's hand.

"I want you to stick around, friend. There are reasons for you to stay. Your life is important, and so are you, even if you don't believe it yet. You aren't going to kill yourself."

"I won't."

"Say it. I want to hear it from you."

Jerry smiled cavalierly.

5

Graham pressed on. "I get it, us depressed people hate sincerity. But still, you know the drill, I want to hear you say it."

"You know I won't kill myself."

"No one knows anything. That's the point of this, as you know, of us meeting, of us all meeting together, our community. It's important."

"I know it is. It isn't easy finding you all, as you know."

"We know. That's intentional."

"Yeah you are only for the doomed cases, the tough ones, the SWAT Team of Suicide Prevention."

Graham bellowed a laugh, a genuine laugh that revealed, in hindsight, that his previous laugh rang a bit hollow, a bit forced. "I like that. Well, you're still here, and you haven't tried anything since, have you." It wasn't framed as a question.

"I haven't."

"So we're doing something right. I'd tell you that we've never had a member of our support group relapse–"

"I'd believe that, for sure–"

"But I don't like saying that because I feel like that might have the unintended consequence of encouraging someone to be the first. You know us, we all think we're so unique."

Jerry made a face to suggest he understood. "If that ever happened for that reason, well, then you'd have to re-evaluate your admissions committee."

As they left toward Graham's car, Jerry looked back at that ticky-tack playground, and both admired Graham's perspicuity while resenting his conclusion: this town was fucking lame, and these people within were, for the most part, stupid, vain, and fundamentally sloppy, in their emotions and intellect. They lacked possession of themselves, and it greatly depressed him to have to go out and function in their world.

Well, he had Graham here, and the others, his online companions, that formed his band of brothers, which at various times assumed the roles of emotional support group, philosophical debate club, or simply his other world he could lose himself in.

That wasn't nothing.

Sure.

*

It's now approximately three months after Jerry's suicide, and something like the new normal has settled upon the family. As a family unit, they attract that aura of attendant sympathy wherever they go, whoever they talk to. They could fail to bring a gift to a housewarming party, or foodstuff to a potluck, or forget to pick someone up, and no one would dare say anything. Not that Andrea took advantage of this, but she could fail to hand in an assignment and have an accepted excuse-at-the-ready.

Everyone processed things differently. No one wanted to go to therapy. Evelyn wanted to scream at them to do so, if only because that's the thing you are supposed to do. She wanted to grab Andrea by the hair and scream at her for never getting along with her brother, even though no one got along with Jerry, and Andrea's approach toward him – reactive, tentative, wary – had been empirically sound.

Was that true, did Jerry not get along with anybody? He'd had friends when he was younger, he could be sharp-witted and clever when he wanted to be, he was a smart boy. He read a lot and spent all day on his computer and playing video games and had friends online. She'd seen him, heard him, talking with people on his headset while playing some shooting games on his PlayStation, and she figured that some communication was better than nothing.

The youngest, Kyle, that nonentity. Truth be told equal attention can't be paid to every child. Kyle had always stayed away from the Jerry-Andrea drama, never had any opinions, didn't want to get involved, silently and unshowily did what was right and what was expected of him, acquired the appropriate interests and temperament, as if just enough to keep appearances without attracting scrutiny. With his silence and withdrawal, Evelyn sometimes just imagined him literally counting down the days until he could leave. He shared that with his departed brother, the feeling that behind closed doors he'd let out a big sigh of relief and pursue some interests he deigned to keep to himself.

Evelyn wanted to curse her husband, his temperament being so quietly reasonable and grounded, his refrains of 'what can we do,' and that nagging feeling that he had processed this, was further along in the healing process and, worst of all, his unflagging, infuriating patience. It was as if her dedication to this emotional wretchedness and profound hopelessness at the loss of her son was the talismanic proof of her love, and was somehow deserved recompense for all the things she hadn't properly done: she didn't poke and prod and investigate enough, she didn't shape his development enough, she wasn't engaged enough in his life, wasn't that it? Why else would a seventeen-year-old, one who never had to worry about money, who wasn't being physically or sexually abused, who had nothing to escape from, do such a thing? By not wallowing alongside her, it was as if her husband was agreeing that the burden of the shame was properly allocated among the deserving parties.

But what are you supposed to do? You can't be a helicopter parent. Was it worth it, for her to have kept her distance, fearful of Jerry's every dismissive, unkind word; was it worth it, her submission in the face of his recalcitrant refusal to reveal; was it worth it, avoiding those eyes rolls, the worst thing she thought he could ever do with his eyes until she found them jutting, distended and now literally lifeless. Apparently, even in death she couldn't avoid his look of ghoulish judgment and disdain.

That neck cracking, those eyes positively lunging from their sockets.

*

It was approximately one month later, and Andrea felt frozen. She knew she needed to proceed carefully. Evelyn, after sitting on the couch next to her under some pretense of small-talk, had just asked her if she knew any of Jerry's friends at school she could talk to about him. Mom had wisely and immediately broadened that request, saving Andrea from the awkwardness of letting it dawn upon Mom that Jerry truly didn't have any close friends.

Mom had, of course, been at the funeral. None of the kids from school who attended could honestly be described as Jerry's friends, in the classical meaning of the word. Family friends; Andrea's friends, Kyle's friends, people who casually knew Jerry and paid him no mind. Sure, many of them knew Jerry and had nothing bad to say; of course, who could say anything bad at a funeral? But likely there was nothing conceivably bad they *could* say, because Jerry kept to himself.

Was there anyone, Mom insisted? Anyone Mom could talk to who . . . the obvious explanation was that Mom was still, and perhaps forever would be, riddled with guilt. Andrea blanched, sensed a dismantling of the assumed understandings that separate parents from children. It was almost frightening: parents provided guidance and made the rules, and inherent in that guidance was the expectation that it would be exercised appropriately. That Mom's request was so transparently a bad idea chilled Andrea to the bone; this was someone she loved, relied upon and trusted, and that the Mother she loved and relied upon so much could be so wrong was a very harrowing thought indeed. So tenuous was the stability that kept the family unit functioning: she imagined no food in the fridge, the family phones cut off due to lack of payment, her Mother on the corner of her bed, knees to the chest, rocking back and forth babbling to herself.

"I can try and find out," was the best Andrea could offer.

Mom smiled weakly and placed her hand warmly on Andrea's face. "Thank you."

Andrea saw then the stable, competent Mom she knew, and Andrea smiled back, as if forgetting that this wasn't the first time that Mom had pursued this doomed inquiry. Mom, so competent, only wanted to hear that Andrea understood and would help and that would be enough. That Mom then asked what Andrea wanted from the grocery store, confirming with her that she'd get Andrea's requested mozzarella sticks, tangerines and crunchy peanut butter, furthered that impression, because here was Normal Mom discussing normal, healthy Mom things.

*

In the parking lot of the Key Food, after the car was turned off and she should be getting out, Evelyn found herself instead unable to move, hands wrapped tightly against the steering wheel, seeking to bend it. She unclenched her hands.

What was she doing? She was a self-possessed, analytical woman. She was frustrated, and in quixotically rending the steering wheel there was that primal satisfaction of physical exertion, of directing that bottled energy elsewhere. Andrea couldn't be relied on to look into anything, Evelyn knew, because no one can be relied upon to do what you want to be done, with the effort you require, other than yourself.

But such activities weren't fruitful, she knew. Just think about it, look at yourself in some imagined third-person perspective. Is this a healthy approach, to sit parked in a Key Food parking lot death-gripping a steering wheel while some geriatric townie gives you the side eye as she pushes her shopping cart of canned soups and cranberry juice or whatever the fuck to her SUV?

No, of course not.

The uncontrollable thing about terrific loss is that the weight of it can creep upon you so impassively, so surreptitiously, and then suddenly it's occupying your gut, your heart, so solidly and so completely. The reality of her son's death, so very briefly forgotten beneath the muddle of her pep talk, reasserted itself with total primacy: your son is dead, and that fact won't change. Psych yourself back up all you like, but that fact reigns supreme.

Still, she got out, fighting through the tears, believing somehow they'd stop because they had to stop, because people didn't cry going into grocery stores. Through the misty veil she acknowledged, remotely and distantly as if observing it on behalf of someone else, a great black shape speeding toward her from her periphery. She paused, instincts taking over, took a colossal gallop backward as a black SUV seemed to swerve toward her. Her heart in her chest, she heard no honk, no screech of tires, became only aware of, bizarrely, some different old biddy, with a crown of soft white hair, silently putting her hands to her half-open mouth in a classic look of shock. The driver of the black SUV only seemed to regain control of its momentum as it pulled toward the curb to exit the parking lot.

Evelyn stayed put, caught her breath, felt the onlook of strangers and sensed the shaking of their head, intuited the murmurings of "can you believe that?" In an alternative world, she thought subconsciously, where Evelyn had ended up splattered in the Key Food parking lot, there'd be at least one good-hearted woman who'd speak truthfully and honestly to the police about what she'd witnessed. And then reality reasserted itself again, and she clenched her stomach, dreading that old biddy coming over to her and asking her if she was be alright, and to think Evelyn could cry and emote and that innocent beautiful woman would think it was because of the outpouring of pent-up relief from that close-call with the SUV, and how lovely it would be to pour out all her feelings upon someone who knew nothing about her.

Evelyn realized with dread that, with the throat-clenching drama gone, what else could she do but go into the store and get her family's groceries?

*

Jerry had shaken hands with all four of them. Graham he knew, of course. Each of their meetings had ended with a handshake, Graham's belief that tactile exchanges had a stabilizing, grounding effect, like a commitment. Until next time, the assumed pledge that there will be a next time.

In a sense, he knew the other three, also, but had never met them in the flesh before. The man he knew online as "Acer" was Steven, probably the closest to his age at twenty-four. "Bizarro" was a well-kempt, fit but otherwise anodyne middle-aged Eric, and "Moebius" was a non-distinct Dan. They'd all traveled some ways to meet Jerry, and, while he was convinced he was intellectually indifferent to social expectations, in reality his palms were sweaty and his heart was racing. He was already accepted, he told himself, but with online interactions he could be collected, calibrated, an expression of pure intellect. Online, he could be charming, comforting and stimulating – as many a cyber-sex partner could attest – but with physical presence came concerns about appearance, his ego, his haughtiness, or just his inherent alien, discomfiting otherness that couldn't be camouflaged.

But if any group of people should understand, it should be them.

"I've been thinking for a while before this meeting," Jerry began, and had the temptation to bail on the opener but he was locked in now, "that it'd be ironic if the sheer pressure and anxiety of a meeting like this would be the impetus for a candidate to off themselves."

They all smiled and laughed.

"Ever think of that?"

"That's never happened before, although I guess that's something new for us to have to worry about," said Eric, unseriously.

"Well, with how our system works, I don't think we need to lose too much sleep about it," said Steven, smiling. "With our terms, our people have to be pretty committed. So don't get any ideas, buddy."

"You can say whatever you like about how extreme it all is, but one thing you can't deny is that commitment is kind of baked into this whole enterprise," added Dan after a pause.

"You can say that again," was Jerry's knowing contribution, like he was an old guy commiserating with his friends about the same ole shit, the weather or untrustworthy politicians or other common pablum. Funny how he hated himself for that comment. Guys all shooting the shit with pitter-patter, the supposed comfort of group acceptance, the strained and forced overreactions and smiles to the banal, the rituals of small-talk. Funny, this suicide support group, certainly the most dedicated and capable such group that ever existed, always reminded him of his inescapable exhaustion with life. Not out of high school and already saturated with embitteredness. He couldn't imagine ever being free of it because the disgust and the tedium was part of – baked into, to borrow Dan's phrase – the whole enterprise of social interaction.

This support group might have worked better if it remained entirely online, although with the type of commitment entrants to its inner circle needed to make, he could understand the idea, at least, about meeting in person. He bet all these guys thought he should be impressed with the sacrifice they were making in traveling however far they traveled to come meet him. He should reflect graciousness, which they should expect, but not overdo it. In conniving, he forgot the clambering, awkward parts of himself.

Graham, as Jerry's ambassador of sorts, made eye contact with whomever was speaking throughout the meeting, and, as everything was going cordially, mostly nodded sagaciously and deeply in concert with everyone's points, redoubling his efforts when it was Jerry doing the speaking.

When the expected lull came, Jerry spoke passionately about how the group's support had helped him, had kept him alive at his darkest times . . . Jerry paused, corrected himself to explain that to describe it as darkest times was misleading, because that implied one distinct low point, when the truth of the matter was that he lived perpetually at the low point, like a little crab "scuttling around the bottom of the sea floor."

"If I think about it intellectually, which I do often, ruminating endlessly and obsessively," – and here the others chuckled, because of course they knew what Jerry meant – "I still come to the same conclusion. I don't, intellectually and objectively, think there is any reason to live. I don't believe in God or Heaven and Hell or a higher power," and of course they all knew he wasn't saying anything that they all didn't agree with.

"But still, I remain here, I persist, if you will, with your help, this group's help, and that's an act of faith, in a sense. I'm not my thoughts, but separate from them. Meditation, self-reflection, exercise, obligation, commitment, tethering myself to reality, faith in action, and I can't, I can't necessarily intellectually validate why this should work but I suppose results speak for themselves and I find it interesting and I'm still here," and, after Jerry finished, they again all chuckled, because again, he wasn't saying anything they themselves didn't daily struggle with and struggle against.

"Process," Steven started, after a dignified pause. "That's what it is. You understand, it's a process. You do the process, your thoughts – destructive thoughts, at least – subside, and you feel better. It is a type of faith, as you say, but faith with results. You don't argue against it, you just accept the negative thoughts as what they are, thoughts, only thoughts, separate from yourself, that come and go randomly like waves in the ocean."

Steven spoke solemnly, as you couldn't be too doctrinaire in explaining anything to the congenitally suicidal, who, by temperament, were skeptical and dismissive.

"It's when you think 'I can't live with myself anymore' that helps to articulate the tension, how in a sense your thoughts are separate and apart from who you are. When you think that, who is the 'I' and who is the 'myself?' You commit to us, and you do what's expected of you, and over time it gets better."

Steven's comments about thoughts coming and going randomly like the waves in the ocean bothered Jerry, because while Jerry didn't know the exact science behind it, certainly waves didn't appear "randomly," but were caused by the wind or the moon or temperature differentials or some shit like that. But he suppressed the rising heat he felt, and when he spoke about the group prolonging his life, the words came easily because what he said was all true, or, said in another way, had he not found this group, he would have killed himself some time ago.

*

Sunday, and the family was making a day of miniature golf. It was that odd type of outing that hovered between obligation and recreation, one that no one seemed to want to partake in but for no good reason. Kyle was withdrawn, his usual fear of failure that now extended even to missed putts. Andrea was more outgoing recently, and spent more time with friends, which Evelyn hated her for.

As if Andrea's years of proximity to Jerry had been whittling her away, and now she was unencumbered by the burdens of her deceased brother, refreshed and rejuvenated for other people. Evelyn kept half-expecting Andrea to start wearing more revealing clothes, because isn't that what teenage daughters do when they are acting out or spreading their wings or sending a message, and it almost angered Evelyn that Andrea wasn't doing so, but was rather perfectly well-adjusted, and, just maybe, was only responding rationally to the absence of someone who had made her life largely disagreeable. It was as if Jerry was no longer here to express his thoughts about Andrea's vapidity and simplemindedness, and with his departure Evelyn, out of some misplaced loyalty, stored his thoughts in her mind.

Evelyn could not remember one loving interaction between Andrea and Jerry; the only peaceable ones had been those occasions when they had been forced to sit in near-silence beside one another, perhaps in a car ride or a school function. But that was childhood, wasn't it, and, Evelyn told herself, it would only be in the years to come that Andrea would learn that she'd lost out on the prospect of a deepening adult relationship with her brother.

Patrick, had recent events not imploded their family, would prefer to be at home watching football with Kyle. Evelyn ungraciously suspected Patrick course-corrected to spend more time with all his family to keep the peace. She felt ashamed at her suspicions when she'd glimpsed the way Patrick laughed at one of their jokes, or the appreciative pride when Kyle let his guard down and joined in for a laugh.

The miniature golf began rigidly and awkwardly, as if they had been forced to play to oblige someone else's expectations, and in a sense this sentiment wasn't incorrect. But they loosened up with their successes and miscues: Kyle's modest embarrassment from an absurdly great putt; the natural comedy of Patrick's patient approach being rewarded by his ball careening into the water; their bated breath and Andrea's yippy shriek when Mom's ball was scooped to the side by the twisting windmill. By the third hole, the atmosphere was loose and genial, Andrea loud and smiling, Kyle unshowily and quietly pleased with his skill. Kyle ended up winning, with Andrea a distant second, Dad and Mom close thirds and fourths, respectively. Evelyn wondered if Patrick partly threw the game to make that so, and joked to herself he may have well gone all the way and let her beat him.

Hot dogs and chicken tenders for lunch afterwards at the shop on the premises, everyone (Andrea especially) tacitly understood that this was no time to be complaining about junk food. Andrea, who had recently been avoiding fried foods and carbs, ate her chicken fingers with particular relish. No one complaining about fat and salt made for a happy family.

Patrick and Kyle lollygagged as they all made their way to leave. Patrick coerced Kyle into getting some frozen Snickers with him, with Kyle countering that, if they were going to bother to get ice cream, they should at least get something they couldn't just easily make themselves. Somehow that became milkshakes, with Andrea and Evelyn "oof-"ing in protest as they patted their stomachs and walked slowly away, waiting around for the boys to get their treats.

"Have a good time?" Evelyn asked her daughter as they stood waiting, half-distracted by the nearby presence of the parked cars. There was something wistfully sad about packing up the day and heading home. Evelyn hoped there was something transferable in the family dynamics that had opened up today. Already, Evelyn saw, Andrea was looking away and down at her phone.

Andrea looked back up. "Of course, Mom, it was fun. I was pretty good at it, who knew?"

"You have many talents."

"And who knew Kyle was a golf pro?"

"Yes. Is there a golf team at your school?" It would be a few years until Kyle went to their high school.

"I have no idea, I doubt it, I mean, where would they play golf unless they went to some course or something."

"True." Evelyn caught herself doing that Mom-thing, finding one possible interest or aptitude her son displayed and poisoning it by schoolmarming it into something careerist or scholastic, or a subtle indication how he should be more social and outgoing. Nothing ruins an interest like dragooning it into the service of responsibility. Bringing up school, the world outside right now, depressed her, and she would not mention it again.

Evelyn saw the boys – lips pursed, eyes closed in ice-cream inhalation – returning with their shakes, and, letting them have their own time, walked a few yards apace with Andrea toward their car.

"Do you want a shake?" Evelyn asked, not knowing why, as Andrea had already said she didn't and, even if she had, Andrea wouldn't inconvenience everyone by going back and ordering.

"I'm good," and this time she didn't look up from her phone when she answered. Evelyn kept her eyes on her, just enjoyed looking at her, a bit unnerved by how quickly and efficiently she typed away whatever message she was sending to whomever.

16

"Imani is having boy trouble again," Andrea said, as if intuiting that Mom wanted to hear something further. Imani was one of Andrea's longtime friends, a pretty, smart Arab girl, whose most noticeable feature was her deep-set eyes, always well-accentuated with eyeliner. Also, Imani didn't drink, which might be a good influence. Evelyn liked Imani, imagined she was chaste, and wondered how boys tolerated chasteness and sobriety these days.

"Oh, that's too bad." Evelyn found her keys and purse and turned toward the boys and their energized movements, where Kyle, with a whitish pukey substance on his jacket, was being dragged backward, Patrick lunging at the two men that were pulling on their son. Now she saw the soaring gash on Kyle's throat, the man closer to Patrick fending him off, as the other man, undisturbed, descending something like a pen knife again and again into Kyle's throat with short, sharp, unrelenting jabs. With each stab, each puncture into her youngest's neck, Evelyn felt something split open in her stomach, the mounting certainty that she'd lost another child.

She saw Patrick's back in three-quarter profile, but now he leaned forward in a way that indicated he was now concerned with himself, despite his son being butchered only a few feet away. She saw his hands go toward his abdomen and he stumbled backward, and she didn't see Andrea in her periphery but filled in an image of her just now raising her head from her fucking phone as her brother lay torn and frayed and essentially neckless on the ground. Patrick backed up into the road where there roared a screaming vision of a shape, a car she'd seen somewhere before, a car that her husband propelled atop of and over and now he lay there in the road, his black jacket the relatively undisturbed lid on something blasted and broken underneath that she knew she couldn't bear to turn over.

*

If her husband wasn't recuperating in the hospital, Evelyn would have insisted they move out of town immediately.

Miraculously, Patrick wasn't in a coma, didn't suffer any brain damage, only –"only" – a broken leg, a shoulder fracture, two stab wounds to the stomach that pierced no vital organs, and a panoply of superficial cuts and bruises. Could people say she got "lucky" that Patrick hadn't died, too? Is that what people could conceivably say she should be thankful for, could people say that to her with a straight face, would people dare, now that her youngest, too young and sheepish to have shed his essential innocence, was dead, throat torn out while holding a half-filled Styrofoam cup. What she'd thought was whitish foamy puke on her son's jacket was actually the contents of his swallowed milk shake, released out of his slit throat onto his jacket, like a little baby with a messy bib, the little baby he still truly was, and now would always remain.

She wanted Patrick to tell her who did this to them.

He wished he could tell her, but he'd never seen them before. One might have been middle-aged, the other might have been younger, and they were both fair-skinned, although one may have been darker-white. He wasn't sure, it happened so fast. Fucking Patrick always had to be so honest and law-abiding and rule-respecting so he told the police the following as if this changed anything or would lead to some break in the case, but he saw something like remorse in the brown eyes of the man who stabbed him. How remorseful could they all be when, a witness revealed, the license plate of the car which had struck him was intentionally covered up with a blurring sheet.

And when the police asked what, if anything, had these men said to him, Patrick just had to tell them the truth: that he was sure one of them had said, unironically and with some exasperation, that he was sorry.

A random, violent attack, so seemed to be the operative theory. Just pointless words, words that never took root, glided harmlessly along the surface of her brain like water striders across a pond. They were leaving town, was all she thought. Even if it had been entirely random, some impulsive crime of opportunity even where the "opportunity" being seized was still a mystery, losing one son to a suicide and another to street-level butchery was evidence enough that the town was cursed; or if not the town, their family was the virus that brought out some latent, violent overreaction in the town's antibodies, and either way they needed to leave.

*

Jerry lay flat on his bed. It wasn't good to be lying in bed in the middle of the day, he knew. That was a classic sign of depression, and he wished he was only depressed. He *improved* to something like depression. It was when he was only depressed where he wondered where this seething cauldron of righteous hatred came from. Perhaps he should request that his brain be donated to science, so it could be studied and, maybe, there could be better treatment for people like him in the future. That premise assumed, of course, that the problem lay with him and not the world, the very nature of existence, and that likely had to be true, because most people functioned, operated and reproduced, and were not like him.

His ennui was so deep that he convinced himself it would be too much effort to request that his brain be given to science. What does that even mean, "to science": it was the type of imprecise thinking, putting the responsibility on others, that he loathed. It was too much work, he thought to himself with knowing, provocative irony, given the elaborate plan he'd already put in motion.

It was in these moments of what might be called reflection that he thought to himself that it must be him, there must be truly something wrong with him. Did other sociopaths know they were crazy, does a man who rapes the corpses of dead animals while wearing a Burger King Mask and nipple clamps ever look in the mirror with post-orgasm clarity and think, "Jesus, maybe I *am* fucked up?"

He'd passed judgment on existence and found it wanting, but he was part of existence, too. That sentiment would lead to nothing, to drifting along, but maybe drifting was better. How could it be that, objectively and existentially, life didn't matter, yet it was still worthwhile devising a revenge that he wouldn't be alive to witness? Was it some kind of intellectual satisfaction, that clicking into place of the last piece?

And what if he were wrong?

But this cessation of hatred was only temporary, and only when he was alone. Proximity to others would remind him of their inherent selfishness, wastefulness, petty cruelty, misplaced priorities. Vapidity, intellectual torpor and the millions of little

19

hypocrisies that he refused to partake in. Even thinking made it all come bubbling back.

Still, he cried. Maybe just the sudden interruption of this placid state of reflection with this rekindled throbbing indignation was too much for his emotions right now. Sobbing like a little boy on his bed. If Mom were home, could he call out to her, would she come comfort him? She'd leap at the chance.

No, he could never do that, because who wouldn't wonder and worry about their malfunctioning sociopath of a son, crying without understandable cause on a weekend afternoon. Nothing in life was unequivocal or unconditional, except God's love, which he admired as a sustaining ideal but knew was nothing but pretty impetus, hollow faith for hollow minds.

He hadn't asked for any of this. The self-loathing turned the corner nicely into hatred, which had the benefit of at least being goal-directed and, strangely, reassuring. Yes, that old guiding emotion.

He actually looked up the National Institute of Neurological Disorders and thought that realistically would make a good place to send his damaged brain, got a private glee imagining writing "send brain to science," something totally daft and innocent, maybe remind his family of the little naïve kid he'd once been.

He thought more about mementoes he should leave, little bread crumbs that led nowhere, lead round and round like a flushing toilet. He thought about penning a suicide note comprised solely of the lyrics to Nickelback's "Photograph" or some other garbage.

He got to work making one such memento, and when he was done stuffed it deep in the bowels of his sister's closet. Greedy, unappreciative slob, she had so many clothes she never wore or kept track of, she'd never even notice.

*

Andrea didn't know how best to tell her Mother. It felt somehow like she did something wrong. Vacillating wasn't her style, and she wanted to be unburdened of this responsibility as soon as she could.

Andrea peaked around the door to her parents' bedroom, where Mom was laying down, reading a book, an assortment of multicolored plastic containers lining the walls, shelves open, clothes and papers abound. "Mom, I, uhh, found something in my closet you might want to see." Dad had been back home for the last month, and they were packing up and moving out east to make both their lives and their realtor's life a bit easier.

"Okay," was all Evelyn said in response and followed Andrea, both in silence, as if both wanted to minimize all facets of this interaction as much as possible. Dad was winding things down at the office, but even if he'd been home Andrea would have gone with this directly to Mom.

"I- uh, sorry," was the first thing Andrea said, as the door stuck on the clothes and other contents piled en masse in her room.

"Holy Hell, Andrea, you have enough clothes to clothe a small army." Evelyn could map out the evolution of her daughter's tastes in the clothes on display. "I remember that strawberry shirt, I didn't know you still had it. You wear that pear shirt still; I didn't know you had that strawberry shirt. Just a couple more fruit shirts and you can be a complete fruit salad."

"I wear this shirt sometime to sleep in," said Andrea, picking the white-and-red T-shirt flecked with juicy red strawberries with green curlicues, "but it's a little too frilly on the sleeves," and she rubbed her frills swiftly as if proving her point. "The pear shirt is classier and a lot warmer, too, it's long-sleeve."

"As long as I never see a peach shirt. I know what that means."

"Mom, ewww," she said dryly, not without a sarcastic love in her voice. "Don't ruin fruits for me."

Andrea pointed at the 8.5 by 11" gray moleskin notebook. It was on the floor by itself, just beyond the entryway where her largest closet began, a distinct, almost dignified island of repose among the mess of clothes and papers and trinkets.

"It- I'm pretty sure it was Jerry's," Andrea stated the obvious. "I found it, all the way like, buried in the back of my closet. I- I moved it up here, it was really deep down there. On the inside of the front page, it says Jerry on the top."

"Good clue that it was Jerry's," Evelyn said quietly, and smiled.

"Yeah," and Andrea smiled back, each smile after each quiet word a reassurance to one another that this was an awkward situation and they were each proceeding as best they could.

"Did you read it?" Evelyn asked.

"No, absolutely not. I knew it wasn't mine, I never kept a journal I don't think, not even for school, but was curious and just opened the front page and saw Jerry's name."

"Thank you." Evelyn took the journal, held it in her hands with a pinched face, overcome with a feeling of oppressive weightiness, hugged Andrea and thanked her again. Andrea was visibly relieved to be rid of it.

*

"You know we care about you, Jerry. I know you loathe hearing things like that–"

"Of course."

"And I know, look, we are both guys, yadda yadda yadda, so I'm sure you're thinking to yourself, 'why do we have to say all this bullshit,' I get it already, but–"

"No, no, I get it–"

"But just the absolute level of the commitment we've all made. That's why our system works. We have truly committed ourselves to the struggle, to the struggle to live, and that's why we–"

"I get it."

"That's why we take this so seriously. You promise never to kill yourself, and it's a promise, not too be too dramatic about it, made in blood. You understand the consequences if you ever killed yourself. You stay alive for others, so this makes that literal."

"I understand the consequences, and accept them. This may sound weird, but I actually like knowing there are actual, extreme consequences. Suicide isn't a selfless act, anyway. You aren't the only victim of your own suicide, anyway, isn't that what they say? This just, uhh, makes that more literal and less poetical. I kind of like how the stakes are just made so high. You don't tempt fate, you don't fuck around when the stakes are so high, when the danger is so clear-and-present."

*

Evelyn lay in bed with the journal, her heart racing. She took a sip of water, enjoyed turning her face from the book, just sipping water, normality, refreshing. She turned to the journal again and, on cue, her heart again started racing, palms sweaty.

How Jerry would have hated her reading his personal journal. Maybe she shouldn't, but that was a farce, because it would only be a matter of time before she succumbed, and she was his mother and he was her dead son and she had the right. Intermingled with her panic was the shame at struggling with the premise that he was the sort of person to even keep a journal. Had someone told her that her son wrote in a journal she wouldn't believe it, but here it was.

The obvious question, and the obvious opportunity for self-reproach: what else did she not know about her son?

She combed through the journal, each turn of the page a new pang of guilt at each fresh violation. The pages were blank, and as she turned came the disorientation, both the mounting fear and strange relief that each page might be completely blank.

Something, more than halfway through, on the top of a page: **THE REASON WHY**, with deep-cut underlines. At the bottom of the page appeared the outline of small, cramped words, arranged with some obvious care and structure, heavily crossed out. She strained to pierce through the morass of black ink that hid her from the most sought-after truth but it was impossible, the treasures that lay beneath were marred and disfigured beyond repair.

But hope, an inkling of a miniature arrow in blue ink, an instruction to turn the page.

More blanks. Blank, blank, blank, and her heart sank lower and lower, but again, another little blue arrow, this one at the top of the page, and her heart soared. She was literally salivating unknowingly, head swimming in a clammy fog, eyes burning with overstimulation.

She found text, scanned it, and then rocketed through the rest of the empty journal. She backtracked, a finger for a bookmark where she found text, and then went back through the journal more methodically, enough times to understand that this found text was, somehow, all there was and all there was going to be:

It read: "I can't live with the cognitive dissonance of being attracted to a shapely ass and then remembering that that's where shit comes from."

An artifice, this was an artifice, she knew without accepting, unwilling to take the psychic leap into what conclusions that would bring. But before structured thought came, Evelyn somehow knew that Jerry's suicide caused Kyle's murder, and that more death was coming.

*

Jerry looked at the single sentence of text he'd written in his "journal" for his family to find. Somehow, this was crueler than the rest of the plan, and, for a blistering moment, he truly hated himself, although that was fitting, in a sense, wasn't it, because he knew he was defective. In time, he'd get over it, and stow it away in his sister's closet to be found after his death, for his family to stew and mull over, or perhaps they would understand the comic absurdity, the pointless of it all, and find it a fitting tribute to their troubled son. If any of them were left, that is, after he'd found himself able to both eliminate his family and these foolish suicide prevention cultists in one fell swoop.

He'd get over it and stow it away and continue with the plan, wouldn't he, because that's who he was. He was stuck in the spider-web of time. Always bored, always anxious, always restless, for what he didn't know; always doing nothing yet somehow always fatigued, never satisfied; always waiting, it seemed, for a resolution that would never come, for just something in his brain to click, some element to appear so he could finally understand and feel the simple pleasure of a sunrise or friendship or travel or food, and then he could think 'oh that's what people see in this' and look back at his dissolute years with a hearty chuckle.

But never, this grinding through the gears of time was perpetual. And that was life, wasn't it? He hated life, and anyone who didn't hate life was, in a sense, an enemy of his. For they enjoyed it, somehow, and because he experienced life as it really was, he'd always be, not only unhappy, but a despised outcast, his existence itself an offense to the established order.

What was wrong with him? The thought came again in a moment of clarity. Where did this resentment come from? Was it just being born with the name 'Jerry,' a party-animal name, a hippie ice cream purveyor name, given to someone born wanting nothing to do with the act of living? That was as good a theory as any, and he thought of replacing his existential poop-joke in the journal with some riff on that.

He'd been right (right again!), the hate-engine revved up once again, and, on what ended up being a few days before his suicide, he hoped his suicide group's incompetence permitted his family to stay alive long enough to find his gift.

NOTES

Well, that story really cleared the room, didn't it? Another J.R. Hamantaschen chucklefest right there. A kind of litmus test, right, if you can get onboard with that story and not go running for the hills (or angrily tossing the book in the garbage, both literal or electronic), then you might be a keeper. I've had an image of someone's throat slashed open while they were eating ice cream for some time and am glad I found a place to make use of it. MARK THAT ONE OFF THE CHECKLIST!

So, the origins of this story. I suppose Jerry's attitude may be an outsized perversion of a juvenile J.R. at his worst, a young J.R. without his moral compass. Like Jerry, I found myself cursed with a strange, pervasive subspecies of feeling permanently bored and unengaged with almost everything put before me. To the best I can describe it, it feels like a type of time compression, where everything feels somehow like a rush and therefore every demand is a burden. For the sufferer, this agony of disengagement escalates easily into a hatred of the contented and satisfied, a type of resentment that still comes perhaps far too easily for me. A related corollary may be a feeling of perverse superiority, as if there must be some special reason for feeling differently, and that reason can be rationalized quite easily as being just too smart or sophisticated for your own good. Anhedonic superiority (if that's not a term I'm coining it) is obviously a recipe for trouble, and I think this worldview might explain the appeal of deliberate self-sabotage: in a world where you feel both (undeservedly) better than others, yet excluded from the happiness and contentment that seems to come so easily or effortlessly to them, forsaking life – ruining things for yourself and others – seems to absurdly count as some type of rebellion or moral victory against the oppressive state you find yourself in.

Jerry's disdain of this unique self-help group he encounters mirrors my own running monologue of skepticism whenever cognitive behavioral therapy techniques are described to me, cognitive therapy being a practice I don't disagree with in theory but, as articulated by a practitioner, always sounds like naïve optimism that discounts criticism as some kind of fundamental misunderstanding or betrayal. Can people really control their own thoughts? Can they, really? Can you, reader? Can you really control your own thoughts, like at night do you choose your mind to be flooded with all types of macabre, downcast, pessimistic worse-case scenarios as you are trying to sleep? Yeah, I fucking "choose" that every night, right? Sigh, still, I read the cognitive therapy books, perhaps today my thoughts will abide by my choices . . .

Well, put that rope down because it's not all doom and gloom: I'm obviously not advocating for Jerry's worldview, just explaining how it all felt in the throes of my youth. Unlike Jerry, I knew these tendencies would lead to nowhere productive, and I just felt guilty all the time for not being better able to fit in. Indulging these tendencies would be some kind of way to find a "moral" purpose, however misguided. And that's where the story came from, I suppose.

<u>House Katz</u>

"I dreamt that I was, like, inside an old strategy game on the computer, like everything was from a bird's-eye view and the graphics were blurry and yet I somehow knew I was a character in the game, and everyone was wearing armor and riding dinosaurs. And I was aware that I was dreaming, and even thought 'this is ridiculous,'" Dan Katz, still groggy in bed, explained to his wife Cassandra as she got dressed for the day.

"Hmm," she said, a few unnatural beats later. He hated when she responded with sounds rather than words. And there'd been a face, too, something that said "well, *okayyy* then."

Hmmm yourself, Dan thought grumpily, though making sure his face stayed inconspicuous. He knew why she said "hmm" like that, it was stupid of him to say he recognized something as "ridiculous" in his dream. Last night, they'd gotten into a fight ("I don't think we're fighting," he'd said in the face of her umbrage) because he thought she was being "ridiculous," too paranoid and unrealistic about this virus going around. Cassandra had heard from her dingbat friend, who heard from some other friend who supposedly worked in the hospital industry, that the virus particles could float in the air for up to five hours, so even if everyone socially distanced as they were supposed to, they could inadvertently walk into a hovering aerosolized patch of it and get infected.

If that were true, he'd countered, why wasn't that more widely known, and why did the government permit people to take walks and go out as long as they socially-distanced? The thrust of it all was that she didn't want them leaving the apartment at all. *Sure*, he thought, be cautious, wear masks, greatly reduce the amount of time outside . . . but to never leave their modest two-bedroom apartment was too great a restriction given their five-year-old son Nathan, plus a cat and two shrill canaries.

Still in bed, he pet Mittens, their black shorthair stray he'd had since he found him outside his Harlem apartment seven years ago, a few months before he met Cassandra, before this domesticity in Queens. Playing with or antagonizing Mittens was always an easy way to distract from or revert things back to their usual course, though that wasn't going to work now. What tension couldn't be lessened by the barely-veiled contempt of a lazy feline tolerating a petting?

Dan had originally named Mittens "Colonel," but Nathan insisted on Mittens, and rather than teach Nathan that you can't change something's name by fiat, Nathan's fascist approach was tolerated on account of his age. Dan had rescued Mittens just before he met his future wife, who happened to be the prideful owner of two beloved canaries, an orange creamsicle-colored bird aptly named Crema, the other a yellow one with a mottled-black face named Brillo, short for brillo solar, Spanish for sunset. Cassandra's grandmother in Puerto Rico loved canaries and something-something-something, and Cassandra had to keep the family tradition alive. And given his surname, Dan joked, how could he not own at least one cat?

So now their combined household consisted of Dan, Cassandra and Mittens sharing a bedroom, Nathan in the other bedroom with the two birds. (Nathan was getting a raw deal but his wife insisted, that whole superstition of cats-and-sleeping-children never having been modified on account of Nathan's advancing age. Dan didn't really mind, let him enjoy the comfort of "Colonel" as his one selfish thing.)

The fight had been stupid anyway, because there wasn't much Dan could do about anything. He worked as a butcher at the International Meat Market, not exactly a job that could be done remotely, and now he was the sole breadwinner, his wife laid off from her office manager job almost immediately after this crisis began six-or-so weeks ago, and no unemployment checks had yet arrived, were still being "processed." (Thank god, he reflected, that he hadn't mentioned during last night's fight that her dingbat friend was unemployed; that'd draw protest, open fresh wounds, although the relevant distinction being that Cassandra was freshly unemployed on account of this pandemic, whereas said dingbat friend was *forever* unemployed.)

He should have known better than quarreling with her before bed, stupid of him given how both of them struggled with their sleep to begin with, and also should have taken into account the tenor of her mood. She was unemployed and scared, ashamed of having to apply for unemployment, had been unwittingly converted into an unpaid homeschool teacher for their son Nathan, all her recent scouring for a bigger apartment in a nicer neighborhood like Forest Hills or Kew Gardens now for naught until this pandemic lifted. With her new diktat against the harmless midday stroll, he'd be housebound today, this fine spring Sunday, and tomorrow, too, which were always his two scheduled days off.

Rather than usually pushing Mittens to get him to hop around and fight, he rubbed the cat under the neck: *us house-bound strays got to stick together*. The only salvation lay with Nathan, perhaps Nathan could wheedle a compromise out of Cassandra. Perhaps, Dan thought, he could conspire with the boy, get him to say what needed to be said to get Mommy to reconsider, but with these close quarters, such a ploy was too risky. Could he trust him to play it cool? He could imagine it now, telling Nathan to innocently ask Mommy if they could please, please just go out for a short walk, then Nathan turning toward him to see if he said it right, already smiling with anticipation. Not a chance, after that they'd have to add a doghouse to their menagerie so Dan could have a place to sleep.

The prospect of the day weighed on him. Dan felt lonely in a way he couldn't describe, lonely in an abnormal, shameful way. *But how can you feel lonely when you have a feisty five-year-old boy who just wants play!* he thought, conjuring society's expected response. All this free time indoors with his son should be joyous, and it was in the abstract, or it would be upon reflection, in some future date where memories are rosied up. What was it: why was it that work at the butcher shop came easier than staying at home with his family? It was the burden of responsibility, wasn't it; here, he was looked at as the go-to, the formulator, the overseer and executor of the plans. (Let Cassandra roll her eyes at that, it was true.) At work, it was enjoyable physical labor and fucking around with the staff. Here, two people and three animals depended upon him.

He cooked up eggs and bacon for the family, Cassandra seemingly haven gotten over last night's unpleasantness (hopefully exorcized through her testy "hmmm"), now running

Nathan through some chores, helping her feed the birds and give them fresh water, and finding some videos about farms to play on the television for Nathan as a reward for his "good work."

"Daddy works with chickens," Nathan said as chickens filled the television screen in the living room.

"Yes, Daddy does," Dan said. Cassandra looked back at him, smiled, glad he didn't go further. There'd be a lot to explain to him someday, what Daddy did exactly with those animals at work. That conversation, add another about what these colorful pictures along Daddy's arms meant, which could be a fun opportunity for Dan to come up with meaningful explanations other than "it looked cool" or "I liked that band."

"You know, Mommy worked in an office that dealt with teeth," Dan said while shimmying the frying pan. "Teeth are real important, right? That's pretty cool, right?"

Nathan nodded dutifully. Not as fucking cool as working with barnyard animals, Dan quietly agreed.

Mittens ran into the kitchen. "I'll make a plate for you, too. Don't worry, ya fat cat," Dan said, hopefully loud enough for Nathan to hear and giggle, but apparently not, the boy focused on his chickens and cows on the screen. Dan tossed the cat a tiny bit of bacon, an amuse bouche.

Mittens didn't give it a second glance. He was at the window that led to the fire escape and the strange quasi-pathway that connected the two buildings, the purpose of which Dan could not really figure out, other than it allowed past building workers a place to loiter and smoke, if the dozens of crushed cigarettes under the fire escape were any indication. At the window were about three other fine-looking cats, two shorthairs and a Maine Coon. Mittens hopped up to the landing and stared out at them.

"Invited some friends over, huh?" Dan was surprised Mitten came over to the window, rather than maybe hissing and backing away or just plain running away into a bedroom. Mittens was a diffident, generally fearful little beast, and had basically rolled over and allowed himself to be scooped up and claimed as Dan's house cat. He never would have survived long as a street cat.

The window was open to allow a breeze, and Mittens pawed at the window screen. Not really pawed, more like slowly stroked his paw against the screen, more like, Dan thought strangely, how an inmate and loved one would caress their hands across the glass that divided them during a prison visitation.

"Hey, don't do that," and Dan lifted and dropped him off the landing.

The three cats all looked at Dan, while another was coming down the fire escape.

"We got a crazy cat lady a few floors up missing cats?" Dan asked rhetorically as he brought over a plate for his wife and son at the couch. There wasn't room at the couch or nearby coffee table for him to comfortably join them, so he sat at the "dining" table and made himself some room. That blue marble table had been their one and only "nice" possession pre-parenthood, now one chair occupied completely with his family's jackets and effluvia. The tabletop, or at least the part of it not covered in paper towel rolls and kid-stuff, was well-scratched and banged up from the kid and cat having their run of the place.

"Cats!" his son yelped, a bit shrilly, giving Dan an unpleasant flashback of teachers about to reprimand him for fucking about in class. Nathan came over, his mom urging him to stay and finish the breakfast that Daddy worked so hard to make.

"That's right, son, with our name, you can become ruler of the cats – it's the benefit of our name," and Dan waved his hands around like a sorcerer.

"Glad there's some benefit to this name," Cassandra said, smiling and laughing, a true 'take that' laugh, as Dan turned to her in mock-shock. "Thanks to you, my name is Cass Katz!"

"Try it sometime, Nathan, you'll see," Dan said, still making sorcerer hands. Cassandra joined him, demonstrating a truncated version of the pageantry, quick and dirty to get Nathan back to his breakfast.

Mittens went back up to the window. There were, what were there now, five or six cats out there. Mittens batted again at the screen.

"Colonel, stop that," Dan stormed to the window, projecting an anger he didn't really feel to scare his "Colonel" from the window, always forgetting that he was dealing with a cat who either didn't notice or didn't give two shits about emotional cues.

("His name's Mittens," he heard Nathan call from the couch.) Dan didn't want Cassandra to notice Mittens was pawing the screen, lest she order Dan to close the window. He needed fresh air; if he shut this window, they'd only have one open window, the one facing the street in the living room.

Just as Nathan approached, the legion of cats outside pawed viciously at the screen. The cat in the lead, an orange Maine Coon, spit and hissed ferociously, his nails between the holes in the screen, pulling and flailing with the almost-frenzied panic of a man who'd just caught his penis in his zipper, or, perhaps more seriously, someone trying to wrench his arm out of the mouth of a ravenous dog.

"Jesus," Dan said, surprised at his own reaction.

"What's going on over there?" Cassandra said loudly, lifting Nathan and placing him back on the couch, as the boy struggled to see what was going on, getting pissy in his frustration.

"These cats might rip our screen. Honey, think I should spray them with the sink hose?"

"Whatever gets them out of here."

Dan did so, putting the water first on that diffuse spritz-mode, and embarrassed at how ineffectual that was, put it on stream-mode, which wasn't much better. The cats meowed sharply and backed up slightly, and Dan spread the water around to the group to make sure this wasn't just one cat getting all soaked. This wasn't supposed to be a fucking cat bath, didn't cats generally not like getting water sprayed on them? Even Mittens, close by on the counter, didn't budge. Fuck it, Dan went to close the window. Shit, these fucking cats ripped the screen, fuck, these were custom screens, like 150 bucks, and a ripped screen was as good as worthless.

"Get the f-, get out of the way," he grumbled, the cats still snaking their paws through the screen to widen the hole. Dan didn't want to crush any of their little hands under the window, so he smacked the screen hard to at least get them to withdraw their hands as he pushed the window down.

He grunted in lieu of blurting 'fuck.' His right hand was bleeding along the top of the palm and the three central fingers. It didn't really hurt, but it was bloodier than he'd imagined, must have been some combination of getting scratched and pinched in the window. He looked out at the furry contingent to see if any one of them looked particularly guilty or, he didn't know, perhaps remorseful, but they all just stared, with their wide variety of expressive cat-eye colors.

"Look at that white cat with the blue eyes, wow I've never seen that before," he said to his wife, who walked over with a bandage. He turned and saw that Nathan was still on the couch. He'd expressed wonderment for Nathan's behalf, thinking he'd come along with Cassandra. As if he cared about a blue-eyed cat now.

"Oh honey," Cassandra said, wrapping the bandage around his hand. Alleviating pains and scratches was her secret calling.

"I thought you were supposed to be a guard cat," she said to Mittens while smiling back at Nathan. "I thought that's why you were a Colonel." Mittens, stripped of his military title, gave the same ponderous, inscrutable stare-back as the outside cats. When either Dan or Cassandra was sad or upset, the other adopted a we-can-do-it, corny-joke overcompensating cheerfulness, part of the steadying emotional seesawing of domesticity.

Dan heard the birds chirping from the bedroom. He could identify their separate trilling, Brillo the more active and robust of the two.

"I wonder if that's why these cats decided to join us on this fine spring day, because of our birds," said Cassandra. The 'fine spring day' part was said to Nathan. "Well, fat chance for them, these cats aren't coming in."

"Yeah, those are *our* birds," agreed Nathan.

"They've never come around before, though," Dan said vacantly. The cats still stared in. Now there were even more of them, and it *was* a fine spring day, and none of them seemed too perturbed about having been doused, as if they knew they'd dry. Dan found himself weirdly jealous of the cats, outside free to roam and explore. Oh well, the cats didn't look as impressive all wet, so at least he'd scored an aesthetic victory.

"What do you think we should do, call the management company or something? Animal control?" Cassandra asked.

"I guess, I mean, is animal control even open anymore? Only essential services are still open. I don't know, I guess I can try but who the hell knows when they will get here."

Cassandra looked at him sternly, 'hell' being one of those borderline words, sometimes okay to say around Nathan, sometimes not. Ironic since, although Dan cursed more, his cursing was harmless, evocative words to fill out or give comedic emphasis to a sentence; when Cassandra cursed, it was scary and meant she wanted someone dead.

"We can call the police if they don't show up," Cassandra answered. Cassandra looked with disgust at the assembled animals, and then at Mittens. She never really liked free-ranging house pets; they never seemed to serve any purpose, stunk up the place and acted like they owned it. Birds were at least beautiful to look at and listen to, and watching their gift of flight, even when only allowed in the bathroom, was still a wondrous thing. What did this fat-fuck cat do other than poop and sleep? He'd never even caught a mouse. If anything, the mice would catch him. Nathan loved him (and Dan did, too), which granted the beast his clemency.

Dan didn't imagine that calling the police would do much, given all they must be dealing with. What would he say, exactly? 'Sorry officers, forget about the looting going on during quarantine, and those dead bodies, too: we have a cat problem here.'

"I'll call animal control, you go take care of Nathan for a bit," Dan decided, and Cassandra was on it, congratulating Nathan for being such a good boy and staying put near the couch.

Dan estimated how many cats were out there, must be about fifteen right near the window, who knows if there were others walking about the landing. The lower half of the screen was effectively torn to ribbons. But even the sharpest cat claws weren't going to do anything about the glass. Having dialed animal control, Dan walked over to the window to get Mittens to come back to the couch, as if the cats were a bad influence, the cats from the literal wrong side of the window.

"Come on Col-"

Pandemonium, some fifteen hairy crabs crawling over each just outside the window, *fuck*, and one inside . . . Mittens. It was the cats. Dan dropped his phone, convinced for a split-second Mittens was having some kind of seizure. Like the cats outside, Mittens was belly-up, crab-walking with oblivious abandon. He scuttled across the counter, tail dragging beneath him, spices and chips and utensils either crushed or fell off the counter in his wake. His eyes were open but unresponsive, inscrutable as always, but worse was his open, gaping, drooling mouth, which on his back appeared like an inverted ecstatic smile.

"Colonel!" Dan dropped the phone and grabbed for his cat, now writhing atop and over the microwave, anticipating the unaware teeth-and-claws that may descend upon his hand when he woke Mittens from this stupor. Mittens' affliction, Dan saw out of the corner of his eyes, was shared equally by the cats outside, now one contorting mound, all bent-backed and upside-down, the same horrifying discrepancy between their blank eyes and their wet, joyous mouths, some gape-mouthed, others nibbling at phantoms.

The cats outside were throwing themselves, face first, into the glass. The sound of the first impact, hard enough to leave blood, almost made Mittens slip out of his hands. The smeared blood didn't stop the next cat, or the next, and the cheap window was already beginning to crack. Mittens was a flailing insect in his arms, a furry sack with possessed limbs, and Dan almost cried, his cat must be dying, how could he have done that with his spine?, and then with a twist, quicker than it takes to blink, Mittens snapped out of it, back to looking around the room in his usual feline resignation, as if there was nothing he could do about being hoisted into the air so he might as well tolerate it.

"Dan, what is going on out there?" Cassandra asked, keeping her voice steady, having obviously waited to voice this question. She kept Nathan close behind her, the boy wiping his face silently, clearly frightened. But Dan could see in her eyes that she saw and that she knew as well as he. She had her phone in hand, and any notion she may have had about entertaining Nathan with the antics of those funny dancing cats outside died almost as soon as it had formed.

Dan babbled, "I think these cats–"

A soft thud came from outside the living room window, then a dimmer, fuller-sounding impact seconds later. Another, then another, as if someone was dropping sandbags outside the living room window. Dan, now furious, as if in a mood to yell at some punk kids, dropped Mittens to the ground, stormed past his family and, it being a small apartment, crossed the distance to the living room window in a matter of seconds.

His instincts had already prepared him for what greeted him, but his mind was still several beats behind, still rationalizing, even now as he looked outside at what greeted him. Their apartment was on the third floor, and he saw about four dead cats, splayed on their side, down on the pavement.

Dan instinctively darted his head as a brown house cat, leaping from a point unknown, smashed face-first into the ledge outside their window, whipsawed its arms to try and gain purchase, failed, and plummeted down to join his brethren. Dan shook his head, as if willing the images to disappear, to reorder the sequence of events he'd just witnessed so as to unmask meaning.

This was the first time he'd looked outside onto the street all day. Dozens of cats walked the streets below, and a few dogs, too, although the two species seemed to be operating without regard for the other. Just now a gaggle of cats froze and some moved out of the way as a German Shepherd sprinted down the street and turned the corner. No human was chasing him, no crying little kid upset about his beloved dog that'd just broken free. Across the street about two dozen cats were piling into a storefront that Dan knew had been closed for at least a week as a result of this quarantine.

"We need to call the police, okay? And honey, why don't you take Nathan into our room and close the door and first throw out any food you didn't eat in case that's what these cats wanted and you guys can watch whatever you want on the iPad, how's that sound?"

Cassandra nodded.

"And how about text me once you get situated in there and we can talk through the door, okay, I have to do something really quick, okay?" Dan was adding exclamation with his face, eyeing the pans and knives he could use as weapons and shields. "Oh – okay, go, go, okay," he placed his hand on Cassandra's back, as if guiding her into action. "You two have fun in our room, okay? You can call from our room, right, and call the police? Go into the room. I'll get the leftovers later, okay?" He just remembered his phone was still on the ground somewhere in the kitchen.

Cassandra hurried Nathan into their bedroom and closed the door.

Dan gathered his phone on the floor, grabbed a steel frying pan, then took two oven mitts and put them on in case the cats tried to bite or scratch him, noted the sauce pot he could wear as a helmet, though that could be a step too far and do more harm than good. He was failing, he knew: be responsible, he commanded himself, because he wasn't tracking the most important development, which was the integrity of the window. That's where all attention should be paid, the living room window posed no threat, as no cat could even gain purchase there. What was the point of leaping by the living room window, he wondered, although asking why was a stupid question. They were cats, solitary and individualistic by nature, who knows why they did what they did. A diversionary tactic, he thought ironically, an unfunny joke to himself.

Oh God, there were so many of them outside the kitchen window, and this kitchen window wasn't going to hold. It really wasn't going to hold, it actually wasn't going to hold, an incredible, horrifying realization that he wasn't prepared to accept. He reinforced the glass by pushing a large pot against it, then thought to boil water, he could launch that at the cats before they got in (no, that would take too long and pose its own hazards if God forbid cats got in and knocked the little water pot over). He started boiling water anyway, could be something, the knockout punch, the secret weapon, like they did in medieval siege defense.

Mittens stood atop the microwave, as if silently judging Dan's performance.

Dan pushed against the splintered glass as the cats, who must have numbered about fifty now, stampeded and thrashed against the window.

"Dan," he heard Cassandra behind him, hushed but urgent, as if there was still some pretense in hiding what was happening from Nathan. "The cats broke the bedroom window and started coming in. Only about one or two came in before we left," she whispered. Fucking hell, the bedroom window, and the bathroom window, too, all faced the same ledge. The bathroom window was tiny and didn't even have a screen. While he hadn't heard anything, he wouldn't be surprised if there were cats mulling around the bathroom right now.

"Oh–" Cassandra put her hands to her mouth, to stifle her emotions at seeing the amassed army outside their kitchen window.

"Did you get a hold of the police?"

"I got disconnected the first two times and now I'm on hold. This pandemic, I wouldn't be surprised if there's no one at the precinct."

Dan knew the kitchen window was a lost cause. Still he wanted to insist that she help reinforce it or ready another pot of boiling water or do *something*, just so the imminent failure couldn't be laid solely at his feet. But no:

"Go into the other room." The window in there didn't face the ledge (he didn't think? it was on the other side of the room?). Actually, he wasn't sure of that, the window in Nathan's room did face the same ledge, didn't it, how could that bedroom not have the same layout? So that was a bad idea, plus what would the plan be, be stuck in a room with two screaming birds in a house overrun with feral cats that could potentially slip under the door?

"Actually," he lifted an arm to stop her movement. "Go right next door to Enid and Gene's. You two need to get out of here." They had two sons, including Will, Nathan's friend who was the same age.

"Okay," and he could see Cassandra thinking, likely the same thing he was, that the neighbors had two young kids and were always wearing masks and wouldn't want visitors, because who knows who was contaminated with what these days. The neighbor on the other side was a single guy they'd never spoken to, and who else did they know, there were a lot of old people, a lesbian couple (they could be a good bet, no kids) or, *that's it!,* Dan thought, Murray and his elderly mother who had that big black dog that would put the fear of god into any feline.

Cassandra yelled as the cats, Mittens included, as if on cue became transfixed in their fervent crab-walk, although the almost-reverent silence that accompanied that previous transformation was replaced with hissing, spitting, and mewling. Mittens fell off the counter, a rolling tangle of limbs. Glass splintered, the squirming mass outside like a collection of screeching, hairy multi-colored pustules. One cat being pressed against the glass was, based on the angle of his neck, clearly dead, but the army outside didn't care, just more weight for the siege.

"Get out of here, go to Murray if Enid and Gene aren't home, get out now. I don't want you to see this," and Dan grabbed the pot of boiling water.

Cassandra grabbed Nathan and ran out of the apartment, wishing she'd thought to grab facemasks from the nightstand in their bedroom but there wasn't time. "I love you," she squawked as she closed the door; she hadn't yelled it in panic, she realized, as if trying to blunt her fear, yelled it more if she were just in a rush, something pedestrian like running late for work.

Dan knew what he had to do but he couldn't, he just couldn't heave scalding water on this sea of cats, with Mittens right in the zone of splash back. He couldn't do it, he couldn't, so he disassociated completely, just swung the pot forward and spilled forth its contents without allowing himself to connect his actions with the screams that followed or the smell that singed his nostrils. Small, emptied pot in his left hand, he steadied the frying pan in his right, still finding it inconceivable he would ever need to use it.

*

Cassandra looked up and back at her front door, could swear she heard clanging, screeching. Why weren't Enid and Gene answering? Were they barricaded inside, so terrified of contagion, just a few feet away behind this door, silencing their children until the knocking went away? No, they wouldn't do that. For all she knew they'd left the City until the pandemic blew over. She would have done the same if they had somewhere to go.

"Will, Will's parents, let us in," Nathan cried. Hearing Nathan's pleas to be let in was too much for her, so she took his hand and brought him down the hall, telling him that Will and his family must be visiting friends upstate, up in the Catskills, where they'd taken Nathan last summer to run around, and that's where they'd go again when this was all over.

"Are there a lot of cats in the Catskills?"

"No, no cats there, it's just a name. Like our last name, nothing to do with cats, just a big coincid–"

Something glass-sounding shattered inside an apartment on the opposite side of the hall. Cassandra was unable to breathe for a moment, heart pounding too hard to regain composure. She just wanted to go back inside their apartment, surely it must be under control now, they were just housecats, for Chrissakes.

Just go to Murray's, midway down the hall. They'd only spoken to Murray a few times, but he seemed trustworthy, he was always at home caring for his bedridden mother, just leave Nathan inside with him until things got under control in their apartment. She could picture it now, Nathan sitting alone safely in a room in Murray's apartment, Murray's big bushy mountain-of-a-dog grazing by the door, making sure no unwanted guests got in.

Tension brewed in her stomach as she prematurely imagined Murray sputtering out reasons why they couldn't come in, his sick mother and this pandemic being especially fatal for the elderly, and if that happened, she'd have to tell him that this was truly and unequivocally an emergency.

She knocked, diplomatically but firmly. No answer, and Nathan's crying began anew, viewing some pattern of doom laid out behind his eyes. "'Sok, honey," and she knocked again, pushing the door to test if it was open. The door was unlocked, and she continued her knocking, pretending to fall forward slightly for an audience of no one as a pretext as to why she opened the door.

The light was off by the door, but lights were on down the hall in the living room.

Cassandra tentatively led the way down the hall, making sure her son stayed just behind. "Hey Murray, it's Cassandra with Nathan, down the hall, I hope you are doing well. This will sound–" they were three-quarters of the way down the hall, and something slinky and agile darted from an unseen corner, losing its balance and slipping just as it made its way down the hall.

A cat.

Time to leave.

An engine was revving.

A foot protruded from the living room, from the source of the engine, and the engine fired up as the foot jerked spasmodically.

"Let's go to the nice couple down the hall, okay Nathan?" Cassandra spoke as placidly as she could.

The engine revealed itself to be growling, and she could see Murray's monster-of-a-dog tugging and twisting, jaws vice-like upon and fully obscuring what was left of his owner's face. There was a scarlet sheen at the end of the hallway where the cat had slipped.

"Come now, and let's be very quiet, the doggy is sleeping," she said as she pushed Nathan back to the door.

As Cassandra and her son headed back toward the front door, Cassandra passed an open room and saw what must have been Murray's mother, flat on her back in bed, body swathed under blankets, one cat atop her head swatting at her face, another by her body and swatting in the air, as if determining whether the corpse before them was just a giant supine rat playing possum.

Near the front door, and the growling stopped. Then a cannon of a bark, and there the dog was, muzzle covered in gore, standing behind them at the opening to the living room, beside Murray's dragged corpse, the face so consumed that the remaining structure had collapsed into itself.

"Run back to Daddy, okay? I'll be right behind you, okay?" and Cassandra underhandedly pushed her son toward the door. She was about ten feet away from the door, the dog maybe triple that behind them. Think, should she make a run for it, push Nathan through the door and slam it before the dog ran forward, or keep the dog calm until she was sure Nathan had made it through and gotten back home. Her life came down to a decision she wasn't prepared to make, a decision that could be wrested out of her hands in a second.

"It's okay, good boy, it's okay, good boy," Cassandra soothed, hands open-palmed. Dan was good with dogs, why couldn't she be with Dan, why couldn't they just be inside, at home, on Dan's day off? Tears welled, the arc of her life up to this point cascading over her panicked mind with impressionistic detail. No, focus. She turned to see if Nathan had gotten through the door, and no he was still here, looking at her, terrified and babbling, and of course he couldn't leave Mommy.

"Nathan, go, go back to Daddy, okay, I'll join you so soon, so soon baby. I'm just – just go, I'll be there in one second, the doggy is okay."

Please, Nathan, please, he was so close. Just slip through the door. "Go, go," she whispered and gestured.

She could run and make it . . . then she studied the animal again and her heart sank. The dog was colossal, its flexed body alone looked like it would halve the distance, a thrust of those powerful legs and the dog would be upon her. If she could only just eke her way over, push Nathan through the door, maybe she could move and the dog wouldn't mind, he already had his chew toy, she thought grimly. The dog – she didn't even know its name – gawped dumbly. She looked to see if its tail was wagging, some insight into the dog's mood. Its tail was an immobile corkscrew.

As if launched, the animal galloped toward her in full stride, not even granting her the dignity of a warning bark. Cassandra sprinted toward the open door, the last terrifying thought as she turned to run was that the dog had already covered the distance, was up in the air, open wet jaws descending upon her shoulder, that she was bound to be another fleshy morsel for this monstrous thing intent on crushing and rendering all in its path, to be dragged backward, grasping in vain to close the door beyond her reach to save her son until a crunch irreparably severed meaning between her thoughts and actions.

*

Dan was in Nathan's room, and the two birds were strangely blasé about the cats pounding, scratching, slipping claws and trying to wedge themselves underneath the door. Dan had killed or maimed several, bashed heads and limbs with his frying pan, lost the water pot and removed the gloves but kept fighting until the numbers became overwhelming and he had to seek refuge behind the locked door. Cats weren't roaches or rats, how many could there be, and why all here, why all now?

Colonel had joined the stampede, the traitor, and that desertment had freed Dan to unleash, do the things he needed to do, although he was sure if he saw Colonel again he wouldn't have the heart to hurt a hair on his head. In his exhausted delirium, he imagined Colonel telling his new friends about the indignity he suffered at being stripped of the name Colonel for the emasculating embarrassment that was Mittens, the only woe-is-me war story that spoiled animal could conceivably have since Dan had taken him in. He'd been so good to that animal, his first proto-child, yet so quickly abandoned.

He looked around the room, at Nathan's toys, books, his Legos, his collection of toy taxi cabs and subway trains and farm sets with the plastic farmers and animals still out, an insight into what Nathan been doing last night, a kind of deleted scene that Dan recreated in his head, eyes wet with tears. Concentrate, he still had his frying pan, its underside caked red. Were there other weapons in here? No, what weapons would there be in his child's room?

The windows were on the opposite side of the room from the ledge. He'd been wrong, they should have run in here immediately. He fucked up, he couldn't believe it, he'd fucked up, one of those tiny oversights with such obvious ramifications, fucking stupid, his fucking stupidity could now have cost them everything.

No, that can't be. It will be fine. His family was safe somewhere. He wanted to call, but shouldn't in case they were keeping quiet. So he texted Cassandra, said he was safely inside Nathan's room, asked his wife to confirm where they were and that they were okay. His eyes stayed glued to the phone.

The gap between the floor and the door seemed larger in this room, and he smashed every questing paw and the more ambitious faces that tried to twist themselves under. A cessation of movement, and then the abrupt, powerfully singular shift in momentum outside the door that left no doubt when they were crab-walking as one, that frightening possession, all-consuming, each time a fresh, simmering agony riving his guts, the reassuring mental defenses he built up came tumbling, as if each time he was freshly reminded of this strange, esoteric hell that lay before him.

Think, think. There had to be something. Something he was overlooking. The pandemic would kill off the cats (no, no). The pandemic caused all this (maybe, but not important).

He checked his phone again, no response. He couldn't stand this, where was she? He would have to call, hear his wife and child, make sure they are situated.

The birds, was it the birds they really wanted? No, this seemed too severe for two birds, but what else could it be? His wife would kill him for what he was about to do, but she would have to understand these circumstances. How comforting it was to think of his wife, reprimanding him on some future date; he could imagine it clearly, "all this, and you just had to go ahead and throw my birds out there, like things weren't bad enough, you know how long- " and he smiled, ruddy-face, as if this imagined scenario was as pivotal and momentous a day as the day of his wedding or the birth of his child.

"Are these what you want?" he yelled, tilting the cage slightly. He opened the windows and screens, made a nest of his hands and lifted each bird to the window to take flight. Godspeed, little guys, he thought as they flapped up and away. They could eat seeds, drink rainwater, be free, or someone else would find them, give them a good home. "They're gone now, so go away," he yelled, to the persistent scratching and burrowing at the bottom of the wooden door.

There wasn't really any heavy furniture in this room. He pushed the sole bookcase against the door, and then the single cabinet that housed some of Nathan's clothes, and the bird cage for good measure. Why hadn't he thought of this sooner, stupid. But these were flimsy, the furniture cheap Ikea-garbage, but still, they were only cats, only cats, still only cats.

He heard heaving growling outside the front door to the apartment, which must have been loud if he could hear it still so clearly, naturally muted by both the front door and Nathan's door. He felt the jerky back-and-forth of something like a big dog slamming around a rag doll. Good boy, good boy, get those fucking cats, bite their fucking heads off, Dan pleaded. Get 'em, tear them limb from limb, and save room in your stomach for more. Dogs didn't eat cats though, did they, just fought them. Fine, just tear them up, be a cold-blooded killer, tear them up remorselessly and then go onto the next one.

He couldn't tolerate the radio silence from his wife, so he called Cassandra. The phone rang five times, went to voicemail. Where the fuck was she, she was always so bad at picking up but even now? Now, of all times? They must be still explaining things in an apartment somewhere, or staying quiet somewhere, or are right now with the police, which could explain the missed call. She'd call back any second.

Dan strained to think as the burrowing and splintering continued. That last possession did a number on the door, all those determined teeth-and-nails against the wood, all those bodies throwing themselves en masse, hard enough even that the bookcase and armoire rumbled, as if caught in an aftershock.

Think, think. His name, did his name have anything to do with this? Katz, haha, could these cats read, and if they did, would it be English? Haha, what else could it be, why them, why any of this, why all the cats in the street, why didn't they care about the birds, think, think?

His hope lay with the dog outside, viciously mauling and tossing something around just outside their door, get those cats, get them, rip their fucking heads off.

<u>NOTES</u>

"COVID STORIES, WRITING COVID STORIES?" Editors and various people seemed to be asking once the COVID pandemic began, although who the fuck would want to read that? I don't get it. So this is my skewed version of a pandemic story, where the pandemic isn't the focus, but just what sets the tale in motion and allows for the characters to remain housebound for a threat that might not otherwise be so threatening. Also, every housecat I've ever met always seemed like it was just barely tolerating its owners but was too lazy to do anything about it, so the idea of housecats coordinating together to enact some kind of frenzied attack just seemed kind of funny to me. Also, I liked that cats are the natural enemies of birds, the titular antagonists in Daphne Du Maurier's quintessential 'revolt of the natural world' story. If you've not read her short story *The Birds*, c'mon, what are you doing with yourself!

A recurring theme in many of my stories is the anguish and weight of responsibility. (I mean, hell, a story from my second collection is called *The Gulf of Responsibility*.) There are those everyday harrowing responsibilities we assume because they must be done – the familial and economic ones we all already know – but then when things go upside-down, all the eyes still turn toward you, even though you are just a dumbstruck as everyone else. You want to disclaim responsibility, yell to the world that you are just as ill-equipped and fumbling as everyone else, but there's nowhere else to turn. It's on you, and that's a true horror, to feel like you had an expectation for how the world should be, find that things have changed, and know that you will let down the people who depend on you. Even in those situations – in situations that no one could ever prepare for – the criticism will likely, as Dan Katz found, turn inward, because where else can it go? When you self-criticize, there's an unspoken assumption that enough criticism may make yourself change course, even where that's not really possible because you've found yourself in an insurmountable position.

Really, that's what this story is about, finding yourself in a situation you could not anticipate, that you did not ask for, and that you cannot handle. Maybe you saw a bit of yourself and that predicament in this story. Maybe that's just a bit too heavy and you just thought the crazy cat formations seemed kind of cool and gnarly (I tried!). Or maybe you hated it, hate me, thought the whole scenario was idiotic . . . . but then why would you still be reading? So I'll just hope for a benign scenario, or at least hope you stick around for the next story because at least that's one that deserves to be hated! (Note I made that comment before finalizing the story order, but it's probably accurate).

The story's original title was "Love is Never Strong Enough to Find the Words Befitting It," which was supposed to reflect Dan's turmoil at feeling like he let his family down and regretting that he did not properly express his love for them before everything turned south. I still like the title, but I didn't want to alter the expectations for the story with that ponderous title. You expect a tragic end with a title like that. And this is about feral felines, after all, so hopefully the punny title got you to lower your guard.

For Most Of My Sad Life I Figured I Would Just Die Alone

Michelle stopped to look at herself in the mirror. Not sure why; she'd been washing up, finished, and now assessed herself silently. What was she looking for, exactly? If there was a trick here, it was working, because confronting herself got her out of the prison of her own mind. She smiled at herself sweetly, almost mockingly, but if there was a joke here, she was in on it. Was this what you wanted? Look at me, all fine, take those prying eyes elsewhere.

She put on a nice-fitting burgundy dress. Not white, off-white, or ivory; not overly sexy, low-cut, revealing or high-hemmed. Her heart wanted green – it was her favorite color – but green doesn't go well with olive skin, so no, and she'd read somewhere that it was a weird color to wear to a wedding.

Michelle opened her bedroom door. Dorothy, her mother, was ready to go, dressed in a blue and purple cocktail dress and heels.

"Oh Michelle, you look so beautiful, so beautiful," she cradled Michelle's slender face in her palms, "just wonderful, look at you, this dress looks so lovely with your hair, your skin, a bright ray of sunshine. I love what you did with your hair, how it flows, so glad you are growing it out again." Mom's right hand traced a pattern through Michelle's chestnut brown hair, which was not well-past shoulder length.

"Thanks Mom." Michelle had been living at home now for over three years; it's not like her Mom didn't see her every day. But it was a special day, her cousin Audra's wedding, and Michelle indulged this pageantry.

Michelle thought she looked nice, too, but her mother's effusiveness was, while understandable, still too much. She suppressed the urge to flee from the rabid fussing and over-attention. Michelle tracked the language her mother used – "bright ray of sunshine" – which as a compliment didn't make sense given Michelle's skin tone, and was more aspirational than anything. You look like a bright ray of sunshine; therefore, you are a bright ray of sunshine; that which is beaming, radiant, a thing that makes others beaming and radiant, a thing that others like to have around.

You are that, be that.

"Have you eaten, honey? Are you ready?"

"I ate a bit, I'm not that hungry."

"It's going to be a long day and a long drive, you'll need strength."

Strength for what, sitting in the passenger seat, making sure Mom paid attention to the road and stopped when the lights turned red? 'Strength' and 'your truth' and 'your journey': everything freighted with such elevated language. She expected to hear about five hundred references during the wedding to the "next step" of Audra's "adventure" and her and her husband's "journey together," as if their honeymoon and e-grifting for wedding gifts was somehow virtuous. Couldn't things just be recognized as ugly and routine? Soon taking a shit will be referred to as "unburdening yourself from the toxins that hold you back from fulfilling your destiny."

"I'm ok. I'll bring energy bars."

"Good idea."

They were heading to a day-wedding reception a few hours away at The Barns at Wesleyan Hills in Connecticut. Audra and her husband nixed all of the eternal-vows part and were just having a celebration; sanctity and the state of grace and holy aspirations being something chucked to avoid boring the guests. They'd never farmed a day in their lives, but Michelle could just imagine Audra going through the grounds, ooh-ing if there were baby ducks quack-quack-quacking about, making faux-exasperated gasp-faces and taking "all part of the drama" pictures if a goat started chewing on a table leg or walked into a shot, loving the rustic-chic interior, pretending to appreciate the ornateness of a chandelier, and surely if there was a sweeping lake on the premises to pose before then oh-my-God it'd all be over *can you believe this*?!

Michelle brought the gift: a card signed from the both of them, containing a generous check drawn against her mother's account.

At various points during the ride, Dorothy would tenderly clasp Michelle's inner thigh and give her a rheumy look.

"It's ok, Mom," Michelle would respond. During the latter leg of the journey, Michelle would whisper some permutation of "it's okay" in response, suggesting to her mother that, like her vocal-strength, the thigh-clasping should peter out.

"Thanks for coming with me, Michelle. Thanks for being here with me."

"Ok, Mom. My – of course, Mom."

The wedding was well-attended, must have been four hundred people, and the interior was gorgeous, abundant overhanging vegetation, brightly-colored roses and violets and tulips counterpointed with the muted root colors of a Thanksgiving cornucopia, Indian corn and curved dwarf pumpkins. Ornamental containers held fragrant flowers and fruits: cherries, strawberries, mangos, some preserved melons, and Michelle noted that some held the occasional cherry seed. When she first spotted a cherry seed, she thought of removing it, a tiny blemish she could fix; then she realized the two or three seeds in each container were intentional imperfections, a "cute" detail Audra certainly insisted upon for some privately meaningful reason.

Michelle went through the parade of distant relatives, distant relations, friends-of-friends, the half-recalled people made real, the animating spirits underneath the social media avatars.

"Michelle!" An uncle's close friend.

"Michelle!" A different uncle's wife, ostensibly her aunt.

"Michelle!" A different cousin.

All saying how beautiful, how wonderful she looked.

"Grown so lovely," Uncle Howard said, holding her hand, as Aunt Catherine and Dorothy and some others greeted and laughed. "Oh oh, giving us a spin now" – it was Howard who was moving his arm in a semi-circle, Michelle just following the route of its passage – and she gave a quick spin.

"Doesn't she look wonderful!" Dorothy said for what must have been the tenth time. Those gathered cheered after her spin, as if witnessing Michelle participating in something corporeal was confirmation that she would remain here, not just passively gliding beyond them, but tethered to this life, this reality, this shared existence, something everyone could look back on and point to if she'd changed her mind, "but she was there, she spun, she looked so wonderful, how could she?!"

She was seated at table 21, with eleven other people, hor d'oeuvres on the plates. All also in their late twenties, also a heavy absence of "plus ones." She didn't recognize anyone except Yvette and Paul, two of Audra's married friends who, like Audra, were a few years older than Michelle. She hadn't seen them for . . . must have been almost five years. Michelle wondered why they were seated with this younger, largely single group. Maybe because they were jovial and good-hearted; or maybe a familiar pair for Michelle; or maybe just a stable presence, two people who had gotten married during college, if Michelle remembered correctly. She noted that Yvette might have a baby bump.

Audra swam upstream against the "congratulations" and "thank you's" and interruptions to grace table 21 with her presence.

"Michelle! So great you could make it, you're here!"

"Of course I am."

"Everyone, this lovely woman – my, Michelle, get a look at you —" she looked at the rest of the occupants of 21 and, curling her lip to emphasize the following in an unnatural sassy-ghetto patois – "get a look at this one, you a fox girl, *dammmn*," and then said normally, "this beautiful woman is my wonderful cousin, Michelle."

The other seated guests seemed to register her differently after hearing she was the "cousin Michelle." They were paying more attention, as if morally obligated to expend some quantum of energy on interacting with her; one or two had a look of confused recognition, the piecing together of what they'd heard and what sat before them. Michelle gave a static, elbow-stuck-to-her-side half-wave.

"This party is really wonderful. It's beautiful."

"Oh thanks, I-I just love barns and farms, I don't know why, I always loved them, there are even pigs out back, we can see them all later, they're so cute."

"My plate will remain pork free. I won't want them judging me."

"Wha- oh-" Audra closed her eyes and raised her head, laughed and slapped her knee, "Oh, that's funny. Not only pork . . . aren't you . . . still vegetarian?"

"No, not anymore. I should be, I should try to, I stopped that a few years ago."

"Oh, great you can enjoy all the food. The meat options are wayyy better than the vegetarian options. Are you still - doing - how are you liking doing with - the massages?"

"Good, good. It's all good."

"All going good?"

"All going good."

"Great! I'll leave you in the good hands of Table 21. All the guests at each table were hand-picked by me, I pored over the lists to ensure just the specific . . . selections of people that pair well."

"If a fight breaks out, we'll only have you to blame."

"I'm sure each table will produce their special brand of alchemy." So said the young man seated next to Michelle, looking up at her as she and Audra gabbed.

"Oh, I'm so glad you two will be sitting next to each other, this whole table is the table I'd want to be sitting at, for sure –" and the competing calls for Audra's attention overwhelmed her and she moved away and into another conversation, waving back at them with a comic "can you believe this?" look of a put-upon heroine in her own romantic comedy.

"No rest for her, that's for sure," the young man said. He was a not-ugly, swarthy man in his late twenties with short dark hair in the earliest stages of balding, dressed in a light blue summer suit with a dark tie with purple music notes. Most notably he had a wide chin and the countenance of a man who always appeared to be leaning into a joke or a jest.

"Mmmhmmm." She kept him in the periphery of her vision, smiled and broke attention as fleetingly as she could, to show that she bore him no ill-will and was certain he was perfectly fine but she was just not in the mood to make small talk.

"So, did I hear you did – worked – in massages? Like, massage therapy, or, like, do you do physical rehabilitation?"

"I've been, yes, I went to the Finger Lakes School, and I'm, I'm doing it until, I'm not sure exactly, I- I'm not sure how long I'll be doing it for. I'm still figuring everything out but it's not terrible."

"Not terrible is good."

The guests at the table almost-imperceptibly oriented toward her presence; rival conversations dimmed, not dramatically but as if the others wanted to give the impression of paying attention, of enfolding her within their group dynamics. She felt she was being treated as if she was unaware of the cues adults gave to children to encourage participation.

"Massage is a great way to meet people," someone else said.

"You hear massage and–" someone else said, a male, and trailed off, and then others laughed, and Michelle figured it was another iteration of the comment she'd heard many times, most often from her mother, that massage was great because who wouldn't want to date a woman who knew how to give a great massage? Her mother, ever utilitarian and adaptable and practical as functional people needed to be, assumed that even if Michelle didn't pursue massage as a career, it was a desirable skill to have, especially in the dating world. That Michelle didn't date, even though she now had this alluring quiver in her bow, was another frustrating perplexity, such a beautiful girl, if only. . . .

Michelle afforded everyone the courtesy of simulating that she was paying attention, and then stood up, indicating that she was going to get a drink from the bar and pretending to be unaware of the ensuing protestation that wouldn't it be easier to get a drink brought to the table?

The young man seated next to her began to stand up as he spoke. "I was just about to get a drink too, actually. I wanted to see what they had at the bar, and at the bar I can get them to add all the maraschino cherries I want."

Michelle checked his table setting and saw that he, in fact, didn't have a drink, but still, his lie was transparent. Maybe he was genuine, it didn't matter, she was beyond caring, although that was a lie because she felt an empathy for him that almost compelled her to acquiesce to his company.

"I'm - actually going to the bathroom first, so I'll be back," she feinted.

"Oh, the bathrooms, best part of being in a giant fancy hall like this is they have the best bathrooms. You could live in these bathrooms."

She almost thought to say "I'll be the judge of that!" She felt compelled to say something overly friendly as if she might actually come back to initiate conversation. Instead she smiled as an acknowledgment of receipt; then, before she fully turned, furrowed her brow and let the smile fade to let him know her politeness was perfunctory. It was no reflection on him but she wanted him to know not to waste his time.

Michelle walked past tables en route to the bar, a peremptory, low-wattage smile on reserve in case anyone looked her way. She recognized a young man sitting at another table: Damian, that was his name, a friend of Audra's she'd seen on-and-off at birthday parties. His younger brother had killed himself, that's why she remembered him. Suicide. Oblivion. The end of all things. The idea seemed so quaint nowadays, all things considered.

She went over to the bar, but kept enough distance so she wouldn't be expected to actually order something yet. She just wanted a breather.

A loud burp caught her attention.

"*Urp* - ooh, excuse me. Lord, must be last night's bar-bee-queee! Don't mind me, y'all, I so sorry. Mmmhmm though it taste good, it tasted good goin' down, it tastin' good comin' up." So said a female employee rapidly bee-lining past the bar; unclear whether she was a server or some type of barback. Another employee laughed and said "girl," while trailing after her.

As always, Michelle was jealous. Any time she witnessed such a lack of self-consciousness, such a delirious, gleeful flippancy, such a sheer reactive enjoyment of life: it amazed her. Here she was, straight-jacketed with self-doubt, and there were unencumbered people all about her, simple, carefree

57

people content in the mystery and magic of just living. The type of people who talked about "great sex"; or who loudly sung along when they heard a favorite song in a store; or the people who go on about the joys of a great sandwich, describing in lustrous detail the tang of the mustard, the snap of a pickle, the redolent firmness of a fresh juicy tomato. To Michelle, a sandwich was just that, a sandwich, food, something to sustain you until you get to the next challenge over the horizon.

How she envied those people. She'd never be that.

She'd resisted the entreaty to abandon this life, kept the invitation at bay. How stupid would it be to base her final decision on oblivious, literally gassy chatter about barbeque? But she just knew she'd never be that carefree and delighted, never even have one scintilla of that joie de vivre.

It was her life, after all. It was her decision.

And she hated them all, didn't she? Wasn't that what it came down to? She didn't want to be here. It was selfish of them to impose upon her this way of life, their way of life. Their system didn't work for her. Small talk and "oh my god, it's like, been so long!" and champagne cocktails and "did you hear who got divorced?" and status anxiety and "when do you think he'll finally propose to her?" and –

"It's nice of you, talking to her," Michelle overheard near the bar. Why she fixated on that, said by someone she didn't recognize, who knows? Maybe it was a sign.

The young man who'd been seated next to her shrugged. "She seems cool, actually. Not interested in me at all, but still, I tried. Can't say I didn't try." He looked around, perhaps even looking for her to see if she came back from the bathroom. He somehow must have missed her, as she was almost directly behind him, just outside his range of vision.

"Well, it's nice of you to try."

Remarkable. Just remarkable. What are the odds she'd hear (most of) that exchange? What were the odds that that exchange would even occur, right in earshot, let alone that they'd just overlook her being directly behind them? Hilarious, in a way. It just cemented the correctness of her decision.

What, had Audra sat them next to each other, kindly requested that this young man flirt with her, try and keep her engaged? Strange Michelle, did you hear all the threats she'd made, to leave this lovely wonderful life. Who could do such a thing?

She harbored no ill will toward him, not at all, none whatsoever.

It was just that her decision was made.

It was remarkable, when you really thought of it. Life was all optional. Nowadays, the option to leave was just right there, open to anyone, but people were just so afraid. Economics, wasn't it? In any competitive market, when an alternative product becomes easier to access, the dominant product needs to stay competitive: upgrade, improve somehow, be better. What was LIFE's improvement, its attempt to keep her loyal? Was it her mother's panicky helicoptering, filling silences with her hollow noises? Audra benevolently bestowing superficial attention?

Fuck them. Good intentions weren't enough. This was her life, her choice.

She would pee, she decided strangely. One of life's small pleasures, right? The pleasure of release, return to homeostasis, comfort.

So she did. That guy had been right, these bathrooms were quite grand.

Peeing burned a bit, no real feeling of release, tepid and dispiriting. Oh well, a let-down. Figures.

She sat back down at the table.

"Oh, hey!" that same fellow said to her, seated in his spot. "No drink? Or just crush it right at the bar?"

She wondered if it would be funny to learn his name before she left. Just, why not? But no.

She closed her eyes while he yammered some more. She didn't need to close her eyes, but it felt appropriate to give an outward appearance of concentration.

I submit, she thought. I'm tired. I'm tired. Let me out. Let me *out*. She succumbed to the voice, the same voice that had made itself available to all who sought it, the same voice she'd threatened to succumb to since it made its presence known. The presence was one of those cataclysmic events that's all a matter of perspective. When the whole world panicked but people of a certain sentiment thought, *finally*, an option.

This life has nothing to offer me. I want out.

She closed her eyes and felt the tingling, and wondered if that was really necessary; was it like toothpaste, where the tingling was introduced solely to let you feel like the product was working?

Are you sure you wish to join us?

She wouldn't really die, she knew. Her body would still exist. But she'd be elsewhere, ferried off to somewhere else, no longer an atomized soul imprisoned in the isolation of solitary consciousness, but spread, intermingled, joined with all the others who heeded the call, who chose something else, something better.

Yes, I want it, a million times over. I want it. I want this. I want it!

She pictured her catatonic face and came to like the idea of her body still existing, being an imposition on others; some payback for all the countless burdens and expectations people had thoughtlessly saddled her with all these years.

She could still hear the voice of her mother, clamoring in protest: How could she feel this way, beautiful young Michelle, the whole "world" before her?

All those people, they were just of a different cast. Their system didn't work for her. She knew her temperament, saw before her a life of leaden gloom, where the guaranteed, ever-present hardships invested in her daily life overshadowed any ephemeral joy she could hope to experience in return, a life that she did not sufficiently value to lessen her sufferings by any active means.

And was it possible she was wrong? Surely, someone else could find the same reasoning unpersuasive; most people would, in fact. But she was her, and for her to find that conceit wrong, she would have to be someone else, with an entirely different frame of reference, entirely different wiring.

She opened her eyes and saw her mother staring from across the room, concern writ large across her face. Michelle considered herself a decent person; in fact, she never disliked herself, only her situation, and always felt empathy and pity for all things. She didn't enjoy witnessing her mother's pain. Any satisfaction she felt was the satisfaction that inheres in equity, of righting a longstanding wrong.

But she could, perhaps, stop this. Just continue on with her life, think of others, they say.

But life wasn't lived that way. It was she who carried her own burdens, in every conscious moment.

She untethered herself, persevered, slavered on, for herself.

The anxiety and depression and panic and expectations and failures and disappointments were, she saw, quite literally saw, a twitching expansive gray cloud, that now narrowed, winnowed, and as it folded in on itself the ambient chattering in her soul diminished in tandem, until the cloud was nothing but a long thin line and here there was – could it be? – a placid stillness. Is this pure consciousness she had heard about, the quieting of the restless mind, one of the zillions of self-help buzzwords she'd encountered throughout her treatment, and the whole time the solution was here and she'd always kept it at bay to serve the demands of other people, think of other people, think of other people, that was her curse, wasn't it, think of others, forget your suffering, as if she wasn't a human being but some other creature that could live a life in psychic concert with others.

But now she could –

The sentiments of millions of others who had taken this voyage spiraled through her, from all across the world, she felt her burdens dissolving, such a sublime stillness, that was it, wasn't it, such pristine perfection to be unburdened, her consciousness spread so thin, floating up and away, becoming indistinguishable, intermingled with the others, so her thoughts were their thoughts, she joined them in great sweeping monuments that beckoned to her.

The area between her upper lip and nose split with a great big tearing sound, and she could swear that beneath the din of the crowd she could hear the satisfyingly slow "pshhhhhh" release of gas from her face, and she smiled a mutilated smile, because that noise served no purpose but was something only for herself to know, carry with her to elsewhere. She held her tongue out and felt jellied chunks of her own flesh and greedily slurped down, not caring about choking or taste or texture and hoped she looked deranged and horrifying because these people's thoughts were nothing anymore, and to her it was the confirmation that her prayers were finally being answered.

Unburdened, and within that stillness there was a fiery, ecstatic rumbling, atonal but somehow musical; no, that wasn't music, it was the ebullient joy of making the right decision, and for the first time in her life she could understand how it was that people bellowed out their favorite song in the grocery store, what it meant to be in the moment.

What Michelle knew of her left arm ended at the elbow, replaced with a pointed splinter interlacing with pulsating deep blue and red veins, the vibrant technicolor she needed to see and it was so delightful, in that delight again was the understanding of how it was that people could feel the urge to bellow and shout and dance.

"And did you always feel like it was that time? That magic time, the witching hour when it's your time to go, the store now closed but everyone's outside still knocking!" she sung aloud, the made-up clauses measured into some kind of melody, an irrepressible song on the fly for this wonderful time. To think, Audra or someone else, hyperventilating over that tune, having no idea what Michelle sung before she left, always turning those phrases over in their mind; what did they mean! what song was that! Audra turning to her stupid selfish husband years later, yelling, "did no one think to Shazam it!"

And at the end of the splinter there lay gagging and sputtering that boy who tried to talk to her, and wasn't that terrible, objectively terrible, in that version of the world where such things mattered and one could be sad, and how was it that it didn't bother her when she knew herself and knew she was a good person?

And it felt so good to not need to care anymore about this world, and she was finally home, to become one who chose to cast their lot with this new presence, to be one with those who felt as she felt, that chunk of ice that for so long desired to melt into some opposite stream.

NOTES

So I'm a Hebrew school dropout. I went for one semester in the 7th grade, dropped out, and then considered re-enrolling due to an unrequited crush I had on a fellow student. (I'll leave out her name just so people do not try to figure out who it may be, but I'll say she has one of the prettier Jewish names. Although it's not one of the three prettiest Jewish names, which everyone agrees are Moishe, Schlomo and Zero. For those wondering, the two Jewish names best suited for a pair of pugs would be Saul and Herschel). I guess my quixotic interest in her was not enough to inconvenience my Sundays. (For the foregoing sentence, as a sign of what an ignorant Jew I am, I had to Google the Sabbath to figure out whether Hebrew school had been on a Saturday or Sunday).

Anyway, I digress. This fellow student was pretty, intelligent, shy, kind, and only half-Jewish, which means she had all of our strengths and none of our weaknesses. I don't really think I ever spoke to her. The extent of our relationship was later becoming Facebook friends, as she eventually went to a rival nearby high school.

There's probably a period in every young man's life when he uses Facebook to add as many attractive female friends / acquittances / not-really-but-maybe acquittances. So, it seems she had a sister who was a few years younger who shared with me several mutual friends, so I added her, why not, right? And this younger sister, like her older sister, was strikingly beautiful. If social media could be believed, the two sisters were best friends and, aware of the exponential power of their combined beauty, took many a manicured and stylized photo together.

The younger sister and I had actually begun to chat quite a bit online on account of our friends in common and some shared interests, and I learned a bit about her. She aspired to be a model and actress, seemed to have a healthy family life and, to the extent social media could be believed, had friends who cared about her.

There were troubles, though, that could be detected. She seemed to be occupationally rootless, never really sticking to anything. She lived at home long after college. She took an interest in my fiction (likely a red flag right there), and when a project was proposed to adapt several of my stories as audio dramas, I recommended her for the narrator's job, largely, to be honest, out of knowing that she could use whatever piddling money the project offered (this project, like most such projects that have been proposed to me, and likely all such projects everywhere, never came to be). She was naturally very busty and had kept her hair long, and then rather suddenly she underwent an extreme breast reduction, cut her hair very short, and seemed to be attempting an Audrey Hepburn in Breakfast at Tiffany's aesthetic.

Our correspondence declined, largely from the inertia of life but also because she just didn't seem as active on social media. A few years passed and a mutual friend informed me she killed herself via an intentional overdosing. After learning of this, I looked at her YouTube page and saw some of her final videos, which consisted of her appearing frightfully skinny and joylessly and rather arrhythmically dancing around. Her second-to-last social media post was "life's good, right?"

I'm not sure exactly how the foregoing inspired this story. As a depressive myself, I'm not naïve enough to wonder "how could a beautiful person with a supportive family ever do such a thing," although, in my more depressed states, I often think, hey if my family had been more supportive or I'd been better-looking, maybe I wouldn't be in this mental predicament? But of course, that's not true. But I do think about her sometimes, and wonder if I should have tried to . . . what, exactly? I had no idea that her depression was so stark or, other than her occupational issues, that her life was unraveling. It's not like I could force an intervention for someone I'd never even met before. I do think about and wonder what, if anything, her family and closer friends might have known or suspected, how they dealt with it, and if they struggled with or wondered how it could be that such an attractive, seemingly well-liked person struggled with such evidently enormous mental health problems. The desire for lonely, atomistic individuals to break free by joining some kind of collective consciousness is a recurring theme in my work, and this sad tale about my digital friend, I suppose, was this story's launching point.

May As Well Blame It On The Heat

When it comes to understanding why people do what they do, not enough credit is given to boredom, either being hopelessly mired in it or making a desperate pivot to escape it. And the power of heat, too, although that just may hasten the speed of descent. Once the decision has been made, and you find your thoughts sweating out of you, it's much easier to stay the course than reconsider where you're headed.

So it was, boredom as the initiating agent, that drenching summer as the sealing agent, that led Sunil and Nakia, both within calendar-flipping distance of forty, to "try" to have a child, because the prospects of midlife and beyond stretched out before them and both had qualms about what they saw. It was Sunil who vocalized the fear, Sunil the one more affected by the loss of their friends who'd decamped to the suburbs, more stung with jealousy by the friends who'd authored themselves a new direction in life. Jealous was a strange word to use, because it was a short-lived, avoidable jealousy, more some cousin of jealousy left undefined on the family tree. One similarity that made Nakia and him so compatible was their mutually held belief in the benefits of childlessness, but recently he could dimly see the diminishing returns ever-encroaching, and as life stretched onward what would he have to show for it?

And those were the conscious thoughts he wrestled with, that flared up when he was careless where he looked on social media and allowed himself to be hurt by others' purported happiness. But it didn't have to be like that, he knew. As he'd gotten older, he'd moved far enough away from the defeatist prism he'd thought himself consigned. The stings and humiliations of adolescence that so imprinted themselves on his formative personality had, if not healed over time, lost the power of narrative.

The conclusion that he'd been an unhappy child still remained, but it was now work to conjure the names and faces and circumstances, the premises for his conclusion. That his father had been a commandeering alcoholic (that word, of course, never uttered within his family), his mother a craven, self-absorbed avoider, that he'd always felt like a burden: that dynamic that had so set him against having a family of his own now felt like the vicarious traumas of a half-remembered movie.

And Nakia, her resistance to having a child had always been less emotional and more primal. She'd had a happy family life, or a reasonable enough facsimile of one. Three siblings, all with children of their own, which had taken the pressure off her. For her, it was the fear of physical transformation, of subordinating her own body to a process she could not control, to those thousands of little experiences one could be warned about but never prepared for, the real education being in the process itself, at which point it was already too late.

*

It was a boring, languorous, sweltering summer. Sunil had always worked remotely, and Nakia's job had just recently announced they were making the same transition. So they stayed at home together, each with their own High Velocity Blower fan directed at their work stations to keep them cool.

It was late spring when Sunil had brought up the idea, which was itself an accomplishment, as he was one to keep emotions close to the chest. Were it a few years earlier, he very well may have kept it all to himself, even though he knew Nature had its own schedule. He knew he couldn't live with himself if he never gave his concern a voice.

Imagine an alternative future with their lovely son, Sunil's own face looking back at him, and now blink and it disappeared, the image broken up and swirling away like dust motes caught in the arc of their High Velocity Blower, all because he'd said nothing. It was as if the future life of his unborn son impelled him, through time and space, to advocate for his creation.

And Nakia, as she aged strangely became less fearful of the expected physical changes; counterintuitively, transfiguration might be more threatening for those most handy enough to withstand it, the young, buoyant and hopeful. She'd *already* changed physically, and pregnancy wouldn't "kill her dreams" or result in so drastic a "sacrifice" as her younger self feared, because those dreams were fulfilled – to live in the City with someone she loved – and by being fulfilled, they died, just as a journey ends once the destination is reached. And, as she was fond of saying to herself as of late when thinking about her oldest sister's quixotic attempt to start her own business, dreams end when you wake up.

Nakia had favorably reconciled herself to the reality that there was no impending, vague but fragile "greatness" that required her constant vigilance to avoid being mistakenly "sacrificed." This was it. And it wasn't bad. And she'd experienced unwanted and unpleasant physical transformations already – to her always waking up tired to the spreading around her waist and the indefatigable flappy flabbiness under her arms – and the gulf between the physical burdens of pregnancy and whatever unburdened physicality she'd once sought to protect had sufficiently dwindled. And the heat, too, it was as if the heat seared out her concerns, those residual fears turned to steam heat that just wafted out her brain up out into the ether.

So they agreed to try. Well, not doing anything overt to "try," other than staying aware of her expected fertility cycles and not using prophylactics. Sunil knew they were older and it could be difficult and a specialist might be needed, but, already so quick to disappointment, he did not want to seek one out, as if to conceal from himself how much he wanted this to be successful. They would let, as quietly gloating successful couples say after having had conceived, to let nature take its course.

*

And by mid-summer, less than three months after they broached the issue and about a month after Nakia suspected, based on her bloating feet and heightened sense of smell, a pregnancy test officially confirmed it. Heeding Nakia's call to come into the bathroom, Sunil stood there, strangely muted, as if the competing emotions couldn't overcome the inviting torpor of the noonday heat. So this was it, the gun in the air signaling the start of the race.

He studied himself for clues as to how he was feeling. Okay, he felt okay, although he had the fierce desire to double-check their finances. This wasn't the bush leagues anymore.

For Nakia, the straight line on the test indicating "pregnant" was a homing beacon to those fears she thought she'd banished, that she discovered had only insidiously obscured themselves, all now re-emerging victorious, all-the-stronger for their dormancy. That straight line was runic code for "we got you now."

No, those were just unnatural negative thoughts from Young Nakia, screaming her last and seeking revenge. Young Nakia, Impetuous Nakia, Noncommittal Nakia.

She remembered who she was, that she wanted this, had agreed to it, and soon like water smoothing over a sand castle the sharp edges of panic washed away. She kissed Sunil on his cheek, which seemed more appropriate, something more befitting accomplishment than a passionate lip-locking, and then they hugged, which felt most appropriate of all.

*

Here they were, a few weeks more into the pregnancy, with a date set for the first consultation with the OB-GYN, and the requisite books on both their Kindles, more reassuring physical copies for reference on the nightstand. Nakia found herself curiously uninterested in sex, maybe a side effect of the biological point of sex being having been realized. She was especially relieved to be pregnant, because her interest in sex had been waning, had already assumed a passionless, functionalist approach before they'd even decided to try and conceive. Nothing having to do with their love fading; nothing having much to do with anything, really, maybe just fatigue, work stress, and both of them having grown more fully into their fairly reserved personalities.

Instead, she thought, inwardly smiling, being feted over and catered to these next months could have its advantages. Sunil had already begun cooking all the meals, perhaps as practice when she was unable to, but when would that be, the last few weeks before delivery? She wasn't complaining.

The stress, strangely, had been lifted. The part they could really control was over. They'd docked themselves on the boat called Biology, and were now following it downstream.

Though it came in waves, there was intermittently that grip of almost-mania, what it must feel like to realize the brakes have stopped working and the bridge has gone out. And then Nakia chided herself because that's an absurd thought, everything was fine. It should mean something that her go-to reference was so outlandish, it should be evidence for the baselessness of her pointless worrying.

*

"How are you feeling?" Sunil asked at bedtime, patting her stomach even though there was, of course, nothing yet to feel.

"I feel good." Nakia thought to herself as if to verify the statement. "I feel good."

"Great. Do you like the prenatals? Should we ask the doctor about what's the best brand or do you think it's okay?" If it were the former, then it'd need to be added to the list on the table, and neither of them wanted to get up. But the alternative would be each struggling to remember to add it to the list for tomorrow.

"I'm sure it's fine. I've been taking them for a while, I'm sure it's fine and it will come up when we talk about what to eat." She'd already stopped drinking alcohol and eating dessert, the first of a series of sacrifices. For Sunil, she knew, proactivity was its own point, his hedge against the turtling avoidance he either inherited from his mother or came to on his own when life's demands proved too overwhelming.

Sometimes Sunil couldn't sleep, and claimed to wake up often in the middle of the night, although he'd never been awake when Nakia woke up throughout the night and early morning, as she habitually did for seemingly no reason. She was too afraid of sleep medicines – it seemed every overdose story involved a sleep medicine – and a sleep study had been on her ever-expanding list of things to eventually do for her own benefit, that list now shunted aside. (Just the beginning.) Why, why did she wake up so often? There was never some discrete, pedestrian worry that crept into a dream, never some character running late with an assignment that forced her to make worrying connections.

She was asleep now, she knew, and her dream-self, if she could visualize it, would have a pinched face of concern. Nakia lay in silent anticipation, knowing, just knowing, that being aware that she was dreaming would break whatever illusion was needed to sustain the dream. Already the environment of the dream was blank, a non-entity, as if chased away by her own

69

presence. But she was still asleep so hold tight, ride out this meta-dream wave, let something pop up and keep her here.

Her dream-self sensed rushing gas seeping in around her. She remembered the air conditioner was on full blast and two fans were running, so she knew that sound was just circulating air piping its way into the dream. Instead, turn that sound into cooking gas, us making dinner, what would we eat? The dream, that recalcitrant, unknowable beast, stomped away from the story prompts Nakia offered.

Let the air glide over her. Sunil's body against hers, hand curled around her hip, the air neutralizing the body-heat, whisking away sweat, allowing them to embrace. Body pressure, connection, relax into the dream, the moment, a hot bath. (Hot baths aren't allowed anymore, she thought, layers beneath the dream, and the fabric of the dream, staid and indistinct, rippled and wavered.)

Nakia knew she was still asleep, hold on to that. Sunil's body, curiously wet, slickened with sweat, up against her stomach. His hand, it must be, but it moved, grooved almost, with deliberate purpose. Not his hand, his lips, a sex dream, she arched back, she hadn't had one of these in . . . Sunil eating her out, no hot baths allowed except tongue baths, wink wink. Dream- self hoped she tasted clean, felt strange about doing this while pregnant; but no, it wasn't oral sex, too high up, the dream became Sunil and her laughing about him not knowing what he was doing. It would be nice if he wasn't always so sensitive and could take constructive criticism, and her dream became her own face laughing about it.

Sunil wasn't near her, she somehow knew, he was curled off on the other side of the bed, and even in testing this theory her dream took a fierce turn. She grew groping tentacles, desperately probing to find Sunil, locate him across the deep, unforbidden ocean of their shared bed.

Not Sunil, and a fire alarm of confusion popped the bubble of sleep.

Nakia waded through the fog into consciousness, propelled by the way one understands, so briefly, the importance of a dream in those brief moments of first awakening. The room was dark and deep enough for her to know it was that dead period of early morning, but their curtains were threadbare and lights from the street always stubbornly found their way in so she could make out what she saw.

She couldn't move. She was so immobilized that her own consciousness in her head, that external watcher, that voice yelling at the screen that was one's internal monologue, was silenced. It was as if all the moisture, all thoughts, all the *life* had been suctioned out of her body, and she lay helplessly on her back, a husk. The room was suffocatingly hot, the only blanket atop her a blanket of heat.

A humanoid face at her midsection, whether it truly had this ghastly blueish-white pallor or it was a trick of the early morning dark she'd never know. She could only see the upper half of its head, vaguely and inconsistently, multiple swaying limbs obscuring her view. No, not limbs, too wispy and chiffon-like to be limbs, and limbs didn't protrude that high up, less limbs and more like the protective canopy of some stunted tree, or a contained, viscous mist. She couldn't see what stretched out beyond and must lay slinking and sliding down the end of the bed and onto the bedroom floor.

Some impulse and her leg fidgeted, she intuited Sunil beside her, asleep, and that juxtaposition, of him by her side while this was happening to her, brought her some fresh new depth of abandonment, desperation, and, somehow, humiliation. When she finally breathed, her dehydration was frighteningly obvious in her lightheadedness, more fluid in her sticky sweat than in her body.

The head turned toward her, and there was a pinch, a *tug* when the face detached from whatever it was doing. The external watcher in her mind returned, instructing her by showing her in her mind's eye what to do: push the face away, wake up Sunil, run. Nakia lifted her leg to kick, and then stopped and screamed when she saw the face more clearly. Time stopped, the face was twitching desperately, protruding eyes doing something like pleading, that absurd swaying canopy retracting intelligibly, as if to give her a full unadulterated view of what lay before her. In several places its skin popped, but symmetrically, like a controlled demolition, from each side of its eyes down to its chin, and little nubs emerged, extended further out and she could only think of Corn Pops, fetid Corn Pops, and they were emerging further; the face became less pleading, there was confidence verging on the triumphant, the nubs were extending and she knew, somehow knew, that what would eventually emerge would be vice-like and crushing, a bear trap reaching outward . . . .

She let out a flurry of bicycle-kicks, screamed, smacked the air and herself and shook Sunil simultaneously, as if a flurry of roaches had just descended upon them. Just before she closed her eyes, she saw the shape disappear, sensed more than heard its added weight on the floor, shifting and sliding away toward the bedroom door.

"Nakia, Nakia, what's the matter, what's the matter?" Sunil steadied her with his body. She pushed him off her aggressively, how fucking dare he assume this pose to calm his hysterical wife, seconds ago sleeping in his ignorance while she was being violated in their bed, how fucking dare he.

"Calm down, calm down," and his pressure became firmer.

"There's someone in the house!"

Nakia could tell, by the way Sunil looked less alarmed than annoyed, that he didn't believe her, but was doing his dutiful best to quell his irritation and get up. He bounded up and turned on the lights. Nothing here. The fans were still on but the A/C was off, he noted, although that sometimes happened, some annoying fucking energy saving function that they always thought they'd turned off.

Sunil disappeared out into the living room. Her anger melted into regret; no, she wanted to reach out to him, don't go, don't go, what had she sent him out to confront? She lay sweating in bed, paralyzed as to what she should do. Please come back, please come back, how long must she wait before going out there? She poked at her gut, the area below her belly-button where she'd felt the tug. The lights were dim in the bedroom, but she couldn't see anything, didn't feel anything different.

Sunil came back with a big mug. "There's no one here. The doors and windows are all fine, everything looks normal. Here, sit up and have some water."

"Thanks." Nakia sat up at the edge of the bed, cupped the mug with both hands. "My stomach hurts, can you take a look?"

"Okay," and he did so. At first he was frustrated, but then remembered the context and was evidently relieved that he found nothing. "It looks fine. What does it feel like? Is it, like, a stabbing kind of feeling, or maybe just gas? Is it getting better or worse?"

She detected a shift in his concern, a shaky nervousness, almost a ready willingness to comply with instructions. *Now* he cared, something with the pregnancy, and *now* he cares.

"It feels fine." She was a bit upset at the admission but not in the mood to pretend otherwise. "It doesn't hurt anymore," she said with finality, guilty about how she'd just felt.

"Do you think you had a nightmare? Why - why did you think there was someone here?"

And what could she possibly say other than dismissible lunacy interpreted as an extreme waking night terror, provide him fodder for psychological speculation about the upcoming pregnancy; and what could she say in response to all that because that *was* the most realistic explanation, although she'd never in her whole life had any dream or vision or whatever anyone could call it that was anything as vivid and bizarre. Which was worse, for that to have been real, or for her to be so disconnected from reality that she could conjure her own living hellscape? No, best to do what needed to be done, convince herself in time that she was overreacting and it was truly nothing but a hallucination.

No, *that* was too scary, a hallucination, crazy people had hallucinations.

Conclude it was some kind of nightmare, stick with that, some nightmare and she'd been dreaming the whole time, even though she knew she'd been awake, she knew she'd been awake, she knew –

*

Sunil wanted to see the OB-GYN immediately. Nakia wouldn't act so withdrawn and sullen then, she'd have to put on her professional face. Then they could tell the doctor this story – Nakia would start out a bit quiet, embarrassed perhaps, but glad to air out her troubles – but the doctor would tell them something about nightmares being common, especially among older couples having their first child, or something authoritative, something like 'I've heard this a million times,' but even Sunil knew that would be a bit much, not realistic. Instead, Sunil imagined the doctor saying something like, 'not as uncommon as you'd think.'

Sunil had Googled about sleep paralysis but restrained from sending her any links, accurately sensing that broaching the subject would be unjustly interpreted as interfering somehow and only serve to get her riled up again.

But Sunil needed her peevish mopiness to end. Not just for her, of course, but it couldn't be good for the baby, for her to be so down and so weirdly antagonistic toward him, as if somehow this was *his* fault. It crushed him to think of his son in there (assuming a son made him feel better), forming in the current of this pumping hatred that now possessed her. And he was a person, too, with feelings, and those didn't just end upon her pregnancy. Her withdrawal of affections hobbled him, consumed him, drained the meaning of every quotidian thing he did throughout the day. What was the point of work, or of doing anything, when his wife apparently hated him?

It would end, he told himself, just be patient and caring, as all fights resolved, although at least every other fight had an understandable beginning. Come to think of it, they very rarely fought, both being agreeable sorts, both knowing the high drama of confrontation over some dumb thing was never worth the cost. In their prior worldview, it was always them, the good, caring people against the vast uncaring world, with whatever challenges representing "the world" always changing: usually work obligations, or just the general mass of inconsiderate others.

Could this situation even be called a fight if one side didn't even know if they were in a fight?

Nakia had Googled sleep paralysis, too, scanned through the same materials Sunil had, some tiny commonality of shared experience that would go unstated. She also looked up nightmares experienced by pregnant women, but really what was the point, because whether she found anything that confirmed or denied her experience wouldn't make it any better, and shit, which was worse? Assume she was the first person on Planet

Earth to Google a medical worry and come away with a wholly satisfying resolution: what then? Business as usual, continue going on until the next heart attack?

Nakia didn't intellectually believe what she'd seen was "real," or, more likely, wasn't feeling equipped to grapple with that question. The paralysis she'd experienced carried over to waking life. Assuming, of course, it was just some crazed dream (of course, of course), what was to come? What dreams awaited her further into her pregnancy? What had she signed up for; and to the extent that she would never stop worrying about her child, had she, in a sense, signed the direction of her life away, consigned to this overarching worry?

And she still had the pregnancy to go forward with, all these changes and complications to her body, watching everything she ate and drank and crossed her fingers and hoped this wasn't the time either of their jobs downsized or who knows what else people such as them must worry about while the rest of the idiots blithely went about their business as things always just clicked into place for them. It was the sensitive who suffered the most acutely.

It was like she'd signed a contract only to now realize she hadn't considered the dizzying, dense array of fine print. Now, into the pregnancy, it was as if some undergirding thesis that secretly supported her worldview had articulated itself to her: she was distrustful of Life, conscious of its burdens and unmoved by its supposed satisfactions, and had always compromised by keeping a safe distance, one foot always back onto the ledge. Leaping into an embrace of Life, agreeing to perpetuate it and take on all its responsibilities and anxieties was not for her, and only now was that fact coming into relief, relief sharp enough to slice.

This was a lot to take while trying to eat breakfast, her husband stealing glances at her. Nakia was not able to give him the reciprocating glances of affection he desired. Why work? Why eat? Why do anything? To continue this process of change within her?

It was as if some hole had been punctured in the ceiling of her life, the water had leaked in and the sanctuary was

75

soaked. The hole could be fixed, sure – time could do that, time, logic, "mindfulness," whatever it is that could do that – but the contaminating water would stay, the rot setting in. Sunil and Nakia would have to navigate their domain with everything soaked and ruined, pretend everything was fine and normal as disease-causing life forms flourished and multiplied and the watery filth rose up above their knees, and at some point Sunil would yell at her to stop complaining, what was the matter? why was she like this? and she'd look down at the swirling muck and all that grew within it and that precipitating incident would have been so long ago that it'd been like this water had always been there.

Calm down. Calm down, Nakia. But she was shaking; something had gone wrong that night, the bell couldn't be un-rung, and she was terrified, afflicted by the stupefaction the rabbit in the open field must feel when it detects the descending shadow of a hawk. Nakia had never felt this way before, so totally in thrall, consumed by this unshakeable knowledge of being irretrievably doomed.

But if she was being honest, during some earlier times in her life she'd heard Doom taking deep sighs outside the door, and things must have been too okay for too long because she'd forgotten that this condition had never left, and she'd forgotten who she was, the person who remained cautious and afraid, and had taken this big leap and forgot all about Doom remaining perched just outside her door, just ready for her to do something foolhardy.

And she had, and Doom was here.

*

But Sunil had told her that the windows had been closed, that there had been no sign of forced entry, and everything had looked fine. And, she knew, that was true: everything looked the way it normally had.

But he hadn't mentioned that the kitchen window had been opened half-way. They usually left it half-opened when they cooked, and there wasn't a screen. Nakia didn't say anything to him, because what would be the point?, but she made a show of forcing the window shut.

Sunil was half-up out of his chair when he realized what she was doing, as those physical acts were his duty and Nakia was pregnant, but the deed was done with a thud and Nakia stormed into the bedroom, grunting about needing to take a work call, although Sunil listened and didn't hear anything. About the time he decided to go and see how she was doing she came out, keeping alive this apparently new tradition of seeming despondent and lost until the moment he tried to say something, at which point she'd become irritable and impatient. The only relief seemed to come that night, when she clutched him in bed, and he was able to tell her that everything would be fine, everything would be fine, and he took her tightened silence as a kind of acceptance.

*

The following day, and Sunil still had to tread carefully. Every action felt freighted. He wasn't sure what she was working on, but whenever he looked, he was sure she wasn't working: she was either clicking away with an intensity too feverish to be work, or staring too listlessly and vacantly to be getting anything done. He wondered what it was that so consumed her. He had suggested she take a couple of days off and that had been shot down, although to what end he didn't know.

Enough was enough.

"Hey honey," Sunil cornered her on the couch as she ate yogurt. Nakia looked as abject as ever, fixated on her yogurt as if it would bring some reprieve, and something both about the absurdity and tragedy before him compelled him to put an end to whatever this was. "What's going on?" He knew, obviously, but didn't know what else to say. He just wanted something to say, something general, something that could ease into something else.

He expected some flurry of impotent score-settling, but as if she recognized the futility of that approach, or caught herself in the remorse of how she was acting, or just needed to do something to escape from the clutches of this depression, her resolve broke and all she said was, "there's a mark on my stomach," and then with a frustrated flourish tossed the yogurt-y spoon onto the paper towel on the coffee table.

"Let me see," Sunil said, gingerly exploring the area as if he had any useful training in the field.

"Be careful," she implored, fighting the urge to become hysterical.

He waited to say the following until he was absolutely sure: "I don't see anything." Her skin was dark brown, and red marks or blemishes didn't show as easily as they did on Sunil's lighter brown skin.

"It's right above the belly button. It feels sensitive to the touch, too. Not, like, any sharp pain or anything, but I can feel it."

This jolted Sunil, as this was something involving THE BABY, that entity now atop the hierarchy of needs. Sunil was intensely nostalgic for those halcyon moments when this was just some stupid spat that would dissipate as all of them always did. Now it affected THE BABY, and his stomach turmoiled with the nausea and anxiety of being on the precipice of some important decision, knowing there would be severe consequences, but not being sure of what to do. Nakia sensed this shift in priorities, and the doom she carried with her re-asserted itself.

With that shift came a realization, as if sprawled, overlooked facts came out from hiding and made their import known. The thing she saw, humanoid but still so outrageous, that shroud on its face, as if designed not to be fully seen. Imagine some species targeting newly pregnant women. A species that had developed traits that would give it the appearance of some kind of blurry insanity, roughly approximating the "shadow people" seen by sufferers of sleep paralysis. A happenstance that would so easily lead to the conclusion of a nightmare or a delusion explained away as happening to someone overly emotional, worried and sensitive. And her, especially, her fear, resentment and second-doubts radiated out of her, a curlicue of scent that lifted its fingers into that thing's nose and carried it through their opened window.

This final "X" on the map might be wrong, but she was groping in the right territory, she felt. And once this course was

78

charted, the belief was set and not bound to be dislodged. No one would believe her, no one could believe her, there was nothing any doctor could do. Go to the doctor, let him take his sonogram, and what would she really expect, some apparent deformity? Of course not, these things wouldn't allow that, they wouldn't have survived for so long if their handiwork could be so easily detected.

No, it would be several more months of agonizing . . . an impossibility, just impossible to foresee sitting idly by these months, knowing this project was cursed before it began in earnest, having to go through the motions of work, the charade of planned maternity leave, the nodding and "yes doctors" and plaintive-fake smiles Sunil would require when he told her she needed to get her folic acid and avoid XYZ for what she knew was a sprouting abomination. Would it reveal itself just after birth, the same ghastly blueish-white pallor and criss-crossing waving growths? Or would it be even more insidious, give her the curse of a lifetime of quiet observation and suspicion, waiting for the truth to be revealed until its mysterious developmental cycle made itself known? Or would it just be plain, simple, and tragic, a stillbirth, with the same tiny mark she bore, that apparently only she could see, and then she'd cry and cry about what she could have or should have done differently.

*

Sunil had been on his best behavior; he truly had been. Patient, as patient as he could be; accommodating, as accommodating as he could be; and he'd done well, never once raised his voice, did his best to lessen the sting of his impatience, sublimate the hurt pride caused by her dismissal and disrespect. Like he was a lodger in their lives, not even an equal member. Why wouldn't she explain? Yes, the dream, he knew, the nightmare, how many more times could he console her, how many more times could he suggest a doctor or a psychiatrist or time off work or a getaway or a visit to one of her sisters' or what, what else was there except at some point you must come to terms with reality?

It was when she suggested without words, just from the shaking of her head, that she didn't want to be a mother. Sunil had felt, intimately felt, the internal wiring that connected his throat to his stomach, and his insides almost lurched out of him. To deter her from this train of thought she was riding along, he diverted, compromised by calling the OB-GYN's office and requesting an urgent appointment with Dr. Savera, explaining that his wife was highly worried about her pregnancy and wanted to come in as soon as possible to make sure everything was alright.

But for what?, as the next day the searing cramping began, and the doctor confirmed with a sonogram the beginning of the miscarriage. These things happen, Dr. Savera told them, with surprisingly less grace than Sunil would have expected. Perhaps that rougher 'it is what it is' treatment was some psychological doctor-trick for the benefit of aggrieved couples, so they didn't think the world had uniquely turned its back on them in their moment of triumph. Dr. Savera assured them that he and his wife had had two miscarriages, and now had two happy, healthy children of their own, and in time, once this miscarriage passed, they could be right back to trying.

He was cursed, Sunil thought, and that was the wrong, unhelpful attitude to have, he knew, but wasn't he entitled to his feelings? Things never worked out for him. It was his fault, somehow, that things didn't work out, as if God or the forces of the universe checked its ledger, realized that *Sunil* was the source of that successful sperm, and the universe did what it needed to do to remedy that oversight, that oversight that allowed Sunil to temporarily think he might just get something that he wanted.

That was the wrong attitude, he knew, and told himself so, but it lingered. He worked hard to bury his suspicions that Nakia had wanted this to happen. That she, somehow, willed this to happen. Sunil thought hotly that Nakia's family might be pleased. They were always disappointed and upset that she married an Indian, and not another proud, successful Black man like the rest of her siblings. They never said as such, but he felt it, the way they were cordial but aloof, their entreaties always feeling like the mechanical bare minimum.

He did his best to console Nakia who, after hearing the news, seemed oddly and quickly reconciled to it. It was as if she forgot that she was supposed to be angry, upset or standoffish toward Sunil, again allowing herself to be coddled and cradled.

Sunil knew to bite his tongue about wanting to try again as soon as possible. Let her get through this, let them get through this, lick their wounds and try again. Anything but the shrinking, decaying course their lives had been on before this pregnancy.

*

For Nakia, as much as she hated to say it, the miscarriage might be a blessing in disguise. A way to start afresh, a chance to reconsider, to not spend a pregnancy in tormented anticipation. She would demand they move, and, if they ever tried again – that itself being a big if – every night every window would be closed shut.

Nakia, despite believing firmly in the truth of something she knew sounded insane, reconciled herself to the lonely reality that no one would ever believe her.

But if there was any silver lining to all this, Nakia thought, Sunil might believe her, just maybe, once he saw her now, now that this bleeding had begun.

NOTES

Geez, there's another crowd-pleaser, amirite? I like relationship "two-handers," or a story that just involves the tensions between two characters. (This may be a result of my self-diagnosed prosopagnosia, which is the difficulty in telling people's faces apart, but even more severe is my inability to remember a person's name. You know how many times I've had to go through stories to make sure I didn't confuse characters' names? However many times it's been, I doubt it's been enough to entirely eliminate the problem, so apologies in advance.)

As one gets older, one cannot help but think about the paths not taken, the weight of society's unspoken expectations, what it means to be a full and complete human. I suppose Nakia represents the classic wary Hamantaschen approach, Sunil that part of me more susceptible and stung by the gradual receding of friendship and affections that comes with getting older. Age dwindles aspiration, and what seems to me now to be this fancy-free, quixotic short story campaign might look deeply, deeply pathetic if I'm continuing it as an elderly old Hamantaschen: alone, dry, stale, on deep discount[2] and with what to show for it? (Don't get me wrong, my short story writing is still deeply pathetic in my thirties, but only one "deeply": it won't be until my forties or fifties until I earn my next "deeply.") What I'm trying to say is that I'm aware that aspirations curdle in the heat of age, and this is a story that deals with that realization: when

---

[2] A hamantaschen is a triangular cookie eaten by Jews, primarily on Purim, and widely available in New York City bakeries. When I chose this pen name on a lark, I foolishly thought most people would be familiar with this, although why I thought that I'm not sure: most people don't even like hamantaschen (I will ignore that subtext). So that's the silly metaphor I'm making up there: an old, stale hamantaschen cookie. It is been kind of cool hearing interviewers try to pronounce that strange last name and ask me about it, not knowing that it's just a prune or poppy-filled cookie (or on very rare occasions chocolate-filled, i.e., the good ones). I used to get them at Moishe's Bakery in the East Village in Manhattan and convince myself that I liked them, enough to have this surname for the last ten-plus years. I don't regret a thing! (or on the list of regrets, it's toward the bottom).

you foresee that what has worked so far is running on fumes, and you plan something dramatic to change course.

I've also always been interested in creatures whose operations have some kind of demented logic: here, one who preys on nervous, pregnant woman, whose accounts people will easily dismiss (in fairness, because monsters that slide through open windows don't exist . . . I mean, monsters that break through windows, now that's a different story, and you'll find about that soon enough one day, when the time is right). And face-canopies, because hopefully that's some scary shit.

Short Bloom, Long Fading

This isn't a story to tell. It's just me. Just what I remember, and what I think about sometimes. Well, some parts often, some parts only sometimes. I think about Elizabeth often. The other parts, I only think about sometimes, and when I think about them, ironically, it's because I feel bad that I don't think about them more often.

I loved Elizabeth. Thinking that reminds me of that classic Mitch Hedberg joke: *I used to do drugs. I still do, but I used to, also.* I used to love Elizabeth, and I still do. I've always loved her, which of course can't possibly be true, but I can't think of a time when I didn't.

Maybe if I'm being literal, I didn't love her immediately as a child, when I first must have seen her in the elevator of our apartment building, when I didn't yet know the difference between boys and girls. I guess I loved her from the moment I became a thinking, conscious person.

I can't say I know what love is. That doesn't square with what I just said, but I connect the feeling I associate with love with Elizabeth. No one really knows exactly what love is, and I've had girlfriends but never felt for them the way I did with Elizabeth. I cared about her, wanted what's best for her, wanted to protect her, wanted her to flourish. Everything about her soothed me.

I remember as a child we used to check for holes together. She's the first person I can remember checking for holes with, but that can't be possible because certainly my parents were the first, and aunts and uncles and other family members, and preschool teachers after them, all would have taught me all about checking for holes. Haha, that could be taken the wrong way: if only! The ole' checkin' for holes. That's an old person joke, they say something like, "I remember a time when checking for holes was the most fun thing you could do with someone on a Saturday night" or something like that.

Elizabeth, at least as a child, was punctual and meticulous like me, and loved checking, re-checking, and making childish maps and graphs, checking off the places we've searched. Everyone "does" hole-hunting and, in a sense, is "into" it in the same way that everyone with basic self-preservation is "into" looking both ways before crossing the street. But we were a cut above, running around our apartment building. It had the benefit of being a scavenger hunt and knowing we were, in a very real sense, helping people out.

Actually finding a hole was rare, but we always sort of hoped we'd find one – I'm talking about when we were little kids and didn't know any better – and made it a friendly competition, each hoping we'd be the one to find a hole and be able to report it to an adult. It was so satisfying thinking about a hole plugged up with caulk – the fizzy sound caulk made when expanding, that concluding suctiony glerpy sound when the hole was saturated – and we both agreed the caulk looked like toasted marshmallows. We'd joke about wanting to eat it; I guess some kids must have actually ate it, because no caulk has that same color and consistency anymore, least not the brands I've seen.

People thought I became so obsessed with hole-hunting because of what happened to Barney, although that happened when I was about nine, and I was totally into hole-hunting before then. I'll never get another dog, even though I'm great with animals, and dogs take a natural liking to me. I know all the dog-appeasing tricks: lay down, expose your belly, rub them behind the ears. But I'm loyal, and Barney was my dog and probably the world's most beautiful basset hound. I feel terrible even though everyone told me there was nothing I could do.

A walk in the park near our apartment. Quick walk, just to let him pee, only turned my head for a second and I only turned back because the leash pulled awkwardly and Barney had fallen on his side. I thought he must have tripped, except dogs of course don't trip like humans do. I was immediately terrified and pulled the leash but he was pinned at the paw and he wasn't moving. Even though I knew there'd be no way of lifting him up off the ground, I went to try, until some others realized what must have happened and pulled me away, which is when I started going berserk with shame and fear. At least I know he died instantly, probably dead before he hit the ground.

I was taken away as I screamed, there's nothing to do once something walks over a hole and gets stung. The stinger goes into the flesh – doesn't matter if it has to go through a boot or a paw to get there – then it splits into two moorings like an anchor, and there's no moving it, just waiting for the hours until liquefaction.

I remember someone threw a thin blanket over Barney, and that somehow made things worse. If no one had done that, I could still see Barney, looking as he always did. I could pet and hug him, because you couldn't tell what was happening underneath for some time, and that's some kind of closure. Instead, I'd see only a lump beneath a sheet, a lump that would become irregular and smaller, being slurped up in the hole.

Barney was a good dog, and he served a purpose, as I suppose it's better we learned of that hole through his sacrifice rather than some kid from the neighborhood. Of course, I'd have traded almost any kid from the neighborhood for Barney. I know my parents got some money from the Parks Department in a settlement, but I didn't care about that, I only wanted Barney back.

Elizabeth helped me get through it. She felt ashamed, too, because she was an avid hole hunter and felt like she failed, too, even though we searched the apartment building, not the park. We could only do so much. Maybe that was the death of some of our innocence, revealing our hole-hunting as just an ineffectual kids' game. No, that's not real, people don't think in terms like that. I'm only thinking that because I'm reflecting, in the natural course of things you never think in those grand terms. That's just my brain pretending there was meaning when there wasn't.

I know that some people can't deal with the existence of the holes, or, really, what they represent. They can't take the fact that there exists something that appeared so suddenly, that we can't eliminate, that can kill us so quickly and remorselessly, and what's worse, how interconnected the holes all are. That's what probably gets people the most and makes them jealous: all these holes, around the world, one species, all working together.

But there have always existed strange, frightening, freaky things: plague-rats, giant octopuses, hammerhead sharks, grizzly bears. These holes began long before I was born, so to me they just are, and I don't think much about the backstory — who knows and has time to think about all that — and people just want excuses to feel dismal and hopeless.

Elizabeth and I never had a falling out but grew apart as we got older, school and all that. Her helping me with Barney was probably the sweetest single interaction with her I remember, but even as we grew apart there was never any unpleasantness. I wasn't the only person aware of her charming sweetness, and I never interfered when classmates — more confident, more direct, more suitable for her, really — made efforts to get to know her. I'd observe her from afar and we'd talk and catch up, although not as often as I liked, like only maybe if my family ran into her family in the apartment building.

I think sometimes that she became more beautiful as she got older, but I don't even know what that means, really, or if that's true, or whether hormones and development distort that perception. I always loved her, and those feelings were unwavering. I knew this about myself, that even if she had become physically unappealing, my love for her would have remained the same. Maybe my shyness would have proportionately decreased, as the way others fawned on her intimidated me, but my love always remained pure. People have told me how romantic that all is, and how Elizabeth would have loved to hear that. I don't think that's true.

Senior year of high school, and I found her on the kitchen floor of her apartment, on her back in a strange position. Her left heel was flattened to the floor as if pinned, the leg bent at the knee, her heel pressed down so tightly on the floor that I remember the toes of her left foot were lifting off the ground, as if reaching upward to the heavens to flee. She was sprawled out, her left bent knee seemed so high up in relation to the rest of her, and her right leg was ungainly splayed out. There was an open box of Frosted Mini-Wheats on the counter.

Her fallen body, even in its awkward position, still fit so snugly in the tight confines of her narrow kitchen. It was odd how if she had just been a bit taller or bigger that some part of her would be pressed uncomfortably against a side cabinet or the dish washer. Why do I remember those details? With the shock I should have forgotten why I was there in the first place, but I remember: our family had borrowed some lightbulbs from hers, and I was sent down to return the favor, and I guess I knocked and then just tried the door.

It was obvious what had happened. Under her left heel I know I'd find a tiny hole, and from that tiny hole, no doubt piercing through the thin fabric of her sock into her foot was some beak-like sliver of a stinger. The hole could have formed just in a day or two. I don't know if her enthusiasm for constant hole-searching had abated as she'd gotten older and busier. You can only spend so much time in the day being cautious.

I know I looked at her for a while. I wanted to call out for her parents, but there's a sense all humans have when we know that a place is empty. I didn't know where they'd gone, but I knew her parents often went on weekends to her maternal grandparents' house, and she didn't always go. It's hard to know if I thought that then, or just thought about that at some later time, when no one came home the entire time I was there.

Looking only at her face, you could think she was only indolently dreaming. Divorced from context, that is; move back and see her all discombobulated and stretched-out, or ask yourself what she was doing on her back on the kitchen floor in the first place, and you knew.

I stood over her and felt I had so much to say to her.

I recognized that my love for her, in a sense, transformed her in my mind from a real-life person into a concept. That wasn't fair. I should have treated her as a real person. What was my love based on if not an idea, an idealized conception? I'm not stupid, I can think deeply.

I felt almost ashamed of my love then, and even of how pure and untouched she looked before me. I knew that she'd been tranquilized to death, that her innards were dissolving and, if I returned in only half a day, the features of her face would have sunken, the symmetry shifted and lost. Maybe that would be good to see, to appreciate her as a real person.

Am I avoiding, excusing, rationalizing?

What did I do, really? All I saw of her would be gone, slush that dripped out of her clothing, down into the hungry sucker that extended through that hole no bigger than what a ballpoint pen makes when driven through loose-leaf paper.

I expressed my love for her. I treated her as a real person....

I made love to her, that's what I did. Yes, that's what I did, and it was beautiful, I'm not ashamed to say it. I put her arms tightly around my body, and I held her firmly, kissing her, nuzzling her, trying to communicate the ecstasy of my love to her, if she could still feel it, feel anything, maybe somewhere deep below in that obscuration where she dwelled.

I'm deluding myself. I'm thinking of smart words I might not even be using correctly. Obscuration, what does that even mean, is that a word? My self-deluding theory being that a smart person makes smart decisions, so if I use smart words, I'm smart, and must have made a smart decision.

I knew she was essentially dead. I like to think otherwise, but I knew.

When I was young, really young, like in elementary school, people would tell me I was sick. I won a "weirdness award" in my 4th grade yearbook, which I'm surprised they allowed, like school-sanctified mockery. Hopefully there is something wrong with me, fundamentally wrong with me, and as she became consumed, my poisonous seed mixed up in the slurry she became, making what lived in that hole sick and diseased like me. Wouldn't that be a thought: saved the world, took our world back to the way it once was, all because our dominant predator inadvertently drank my cum.

Making jokes to myself. Lightening my own mood, when you're laughing, you aren't thinking clearly, or sugar with the medicine or whatever the apt expression is.

This was years ago, well over a decade now. I'm a different person. No, I'm not. People don't really change. Yet I don't feel bad, not really; I only feel bad when I think about details that, if I told others about, they would act like I did something terrible.

But they don't really know. I loved her, this much is true, that still remains. I know what I felt, I know what I intended, and I know that I loved her. Excuse-making, maybe, but I think about how some people reacted when I told them how my love for her stayed pure, and how they said how romantic that was. I thought that well before I did what I did — even that phrasing, *did what I did*, makes it sound like I did something wrong — what did I do except take the last possible chance to convey my love for her?

NOTES

This story was originally published in an anthology with the title "Victims of a Transitional Time in Morality," a title which in retrospect I'm unsure of, since the plural makes it unclear what "victims" I'm referring to. (I intended it as referring to everyone suffering through this horrific new paradigm of perpetual uncertainty and instant death, but didn't want it misinterpreted as referring equally to the narrator and Elizabeth.)

In terms of interesting factoids, like our narrator here I too was voted "most weird" in my sixth-grade class, although if memory serves there was one weird male, and one weird female, and maybe "weird" was supposed to mean quirky. That's the type of award that naturally no public school on Earth would allow today, and I kind of wish I'd kept that yearbook. Naturally, my parents were none too proud

This is just a short, horrible little story with an unstable narrator, a world turned topsy-turvy and a highly unpalatable ending. Oprah Book Club Invitation I'm still waiting!

Nothing Goes Wrong From The Couch

Chapter 1: In the Great Western Tradition

Two post-collegiate American male roommates, in the great tradition of post-collegiate male roommates in developed Western nations, slouched on opposite ends of the couch and played video games. It was a Sunday afternoon and they'd drank the night before, but they weren't hungover, unless you count the moderate combination of alcohol, marijuana, sleep deprivation, and yesterday's diet of cheap, heavily-salted-and-carb-heavy foods as a kind of perpetual motion machine for an ambient hangover. Of the two, Casey at least went to the gym three times(ish) a week, and had the dawning awareness that this post-college pizza-and-beers lifestyle had an expiration date, as his innate leanness was filling out in unflattering ways. Ben, shorter, naturally stockier and blessed with a strange reserve of unearned muscles that kept his metabolism churning, was happy to let it ride.

Casey's girlfriend Debra was at some drink and paint class with a friend and then off to the gym, which didn't seem like the smartest combination. Debra was often busy with these random classes and events – fun "asides," they called them – and Casey usually joined her, even on events that didn't really interest him, but perhaps less so since Ben moved in and gave him a handy alternative. Couples needed their decompression time, anyway.

Ben was making a good salary selling advertising for Google, which seemed like one of those jobs which shouldn't exist: didn't Google sell itself? Not six-figures-great or anything, but still, Casey was surprised how well Ben was doing. Better than Casey was doing as an account executive, which was just being a glorified secretary for finicky and demanding corporate clients; and better than Debra as a junior architect, architect being one of those demanding, low-paying jobs that may be a great signifier for television characters but not so much in the real world.

The video game session had started as laconically as always. Casey had come home with some items from CVS. He saw Ben, nestled in his corner on the couch in the T-shirt he woke up in and the gym shorts that should lose that appellative descriptor, given they were worn almost exclusively as loungewear.

Ben was playing the newest version of Mario Kart online and doing well with Princess Peach, as he often did. Casey recognized the track, Coconut Coast, as the last of the set for Egg Cup. Ben was silent in concentration, although even in "silent concentration" there was something goofy, carefree and inviting about his presence. Maybe it was his wide-set masculine chin that lent the impression he was somehow always in control of the situation, counterbalanced with his boyish semi-fro of brown curly hair that wouldn't be worn by anybody who didn't have a sense of playfulness. It was that combination of competence and ease, Casey had to concede, that likely made Ben a good salesperson.

Ben's Princess Peach came in second. "Awwww hell yeah!" Ben said when he saw that Luigi came in third. Ever since 'Luigi's death stare' became a meme in an earlier iteration of the game, Nintendo kept embellishing upon Luigi's various stares whenever Luigi came up short.

"That cold-blooded killer," said Casey. Luigi's death stare this time was the stony slow-panning glare of vaguely morally superior contempt.

Ben nodded to Casey's corner and motioned with his controller, and asked "Kart?" even though words were superfluous between them. Casey picked it up, logged into his account – Casefiles, which he always thought to change because it wasn't clever or had anything to recommend it – and they started playing, both old pros who chatted and played reflexively, only going silent when they were concentrating on passing somebody or when something traumatic happened, like the inopportune timing of the purple shell that landed Ben's Princess Peach into a ravine.

"So where's Debra at?" Ben asked.

"She went to some drink and paint class in the afternoon with that girl Elva and then I think she's going to a rowing class."

Debra had shared a bedroom with Casey for the past two years in their two-bedroom apartment. Ben had moved into the spare second bedroom about six months ago, after their Craigslist roommate graciously left without warning. Sharing one room between them in a two-bedroom apartment wasn't ideal, and once the lease ended Casey and Debra were going to get their own apartment. They were saving money, as Debra always said whenever Casey groused at the situation that had become, to Casey, mildly embarrassing and emasculating. They could save money in their own apartment, Casey would grumble, if only in his mind. He liked living with Ben, but the extra space would have been worth it.

"Debra's drinking and then working out? Debra gets drunk off one drink. So even assuming she had just one drink and then worked out, that could be risky. I mean, we've done way worse."

"Way worse," Casey echoed his friend.

"But that doesn't sound like the Debra I know."

And Debra knew them both well. Ben and Casey had actually both met her at approximately the same time, as they'd all shared an English class sophomore year of college. Casey, however, had lucked into sharing a dorm building with Debra that same year, and by the end of the year were a unit, which Ben wasn't initially thrilled about. He'd liked drunkenly carousing with Casey, his best friend since high school. Well, sure, they'd still drunkenly caroused, if you could call it that, but then often with Debra, who took it upon herself to try and hook Ben up with somebody, her proposed prospects of such a standard deviation below what Ben fancied a suitable potential partner that it made him question what Debra thought of him.

Casey made a face that was the equivalent of a shrug. "What can I say. That's the story I was told and I'm sticking to it."

Track one, the Shy Guy Shallows, ended with Ben in first, Casey in third. As the closing race animation played, Ben got up and walked to the fridge.

"Beers?"

"You know it."

Ben peered into the fridge. They all shared the top row, which was for drinks, and the crisper drawer for fruits and vegetables, although since Debra's purchases consumed the crisper, Casey and Debra as a unit ended up with a disproportionate amount of the refrigerator space. Not that Ben cared, but it was impossible to go through seminars at work on awareness trainings and recognizing inefficiencies and not become, well, aware of distribution inefficiencies.

"We classy or trashy tonight?" Ben asked, body mostly concealed behind the open refrigerator door.

"I mean I feel like by nature we are trashy bitches, but it is Sunday and we both got to go to work tomorrow, so let's pretend we high class."

"And we are playing Mario Kart tonight, the gold standard of kart racing games."

"True, not like we are playing, what, Beach Buggy Racing like a set of common whores."

So, classy meant breaking into the dwindling supply of Schlafly Summer Lagers, not the surplus of Coors Lights.

For Casey the onset of beer drinking always had a liberating effect. In intoxication there was that scaled-back feeling of being exactly where you need to be, knowing everything that needs to be known on any given subject, and a rosy sensation that whatever you don't know, you'll learn.

"Does it ever happen to you that you get horny and then all of a sudden you have to take a shit?" asked Ben.

Casey paused a moment and looked thoughtful. "Funny, I always have the opposite problem," he said dryly.

Ben snorted a laugh, that wide mischievous smile of his. "Guess your shit really don't stink. Sit down to take a shit, hard-ons sticking out at both ends."

Casey laughed and, not having any wittier repartee to add, stated, more glumly than he expected, "well, I don't really have to worry about getting too horny anytime soon."

"What do you mean?"

Casey usually kept any personal troubles or disagreements in his relationship with Debra private, even from Ben, but this one could be excused as darkly amusing, and maybe he could benefit from Ben's advice. He'd wanted to get Ben's opinion on this but had no natural way of bringing it up; a shit joke had been the natural entry point.

"So Debra got kinda mad at me, well maddish at me, I don't know what the word is, but as you know I never use Instagram, really, I think I follow only like five people, including Debra."

"Debra never posts on Instagram."

"True." Casey fleetingly noted and moved past how quickly Ben knew that. "Well, she noticed that the people I followed, they are all basically hot girls, although I didn't even know or remember or really look at it. Like remember Mallory Brenda?"

"Oh yeah, I remember her."

"Well, when she was trying out modeling, she asked for everyone to follow her account, so I did."

"What a sacrifice. 'I'll subscribe to see your perfect body, Mallory, but only to help you fulfill your dreams.'"

"She's still actually trying to model and posting pictures."

"Oh, I know. Unfortunately, no one ever told her that no one can be a professional model with the name Mallory."

"Well yeah, and there were some other people who I added on Instagram like that for whatever reason, and I never even look at it, I think it's only like six people in total but Debra noticed and, well she wasn't mad really, but hah, I don't know, like, disappointed?"

Ben leaned into a tight curve where he overtook a CPU-controlled Bowser. "Well, Instagram is a visual medium. Doesn't really sound like a big deal at all."

"It's not, but you know, it's one of those things. She just said like, 'why are all your Instagram friends hot girls?'"

"And she didn't say it in a fun way, I take it."

"No, no, definitely not a fun way. She didn't say it as some kinky prelude to sex, like she was impressed with my taste or something. And she believed my explanation, which is true, but eh."

This track was over, Ben again in first, Casey fucked it up in fifth and was awarded no points. Ben took a swig of his beer and gesticulated with his beer-holding hand, which was fun because it made him feel like he was dispensing well-worn wisdom.

"Having hot Insta friends is just one of those silent things that's not great or pleasant to think about and maybe you don't want to hear about it but it's not like a bad thing, just one of those things that aren't supposed to be commented on, you know? It's like, taking a shit. Like if you texted Debra whenever you took a shit she'd be like 'what the fuck is this? I don't want to hear about this' but it's not like you're doing anything wrong, it's just one of those unpleasant things that just happen."

Casey's beer was held between his legs as the next race started. "Wait, what? You know that made no sense, right? I mean, I think it's quite possibly the worst example anyone could have possibly ever given."

Ben, stone-faced, kept his eyes duly fixed on the screen as if something caught his interest. Casey and Ben could banter and exchange insults interminably. But every friendship rests atop a sensitive fulcrum of power and perception. Even though Ben would have relished mocking Casey for saying something so admittedly stupid and sloppy, it felt different when Casey attacked his intelligence. Objectively, there's no excuse for this double-standard, Ben understood. Ben could never explain it to a non-interested party and expect to be viewed as in the right.

But with the history between them, Ben had the distinct impression that Casey always thought he was better than him, somehow; with the girlfriend, with generally being more academically inclined, for being just generally busier with activities and events, as if activity itself – no matter how pointless or stupid – was inherently virtuous. Which was doubly obnoxious because they both knew that Debra was half – no, three-quarters – of the reason he was so busy, like Casey really cared so much about alumni events or museum receptions.

What it really came down to, Ben knew, was that Ben was making more money and having more success in his career, which overthrew Casey's expectations for how he felt the world should be operating, as if there was a 1:1 correspondence between Casey's academic effort and post-college professional success. Poor Casey didn't realize yet that the world operates on more than just book smarts and needless labor. Casey, taller, (arguably) smarter, who took college at least semi-seriously, who had it all together with the responsible lovely long-term girlfriend, wasn't doing as well as Ben. Ben, with his strong jaw and strangely cavalier, ingratiating style of relaxed confidence, found a niche where he excelled. So whenever Casey took too much enjoyment in a Ben faux-paus, Ben couldn't avoid feeling burned by the subtext, or see it as some sublimated way for Casey to recover some aspect of his lost manhood.

Ben, reflecting upon all this instantly, took the stoic approach, less for its own virtue than because he knew it would deprive Casey of whatever victory he thought he'd achieved. "Like flirting, is what I mean, like flirting, a harmless thing that everyone does, is what I meant."

Ben was probably being too hard on his friend in glimpsing these sinister psychological motivations. With Mario Karts a kartin', both resumed their drinking and hallowed shooting-the-shit pastime, any unpleasantness over Ben's shorn feelings or Casey's air of superiority vanished.

Ten minutes later and Debra was coming back into the apartment complex, unloading the day's lucre from her car. She came home too late to hear Ben stating that from all the beer and chips he couldn't stop farting, with Casey reminding him that's how a loser talks, a winner would say 'I won't stop farting.' Ben agreed then narrowed his eyes in ominous concentration, Casey begging for him to reconsider what he was about to do but as luck would have it Ben had run dry.

And they all missed what was going on in the apartment directly above theirs.

Chapter 2: In the Apartment Directly Above Theirs

Enter the upstairs apartment, and you'd hear the shower running. Peek around the bend from the front door and you'd see an outstretched foot, extending out from the open bathroom door.

Closer, feel the steam heat of the running hot water. Turn the corner, see sprawled on the bathroom floor a very naked, water-slicked heavyset woman in her sixties, her poor health and skin folds making her death seem all even more unseemly and pathetic. Ms. Verona, lived alone in this apartment for over a decade, and died alone, too; or at least without another human around.

Before your eyes took in the relatively placid, puffy moon-like visage of Ms. Verona, you couldn't avoid the gaping gore of her lower-half. The blood black-red, the damage too total and complete to note specifically that her perineum, or the area between her anus and vagina, had been demolished, burst through with such force that her adjacent structure could do nothing but obey the laws of physics and collapse inward.

Notice a particular blood spatter. Not a heavy spatter, more like a single outward light-spritzing, almost as if a cute little dog had unexpectedly stuck his wet little black-button nose in the rain of her blood and shook itself vigorously one time before being dragged away by an impatient owner. The damage was repellently captivating, could only catch maybe a single telling detail about her body before revulsion forced you to look away. That observed detail would likely be the narrow, bloodied striations along the belly, the delicacy of those marks a jarring juxtaposition given the carnage of her vaginal area, that most guarded and sacrosanct of areas, that body part that gets deemed from childhood as "private." Seeing those striations would make most people think of garrote wire, those thin wires movie assassins used to choke countless unnamed henchmen.

Given this scene, maybe you wouldn't have noticed the fleeing, panicked animal. What it resembled you couldn't be sure, too much was going on there, too much was moving just on the periphery in that scramble of newly-birthed, frenzied life, with all the torque and contortion of a flipped-over beetle righting itself. But whatever it was - maybe you'd remember it resembling a small, blackened horsetail - it would have glided past you, out of the bathroom and under the apartment door.

Chapter 3: Threesome

"Coming," Casey paused the game, bounded from the couch when he heard Debra knocking on the door as if he was being paid based on his efficiency. In a sense, Ben figured, maybe Casey was being so paid: that's what relationships are, and even though Casey and Debra had been together for a while, it was good Casey still put in the effort. Debra was his world, really. To be fair, Casey was Debra's, too. Although, Ben added as a caustic closing line to himself, Debra's potential world seemed larger than Casey's.

Whenever Debra entered the picture, Casey's demeanor softened appreciably. His speech slowed, his body language became more nurturing, he became less quick to judgment, even his eyes seemed wider and gentler, all in service of the kabuki theater of fidelity and companionship.

"Hey babe," Casey opened the door, wondering to himself why Debra just didn't open it herself, until he saw her lugging back her artwork, with a gym bag slung over her other shoulder. Great, something else to take up space in their tiny bedroom.

"What do you got there?"

"Can't you tell? I'll give you an obvious, obvious hint: we were drinking Napa Valley wines." And she put her gym bag against the kitchen table and lifted up the painting. It showed a respectable if amateurishly simplified view of an elongated orange suspension bridge in three-quarter view, with some nebulous patch of green and purple hilltop in the distance to suggest the fog-shrouded land beyond.

"Damn, that's pretty good." It was better than he could ever do. Casey wasn't a skilled artist, and attempting painting, even at a drink and draw, would only frustrate him. Becoming better at it wouldn't benefit his life in any quantitative way, so why bother, a philosophy which Casey and Debra had several good-natured arguments about. Debra felt you needed to have an open mind, and there were cross-disciplinary benefits to trying new things, and also something about brain circuitry and longevity. Ben, if participating, would take an even stronger position than Casey and posit that since life was short, it was more efficient to focus on what you could become good at and which could actually directly benefit you, and it was wasteful to fritter away precious time on a constellation of random activities that won't lead to anything. Casey would usually eventually concede Debra's point and admit that her philosophy led to more fun activities.

"Oh, hell yeah, the Golden Gate Bridge, that's pretty good!" piped Ben from the couch.

"Oh, hey Ben, I didn't see you there, hah. See, he got it!"

"It's Sunday, I blend into the couch."

"I see, rocking the shorts still. I'm jealous, have you left the house today?"

"Nope."

Casey had obviously known it was the Golden Gate Bridge. "I knew – c'mon, give me more credit than that."

"I know."

"You can hang that up in the main room," Ben offered. "That's an above-the-alcohol-collection addition for sure."

"Noice! Maybe one day we can actually add wine to our collection."

Ben raised a beer. "Well, I've been doing my part by drinking the beers so we can clean house and get more alcohol, maybe some wine."

"Hey, credit to me, too," Casey chipped in, "I've been playing video games with him and drinking too."

"Following my lead, though."

"Fair."

"We all know if Casey's drinking and I'm not around, that means he's following your lead, Ben. But I truly thank you both for your service."

Ben gesticulated knowingly. He was a bit disappointed that Debra hadn't come home all sweaty and fragrant, in some crop-topped elevated sports bra and some tight-fitting workout pants.

"Hey Deb, you worked out *before* the drink and draw, right?"

"Hey Ben, of course."

"See?" Ben gave Casey a knowing face.

"Casey, you thought I'd drink, then work out? Hah, do you even know me?"

Casey shrugged defensively. "I misheard this morning, but figured it out." That means she did technically have something to drink and then drove home, not sure that's much safer than drinking and then using work out equipment. But yes, the idea of her being tipsy and working out was unfathomable. Knowing her, she probably actually had only one wine early in the class and drove home about two hours later.

"Ok, I'm gonna go shower."

"Well, you'll know where to find us," Casey said as he took two beers from the fridge.

"I hope you haven't drank too much, we should think about dinner in a bit."

"This is only my second."

"Yeah, I've been keeping watch. Don't worry, he's speaking the truth. Hey Deb, you want a beer for the shower? It'll keep them away from Casey," Ben offered.

"Hmm," she pretended to consider. "Maybe I should bring a Coors in there, I mean is it even possible for a Coors to get even more watered-down? I think that's actually how they make them, they make a normal beer and then the workers leave it in a shower overnight."

Casey, back on the couch, dangled a beer suggestively toward Debra. "And the more beers we drink, the sooner we replace it with wine," Casey added.

"And then if you poured beer on yourself in the shower, it'd be like an actual beer commercial. A Coors commercial," said Ben, too quickly.

"Good way to convince me not to do it. I had one wine so I'm good for the entire day, I don't want to go buck wild and trash the apartment and break my beautiful new art before it gets to grace our walls."

Ben smiled. "You sure? Could make the shower more fun."

"Positive."

"Suit yourself."

"More for us. And this is the good stuff, the fancy beers," Casey added. He didn't like feeling like he was supplementing conversation rather than directing it.

"Well you two fancy boys can enjoy." And she went into their bedroom and, as Casey and Ben resumed their gamin' and drinkin', slipped into the bathroom with a change of clothes. Both Ben and Casey looked at her as she went in, Casey directly, Ben subtly, the latter disappointed than she hadn't done something like undress and wrap herself in a towel. She never did that, but he always held out hope. When he'd first moved in, she'd sometimes casually come out of the shower wrapped in a towel before swiftly retreating to her bedroom, but that'd quickly stopped, he suspected at Casey's request.

"Any dinner plans?" Casey inquired. "And when Debra gets out of the shower, want to see if she'd be down for Overcooked?"

"Sounds good." Overcooked was an isometric, cartoony cooperative cooking game where each character controlled a little chef, and they had to work together, avoid environmental hazards and obstacles to jointly prepare meals before time ran out. It was winsome and breezy, unlike Mario Kart, which was deadly serious and played-for-keeps.

"And no dinner plans, probably I don't know just order in a sandwich from Stu's, feeling lazy. Might have some leftover shit in the fridge. You two going out or doing something?"

"Sounds like it. Maybe we'll just make something."

"If you do, make extra."

"We'll see." Which meant that they'd see what Debra wanted to do.

Casey was doing better this round in Mario Kart. Ben felt strangely bad about overreacting internally to Casey's prior good-natured insults.

The warm purring of the rushing shower could be faintly heard in the living room.

"So Casey, you were kind enough to share that thing you told me about earlier," and he indicated toward Debra in the shower, and it took Casey a moment to figure out what Ben was referring to. He realized and appreciated Ben's subtlety in not blurting "YOU KNOW DEBRA AND THE INSTAGRAM THING."

"So listen to this. I was at lunch with Bill and Dan from work, you remember them, right?"

"Yeah, I remember. I met them at a couple of your work happy hours. Seem like good dudes."

"Yeah, they are. So, we were out to lunch at work, and Dan, you know, he's all into this healthy eating stuff, and he's pretty ripped and goes to the gym like every night-"

"Oh yeah Sexy Ripped Dan, how could I not remember Dan now."

"And he's also always reading this health advice stuff, so he told me that he read this study that men who keep their phones in their front pockets have a greater risk of getting testicular cancer."

"Is that true?"

"I don't know. It makes sense though, I guess. Radiation from the phones."

"I don't really think phones are radioactive but I get what you're saying."

"Then, I don't know, electronic wavelengths from the phone or some shit, I don't know. Anyway, so he tells me he looked it up afterward and it seems legitimate, and men who keep their phones in their back pocket don't have the same risk of getting testicular cancer."

"I wonder if those guys get ass cancer."

"Hmmmm. You know, that's a good point, although it's not like the phones are up your asshole, whereas in your front pocket they are pretty close to your balls. Anyway, so later that day the three of us are at our mandatory Wednesday all-hands-on-deck meeting, which is basically as it sounds, the entire office, and I start thinking about my phone and patting my legs and freaking out because I can't find my phone. You know when you check, re-check, triple-check and just in the pit of your stomach realize that you lost your phone and you are truly fucked, to the point I start telling people 'lost my phone' as I'm searching the immediate area, retracing my steps, thinking about the fucking restaurant and all that, worried that people might realize I had a drink or two at lunch."

"Oh shit."

"And then of course I find it. I'd taken Dan's advice and put it in my back pocket."

Casey nodded sympathetically, doing that exaggerated exhale to acknowledge the punch line of the story. "Well, now you get to-"

Something moved abruptly in the unfocused outer reach of Casey's periphery, the spatial sense in your brain reserved for noticing a tiny flying gnat or some other unexpected zipping thing. It was at his back-right, and he turned his head slightly, expecting a quick resolution, but no, what was it?, and turned his attention fully to the front door where he sensed the motion. He saw mail being pushed under the door slot, no, that wasn't it, that wasn't mail, like a black mop-head or something, a tiny, what could it be?

"Dude," was his piddling attempt to encapsulate all that he saw.

Ben followed his line of sight, eyes arched in bewilderment, face blanched, mouth slightly open in a small "o" of something like excited anticipation, as if soon he'd have a new story to regale clients with, about that crazy time an animal just slipped in under their door. A little black dog's snout....

No.

"Jesus!" Ben shouted.

An approximately foot-long bristly black line seemed, after a second or two of resistance, to wrangle its way under their front door.

Chapter 4: Bug Wrangling

"Is that a fucking millipede, dude?" Ben asked with some alarm.

"More like a fucking billion-a-pede," Casey answered.

Casey only got a fleeting glance, but the impressions loomed and enlarged in his mind with the certitude of gospel truth. Whatever it was, it was at least a foot, for sure. It was too coarse and too thorny-looking to be a millipede: those had functional legs on only one side, not legs all over their body, right?

"A billipede," Casey mumbled, as if clarifying to himself.

It glided across the floor. Bugs always seemed to move with unexpected, the gun-shot-just-went-off speed. Even with that expectation, its speed was startling.

"Fuck, dude!" Casey yelled, both of them instinctively lifting their feet off the floor onto the couch, Casey's feet folded up so he was sitting on an ankle, Ben in an ungainly, withering Lotus position.

It ran to the opposite wall, darted about halfway-back toward from where it came, pivoted some slight distance in an angular direction, then rocketed with brilliant speed to the protective shadows in the kitchen. Its motions were too precise to be solely instinctual, and there seemed to be some underlying mathematical cohesion in each traveled segment of distance.

"What the fuck is it doing?" Casey could see the outline of the insect in the shadow created by the fridge; or at least thought he saw a slightly darkened string-like shape that he told himself was the unwanted guest. Casey's position naturally made him the dedicated sentry. Ben, on the farther side of the couch, had no hopes of seeing where it went.

"Let's both go there and crush that thing."

"Word," Casey replied.

"Debra's lucky she's spending so much time soaping herself up in there, she's missing all this fun. Maybe we can get it alive and become Instagram-famous."

Ben seemed weirdly giddy, maybe just seeing this as a novel form of excitement. The way the two hung out often created a kind of force field of jokey irreverence, which made otherwise unpleasant or boring episodes fun. Or perhaps Ben had the added comfort knowing that, whatever else, the insect had to get through Casey first, like that twinge of security one feels walking at a crosswalk parallel to people closer to the source of traffic. If someone blows the light, hell, at least there's a few bodies as buffers.

"Casey, if we do capture that thing, you should post the pictures online. Post a couple of disgusting giant insect pictures, and no way Debra is going to be spying on your Instagram accounts anymore."

Casey was silent for a moment, trying to spot the creature in the shadows. "I don't think it moved. Unfortunately, don't really think there's time to put out a 'Wanted Dead or Alive' poster on him. I think we gotta go in there and take it out. I don't think it's moved, let's go."

"See isn't it a good thing I kept my shoes on?" Ben said as he slipped one off and held it in his right hand. Debra always demanded that they not walk around the house with their shoes. Casey always, always complied, and made a show of his compliance. Ben often did, and when he didn't, it was usually Casey who would have to deal with Debra's bedroom complaints, Debra's frustration channeled as an inexplicable sourness toward Casey, as, after all, Casey was Ben's friend, and it was Casey's idea originally to have Ben move in. At Casey's self-preserving insistence, Ben was usually good about the shoe thing, but fortuitously, not today.

"Dude, you're lucky Debra didn't see that," Casey told him distractedly.

"Eh, it's a flip-flop, it's not really a shoe. And you mean *you're* lucky Debra didn't see that."

"Fine, then we're both lucky."

"Well, buddy, let's see if our luck runs out."

They looked at each other, Ben's flip-flop gripped in his right hand, Casey armed with a bare paper towel roll left near the couch.

They baby-step skulked toward the kitchen, figuring out how to proceed. But just as Casey crossed the threshold of the kitchen, the intruder practically skidded onto its hind quarters, its multifarious legs moving with such countervailing fervor as to propel the lithe creature, if only for a second, clear off the ground. In the blink of an eye, it seemed to clear half the distance between them, and then scrambled and rolled in short, forward-progressing circles like a man on fire.

"Holy fuck!" Casey yelled, these unexpected moves more than they'd bargained for.

"Fuck dude, kill it!" Ben responded. Ben pivoted around Casey and launched his flip-flop, which didn't come close.

"Fuck!" Casey steeled himself with his paper towel roll, knowing he had only one opportunity to strike, but upon realizing he was wearing only socks, jumped out of the way rather than face the possibility that this skittering mass of stringy shapes might crawl over his feet. And in that moment of retreat it was gone: only a second after it disappeared did they both realize, based on its trajectory, that it must have slipped under the bathroom door.

Chapter 5: Uh-Oh

"Debra, don't freak out, but we think a biggish bug might have just gone under the door." Casey was trying to keep his voice calm, and it wasn't really apparent why the prospect was so terrifying; it was, after all, just an insect, and over the years he'd killed a few roaches while Debra overreacted with histrionic terror that Casey used to figure must have, in large part, been a way to make him feel like a hero. But he later learned how truly terrified Debra was about the more repulsive looking insects. Her terror had been that of someone who really must have thought that a little spider would, say, grow to dog-size, tackle her, subdue her with venom and make her watch as it feasted on her organs.

Ben stood back, understanding that the situation behind the shower had become exclusively Casey's domain, although still making subtle motions of movement as if he was going to help. Ben kept his eyes on Casey and the door.

"What?" Casey heard Debra ask, muted first by rushing water and then the door. Figured it'd go in the bathroom, he thought strangely, the hot-house humidity of her overlong shower a fitting environment for some kind of Amazonian nightmare.

"A big bug, we think it's a millipede or something just might have crawled under the door." He very well knew it wasn't a millipede.

"Don't worry, Deb, it was just like, yeah, a millipede or something," Ben barked from a few feet away. Casey looked back, Ben offering an *I tried* shrug.

Some muffled words unheard, a "hold on," the water abruptly stopped, and then, screaming. A startled, even a highly-frightened initial reaction was to be expected, but not this: This was a scream that could not be tempered or consoled with assurances alone, this was a scream that could not be reasoned with. The piercing pitch of this scream could only end with the bloodied dampness of a torn vocal cord.

Ben came beside his friend and paused, almost thinking he must have missed something, like there must be two strange occurrences simultaneously.

"Debra, open the door! Open the door!" Casey was attempting to turn the locked knob, pointlessly.

"Help me! Help me! Please help me!"

"Just, just hit it, hit it with the shampoo bottle or something!"

But when Casey heard the thump that could only be her entire body taking a hard fall in the tub, there stood only churning panic, as if it'd been hiding in plain sight beyond the protective coating of their aloof irreverence.

"Fuck," Casey muttered to himself, took a step back and in the process collided with Ben, then just started front-kicking the door, just under the knob. Once, twice, three times, and still she was screaming, and he heard scrambling, and he wasn't even sure his kicks were working.

"Here," he heard Ben. Ben, squat and stout, kicked twice in the interstices of Casey's attempts, and with the second blow his foot pierced the door. They both started kicking over each other, until enough space was opened for Casey's hand. He unlocked the door, Ben right behind him.

Casey didn't know what he planned to do, but Ben's constant motion behind him seemed to force him forward. The shower was still running, and the beaten looking baby blue shower curtain with the rubber duckies was largely amassed to the left, water spraying all over the bathroom floor. He couldn't understand why, until he saw Debra, and envisioned the scenario where she'd swung the shampoo bottle, missed, and half-knocked off the curtain.

Debra was on her back in the tub, stark naked and body slickly wet and dewy, kicking up in the air, shampoo bottle held upside-down like a club. She was in strange hysterics, eyes glued to the leftward wall by the sink.

"Debra, Jesus what is it, what's happened," Casey whispered, some combination of consoling her and respecting some subconscious privacy of her vulnerable nudity.

"It's still here, it attacked me and missed, it attacked me again, I hit it, it's still alive I saw it crawling!" She answered in halting gasps.

"Honey," Casey lowered his voice, feeling a surging combination of anger and embarrassment, "it's just a bug."

"No! It leaped at me! It leaped right at me, it landed on me, and was crawling directly toward my fucking, my, my, my pussy, like it was trying to, to kill me that way." In some split-second of discretionary word choice, the playful word 'pussy' seemed more benign than the clinical and stolid 'vagina.'

Casey turned and saw Ben looking under the sink, although he had the distinct impression that Ben was deliberately avoiding his gaze and that a millisecond before, his attention had been on Debra. In the reflection of the mirror Casey could see that Ben had a flushed, almost dreamy look to him, perhaps overcome by the strangeness of the situation.

Debra was calming down, scooted up her back against the backward curve of the tub, calming herself down with the fanning-flutter of her left arm, her breasts jiggling in tandem. Casey said "here" angrily and shut off the water, then, facing her, began to lift her to her feet. His stomach roiled with acid, but he wasn't nervous; there was some surging undercurrent of hatred and anger, the wish to strike out at someone, and as he looked at her there was an unaccountable feeling of shame and humiliation at her smoothness, the upturned points of her hardened nipples, the movement of her full breasts, the rounding outline of her hips.

Then she screamed simultaneously as Ben yelled "oh fuck" and flung himself backward away from the sink in one sudden swift movement. Casey turned and couldn't account for what he saw. The black shape that he was sure had seemed at least a foot now seemed no more than six inches at most. It sped down the wall where the mirror hung, extended itself half-off the wall, its little limbs a flurry – what was it doing, bracing itself, greedily shoveling air into its mouth? – and, almost as if traveling via suction, flicked itself onto the shower wall. It slithered through the forest of miniature conditioner bottles and body washes before anyone could say anything, and Casey blinked and Debra was all crazed motion and moving limbs, and she started smacking her inner thigh and groin as if battling a swarm of mosquitos. She spun once, as if something was actively hanging off of her, and screamed and continue to smack almost every part of her body as Casey lunged for her, though she slipped wholly out of his grasp.

In one flowing sequence Ben bounded into the shower and appeared to scrape something off her chest. At the tail end of his movement he panicked, and flung whatever he'd touched hard against a wall, and then Casey saw it. The insect smashed against the wall and then twitched spasmodically, fell back to the tub, and was segmented into triple its size. Now it was definitely over a foot.

Around its whole circumference tiny, skinny legs spun and churned, with certain longer, brambly appendages sticking and jabbing into the air. Its middle segment was more twig-like and brittle. What could be called the front of the creature was so identified by two antennas, so wispy-thin they were distinguished only by the disorienting effect of their rapid movement. Ben and Casey subconsciously both realized the creature was purely black, whereas before, maybe an illusion created by its speed, it appeared to have some uneven, reddish-mottling sheen.

It lifted itself and stood up, a narrow, vertical line of writhing insectile chaos. The motion was transfixing and Casey was thinking to move, to act, to kill it, but found himself stunned into a momentary stupor, thinking only that he was witnessing something incredible. It truly stood up in almost a perfect vertical column, certainly above one foot, and it was so repugnantly disgusting it was almost inspiring. Out of the corner of his eye he saw repulsion and terror mixed in Debra's face, and a sort of disequilibrium on Ben's, as if he now realized that his display of temerity hadn't solved the problem.

And again, like a suction, the creature flung itself forward and upward, its antennaed front half projecting directly toward Debra's crotch. Ben wrapped both hands and arms around Debra and leaned into her body. She collapsed under his weight, and they scrambled and both screamed, Debra more frantically and hysterically, Ben more a groan of pain. Casey bounded over to them, not sure what to do, looking for the insect to slip into view and ready with a conditioner bottle when it did. Ben's movement became more animated and he stood up to his feet and started stomping while Debra hunched against a corner.

They all saw the wounded insect roll from the corner and then, as if it were never there at all, disappear down the drain.

From all fours, Debra pounced and plugged the drain with the stopper.

"Get bleach! Pour bleach down the drain, we have to make sure it's dead we can't have that thing alive in this house!" Debra was putting her weight on the stopper, as if she was bracing for a returning onslaught.

Casey, as the least active of the three, felt like her orders were directed toward him. That sounds like a terrible idea and for all he knew could destroy the drains, but, ashamed at his inaction, didn't want to compound things by refusing to do as she asked.

While still looking at her but moving toward the door, Ben said, quietly, "let me go get it," and shared a telling look with Casey; then, as if reconsidering, said "maybe we should just get out of here, the drain and the water is going to push it out of here."

"Yeah, let's get out of here," Casey agreed. "Let's get you dressed and out of here," and was finally able to conceal her nakedness with a towel. There was something pointless about covering her, he felt without thought: every permutation of her nakedness, every available glance in every available position had already been offered on display. He rubbed her dry, and in being the only one privy to touching her felt a re-established connection.

Ben walked out of the room.

"Do you want to go to the hospital?" Casey whispered in her ear. She nodded plaintively, and he sighed internally, not expecting her to accede. "Are there any marks on your body?" Casey asked, but then thought better of pressing the point and instead figured the best approach would be to let her have peace of mind. It would be a long night, emergency rooms and everything, why had he said "hospital" and not "urgent care," maybe one of those urgent care walk-in clinics would be fine.

As she dried and dressed, Casey told Ben, who was now sitting on the couch in silence, that the two of them would be going to a hospital. Casey thanked him, and Ben said "of course, of course," and then Debra, as they were leaving, turned to thank Ben also. Her thanks seemed at first perfunctory, maybe she was still dazed from the bizarre enormity of what happened, but, as if catching herself not giving credit where credit was due, hugged him and repeated the thanks, voice redolent with an unusual emotional solemnity.

Ben didn't really hug her back, only an ironic patting, and both he and Casey gave each other knowing, undercutting smiles, as if both in on the same subsurface joke.

Waiting for the elevator with Debra, saying nothing of substance, Casey realized his throat felt very sore, and he ached for this pointless, lengthy visit to the ER to be over and done with. His only job now was to be supportive, he knew. There was an unacknowledged distance between them, and every overly-attentive act felt like a tiny atonement, for what he wasn't exactly sure.

Ben went to his bedroom, thought about what to do for dinner. He had a nervous, impatient energy. He couldn't wait to go to sleep, sheets over his face, to have leisurely time undisturbed with his own thoughts.

Chapter 6: A Night Together, Alone

Suffice to say everything at the ER checked out. No one was surprised. What had she expected, that Scary Story to Tell in the Dark come true, a cheek full of spider eggs?

That night in bed Casey held Debra in his arms. He had the impression she didn't want to be hugged, and was making a show of her begrudging acceptance. He felt both hostile and constrained. He thought of a circus bear on a rampage, with an explanatory, rationalizing flashback showing the bear suffering the indignity of being forced to ride around in a little car wearing a fez. Stupid. That was too cute an image for what he was feeling.

He kissed the back of her head and said he was sorry, and the first few times she didn't acknowledge it, only patted his hand, until eventually she assuaged him with how he had nothing to be sorry for, it was okay. And he *was* sorry, but in the higher regions of his brain he knew it was a kind of shame without culpability, operating more on the logic of where remorse was present guilt must be found, just as one can be confident that where there was a tree, that buried down in the soil there must have once been a seed.

Who could really be prepared for such a crazy situation like that, though? He'd stomped roaches and swatted bees out of the air and thrown out mice found in traps: the expected masculine responsibilities. How could he ever expect to know how to handle a rampaging nightmare bug that really did seem to manifest, as impossible as it sounds, a singular interest in biting Debra. And, if we were being truthful, wasn't she sort of overblowing things, making it all seem more significant than it was? It was her conflation of an admittedly big weird bug to some kind of masked intruder that exacerbated his emasculation and incompetence, like the embellishments on a rumor that ruins one's reputation.

He knew it would pass, give it a few days. But he was a worrier, and this felt, somehow, like the uneasy aftermath of a fight. A strange pall was cast, a distorting slime that worked in several insidious ways. It hid from view the irreverent, understanding Debra he so loved, replaced her with this grave stranger who seemed to be processing some kind of loss. Worse, it seemed to negate all the considerate acts he'd always undertaken on Debra's behalf, like he'd, in the blink of an eye or the mistimed turn of his head, worked up some relationship debt that must be repaid.

Don't be insecure and stupid. Try and think of it from her perspective. What was she thinking, actually? It would be idiotic to voice his concerns now, but don't overdo it, stop apologizing. If you apologize, she will assume you did something wrong, even if only subconsciously. She wanted to be alone, he could tell, and in a perfect world he'd sleep on the couch, just to give her that alone time, if "sleeping on the couch" didn't connote all that baggage.

So he decided the best course of action would be to just hug her and be supportive and whisper some more proactive plans to put her mind at ease: handle the process of fixing the door, get an exterminator pronto, and shore up some masculine credibility by, *for fucking sure*, sending that exterminator bill straight to the fucking management company. Also be a good idea to pour bleach down the drain, and come to think of it he should do it now before they forget, offering while knowing of course she'll say just to stay in bed and do it tomorrow, which she did but, again, kind of reluctantly. He felt he should have pressed on and insisted, or just gone and done it, and there was another minor loss in his staying in bed.

She still felt so distant. His concern for Debra, his concern for their relationship and his self-pity and emasculation were all sinking, leaden feelings, that type that leave you immobilized. There was another, equally unpleasant but altogether different feeling stirring inside him: one of fiery, acidic injustice, the recognition that something had been taken from him, and no one would do anything about it except himself.

Chapter 7: No Time Like the Present

Things didn't get any better the following day.

First thing in the morning Casey poured bleach down the drain, and then set the stopper firmly to make sure nothing could squeeze through. He knew pouring bleach would do nothing, and he also knew that the insect could come back up the pipes and get around that stopper if it really, somehow, had a desire to, if that were possible, if they were truly living in a world where insects had conscious long-term goals.

He searched online and found an exterminator who could come that night. The exterminator's price was a huge rip-off, and he'd be embarrassed to submit that to the management company for reimbursement; he hoped Debra wouldn't be madder at the expense than anything else.

Casey sent Debra texts at work detailing the arrangements and what he'd done, waiting for her affirmations and sifting through the meaning in each response or choice of emoticon. Gone were the exclamations and exaggerations of her oft-animated texts. Was a curt "ya" dismissive? Was an "ok" a signal that these texts were annoying, that she wanted the conversation to end?

"I think we should move out immediately," Debra told him in their bedroom later that day, after they'd both returned from work. His heart exploded in his chest, until he realized she'd said "we," not "I."

"Okay."

"I spent like half my day at work looking up real estate listings. I'm putting together a list of good ones to send to you."

"Okay. Great!"

"Yes."

Usually she loved considering real estate. Debra squeezed his hand and smiled slightly. It was like the blinking a machine does to let you know it's still on.

"That's a good step! It's good, a great start, we'll get on this and have a new place all to ourselves before you know it." As she'd recently adopted the sullen role he usually inhabited, he took on the chipper, we-can-do-it positivity she often provided.

"I hope."

There persisted a constricting sobriety that he couldn't quite identify, as if he needed to carefully pre-select his words. He was stepping into dangerous ground, he knew, but as momentous a decision as breaking a lease deserved some airing out.

The best he could muster was, "Is everything alright?"

"I just feel," and it was obvious the dam had broken on the emotions she'd been restraining, "so fucking stupid and embarrassed and–," and when he went in to console her, he could tell, by the pinched look on her face, that there were obviously additional feelings, hard to process, of a different, more troubling cast. "And it's just so, I feel just so weird and ashamed and I know it was my fault by overreacting–"

This cued the easiest good boyfriend line: "You weren't overreacting."

She nodded in acknowledgement of the expected, proper response, hasty to continue: "And now everything just feels so weird, you know," and her pressing eyes filled in the details. Yes, Casey knew. Frustrated, fatigued, and trapped in consciousness all throughout the overheated night of the incident, he'd enraged himself with his helpless thoughts about Ben; but the demands and seeming normality of the following day had cooled his temperature. He just avoided thinking about it, a strategy that usually never worked but, strangely, was finding some success here.

Maybe moving out would be the best idea: not see Ben, not be reminded of it. A portion of him found her exposed nudity exciting, as he'd always wanted confirmation from another on the appeal of her proportions, which he always thought were disserved by her choice of clothing. In his overheated tossing and turning his heart would skip a beat and he enjoyed a troublesome erection whenever he replayed certain portions of this whole shit-show. That was a developing avenue of his mind best left decommissioned with a prompt moving-out.

He'd not really even talked to Ben all day, except texting him that an exterminator would be coming by later. While speaking with Debra, he'd heard the front door open and wondered if Debra heard, too. Must not have, because when Casey said he'd go speak to Ben and let him know the plan, Debra shook her head as if she now just realized that the expected completion of an unpleasant task just got dramatically expedited. She even put her hand to her forehead, a move that seemed inherently comic.

The atmosphere in their bedroom was suffocating, and Casey needed to get out. Debra impassively moved to her computer to joylessly watch YouTube videos and re-read the same websites. No, she didn't want anything from the kitchen, as she'd eaten a late lunch at work. Casey knew that but preferred the pretext of going to the kitchen and oh, look who's home, it's Ben, two birds, one stone.

He wondered if Debra showered today or used the bathroom this morning. She must have brushed her teeth and washed her face, at least. Would that now be a whole thing, would she need to be accompanied to the bathroom every time she went, Casey standing guard outside with a flashlight every time she had to take a late-night dump?

The showering part wouldn't be so bad; "need company," he could ask, although joint showering actually kind of sucked, one party always cold and waiting for the water, can't really properly clean your asshole and genitals with someone else there, and some of those contortions like bending down to clean your feet is never a good look on anyone. He couldn't picture her wanting a joint shower these days anyway, not the time to ask that, anyway.

He was fucked even in his fantasies.

Chapter 8: That Bug's Never Coming Back

"Hey Ben," Casey greeted him after knocking his way into Ben's bedroom.

"What's up, Casey." Ben turned away from his computer and stood up, butt languidly leaning and resting against the desk. Casey sensed an unexpressed smirk, which seemed to lift off Ben's face and disperse throughout the atmosphere.

"You just get home?"

"Yeah. Ate wings at Foxhold's with some guys from work. Exterminator come yet?"

"Cool, cool, cool, what? No, sometime later tonight, you know that whole sometime between six and ten bullshit. You don't have to worry about that if you plan on going back out or something, we'll be here."

"Didn't know exterminators worked so late."

"Well, you know, for the right price, I guess."

"Got you by the balls."

"Right." Surely, he meant the exterminator.

"So, Ben, I feel like I should just let you know that whole situation in the bathroom really freaked Debra out, so she wants us, meaning me and her, to find a new place as soon as possible. You know we've been thinking of getting a place of our own for some time, you know, next steps and all–"

Casey wasn't sure what he expected. Maybe an impassioned "what!" or its equivalent, "dude!" Instead, after a beat: "And leave me here with the bugs, I guess?" It presented as sardonically off-the-cuff, but there was a pregnant pause, almost a moment where the comment caught, flared hot until forced to come out.

"You should leave too, maybe, not the worst idea?"

"So you're just going to bail on the lease? Why not just wait until the lease is up in a few months rather than breaking it and, it's just a bug, dude, apartments get bugs."

"That was no ordinary bug, man, c'mon. And, anyway, you know, Debra is pretty positive about getting out of here, so you know, can't really–"

"Decision been made, then."

"Yeah man, you know how it is."

"I guess I understand. I mean, maybe I don't. How definite is this, maybe give it a week or so and when she realizes that bug was stomped and flushed down the drain, I mean, I killed that bug straight disrespectful warrior style."

"I don't think it was dead, dude."

"Maybe not, but it definitely learned a lesson. It'll tell all its freakish bug friends not to come back."

"Oh, don't get me wrong, I'm sure it had to go to bug ER, get a bunch of stitches and a walker."

"A bug walker for all one thousand legs. Bitch'll have a limp for the rest of its life, better learn to roll up in a ball. Imagine, going from a centipede-thing to a pill bug. I took that bug's manhood. That's emasculating, his wife is going to leave him for sure, kids won't want to talk to him."

"All ten thousand of them, I'm sure."

"Speaking of hospitals, Debra is alright, right?"

"Yeah, she's all good."

"Cool." Ben rubbed his nose and fidgeted, not a shrug exactly but serving the identical purpose. "Well, I guess that's it, then."

"Yeah." Casey nodded, continued speaking both to fill space and as if he owed an explanation, even though he knew he didn't. "Debra just feels all freaked out about the whole thing."

"About what, exactly, the bug?"

"The whole thing."

"What do you mean. It's just a bug."

"You know, man."

"Okay. And how do you feel about it?"

It didn't matter how he felt, is that what Ben wanted him to say? Because in a relationship, when one party's zeal greatly exceeded the other's indifference, you did what the more passionate party wanted, because that's what you do to keep equipoise. They were planning on moving out anyway so if anything, this just put a good fire under their asses to do it: it accelerated plans, it didn't transform them. So whatever righteousness Ben was aspiring to convey was contrived at birth.

And you know what? Fuck him, he knew what "the whole thing" meant.

"Truthfully, I'm not super crazy about how the whole thing went down, either."

"Okay, well, sorry man, I was only trying to help, you know, I was just following your lead."

"Okay man, well, fine, still, it's–" and he was going to say it wasn't a big deal because this was his good friend, and his indignation had a showy, brittle hollowness, like he was performing more out of duty than genuine emotion, although Ben's obstinance was renewing some of the flavor to last night's overheated anger. That smarminess, that was it, that . . . he thinks he's gotten something over on me, that's what it is, that's that fucking unexpressed smirk, he doesn't even need to smirk, it's like a perpetual victory he can return to, memories, fuck, that's what it is, isn't it, memories of my girlfriend in his mind, completely naked and bouncing and . . . completely shaved, he now knows Debra, my girlfriend, has a completely shaved pussy, maybe even saw the two beauty marks a few inches above her left nipple, separated in such a way that they looked like little shadow imitations of the nipple piercing she had in college; maybe he saw that her vaginal lips were a bit larger than average; contented knowing he had a go-to cruelty to unleash at the appropriate time.

Well, no, Ben wasn't really like that, but who knew what Ben shared with his friends at work. Now anytime Casey or Debra met anyone of his friends, who knew what'd they'd be thinking, chuckling at; would they be sizing her up, trying to fill in the details of Ben's narrative.

"I mean you didn't need to grab her like that," and the words sprouted spikes in his throat.

"What! Are you crazy? I was protecting her."

"She didn't need protection, man."

"Well, you were free to do it if you didn't have your thumb up your ass the whole time. Dude, there's a fucking bug jumping around at her, I got her out of the way because you sure as shit weren't doing it."

"Oh, I thought a second ago it was 'just a harmless bug' or something, now it's a supervillain bug so you had to grab Debra's tits in order to save her, right?"

"I didn't grab her tits, man. Can you listen to yourself? Do you think I'd do that? You were there."

"Okay, fine." Casey wanted to believe what Ben was saying: he didn't want to imagine his best friend indulging in his girlfriend's body. So he passively conceded the point, and felt the following was a fair middle ground of their respective positions: "You took some liberties, though."

He regretted how it came out: something about the arch language added a layer of opportunistic calculation.

"Liberties! What!? I got her out of the way, and she was naked, that's all. You're making it sound like I'm at fault here. Where is this coming from, anyway. Is this coming from her? If so, let her come and talk to me if she has something to say."

Casey shook his head and instinctively rolled his eyes, less at the merits of Ben's suggestion and more as to what a clusterfuck that would be: no, no, no, can't have that.

"Honestly, do you really absolutely care that much? It's a body, calm down. Tell you what, I'll show her my cock if she wants. I'll show you and her my bare ass and cock and balls and I'll go out in the kitchen and dance on the counters for you, you can both look up to the unflattering underside of my hairy ass and low hanging balls and spit water up at me."

Casey looked skeptically. "Oh, so you're saying we should reward you, then. You'd like that too much, you sick fuck. Having water sprayed up your asshole, that's probably, like, at least top five in your fetish list."

They were both half-smiling, back in the unforced habit of their beloved bickery antics.

"Look, honestly man, do you really even care? Like, you know, sure, it's a bit embarrassing and awkward, but honestly, it's not a big deal. We're all friends. I mean, it's not the first time I've seen her not wearing much."

"What the fuck is that supposed to mean?"

"Dude, calm down! I meant, remember, that picture you sent me?"

"What?"

"In college, remember, when you started dating? She was like, wearing only a bikini bottom and hand-braing herself on a beach somewhere."

"Dude, what? What, was that like, when we first started hooking up like, fucking a million years ago? I sent you that? Anyway, this is obviously a million times different and I shouldn't have sent you that, anyway. Wait, I think I had originally just taken that from her Facebook page anyway."

"No, that was never on there."

"How do you know? What, did you study her Facebook page?"

At this Ben rolled his eyes but tellingly turned away for a brief moment to adjust his computer. What, he didn't want the screen to go black all of a sudden? Yeah, right, more likely Casey had struck a nerve.

"You still have that picture, Ben?"

"I don't know, man, I doubt it."

"You have pictures of her saved on your computer or in your emails or something? You seem to know her social media pictures pretty well."

"Oh, get fucked, dude."

"Show me your computer, dude, show me you don't have that one or any other ones of her saved." Debra had erased all swimwear pictures or anything else that could be perceived as debauched or just unprofessional around junior year, after she started applying for internships.

"Oh, what are you, fucking McGruff the Crime Dog? Casey, fucking bikini photo sniffer. What are you going to do, search all my emails and pictures?"

"You still have them, don't you? I bet you have all those pictures of her from back in the day. How else would you even remember that one?"

"Why don't you remember that?"

"Oh don't fucking reverse it-"

A crazed orchestra at different pitches:

"No really-"

"No guy ever deletes-"

"Fucking squirrelled away like some fucking squirrel."

"Okay, you're a lunatic man, it's official–"

A heavy knocking. It was coming from the door of the apartment, the sound muted by the time it reached through into Ben's room. Casey heard movement and went out to see Debra, timid and uncertain, looking at him hesitantly.

Chapter 9: Don't Worry, He's a Professional Exterminator

"I think the exterminator is here," Debra said. She'd been watching Casey as he came out of Ben's room and been peering in; there'd been some eye contact between her and Ben. He hoped Ben didn't give any kind of fucking smart alecky look, or worse, offer some little aside. Last thing he fucking needed.

"Okay, I got it."

As Casey went to the door, Ben followed, casually smiling as if expecting a delivery.

Unseen by either of the two boys, upon Ben's emergence Debra's blanched expression wilted even further. She took a step forward, as if to get away, then stopped, turned and drifted toward her bedroom door without going inside.

Casey didn't know whether to continue to the door or see how Debra was doing. So he unsuccessfully attempted both, took a step forward, with a detour to whisper, "everything okay?"

"I'm fine, get the door." Debra's resolve appeared reoriented by being able to shush him away: funny, by providing her something familiar, Casey thought, I was able to renew her. I should get boyfriend points for both trying to help and inadvertently doing so.

Just please don't let Ben do or say anything stupid.

On a superficial level, Ben wasn't doing anything to complain about. But his mere good mood was a provocation.

Casey beelined to the door, not sure if Ben was en route, but wanting to beat him anyway.

The exterminator, a scraggly good-natured man in his early thirties, naturally bulky and made even bulkier carrying his rucksack of traps and ointments, confirmed he was in the right place and came in.

"You know there's a bunch of police outside your apartment building?" That was the only pertinent information he really offered, and not exactly the kind of information that would help to restore balance to the apartment. The initial courteousness brought by having to be civil around an outsider quickly evaporated, and the momentum of concern shifted; now Casey wanting nothing more than to accelerate the exterminator's departure to find out what was going on elsewhere in the building.

Ben didn't share those concerns; not Ben, of course. Oh, he asked all about what that bug could have possibly been.

Casey could sense Debra leaning in, straining to hear without stepping into the conversation. When the exterminator – Exterminator Bill, seemed an appropriate name – seemed stumped and pressed for further details, Ben turned to Debra, as if drawing her out into a normal conversation would extend normalcy among all parties. Debra spoke meekly, but then regathered herself, describing the size, speed and color of the insect, the way it jumped around the shower and seemed to be deliberately targeting her.

It didn't help much when Exterminator Bill guffawed at the state of the door. "No bug could be worth all that." (Avoid eye contact with Debra, avoid eye contact with Debra, Casey commanded himself.)

"The shower?" was how the exterminator reacted to all the information provided. Beats him, sounds like some kind of flying cockroach, maybe, but certainly wouldn't have that many legs or be that big. Exterminator Bill deposited his ointments and traps in all the expected spots, sealed some corners and cracks in the bathroom and kitchen.

"Can you spray anything, like, bug spray?" Debra asked when he was done.

"Can't use the spray anymore. It's not good for pets."

"We don't have any pets."

"Sorry, we just aren't allowed to use that anymore."

Debra, unconcerned even about a hypothetical animal possibly coming into the apartment – or a neighbor's pet – meant none of this pantomime salve was worth a damn.

Ben walked the exterminator out.

"Debra," Ben said when the three of them were alone. Casey could see immediately that whatever gloating fun Ben enjoyed with the exterminator had been only at Casey's expense. Upon addressing Debra, Ben's demeanor softened considerably. "Is there – can we talk about – I don't want any bad blood between us."

Debra's expression was hard to read. She seemed leavened with an obvious desire to avoid the conversation, but also a countervailing wish to get it done, as if she knew the responsible thing would be to address whatever it was that compelled her so strongly to leave. Casey held his breath and wanted Debra's sour feelings directed exclusively at Ben, for them to have a united front in their distaste, to elevate himself in her eyes through commiseration. But her feelings, he realized, were more complicated than that, and perhaps too complicated to be expressed, competing forces that resulted in inertia.

Casey could guess at what these feelings entailed. The topmost feeling might be an appreciation for what Ben had done. Maybe this was the type of appreciation that would leave a permanent impression upon her, Ben now being permanently associated with a type of appealing competence that made her uneasy, and somehow, feel a great diminishing of herself, like she became less than herself whenever she was in his presence. And this pained her for multiple reasons, and Casey, too, because he felt the worst about his friend: he still felt Ben had taken a kind of advantage of the situation, but his reasons for believing so were weathering away the farther removed he became from the incident, under the natural good graces of their friendship, his expedient desire for forgiveness and reconciliation, and his creeping suspicion that his reactions were colored more out of frustration and shame than accurate recall.

"There's no – we're just going to move out, is all. I don't feel safe here anymore."

"Because of me?"

"I don't feel comfortable at all for several reasons. You should understand that and please just let me process this how I need to."

Ben nodded, tight-jawed. Clever girl. The request to allow her to process, the use of that therapeutic language currently in vogue, allowed her to shut the conversation down and make Ben look like an asshole if he wanted to press forward. Casey would congratulate her on that later.

Debra returned to her room, giving them both sorrowful glances. Ben, jaw still tight, turned to Casey and tilted his head back as if staring down a hostile stranger on the street. Why, exactly, Casey didn't know, or care to know right now. Let Ben be pissy, Casey was out of here.

"I'm going to check the mail and see what's going on outside."

So Casey left.

Chapter 10: A Most Reliable Source

With the junk mail thrown away and no police vehicles outside, Casey went to superintendent Vikram's apartment on the fourth floor.

Vikram answered, door opened enough only to reveal a sliver of his body, as the family havanese stampeded toward the door. Vikram said foreign words back to his wife, who, Casey sensed, was now backing away from the door with the animal.

Someone was found passed away on the third floor earlier today, Vikram explained, and police came by to pick up the body and look around. The natural follow-up questions: Who? Which apartment? And, the big one, which Casey couched in a strange way as if foul play might reflect badly on Vikram, as if he wasn't only the superintendent but the sheriff of the building: was she murdered?

Casey didn't know whether it was because he and Debra were generous holiday tippers; or Vikram looked back fondly on that one time Casey nodded along uncomfortably when Vikram shared some rather politically incorrect views about Pakistanis and the trouble they caused back home, all while Casey thought, okay, okay, whatever just nod as he installs the air conditioners; or just that Vikram wanted to close the door and get back to dinner; but whatever the reason he spilled the beans: not a murder, but a "big mess." The woman, a name Casey couldn't connect to a face or body, must have been deceased, unfortunately, for quite some time. That's why it's important to have a wife and family, Vikram proffered; that was the other thing about Vikram, always asking when Casey was going to get married, start having a family. So he spilled the gruesome beans so readily and perhaps too eagerly as a kind of teaching tool: she died alone, must have been there for a long time, and was found practically in pieces.

Perhaps realizing he'd divulged too much, Vikram then added as a chaser, "very sad, very sad. She was a nice woman," swatted away at an invisible dog (as the havanese was now nowhere near the door, instead begging at the dinner table), said his good-byes and closed the door.

What to do with this information? What to do? Certainly they didn't need a death in the building, that wouldn't set things at ease. But maybe, let's think. Perhaps telling Debra and Ben could put everything in perspective: let's forgive and forget, and be grateful we have our lives. Why waste our precious time, we all love each other, all dear friends. Yes, that could work.

And realistically, they will find out eventually. But the issue was, when: should I wait to tell them? Better to let everything return to some kind of equilibrium first before introducing this news. And telling Debra about a death will shoot their plan to leave the apartment into overdrive. He didn't want to leave, he realized, at least not yet. Leaving would confirm his worst feelings about Ben, and maybe the worst feelings about himself, and was more about caving-in than thinking-through. He wasn't sure why, but he felt unsettled, and leaving now felt like losing.

Who was he kidding, he knew he would tell her what he learned. He had always been honest, and the risks of deception outweighed the rewards: since he was already in the dog house (okay, well, if not in, then at least adjacent-to), it was best to play it straight.

He believed that Ben still had those old pictures of Debra saved somewhere in his email or on some computer. It didn't affect him, really. But he felt like he should be upset, like there was some kind of, well, not betrayal, but . . . something untoward about it, let's go with that.

And those were the thoughts he was thinking when he came back to the apartment and started telling Ben that the lady above them had passed away, so his tone wasn't as friendly and conciliatory as he had planned. It went awry, suffice to say. Not terribly so, but it wasn't a bonding experience. Maybe Ben shouldn't have teased, saying, "I bet it was that bug who did it!"

Casey ended it like this, which he regretted instantly, before the words were even out of his mouth:

"Just tell me the truth," he asked in a voice low enough not to be heard by Debra in their bedroom, "you still have those pictures of her?"

Ben just shook his head. "Fuck you, dude." It wasn't hostile, but reproachful, like Casey should be the one apologizing. Hadn't Ben essentially admitted he had them? And again, Casey didn't care, he should have asked it lightheartedly, like a parting buddy shot, a good-natured ribbing, but he didn't. Anger again, suspicions about Ben getting away with something flared up, but almost out of obligation. He didn't feel it, and he regretted how it ended. When he left, he heard Ben locking the bedroom door.

Things didn't go much better in his own bedroom. It was obvious Debra was displeased; she looked burdened just by his presence.

After extended periods of awkward, isolating silence – it was obvious she'd also gotten ready for bed without him – she stated, almost without feeling, "I heard you and Ben talking before, by the way, earlier tonight before the exterminator came."

"Okay." He wasn't sure what he'd said, but certainly she wasn't bringing it up to compliment how he handled things. Should he preemptively apologize, or wait to hear the specific grievances?

"It's fine," she stated blankly. "I don't want to make you feel bad. I just feel so uncomfortable about everything."

The subject was depleted. Talking about this, at least now, wasn't going to do anybody any good. Thank God that old woman had died, he thought macabrely, because now he had a way to pivot from under where this dour conversation was going.

He instinctively stored that joke away to relay to Ben later; it would take his sense-memory time to adjust to the new reality of their strained relationship. Maybe once everything was back to normal.

Turning his head and pretextually fiddling away with some other thing, Casey casually explained the presence of the police officers. When Casey turned, Debra was staring at him, wide-eyed.

"Miss Verona, right above us? I just saw her, like, two days ago!"

That couldn't be easily reconciled with Vikram's account. He'd said she must have been laying there for a long time to make such a mess. He didn't know exactly what that meant. He imagined a douty, fleshy old woman dead on her back, wearing a simple dark-colored sweater and pajamas, then imagined repeated time-jumps into the future, revealing an increasingly dissolute, congealing decomposition, a gradually expanding thickening puddle of sludgy matter where those flesh colors and dark clothing colors spilled into and through each other.

He approached Debra as she sat at her computer desk as if to console her; his proximity snapped her out of her calm of her mourning. I helped again, he joked to himself.

Casey did his filial duty by truthfully telling her about the recent death, even though his better judgment rebelled against the admission. That duty didn't go so far as to report the unverified speculation of their Pakistani-hating superintendent who took his sweet time responding to repairs. Maybe Vikram was just exaggerating? Or who knows, maybe in two days an old woman could decompose (he added a rotund, gassy belly to his sweatshirt-and-sweatpants speculation).

"I believe she died of natural causes, I think."

Debra nodded gravely. She treated this spontaneous utterance suspiciously, and with good reason; he was obviously trying to allay concerns without deigning to first recognize them.

This was brutal. He wanted the old Debra to return, their old relationship to return. Where do our real selves go, in this, what was this, this fog of bullshit and discord between us. Where was the real Debra, the real me, and that blessed entity: the real us, of love and affection and fun and joking and planning. When things were going sideways, he wished he could just take Debra by the shoulders and shake her like she was on the fritz, like these bad attitudes and misgivings were just some personality blip that needed to be reset.

That would have to wait, because the iciness in the room couldn't be ignored. He made to hug her and she wasn't responding, just lying listlessly. Enough, already, he thought, enough, and she said she wanted to be alone, but he could read the subtext, or at least he thought he could: it'd gone from some kind of sexualized anger at Ben and disappointment with him, to some kind of shame and resentment toward both of them, blended with persistent paranoia about the illusory dangers of some flushed-away bug.

Yes, yes, the bug was creepy and gross – what bug wasn't – but enough. Enough. He'd dealt with a lot, too. Fuck, he was practically losing his best friend over this. He needed to get inside her head, if only she would communicate with him. Could he be missing something? What approach could he take that would be respectful enough (or appear respectful enough) to get back into her good graces, to give him the benefit of the doubt? Would just the passage of time be enough, allow her to re-center herself and come to her own realization? The problem with waiting is that all you do is fill your time with worry; being proactive, even if wrongheaded, at least provides the comfort of distraction.

"Maybe I should sleep on the couch tonight?" Relations are partly a game of chicken. He made his counter-move. Taking things to their logical extreme is a kind of challenge, whereby the other party realizes they are courting a precipice, and wisely pull back before the brink.

She didn't blink. "Maybe that's a good idea for tonight."

He instantly regretted it, and it dawned upon him how serious this might all be. How could he explain that OF COURSE he didn't want to sleep on the couch; by even posing the question, he was trying to get her to console him, reassure him that of course he was needed here, that he was trying to bring her back into the fold by showing her the ramifications of where they were heading? How could you explain that? You can't, not sensibly, and not now.

He skooched over and hugged her, as she faced away from him and patted and rubbed his arm listlessly, if only to show that there still dimmed some spark of connection. He took that little show of affection to heart.

"I guess it's better if you just really want to be alone tonight. I'll miss you."

"I'll miss you, too."

"I don't really have to go on the couch."

"I just, I'm sorry, I just feel so shitty and uncomfortable. I just want to be alone."

"I'm sorry about Ben, and everything that happened."

"It's not your fault. You can't control nature, you can't control him, you can't control – it was all such a split-second thing. And you know how I, I worry, I just want to get out of this apartment already, I'm sure soon things will be back to normal, I – I just have to admit I feel uncomfortable, even around you right now, and upset and disappointed."

Okay. Truthfully, he was wearying of all this, and maybe it would be best to leave. There was so much to unpack there. By "you can't control nature," he hoped she meant that he could not control the physical world – of creepy-crawly insects – and not control "nature," meaning her biological responses to what happened: a strange repulsive attraction to Ben. No, that couldn't be it.

So he kissed her and indulged himself in a long hug – and she indulged right back, hugged and kissed him, which he appreciated – and, after grabbing underwear, socks and a t-shirt for the next day, he went to the couch.

Chapter 11: The World Doesn't Stop Because You Had a Bug in Your Apartment

He hadn't slept on a couch in a while. It wasn't as uncomfortable as he thought it'd be; or maybe the discomfort wasn't sufficient to overcome his mental and emotional exhaustion. Turning the lights out and darkening a bedroom felt like an artificial manipulation. The darkened living room, with its concealed tables and chairs and rugs, whose proximities were never encountered in pitch-blackness, made him feel more alone and the darkness more complete. Tucked away into the curve of the couch's armrest reminded him of being a child, when nights seemed to stretch onto infinity and he'd never wanted them to end because he relished the time to think and reflect and the new day brought only burdens and obligations.

He awoke into the familiar humdrum of his living room, made pedestrian in the daylight. He imagined himself an alcoholic for a moment, isn't this how drunks are portrayed in the movies? Waking up after passing out on the couch. Funny, that movie drunks are usually figures of pity, even though they're selfishly killing themselves and ruining the lives around them. He wasn't a drunk, just someone who'd not reacted fast enough, didn't always know what to say or do, and found himself with a predicament he didn't know how best to navigate. That was all, really, wasn't it, and now there was some kind of stigma he just couldn't shake. This stupid fucking insect had temporarily exploded his world.

He left for work before Debra did. He changed in the living room into his undergarments, and was going to wear the same black pants again for work (which he did quite often, only just making sure no embarrassing telltale stain had cropped up which would out him as being a pants-recycler). He needed to go back into the bedroom, though, to change his shirt and, come to think of it, grab his charging cell phone off the desk.

He entered as furtively as he could and didn't turn on the light, as it was easy enough to see in the morning's sunrise. He plucked out a button-down and put it on.

He watched Debra sleeping on her side facing the inner wall, just as he'd left her, and thought to kiss her on the cheek as she slept. It seemed hackneyed, and he wondered who was it for – was it so he could tell himself he was a good person?; or would he be waiting for the opportunity to tell her, once they patched things up, that he'd kissed her in her sleep, and she'd say how sweet he was and embrace him? And no, it wasn't for that, he concluded, and he felt good about himself. As someone aware of the mercantile and kabuki aspects of relationship theater, he so often questioned himself about his own motives. But here, he wanted to do it because he loved her and wanted to be close to her. He wanted to hold her and hug her, as if to reduce them back to their essence, so all the shame and tension and unease riddling their relationship would squeeze out of them and they'd be back to who they were.

He saw her turn and shift, and didn't want to interrupt her sleep, as it was often troubled and deficient. It would serve her better to get her sleep, to be better rested for the day, and that's what true love was, wasn't it?: the ability to silently prioritize someone else's well-being over your own. He felt good about himself, hugged and kissed her in his heart, and left.

Riding this slightly cresting tide of warm feelings, he placed his hand delicately on the knob of Ben's door, felt resistance and wasn't surprised, apparently this would be a talk for another time.

He left work around 5 p.m., which was early for him, and really, early for any young middle-class professional these days. Six-thirty or seven was the norm, a fact that was still incredible to him: all that time they spent at work. No wonder personal issues seemed to drag on interminably, there was no free time to resolve them. If only they'd all taken off a few days of work, just to lock themselves in a room and air out their grievances. With that time off, he could have done a deep cleaning of the apartment, perhaps convince Debra that the apartment was safe, and – not sure how this would work – but at least alleviate whatever bad tidings and tensions existed among them.

Back at home, and the apartment looked like he'd left it. He still felt calmly contented with himself, secure that he was trying to do right. He'd looked up some of the real estate listings Debra had sent him earlier and took some good notes, made a little spreadsheet of people to contact, and looked up some places on his own, in the same general locations and price ranges as she had.

He hadn't told Debra that yet, and thought to text her about it during the day, but had only sent one text during the workday that she hadn't responded to: "thinking of ya." He wished he'd had said "I love you," because they had a rule that, when one of them says "I love you," the other, no matter how they are feeling, has to say it back. It's a way of letting the other know that, no matter how the other party was feeling at that time, they were secure in each other's love, and it was the spats and disagreements that were passing.

He made himself a glass of water and grabbed two Polly-O Mozzarella sticks. Not knowing when Debra would be home but wanting to eat dinner with her, he chomped the two sticks down while sitting on the couch, thinking that would be enough to tide him over. He sent Debra another text, this time just asking when she'd be home tonight and if they could get dinner together.

He tried Ben's door again, and again found it locked. So he texted him too, just asking, "any chance you're around tonight," taking the time to make sure auto-fill didn't fuck up the grammar. The proper grammar was important to him.

He grabbed an apple, too. Debra could work late sometimes. It was rude of her not to get back to him; he had often waited around for her, only for her to text, fairly late in the day, that she wasn't going to be able to make it out of work at a reasonable hour, or that she was just going to eat in the office, or sometimes that she had some other plans he'd forgotten about.

Apple in hand, he picked up the crinkled cheese stick wrappers from the living room table and opened the kitchen garbage. Tossing them in, he saw something out of the corner of his eye, but, no, he didn't. He was wrong. Subconsciously, he was noticing something, something to give him pause, but what was it, near the apartment door.

It was nothing.

It was Ben's shoes: three pairs of work shoes, all by the apartment door.

Ben only owned three proper pairs of shoes and a pair of flip-flops, and kept one pair of ratty gym shoes at the office.

Ben's door was locked.

Okay. So, that means Ben had to have come home from work, taken off whatever work shoes he wore, locked his door, and left to go somewhere: in flip-flops, perhaps, across the street to do laundry.

That didn't make any sense. He never wore flip-flops out of the house. That's when you knew you were in deep for a good apartment hang, a Ben in flip-flops.

Maybe he went to the gym. He could have, let's see, gone to work, then gone to the gym afterward, where he uses gym shoes, but . . . but, those are additional shoes he doesn't keep here, that doesn't make sense, still the three pairs of shoes....

Okay, he went to the gym, brought his gym shoes home, left his work shoes – accounting for all three pairs of shoes – then left somewhere in his gym shoes. That's not crazy. And maybe Ben is stressed out too by all this, the gym could do some good.

Ben hadn't gone to the gym in a while, though. Although I guess that doesn't mean much, Casey thought.

Ben wasn't at the gym, was he?

Apple in hand, Casey knocked on Ben's door. No answer. Yes, locked.

Apple in mouth, he shot Ben another text: "let's grab a beer if we can. I'm sorry about all this going on." He needed to be careful: he didn't want to say anything that could put him in an uncomfortable position with Debra.

He sat down on the couch. He gripped the apple with his right hand and bit out an unexpectedly big chunk, down to the hardened core. Looking at the seeds, he had a thought, how it could be that both Debra and Vikram had been right: just an old, fleshy lady on her back, dead, just a normal dead body to be carted off to the morgue; then, black insects erupting all at once on every square inch of her body and, as necessary, right through her clothes, each about a foot long, all fastened to her body, all waving in triumphant unison, their shrill little screeches of triumph all inaudible on their own but united into something resembling the squeak of a substantial rat, if you kept your ears peeled and knew what you were listening for.

No, that was absurd. But it was equally absurd that an insect had been making a deliberate beeline for his girlfriend while she was in the shower. At her privates, really, that's what it'd been doing. Beeline, hmmm. He never really thought about that word: did bees really charge in a straight, uninterrupted line? Why not "birdline," unless there was something specific about the way bees – or insects – had been observed on the hunt.

No, that was absurd, too. All absurd.

He got up and threw out the largely-eaten apple.

He went to his bedroom.

It looked the same as when he'd left it. Nothing new, no new sights, no new smells, no unexpected surprises.

No new sights. The same . . . the same . . . the bed. The clump of sheets.

Debra was still sleeping in bed.

He furrowed his brow and his heart lost its moorings. He felt its absence in his chest as it splashed down into his stomach.

Replaying this morning. She'd shifted in bed, turned over, troubled sleep.

No, he saw it again. He stood near her, and she had moved, shifted in bed, turned over. No, no, the sheets had shifted. Her face had stayed fixed on the inside wall. She hadn't been turning, she'd, she'd been shifting her legs, that's all, legs probably gotten hot, that's it.

She was still there, facing the wall.

She must be sick, must be sick and stayed home today.

Legs still must be hot, shifting, that must be it. Whole body, too hot, she must be sick, legs, body, neck, her blanket the surface above an invisible ocean, all shifting under the sheets.

NOTES

I'm a fan of what Quentin Tarantino has called "hang out" films, films with a kind of deft lightness of tone and a languid, meandering pace, where the primary attraction is just hanging out with a set of characters. I was trying to depict a typical hangout session between a group of friends, allowing you to get to know these people as they just fuck about. That is, at least, until everything gets complicated – as everything eventually does – when a triggering event puts into sharp relief the tensions lurking below the surface. This novella was originally titled "These Silent, Coherent Conversations," although that seemed too heavy for what I wanted to begin as casually as possible. I like stories where there aren't bad guys, where the tension comes from legitimate competing grievances.

Ben's personality and appearance (particularly his curly hair and strong chin) were roughly modeled on retired UFC fighter Ben "Funky" Askren, who exudes a likeable if somewhat smarmy brand of confidence (although he's now most famous for being knocked out in five seconds courtesy of a flying knee by now-superstar Jorge Masvidal). Although, that setback hasn't humbled the indefatigable Ben Askren, who is just as cocky and trash-talking as ever in his retirement. I wanted my Ben to have that same aura of breezy competence edging-toward-but-not-quite-reaching smugness, a personality that Debra would find appealing, maybe even despite herself, and Casey would, no matter how long or close their friendship, always feel slightly uneasy around and perhaps jealous of.

<u>Grab More Knives</u>

It'd just been there, and now it wasn't. Clare was sure of it. Where did the knife go? She froze, body paralyzed, still sifting through the innocuous explanations, awaiting that moment of simple clarification. She made a face, a kind of mildly confused-grimace, as if it signaled to an imagined audience that this was just so stupid, such a nothing; but it wasn't a nothing, was it?

*

Earlier
*

Clare Allende had spent this mid-summer Wednesday at nearby Capewell Park, doing her middle-aged best to chase her seven-year-old son Cody around the pond and playground and hem in his instinct to rouse the ducks into flight. Cody, his sweet nature complemented by his hug-encouraging cherubic plumpness, upon her suggestion took her hand and accompanied her on a little "hike" up the park's gentle "hills." He responded positively to the suggestion, Clare bet, because it sounded like a big-kid activity, something his siblings Isabella or Gabriel might do.

Summer break, and the responsibilities fell upon her, as her husband Andres continued working his ungodly hours at Cobson LLC in Midtown Manhattan. Not right for an executive in his late fifties, she thought, and part of her, even though years removed from student life, still felt the summer, if not an excuse for outright vacation, should still be an excuse for at least some sort of reduced schedule, "summer Fridays" and all that.

But her husband's work had been chaotic. Heads were rolling, especially down in the Jacksonville, Florida headquarters. The recent press had been excruciating, following "revelations," as the media put it, that Cobson-manufactured tear gas had been used by the French military to quell ongoing race riots in the migrant-heavy Paris suburbs, riots that began after a migrant who, after allegedly stabbing a police officer, was then allegedly shot unarmed. Then, whipping the fire into a conflagration, articles came out about how Cobson-manufactured tear gas was deployed by ICE agents at the U.S.-Mexico border. In response, the trustees at the New York Museum of Modern Art, Columbia University and Yale had all just rejected Cobson's annual philanthropic donations: if voracious, mercantilist and land-gobbling institutions such as those were turning against them, then the optics must truly be bad. If firings were taking place in low-cost Jacksonville, the thinking went, all the high-cost New Yorkers would have to work even harder to prove their worth.

Clare didn't know what to make of any of this. She just hoped it was resolved, and quickly. Let Cobson just end the tear gas accounts. Tear gas was only one of the hundreds of products Cobson made, her husband had explained, and for years the federal government and foreign police forces allied with the United States had been dutifully served by their products with nary a peep. The breathless tenor of the articles made it seem like this was some dark industry secret. In reality it had been a badge of company honor, a perpetual prong of the P.R. campaign, like when Cobson-brand tear gas had been deployed by the French military a few years back to end an Islamist hostage situation at a Marseilles concert hall, which helped prevent another Bataclan horror. Framed photographs of thanks from the French government and photographic stills from the victorious operation immediately came off company walls in the midst of the latest news, Andres had explained with some sadness (as he'd played a sizable role in maintaining the French accounts), lest reports leak about the company "celebrating" its relationship with the French authorities in the wake of these riots.

All of that would hopefully come to an end soon. There were only so many days for playdates for Cody, not so easy to arrange in Shelton, Connecticut, with its isolated manor-style homes, filled with busy professionals with plans-upon-plans. Many of their nearest neighbors had already gone on their family vacations to Italy or Northern California or wherever this summer took them. Cody was too young for sleepaway camp. About four more years to go, and then, like their now twelve-year-old Isabella and thirteen-year-old Gabriel, he could spend his Julys if he wished at sleepaway camp. Gabriel was at Camp Awosting, and Isabella at Camp Chinqueka, camps exclusively for their respective genders. Both Clare and Andres knew that if Gabriel was going to agree to go back to summer camp next year, it'd have to be somewhere co-ed. That'd be a decision for another day, when Andres had some time to focus on anything but work.

The park had killed off a good portion of the day and the beginning of the afternoon was spent out in the backyard, where Clare encouraged Cody to read one of his *My Weird School* kids' books. Even though she could tell he didn't feel like reading, he was a good-enough kid to stare at the open book and mime reading, every so often turning a page to show some progress was being made. He'd been too worked up at the park to focus now, and, using the excuse that it was getting late anyway, they were soon downstairs in the living room searching for a movie to watch.

He had his repeat favorites but was always amenable to suggestions, which provided at least enough variety to prevent Clare from going insane. She had to catch herself sometimes, as the third go-round raising a small kid didn't seem as magical as the first two. She was older now, and Isabella and Gabriel had each other while growing up to fill their time.

But Clare's issues shouldn't be foisted upon unsuspecting Cody: her poor time-sequencing wasn't his fault. If anything, her fear that his childhood would be drabber and lonelier with this age-gulf among his siblings compelled her to push past any of her grumblings, be especially doting even, although she was always unsure if that was the right thing to do. She was trying to build up that early reservoir of goodwill, living in quiet fear that one day he'd intuit, if only based on the timing, that he was unplanned.

So now it was early evening, and she was making simple "nachos'" with salsa while Cody stayed downstairs, a specifically requested "or-derve" in their gleaming kitchen, which gave her some time to think about what to do later about dinner. Let's see, if recent history served, dinner would be a simple pasta, grilled cheese, a hamburger, or tuna fish, which was all this expansive, state-of-the-art kitchen had been used for as of late. Let Cody forever be so easy to please, let him forever bob his head with such toy doll enthusiasm for something as simple as Tostitos with melted cheese.

This reverie disappeared in a flash; the moment she noticed a knife she'd left on the cutting board was missing. She'd cut a pear for herself a few hours ago while they'd been lounging outside. In the kitchen there was a horizontal window above the sink where she could see out to the back patio. She glanced out, despite knowing she'd not brought the knife outside. She'd used the Kinzoku 8-inch slicing knife, wildly overqualified for petty pear duty, and left it, resheathed, on the wooden cutting board. Yet if it was so simple, then where was it?

Holding sharp knives, despite the hundreds if not thousands of meals she'd prepared throughout her life, always gave her a bit of worried pause, as silly as she knew that sounded. Submerging her worries as nonsense, as is required around children, she'd told Cody that if Disney ever made a fanciful cartoon about their knives coming alive at night, that knife, with its stylish, grooved and marbled blade and its black resin handle (whereas all the others in the series had brightly colored handles) would be the cocky, evil one. That only made Cody like it even more, as little boys are forever drawn to cool things, so it was dubbed the "Batman knife." The sink and counters were perhaps inexcusably messy, given that she'd had all day to clean and tidy, but she always knew that knife's whereabouts. She looked at the cutting board, saw the slight streak of dark in the wood grain from the spilled pear juice.

But she simply has to be wrong, she told herself. The knife very clearly wasn't in its holster. She opened the plausible drawers and, still, nothing. She made a face to herself, a self-deprecating klutz face.

A piercing shriek and she flinched. Just the microwave, Clare was right next to the microwave and the nachos were done. She checked to see the cheese was melted and kept the door ajar until they cooled down, got the salsa from the fridge, although that seemed wrong to do since the knife hadn't yet been located. She debated whether to bring down the nachos or call Cody up here. It was beyond rational consideration to think that Cody knew where the knife would be, but it just didn't feel right to leave the kitchen without this resolved.

She called down for him, that balance between being loud enough for her voice to get down the first short set of stairs and snake around the bend to the second and still be heard, all while not sounding alarmed.

(*What if he doesn't come upstairs*), came the evil thoughts. (*How long would I wait deluding myself just that he didn't hear me?*), continued those malicious thoughts, her heart already convinced of their certitude, fluttering away in terror. These panics, how she remembered these as a young mother, so aware of all the things she could be doing better, motherhood her only "job" since their first child had been born.

(*You had one job*!, or however the meme went.)

Now middle-aged in this third go-round, she was too experienced to be lured by these negative thoughts. She was the grizzled special agent called back from retirement, she and her husband had joked, for just one more job.

Cody dawdled up the stairs. What a sweetheart, his stocky chubbiness proof of his guilelessness, something always admirable in a boy his age (that of course she hoped would vanish by the time he started liking girls).

"Hey sweetheart, do you know where Mommy put the Batman knife?"

Keeping his shoulders still, Cody put his hands up and out and shook his head, then moved his neck in tandem with each alternating hand, almost like that ancient "walk like an Egyptian" head-bob, no doubt this being some Internet reference or something lost on her.

"That's a no, Mr. D.J.?"

"Yeah, I don't know. Are the nachos done?"

"Mr. Direct, too. Yes, they are, just need to put the salsa on them."

"Cool," Cody walked past her into the kitchen. "I can do it."

"Okay, let me just open the salsa and you can put it on."

"I can open the salsa, geez Mom," he said, laughing for no reason other than maybe summer giddiness.

"Make sure the plate still isn't hot. Do you know what you want for dinner later?" With Andres eating dinners at the office, even sometimes coming home past her capacity to romantically stay awake for him, their dinners had taken on a real piecemeal approach, which Cody didn't mind, as there was nary an unpleasant "eat your vegetables" side dish in sight. Again, "orderves."

Cody took the salsa and said "this won't open" only seconds after giving it one ineffectual attempted twist, inviting Mom to do it for him. She wordlessly opened it, mind vacantly elsewhere. She looked out the kitchen window again for something to do and did another quick canvass: no counter, no drawers, not somewhere weird like next to the fruit bowl on the center island.

Jar opened, Cody completely covered the center nachos with deep clumps of salsa.

"That wasn't supposed to happen. It came out so fast," he giggled.

"Honey, come with Mommy to the bedroom, I should check my phone to see when Daddy might be coming home."

"I think Dad is still working really late this week." When Cody spoke about Dad, it was usually with a somber attempt at sounding informative, analytical, or helpful, perhaps in tacit reflection of what he either imagined Dad wanted out of him or what he believed Dad's personality to be.

"I know, honey, but still, leave the chips here for a second, okay?"

The hallway ended in a roundabout, where the four bedrooms fanned out in a semicircle: the master bedroom that she and her husband shared to the left, toward the back of the house; then Cody's and Isabella's rooms fanning out at the top of the semicircle, respectively, then Gabriel's, which was across the hall from the master bedroom. Appropriate placement of the room, given their dispositions, that Cody's was closest and Gabriel's farthest away.

Halfway down the hall, just past the bathroom, she felt a presence from the closed master bedroom. Humans have an intuitive second sense for vacancy. She couldn't hear anything, exactly, but there was just a feeling, something about the *vibrations* through the wall, as if the air itself emitted the subtlest *something* by having to move around some foreign object (or person) taking up unexpected real estate in the master bedroom. Or a shifting, perhaps, some unheard-but-only-felt creak.

Clare stood still, instinctively putting her arm out behind her, barring Cody from continuing forward, as if he wanted to or cared. She swallowed hard, waiting.

"What are we doing?" Cody asked, the giddiness of before still evident in his latent chuckle, but attuned enough to the change in mood to speak in a hushed tone.

Clare kept her hand up. She was sure of it, she sensed something, enough of something to not want to go farther. This was ridiculous, but then again, it wasn't, because she could tell herself so many times this was ridiculous, but her clamminess, this inexplicable wooziness and fatigue that had manifested, this tension and acidity in her stomach, none of those cared what was "ridiculous" or not. Her cell phone was in the bedroom, she could imagine precisely where it was, resting on the drawer right by her jewelry box.

The master bedroom had a door that led out to the back patio. She tried to think if it'd been opened before or if they'd only used the door that led from the kitchen. They definitely came back inside from the kitchen door. Yes, now that she thinks of it, she did at one point come back inside from the master bedroom door, to grab a book and also use the bathroom inside the master bedroom, their "private" bathroom, whereas the kids shared the hallway bathroom or used the one downstairs in the den. She wouldn't have locked it, why would she . . .

"Let's go back to the kitchen actually, the nachos are probably cool by now, especially with all that salsa you put on them."

"I did put a lot of salsa on them, didn't I?" Cody said in that way where he wanted to laugh at the confirmation of his own blundering silliness.

As they walked back, she imagined someone finally unclenching their breath, a deep sigh of relief coming from the master bedroom. She more than imagined it, she frightened herself into believing it, even though she knew it was crazy, it was crazy, but if she was crazy, why was she so nervous? Because she couldn't find a knife she'd misplaced?

There was a phone in the kitchen, of course, how, how did she forget, a corded house phone that no one ever used, that she hadn't used for God knows how long. Clare became immediately terrified that they'd actually disconnected the phone line, as no one used it other than telecallers. But she remembered just now, thinking not long ago how weird it was that the recent telecallers seemed to be speaking Chinese – why bother calling to speak in Chinese, how could that be a viable business plan? – and, as that was a recent memory, that meant the phone was still on.

She lifted the phone and felt an impotent despair, realizing with crestfallen frustration that she didn't even know her husband's work number or even his cell phone by heart. Had she ever called him from the home phone? (*Of course not*), so the only option was to make the plunge, call 911.

No vacillating after calling 911, that was an undeniable affirmation of what she still didn't want to accept, that there was something wrong, even if she didn't have proof (*what would I say, I can't find a knife and – no, just say you need police here there's someone inside the house, that's fine, they don't charge you if you're wrong*) and yes that's what she'll do, call 911. Then leave with Cody out of the back patio, run to the Websters' house, their nearest neighbor. Think, if they ran, they could get there in five minutes. The Allendes had a fence in their backyard so they would need to run down the driveway out the front of the house (*a bottleneck, right there, all roads leading to one exit, pinned themselves inside*), maybe that was fine, just taking precautions, why not just go out the front door anyway?

Cody was standing by the kitchen island, plate half on the counter, sloppily eating nachos, one oversized bite at a time. The ease with which she lifted the phone, the lack of tension, that's when she noticed: the bottom of the cord had been cut.

A maelstrom of thoughts, flooding panic, a jumble, everything at cross purposes. (*How stupid, wasn't even a dial tone*, flared one identifiable thought.) Primary thought: gather Cody and leave, get out, get out, cord cut, someone's been in the house, that's why the knife is missing.

She signaled Cody to come to her with a clawing gesture, nothing too abrupt, as she panned the kitchen, saw nothing, already coaching herself to speak calmly so as not to send him into a panic.

"The Websters invited us over for or-derves, so let's leave your nachos and let's go, okay." Seeing nothing but his placatory nod, she quickly turned around, grabbed the sheathed Boker Solingen chef's knife from the drawer. (*Grab more knives*, she thought, but most didn't have sheathes.) She took a smaller, sharper unsheathed red knife that had an approximately 3-inch blade which she often used for cutting lemons and limes, and balanced it upright in the pocket of her jeans. Not a good idea if she tripped and fell on it, but she could pin it in place with her right hand.

"Here honey, I should bring this cutlery I borrowed from them, okay?" And she handed Cody the other sheathed kitchen knife, the Kinzoku chef's knife, horrified at both herself and the doomed prospect of Cody, her sweet uncoordinated seven-year-old Cody, ever protecting himself with a knife. She wondered if she worried him by using the word cutlery, a word he likely didn't know, but no time for that.

"That's right, the Websters have that missing knife of ours, we have to give them the others, okay, now hold my hand, stay down, okay honey?"

Right hand cupping the red knife, Baker Solingen chef's knife wedged into her left armpit, left hand clutching a few of Cody's right fingers, she crouched and moved toward the stairs, Cody just behind her, so close as to be brushing against her. The moment she no longer felt Cody brushed against her left thigh she'd freak out, if only for a second, even if for entirely natural reasons.

Stay calm.

She didn't even make it out of the kitchen.

She flopped back hard, pulled Cody and dove into the far interior corner of the kitchen near the sink, where she'd been when she first noticed the knife missing. "I'm sorry, I'm sorry," she muttered, seeing Cody's pain and confusion, knowing she must have twisted his little wrist, and she couldn't look at the pinched expression on his face, please don't cry.

She'd seen a shape on the other side of the front door. Oh God, she saw it still, a shadowed human shape, looked to be resting on the front door. *Oh God, Oh God.*

Clare freed the chef's knife from under her arm, unsheathed it, gripped it with her right hand.

A tittering, a muddled, almost sarcastic laughter outside, coming from the back patio. She could lift up from this crouching position behind the counter, look out the window . . . there was a macabre appeal to just ending this mystery.

Please don't cry, she prayed for Cody. He'd have to run with her. Should she order him to run and hide in the closet, under a bed? No, she played that out, not able to visualize the grisly end, only saw enough to conclude that wouldn't work. He couldn't hide, she couldn't leave him alone.

Clare could hear Cody's deep, panicking breathing, and saw enough of his reddened face to know he was scared and crying.

Metallic tapping on the glass above her head. Oh God. She couldn't see directly up and behind her, but she could imagine: the tip of her missing knife, mocking her.

She pulled Cody even closer to her, arms shielding him, knife up at the ready, just making sure she didn't lean and pierce herself on the knife in her pocket; no, move that knife, so she did, kept that in her other hand. Small red in the left, chef's in the right.

"It's okay honey, it's okay, we'll be okay," she kissed Cody's wet cheeks, grateful his back was to her chest and she couldn't see the blubbering terror writ large across his face.

Where to go, what to–

"Not so much fun now, is it bitch?" She heard a youngish female voice say from the back patio. And then, she couldn't tell if it was the same voice or not: "Murder there means consequences here!"

What? She processed what she'd just heard. No time, she couldn't stay here. She could see the front door down the stairs from her corner, saw the same stationary shadow. Would that shape attempt to force its way in? That door was certainly locked, she didn't hear or see anything to make her think the lock was being tested.

She heard a fevered metallic tapping up above her at the window, a pause, then a "woohooo" and then other voices, one urging something like quiet, another laughing, and then something blocked the light coming from outside the window, something moving up and down, followed by a vapory hissing.

No time to think, she stood up, first instinct to drag Cody and run out the back door, stab and even kill whoever stood in front of her, then confusion at what she thought she saw from her periphery: what bobbed outside the kitchen window moved with the vertical motion of some kind of bucket, then a hiss again, a hiss like the sound of steam or a can of spray paint, and she heard a laughter again. There must be several of them—

and then something hard and wet collided with the window and she grabbed Cody and ran in sheer unthinking terror in the opposite direction, down the stairs, Cody keeping up enough to almost be running in front of her, almost tripping them as they ran down the stairs. She heard yelling and the abrupt shift of movement from the back patio, the blob of a shadow at the front door became more vertical and restive, and she could see it move back from the door.

Running down the stairs, unable to breathe, contemplating in micro-seconds, should they run down the second flight of steps, go into the garage (*no no, garage closed, no quiet way out*) was there a back door from the lower level she was missing (*no no no*)—

and she flung open the front door and saw a bearded man in his twenties wearing a bandana, thinnish but not fit, now a bit farther back from the door and leaning on the railing that led down the driveway. He was looking shiftily to his right, an uncertain nervousness, a bit of a smiley leer on his face like he was so clever, and he looked again to his right, tilted his head back, as if waiting for something, and then turned to her, began to speak with a voice of deceiving calm—

"Hold-"

She drove the 3-inch red blade straight into his neck, and it was the millisecond before the knife made contact with his mangy throat that she saw his eyes widen. He must have only seen the sheathed kitchen knife in her right hand, thought he had a window to attempt his smug, calming sophistry, and he'd realized his error just as the blade tore the flabby-milky-paste of his throat.

"Veron!" he shout-gurgled, blood spurting through the fingers he pressed against his neck. Falling back, eyes widening even further as he realized he was going over the railing. Clare only saw his arms flailing in the periphery as she grabbed Cody and led them down the steps, just now seeing, through the dusk, four other shapes coming from around her house.

Four equally young white adults, three women and a man, one woman with gloopy-looking braids carrying something that looked like a picnic basket; another woman with a bandana carrying a shape that must have been the missing knife; a man with a scraggly beard, holding an aerosol can; the other female indistinct behind the man. And it was *they* who all looked horrified. The bandana-wearing woman put her hand to her tearful face and then dove face-first, inconsolably, into the chest of the bearded man, who embraced her in a mournful hug.

"Fuck you, you fucking fascist fucking murdering bitch!" one of the women screeched,

as Clare dragged Cody down the street full-bore in the opposite direction, although Cody now ran on his own, face bright-red, the terror on his face mixed with something else, something like confusion, something like exhilaration.

<u>NOTES</u>

This story was just intended to be a fast-paced riff on a common fear of the "there is someone inside the house!" trope. I thought the implied motivation would serve as a modern-day variant of the Manson Family's practice of "creepy crawling." (If our fair reader is not aware of that, why not give it a Google?)

As some of the other stories in this collection aspire to be more cerebral slow-burns (or whatever other synonyms artsy people use to euphemize boring material), in the interest of balance this story is just here to pep things up and hopefully give the reader a quick jolt. Nothing more, nothing less (unless you were crafty enough to string together the first letter of each sentence to understand the *true* meaning of the story).

Additional note: Don't do that. FOR YOUR OWN SANITY. Or because I'm fucking around and it's a waste of time. OR AM I JUST TRYING TO HIDE THE TRUTH I'VE INADVERTENTLY REVEALED!

No Hole In A Small World Can Truly Be A Small Hole

To be married to someone for a long time is to create a separate universe. Each marriage is similar only to the extent that people everywhere, I suppose, have common motivations and emotions. But to explain the dynamics of your marriage to anyone in any real way is impossible: the words make sense on paper, but the words are animated from beyond, from an endless well of lived experience, understood only within the universe of that marriage.

Within your own universe, it can make sense why you become angry when, for example, your husband pours out your water at night before you've finished taking all your pills. He probably assumed you left it out, even though, why would you leave out water that was half-filled? It makes you wonder what he must think of you: lazy, forgetful and inconsiderate, because he's the one who makes the money and you let him do most of the cleaning because he likes to do it.

And he thinks he's being considerate by pouring it out without asking you, as if that's something that he's contributing to the marriage: unfussily disposing of unnecessary items. And the internal critic asks: why make such a big deal out of it, surely he didn't mean anything by it?

But to give a full accounting for that answer would require you to go through the years of your marriage, and lay out each and every little inconsiderate indignity that has led you to this moment, to explain to yourself why this all makes sense; but if you do that, you are shrill and unhinged, and, fuck, maybe you are?

Do you understand the point I'm trying to make?

So life went on and I never really complained, so the perception built up that it was my increasingly gloomy husband who, as we crept along into advanced middle age, was the one who'd been suffering the most under the weight of life's accumulating privations. And maybe he had, actually, and I'd never noticed.

Which is maybe what you are thinking, because here I am, the one explaining myself.

It's no secret that I'm talking about what happened with Robert. And it's no secret that first impressions are largely unchangeable. It's like a playing field, split in the middle, with one side colored green for GOOD, the other red for BAD; now Robert is on the BAD side, based on how I just described him.

I can tell you all the great things about him: how I fell in love with him, why I married him in the first place, how he's taken care of me, how he's always been faithful even through what I admit were long sexual droughts, has always been a good financial provider to me and our two children, and all the other reasons, basically, why I love him. All those explanations get me indulgent nods and comments about how things are complicated, and maybe that will, in your mind, claw him back some toward the center of that playing field but the die has been cast and the impressions have been made. I'm the silently suffering, put-upon wife, he the boorish brute (perhaps ignorant of his own privilege, or a well-meaning brute, you think, but a brute nonetheless).

And when you begin to make impressions, let me just remind you of my analogy about marriage creating a separate universe, as clumsy as it might be. I think it gets to some essential point: we had a universe of two, and you're on the outside, looking in.

I'm trying to be honest. As honest as I can be, knowing still that the first impressions I gave are likely to remain. I regret how I began this, and wish, somehow, that someone could look back over the course of our marriage, learn the laws and customs native to our private universe, and render fair, impartial judgment, to provide me with some . . . I mean to say closure, but that's not the word.

Our two adult children are grown and gone away. Amy, our oldest, lives four hours away, Erin just under three. I've felt guilty that we only had daughters, as all men want a son. Over two decades ago, we'd talked about a third, but my heart and body wasn't in it, and while he never explicitly indicated as such, I wonder if he bore any resentment. Maybe that played a factor in what happened? No, I don't think so, but things like that you just never know.

I had noticed generally that he'd been keeping more to himself. He read alone without coming out to the couch and asking if I wanted to read alongside him. Or I'd come home and he'd be in the middle of a movie that I'd want to watch, whereas in our younger days he'd never start a movie he'd even conceivably suspected that I, just maybe, wanted to watch alongside him. Maybe he was just extremely considerate back in the day and I'm spoiled because who can maintain that?; or maybe he became too preoccupied with other things to give the subject much attention.

In our advanced middle age, we've become sexless, which might be important to mention. But all couples become so, really. He didn't query, so to speak, and I don't know . . . I didn't feel the urge, honestly, and I didn't want to embarrass him, so that entire aspect of our lives laid dormant.

Also, our health hadn't been great. We were both overweight (as you can tell with me, obviously), but for a woman it just feels different: I feel disgusting, this dumpy garbage-bag gut. Maybe that's where it all started? No, of course not: that's way too simple, way too pedestrian, but what is a rational mind for if not to rationalize?

Since our health wasn't great, we were watching what we ate. I always thought we ate pretty healthy, by American standards, but my impression from the start was that the onus seemed to fall more on me because I cared more.

To please me, he would eat more salads, chew slower and avoid fried foods and desserts. He was always someone who seemed to want praise, and in the beginning he'd call attention to his good habits, which could be charming, although it's dispiriting to think that the needy habits of our youth remain essentially unchanged.

I did notice over the course of several months that he took pride in disciplining himself enough to stick with something. He was always someone who prized order and routine, the type who hates rowdy crowds or loud spaces (not that I'm much different in that regard), and always at least aspired to maintain some type of discipline. Such as, he didn't like watching two movies in a row, thinking it was indulgent and undisciplined, like the greater balance of a night was being upset. Stupid things like that. He used to listen to podcasts about discipline and routine and working out, but what he ever did with any of it, I have no idea. He certainly wasn't working out to my knowledge.

I wish I could say I know with certainty that we had the following exchange the night before everything went awry, but I can't be sure. It was close to it, at least. We hadn't eaten any dessert for some time at this point, probably something like six months. I had more of a sweet tooth than he, and there used to be these chocolate fudge cookies, made by Feinsteins', that I used to just love.

Robert turns to me one night while we are reading in bed, and asks me:

"I was wondering something. Say the world was going to end in exactly one week from tonight, and we knew this. Would you still stick to our diet and avoid desserts?"

Why'd I bring up those Feinsteins' cookies? He must have mentioned them, that's why, he must have said something like "even those Feinsteins' cookies you love so much?"

I thought about it, and when I became self-conscious about my failure to quickly respond, I said "hmmm" as if that overt act of reflection reset my time to answer.

"No, I think I'd have the cookies," I finally answered.

Robert nodded solemnly. I'm not sure if this is just retroactive imagining, but I felt that question carried some importance and my answer had been disappointing. Even worse, it was as if he expected my answer to be disappointing, and he lingered on me for a moment, as if reluctantly processing confirmation of that disappointment.

"See, I wouldn't. I'd stick with the pledge. I said I wouldn't eat any desserts, so I wouldn't," he said in an unadorned way that I know means he was proud of himself.

All I could think was that it's a strange world where an atheist, who has never articulated any belief in any objective meaning or higher power, finds transcendent value in refraining from eating cookies.

"You wouldn't eat cookies with me, with only a week to live? Cookies and Phish Food ice cream, a movie on the couch, maybe a classic, and some nice drinks? Doesn't that sound lovely, though?" I said it in a bubblier voice than usual, a bit faux-wistfully, a voice I used when I was cuter and which used to induce in my husband a masculine, protective instinct to embrace and love me.

He paused, half-smiled, and said, "when you put it like that, for you, I would." And he touched my hand warmly, kissed the area of blanket which covered my upper body, and turned over to his side. As we said our goodnights and turned off the lights, I thought to myself, maybe he'd do as he said, but he wouldn't *want* to. He'd be disappointed. He made a promise and wanted to stick with it. The world ending would create the opportunity for him to be recognized as disciplined, even for something so petty. To him, that's still some kind of accomplishment.

We often wake up at the same time. When one of us wakes up before the other wants to, we usually go back to sleep until our alarms, reset for the agreed-upon time, wakes us both up.

The day after that dessert conversation – in my mind it was the following day, I'm not sure but that's what I'm sticking with – it must have been a Saturday or Sunday, because he didn't go to work. I don't remember why but I got out of bed before him. I was doing something insignificant in the living room, like reading the paper, holding out making breakfast until he woke up. That was it, must have been breakfast, because I must have gotten hungry and went back in to ask him what he wanted, which also doubled as a way of waking him up.

He was already up and I remember, first thing I see, is him in his white T-shirt and boxers from the night before, back toward me, crouched over and staring out the window. He had uncharacteristically opened the blinds. After waking up, he always first takes his pills, heads to the shower or, if not showering that day, at least changes his clothes. But I recognized this T-shirt as the same one he wore the night before because it had a little red pus stain on the back near his neck, from where he must have popped a swollen back pimple.

I could see the folds at the back of his neck, the thinning grayish-brown crown that was the back of his head, and his knobby, pointy elbows, which seemed ill-proportioned given the supple fatty thickness of his arms.

"I was thinking of making shakes. Want one? I can make it with frozen bananas in the freezer?"

I remember acting timidly, as if the unusual act of sleeping late, keeping his back toward me, and looking out a window in the morning suggested something disquieting. He wasn't a man who tended to look out windows, other than the sporadic observation about an unusually pleasing cloud, the type of rote comment that anyone might make.

Turning slightly to signify my presence, but not enough for me to see him any better, he only said, politely and almost with a sense of guilt, "I'm not hungry just now," and before I moved or responded, as if changing course, he asked, "Could you please close the door?"

I didn't know if that meant with me in or out of the bedroom. Without turning around, he must have sensed this confusion because he quickly clarified: "Please come in, and close the door."

The obvious protest was that I was hungry and just wanted to get started making breakfast. His voice wasn't severe, and I didn't really expect him to drop any kind of bombshell on me. He wasn't that type of person. If history was any indication, he'd ask me to look at something on his body, convinced he found some kind of cancerous mark (which, thankfully, such marks had never amounted to anything), or perhaps, at worst, tell me about some minor remark or perceived personal failure of his that was making him distraught.

"Are you okay, honey?" I asked as a matter of course. I don't want to give the impression I didn't care. Of course I did. But I do remember thinking that I was hungry, he likely was, too, and we'd feel better after eating.

I sat on the bed, facing his back. I noticed he still hadn't turned from the window, or given any indication he planned to.

"Come sit with me, honey. What's bothering you?" I tried again.

"You know I've always loved you so, so much. You've been the light of my life."

There were directions this could go. I was getting nervous from this ominous build-up, but also found myself a bit peeved, if I'm being honest, but in an anticipatory way, as if I knew this was going to be something of a deflating bit of deferment. Unless he had been hiding a terminal diagnosis from me (unlikely, since I knew every doctor's appointment he went to), there was just no way this could be as dire as he made it seem. We had aged out of the instability that allowed for betrayals and secrets. I just wished whatever this was, we could resolve it swiftly and eat breakfast.

"Honey, what is this about?"

Such a question is inherently direct, but my tone was, I hoped, gently accommodating.

He shifted his weight slightly. I saw his shoulders rise and fall as if swallowing a great load of air, and he fidgeted, as if not sure how to proceed.

He turned partly. I stayed still, only noticing his eyes were still closed.

He turned fully, came to me, and opened his eyes.

"Oh," I said, and I'm sure my hand involuntarily came up to my lip, as one does naturally to cover the unarticulated gasp, and then, realizing this, I immediately brought my hand back down so as not to scare him. He had always been a nervous person, and, to me at least, unduly sensitive to physical ailments.

And this one looked, frankly, terrible. All I saw were his eyes, and I wished I'd been more observant, so as to understand fully the expression he was conveying.

I'm thinking of the euphemistic descriptions I first thought up. Both of his eyes were puffy, dewy, and swollen. That's what I imagined telling him if he asked, prepared to hear him telling me his eyes were burning or he was having trouble seeing. Yes, your eyes look swollen, a bit puffy . . . then I'd trail off, try to get him calm, and get him to a hospital right away without allowing him to obsess in the mirror.

His eyeballs looked like peeled lychee. An off-whitish pink, translucent and glossy, with wrinkles and folds I was not accustomed to, and generally appearing more globular and fuller, as if there was more eye mass than usual in his sockets. When he blinked, I wondered if his eyes fully closed, or if some part of that enlarged, moistened flesh prevented his lids from making complete contact in their coverage. That lychee description was perfect, really, because it captured the red seed, too; inside a lychee is a red seed, which looks like a hardened kidney bean. And behind both irises, I saw a faint, dull red nubby protrusion that looked somehow too neat and orderly to be a cyst or other, normal inflammation.

That sounds terrible, I know. It was terrible, it was.

"Just stay here with me for a bit," he said, a cordial request.

This was when I first noticed his strange calm.

"Dear, listen to me. We need to go to a hospital immediately. I'll drive us. Just stay calm, I'm sure it's just an infection. Can you see?"

At that last question, he smiled: the smile of an inside joke. I'd seen it before: someone says something that brings to mind something else, and you smile to yourself and think it's not worth the effort to explain, that's something just for me.

That smile excluded me, and seemed especially inconsiderate given that I was trying to help, but I fastened my mind on this being an emergency and how it's important to keep your cool. Let him just consider that improper smile as creating one big IOU.

I'll get to pick the dinners for the next month. And I could eat as many fucking Feinsteins' cookies as I damn well pleased.

And, behind those thoughts, I chastened myself because I loved this man. A mistake, because it was when I thought about how much I loved him and so desperately wanted him to be okay and safe, and for this medical anomaly to be over and behind us, that I began to freak out. Focusing on the logistics, and even my petty feelings about being hurt by his inside-joke smile, let me concentrate on something other than the panic fomenting inside me.

Here was my husband, my companion and father of my children, with bloated eyes.

"Dear, I - I want to stay here. It's okay. Let me explain. This is . . . this isn't bad news, okay? This - this is, in fact, quite good." And he took my right hand and rubbed it between both of his hands.

I shook my head as he spoke, not so much in disbelief as for waiting for my opportunity to interject and disabuse him of this .

. . whatever it was. As I heard him out, I almost gagged on my next revelation, felt it as a physical obstruction down through my throat into my chest: this inflammation must have affected his brain, because what he said made no rational sense.

"I wanted this to happen, dear. I've . . . this-this is what I've always wanted, what I've been waiting for my whole life. Dear, I can't cry now but if I could, I would," and he laughed self-deprecatingly, giving me the painfully fleeting vision of the wryly humorous man that I had married and loved, immediately replaced by this stranger who spoke of ocular inflammation like a blessing from God.

"Just, please, stay here with me, for today. We can spend the entire day together."

"What on earth are you talking about? Please, look at yourself, we need to take you to a hospital. I am going to call 911."

It was becoming difficult to look at him. I could imagine him being mugged and, in the recuperation process, left with these jellied eyes.

"Don't you do that, please, just, let me get this all out. I'll be - I can't say much but soon I'll be gone. And I don't mean deceased, honey," he tightened his grip on my hand to emphasize this point, "I just mean I'll be off in a better place."

"You owe me an explanation. A real explanation, right now."

"Just please, sit here with me."

"I'm fucking starving." I was shaky, and struck with that weightless, dizzying feeling that comes from low blood pressure. Forgive me, but I've always been insecure about saying when I'm hungry, since I'm overweight and still not used to that. I still hold onto that child-like notion that an overweight person would burn through their stored fat before becoming hungry again. I got ahold of myself and explained: "I'm hungry, dear. I want to make a shake, and I need coffee. I can make some for you, too. Then we'll continue talking."

I could tell he didn't want me to go but smiled and said sure, as if he was indulging me out of remembered fidelity.

I was sure somehow that after breakfast and coffee he would come to his senses and allow me to take him to a hospital. There was no house phone; instead, we each had a cell. Mine was still charging in our bedroom, and I assume his was in the bedroom as well.

If he wouldn't let me call the hospital, then I'd first call 911, then our daughters. I didn't care what he had to say on the matter. I should have demanded he call 911 just then, but I was famished and my head was already beginning to hurt, that type of headache where your eyes burn and your temples pound and your solid thoughts break apart into fragments and a great cloud seems to hide from you the next point you were going to make.

Miraculously, I made the shakes as usual, and could pretend this was just any other normal weekend morning in our kitchen. I called out to him a few times, asked if he was okay, and he responded affirmatively each time in that upturned, doing-great voice we use to let each other know that the other person is perfectly contented being alone in the other room, no offense implied. I wanted to get back to him quickly so I didn't make any coffee.

I came back to the bedroom and he was laying on his back, smiling, eyes closed, face widened and contorted as if he'd been crying tears of happiness, although of course, there were no tears to be found.

I returned with our shakes, which he sipped and cooed, "Mmm, I can taste the bananas." I had used extra bananas and peanut butter, which were his favorites. I'd stopped using pineapple and blueberries because those are acidic fruits, which aren't good for our stomach conditions, and remembering that bit of marital logistics made me extremely depressed and heartbroken. We had shared responsibilities, we had shared customs and etiquette, we had shared jokes and references, we had, basically, a life together, our own universe as husband and wife, and now this. This was more than an eye infection. This was, I was beginning to understand, some act of betrayal, and somehow even worse, an act of betrayal that wasn't even being recognized as such.

The taste of the shake seemed to be making him nostalgic, as if he really believed he was drinking my shake for the last time.

"You owe me an explanation."

"You're right. I know, you're right," and, putting the shake aside, rolled over onto the pillow for a moment - with his eyes covered, he appeared absolutely normal - and he turned back over, seeming to gather his strength.

If this was truly the beginning of some miraculous new development in his life, then I was the obstacle in the way, and I could read that conflict in his reactions: the elation in the waiting, if only he could move beyond this present remorse.

"I cannot say much, only that I'm sorry. I've waited my whole life for this. I've studied, and researched, and I've worked for this, if you can believe it. I've worked for it, long nights of study and research and" – the streak of defensive pride that had been building was quickly smoothed out by self-deprecation – "and prayed even. Yes, me, praying, I know. Hard to believe. But I prayed for this, which is, trust me, especially ironic. I'm being taken to a better place. This is a sign, the narrowing of the senses, it's called."

I was shaking my head and visibly fuming, hoping my expressed disgust would correct the situation. In our marriage, it didn't matter who was right or wrong: whenever one party became visibly distressed or angry, the other would become more accommodating and deferential, just to allay the situation and make peace. Because marriage is a partnership, and it's better for the partnership to function rather than for someone to be right.

But not only was I furious, but I had the added benefit of actually *being* right, and my performative anger only served to make me even more legitimately angry.

One thing I realized, though: Robert's explanation seemed too detailed to be complete derangement. I had to approach this as something that he believed was credible.

"What *is* this?! You have a family! Think of our children! And what am I supposed to do?!?"

My goal was to get him to come to his senses, to go with me to a hospital, and, even more importantly, to acknowledge that he was somehow wrong in all of this, that everything would be fine and we would resume the course of our lives.

Robert, sneaking about, studying and "working" and "praying" for, what, exactly? Some crazy cult beliefs? And when was he doing this, exactly, and how had I never known about this? For all I knew, he might have been laid off from work years ago and we'd been paying our bills off savings and he, what, skulked around libraries and went off to meet fake gurus who fed him mumbo-jumbo?

"And I'm very sorry, I'm truly sorry. This, if this makes any sense, or means anything to you, you are the absolute love of my life. This all began before I'd ever even met you, and I know that's no excuse to you, but . . . I cannot explain to you what this means to me.

"You are the absolute love of my life. But this is beyond life. Before I even say this, I know how it's going to sound, but it's like at the end of *Close Encounters of the Third Kind*, when Richard Dreyfus just has to go on the alien ship and explore other worlds.

"And here, I'm dying on the inside. This has been so, so hard for me. I almost wish this miracle never happened, because I know what I'm going to have to give up, and I thought it would be easier, but it's terrible, a terrible sacrifice, and I will miss you so, so much."

And I could tell he was crying without tears now, heaving and pathetic and desperate and I wanted to hug him and console him and stop this suffering, to tell him I understood, even if I didn't. I thought, perhaps, to consider him as if he had a terminal illness and just provide palliative love, and maybe in a sense, he *did* have a terminal illness.

So I hugged him, and he hugged me back, tightly and devoutly. Before we'd embraced, I looked into those swollen eyes and my stomach turned, because in all this drama I had forgotten what pain he must have been in; no person could comfortably have rubbery eyes like that and still have their wits about them.

"Honey, we both didn't like that that movie, remember? It's boring."

"True."

"And, honey, if I remember correctly, didn't Steven Spielberg say he regretted that ending? I believe he wrote that before he had a family of his own." I kind of remembered reading that somewhere; we'd both found that movie so treacly and dull and wondered what the hell the fuss was all about.

"True. But-"

"Now honey, this isn't a movie. We-we can write our own endings, don't you understand? There's nothing that can't be fixed, okay?"

To this, he didn't respond, and I wished I could see his face as it rested on my shoulder. Was he coming to his senses?

"Now I'm going to take you to the hospital, okay? Don't you want to . . . let's assume what you are saying is true, about all the work and studying and praying you've done. Wouldn't you want to know whether it's actually true, whether what you think is going to happen is actually going to happen. Well, if we go to the doctor's and they tell you that you just have, I don't know, some kind of conjunctivitis, then, well, that's something that's important to know, isn't it?"

"No, dear. I have to remain right here, by this window. I bet that in less than a day, I'll be gone, or unable to move, anyway."

"Okay, well, how do you think that sounds to me? Imagine you were me, and you heard that, how would that make you feel?"

"I don't disagree with the point you are making," he said, and I could hear a hint of exasperation. It's morbidly funny, if you think about it; he might be thinking he's heading off to his version of heaven in the next twenty-four hours, but, well, not yet. There may be no sighing in Heaven, but there definitely was in this bedroom.

"But this is something I can only do alone. If you have ever needed to trust, believe, and love me, then this is the time. This is the time."

"I'm not going to let you stay here for a day, okay? I'm not going to let you because I love you, do you understand? Maybe you are right, okay, and then won't I feel silly when I come back here and you've been taken away by a magic sunbeam, but until that happens, you're my roly-poly and I'm your hug-a-lump, and you can call me a hug-a-lump even though now we're both fat and our youthful nicknames don't sound so cute anymore."

"Not like roly-poly sounds flattering to me, either."

165

"Exactly. And we'll still watch our movies and read our books and eat our healthy foods and you'll indulge me sometimes with antique shopping and we'll have Thanksgiving with the girls and you'll be around to become a grandfather one day and we can resume bargaining over what type of dog we might get."

"That sounds nice, dear, it does sound nice. But I won't be going to any hospital, and I can't have you calling 911."

I gracefully separated from him, still next to him on the bed. Then I stood up, feeling his eyes on me, even under all that bloated, engorged flesh. He watched me as I went to the opposite side of the bed, also known as "my side of the bed," the side closer to the door and where my cell phone was charging on the night table.

"Honey," he pleaded.

"I'm not doing anything yet, honey. Now, please, will you come with me? We can take you to the emergency room at Mercy Hospital, it's only twenty minutes away, at most." We'd gone there for every operation, most recently his hernia surgery a few years back. "Or if you'd prefer, we can call Dr. Harmon, I believe you have his cell phone number, right?" Dr. Harmon had been our ophthalmologist for over a decade, and we'd seen him annually ever since I was diagnosed with prediabetes.

"I can't, honey. For all that is good, and just, and pure in this world, just please, please, please indulge me and let me stay here for the next day, and stay with me, please. I want you to stay with me. Just please, let me enjoy this day with you, and you with me."

And there isn't much to say except for what you already know. I couldn't take that as an answer, which he understood. He had his senses about him. And you know that. And you know what happened next: I've explained it enough times.

He wouldn't let me get to my phone, and he tried to restrain me without hurting me, and I tried to simply make enough space for myself to use my phone without hurting him. He perhaps thought that any sign of physical aggression from him would keep me from calling. I can honestly say I'd never seen that side of him through all our years of marriage; I'm still not convinced he even had that side to him, which is why his whole attempt at physical intimidation was so toothless and ineffective.

Maybe he thought that I would just give him that one day, and if he was still there in 24 hours – and by "there" I mean physically there, not transcended or morphed or whatever he thought he might be doing – then he would realize his error, relent and go to the hospital. But I wouldn't allow myself to sit in silence and allow my husband to suffer, so I insisted.

As he was coming toward me all lumbering and uncoordinated, I darted out my free hand only to defend myself. I freaked out when my aim proved wrong and my outstretched fingers *should* have made contact with his eyes.

Should have. I've explained that part, too, enough times, and maybe I was more convincing the first time I explained it. You can only be told you're wrong so many times before you lose all enthusiasm to explain yourself, so don't be offended if I don't give it my all. Go ask my daughters; they believed me, at least the first time.

Do you ever think: why would I volunteer that detail about how my fingers should have touched his eyes? How would it benefit me to say something that sounds so crazy that no one believes me?

But yes, as I said, *should* have made contact with his eyes. The hardened red seeds protruded further out, the slick, rubbery flesh withdrew defensively. Or putting it another way, his eyes contracted.

None of that has to do with how he died. I stabbed him, you know that, things escalated and I stabbed him with a kitchen knife. He did everything in his power to stop me and I defended myself. I'll leave it at that because saying anything more is going to make me vomit and weep. I'm not even being accused of murdering him; the 911 operator heard enough to vindicate me.

It's always about the eyes. That's what it's about.

And the worst thing? I wish what he'd been saying was true. You know that his brain has been studied and they tell me there was nothing wrong with it, at least nothing that they could see in an autopsy. So maybe he was in his right mind. I wish I could say that when he fell, helplessly and pathetically as you'd expect of an overweight, unathletic middle-aged man who never played a sport in his life, there'd been some giant omen, some corroboration of what he'd been saying, like the thunderclap of an anguished God.

And I can't help but think that it was my fault, that I was too prideful just to let him be. I know, stupid. But that was my husband and the father of my children. Maybe in some alternative universe I could have given him his final day, and I'd leave and I'd come back to find him gone, and it wouldn't be hard to explain that. People are ready to accept a middle-aged man disappearing from his family for any number of understandable reasons. I'd tell people I always suspected something, some other woman, or, more painfully but more credibly, some exhaustion, depression, and dissatisfaction that he just couldn't deal with anymore. That becomes more believable with each decrepit year.

That's what I'd say if he'd disappeared, but each night I'd look out that window contemplatively, up toward the sky - even though I'd had no reason to believe he'd have disappeared northward, but isn't that comforting to think? - and I'd do it so often, and freight it with such significance, that I'd start to believe it myself. I'd convince myself that my darling Robert had fulfilled whatever mission it was that he'd set out for himself, and disappeared into some sublime satisfaction.

Instead, there's a body.

And they'll come up with some way to describe his eyes.

<u>NOTES</u>

It goes without saying that you can never truly know all of your partner's secrets and ambitions. I liked the idea of an older man, who perhaps had earlier in his life forsaken the world to seek some kind of transcendent or divine truth, had since given up that pursuit and found a partner he truly loved, but suddenly now finds that all of his previous attempts were vindicated, and he now needs to make some kind of attempt to explain this bizarre development. The sought-after truth, he realizes, is his first and most paramount love. The cosmic meeting the mundane.

I've always kind of wished I believed in Lovecraft's cosmicism, finding it, as I think most natural pessimists do, as a handy way to explain away or minimize the psychological feelings of failure and insignificance. Surely, if all human life and endeavors are insignificant in the face of the materialistic and mechanist universe beyond our comprehension, then why spend one iota of concern upon our own failures? I believe in this cosmicism intellectually, but life isn't lived intellectually.

And here, my thoughts were of some kind of classic Lovecraftian seeker after truth finding himself finally, after giving up hope, on the verge of just such a cosmic discovery, but he has a different life now; and say what you want about cosmicism, but the divorce from emotions and human connections, to me, is easier theorized about than done. At least that's what I was going for: whether I was successful is up to you.

More As A Knower Than A Sufferer

The sensation of getting run over was both fundamentally unexplainable yet, somehow, exactly like he'd imagined it to be. Joel had consciousness enough to know he was very badly hurt without understanding it as pain in the ordinary sense. The closest parallel would be when as a child he'd been plowed over and lost within an unexpectedly powerful wave, except this time the forward momentum never seemed to end.

Even though he'd *actually* experienced getting crushed to death by a car (still remarkable to contemplate), if Joel ever seriously reflected upon it, all that came back were hollow half-remembered scenes from movies. As if someone had smuggled out his memories for these ersatz imitations, and his mind – or whatever functioned as "his mind" these days – recognized but accepted these frauds, just too much work to investigate further.

A wide panning shot of him in dark clothes, giving chase in the night (it's that part he most remembers, because he was finally taking revenge, taking *action*); a closer shot in focus, disrupted by a cutting light around the bend and abrupt, urgent honking; an extreme close-up of him looking up; the sound of collision; and, perhaps if for an R-rated audience, the briefest glimpse of his body upended and mangled, head about to be crushed, then fade to black.

Fade to this.

An ignominious death, one would think. But when Joel thought about it, the pathetic details became less important than the gestalt of the injustice, which reaffirmed both his essential view of the world and paradoxically made him feel better. He'd finally stood up for himself and got run over like roadkill for his troubles. Viewed in the satisfying light of confirming what he'd always felt about being essentially cursed, well, it was quite the appropriate way to go out.

*

"Hey," Joel said, standing over the man before him, who was down on his equivalent of all fours. Not "hello," not "hi," not "how are you?" but "hey," authoritative and a bit imposing.

The man (more an overgrown kid, really) timidly shifted in response to his voice, both trying to make something like eye contact while "looking" around this perturbingly blank environment. Joel knew what questions the kid had. The kid seemed like the type too embarrassed to ask, too afraid to voice the cliches. The same questions anyone would have: where am I, who are you, what happened?

"I'm Joel." Just as Joel communicated his name he regretted it, too impulsive, just as he'd always been. He should have said Magnusson, something sweeping and strong. Or something like Socrates, except not as embarrassingly transparent an attempt to connote wisdom. Instead, he'd just gone with his living name.

Joel reached out a hand for the kid to gain his bearings. This was all metaphor; they had no bodies, just a phantom memory of a body which inspired their spirits, their essence or whatever they now were to move and contort the way they did; no lungs or vocal chords with which to speak except yet communication was made; no physical way to discern their environment, yet its torpid blankness was still undeniably understood by some other means, with a crushing finality greater than could be conveyed by sight.

"As you might have figured out, you died. The good news is that your being, so to speak, survived. That's-" (Joel refused to say 'a blessing') "something to be hopeful about. So, what can I call you?"

The kid, Joel could tell, was immobilized by dual instincts: the need to brush him off and sulk alone, but also an obsequious fear of the consequences from rebuffing what passed for an authority figure. It was as if the kid was back in the storied locker-room of bullyings past, as if Joel was some muscled aggressor leaning into the kid's face while threatening, "so say that again, what can I call you?" the kid trying to appear outwardly calm while inwardly squirming.

"You don't have to worry," Joel said. "It's alright, I get it, it's a lot to take. It sucks that we can still feel nervous and anxious here."

"I noticed that," the kid finally communicated.

"I wonder if that means something significant, like if that was something that would be helpful to, like, researchers or scientists

172

back on Earth. It's cool to know something that others don't. It's cool also to know what it feels like to be dead. It's like what every living person has thought about and wonders about, but we get to know, you know?"

The kid was still obviously despondent about realizing that anxiety and depression didn't end with the physical body, as if mental health issues were some essence of themselves that couldn't be stripped from the equation.

"Vincent was my name, by the way."

"Nice to meet you, Vincent. And how old were you?"

"Nineteen."

Joel was surprised to learn Vincent was nineteen. He sensed something younger and less developed, like a sixteen-seventeen, maybe even as low as a fourteen-fifteen. By nineteen the kid should have been mentally freed from whatever caste system high school had placed him in.

"It's interesting, I could somehow tell that you were younger than me, although there's no way I've yet understood as to why that should be. No eyes, no senses, as you've figured out. But still pretty accurate impressions. It's like gut feelings without the gut, and I've always found, and even read about, how gut feelings are actually pretty accurate."

Vincent stayed motionless. Joel felt a twinge of antipathy toward the unappreciative kid. He didn't need to be mentoring him like this. Think this kid ought to be a bit more, what, engaged? Sure it's a head-trip to wake up here, but this environment was at least different from what was expected, and difference is inherently interesting, even when it represents a worsening.

Joel offered an olive branch. "I was twenty-four, had just started graduate school when I died."

Vincent stood up, animated by some positive insight. Joel felt proud of himself, as if his tutelage had caused this reversal in the kid's outlook.

"I had a friend, growing up, like a best friend, who died of leukemia when we were children," Vincent began. "I suppose I could try and visit him down – wherever this is. And my grandparents," Vincent said with an afterthought, "on my father's side, I didn't really know them, they died when I was real young, but I could reach out to them. And, pets?" he said hopefully.

"Well, if your friend died of leukemia, he is definitely not surviving down here, if he's surviving at all. I think he ceased to be at the moment of his death. And your grandparents, I assume they died of something like natural causes, and they would, by being grandparents, naturally be pretty old and weak and everything, so I'm sorry to tell you but they aren't going to be here either. This isn't like the afterlife as you might have expected it."

"Oh." Vincent looked around, and Joel could tell that Vincent might be becoming reacquainted with that other grave affliction that he'd hoped would have ceased upon death, that of boredom. "So are there any other people down here with us? What do we do?"

"That's the good news, at least. There's a lot to do. But before I tell you, tell me, how did you die?"

Joel was unexpectedly enjoying his time as a mentor. While alive, he had always assumed people enjoyed mentoring or teaching for purely predictable self-interested reasons, but there was a psychological distinction in becoming a teacher that he hadn't anticipated. Assuming the mantle of "teacher" made him almost a different person, and it was not self-interest but rather a satisfying obligation to rise to the occasion of his title.

While all the little verbal and bodily tics to demonstrate openness and camaraderie were lost without the benefit of a body, Joel did his best. "Don't be shy, man, nothing to be ashamed of. We're all dead down here, after all, and came down here only in so many different ways."

It worked, Vincent's protective walls shimmered out of existence for just moment enough for him to reveal: "I killed myself," and, in the grips of his second-hand embarrassment, added "so fucking stupid, I guess. I can't believe it. I overdosed on sleeping pills and alcohol. I always told myself that before I'd kill myself I'd take every drug I was always scared to try. Who knows, maybe acid or mushrooms or something would have reworked my brain chemistry and I'd have lost the urge to kill myself altogether. Who knows? Pathetic that even while planning to kill myself I never did the things I wanted to. I guess I made the decision pretty suddenly."

A suicide. If Joel had a body, his heart might be skipping a beat. He'd not met yet met a suicide.

"Why'd you do it?" the question propelled as if by some accelerant, before Vincent had time to return to post-mope equipoise.

"That's a long story. I don't know, who knows?"

"All we have is time, right?"

"I don't know. I was unhappy, I guess."

"I mean, c'mon, obviously. I don't know how many happy suicides there are."

"I just mean, I don't know, I was always unhappy, stressed, sick with anxiety about nothing and every small thing, the future in general I suppose, and without much of a present to rely on. I was bullied, scrawny, always kind of sickly, I don't know why, but always sick."

Joel waited with a pregnant pause. "The bullying though, is what did it, right?"

Yes, it had been, and Joel knew it without needing Vincent's confirmation. Being sickly and scrawny and generally anxious; well, that that was tough and everyone had problems. But being bullied without any sort of recompense was an invasive reminder that not only was the world inherently unpleasant, but rather unremittingly unfair to those outside the approved social strata. The abiding lesson learned was that you, the bullied, were despised, that forces were actively arrayed against you, and no one was going to step into help. It rubbed the unfairness of life in one's face. You are not one of those also joined into the collective humanity of life's struggles: you are less-than, and must be punished for it.

So yes, it wasn't just the mere fact of being bullied. Vincent hadn't killed himself while it was happening. It wasn't until a few years later, when it became clear that his victimizers would proceed with their lives unscathed, that the universe seemed oblivious or indifferent to this moral crime that defined Vincent's psyche. Not only had his bullies not been punished, not only had no one seemed to care, but, if anything, they had *improved* their social status off of him. Supposedly loyal friends of his looked the other way or did what they could to save themselves; female students who made such an outspoken stink about progressivism and equal rights turned out, like everyone else, to be attracted to the strong and repulsed by the weak; what he'd thought was the rule of law would have amounted to "snitching," which was somehow perceived as somehow wretchedly and dishonorably emasculating, somehow worse than the apparently understood paradigm of the violent pecking order.

And the one time Vincent defended himself, with a frantic stab in the eye-area intended only to dislodge the hand wrapped around his neck, *he'd* been the only one suspended, for three months. His nerdiness had been part of the pretext for his bullying, and ironically after being suspended his modest academic success was all for naught, as whenever a college admissions officer saw that suspension for the "violent" act of self-defense his hope of some kind of academic vindication went up in flame in that same short amount of time it took his hand to lunge with that pen.

Joel listened with a combination of empathy and that excitement that comes when one has a private insight confirmed by another. At the conclusion of Vincent's story, which was partly expressed, partly intuited, Joel said, "You know, Winston Churchill was, by his own admission, a big bully growing up. He bullied someone so bad the kid stabbed him in the chest with a pen knife."

It was something of an irreverent line, and Joel wasn't sure why he said it. Maybe it was baiting, but baiting in the way one might wiggle a piece of bacon toward a dog to get it to run out of the street.

"Well, the kids who bullied me are no Winston Churchills, trust me."

"They got to go onto college, or have their normal lives?"

"Yeah. It's a nice fantasy that every bully is someone who was, like, abused as a kid and that's why they act out, or just someone distracting themselves from their own inevitably dead-end life. But it wasn't like that here. They're still breezing their way through life. They did what they enjoyed and got away with it."

Joel knew there was a pivotal fact missing in the tale.

"And before you killed yourself, you were planning on doing something about it, weren't you?"

Vincent's natural sheepishness returned. Joel could imagine Vincent coping with some pet or some other totemic consolatory figure or private obsession that Vincent would pour himself into to avoid reality, his guilt about those hateful thoughts of vengeance never abolished, only redirected. Someone so used to scurrying into some interior place to narrate some significance upon his dilemma wasn't someone so willing to express something so seething as a plan for revenge.

"Yes, I had a plan. Wrote a list. On paper, which is so stupid, but felt more dramatic and important, like a bigger step, more 'real.' I tore it up, though. I wasn't going to do that, hurt anybody, really, I'd probably just end up hurting some innocent person and even if I didn't, I don't know. What was I going to do, really? So yeah."

"You must have come pretty close, I bet."

"I mean, I don't know." It was true: even through all the fixation, he just didn't really know if he was capable of it. He never wanted to hurt anyone, he only wanted to be left alone, to just be allowed *to be*. He hadn't believed, as naïve as it might sound, that the world could be such an unforgiving place until that reality had been thrust upon him.

"What was your weapon going to be? I'm sure you thought about it."

Vincent didn't respond, and rather than let the question linger, Joel continued:

"Well my man, it doesn't matter. You don't need to answer. And here's why, and here's the good news: that's why you're here! That's why I'm here, that's why we're all here. There are more of us, you'll meet them, don't worry.

"Turns out, sometimes things do work out, because here's the best I can figure. The people who've been 'saved,' so to speak, are the people who *acted*. It's that *boldness* that saved us. So, say whatever you want, but I'm pretty sure you must have come pretty close to doing what you planned to do, even if you eventually didn't do it. That's an interesting wrinkle in all this, I guess you came close enough.

"It wasn't prayer, or mindfulness, or suffering, or good deeds that saved you, that saved us, and it certainly wasn't turning the other cheek or whatever it is we thought or expected might save us, assuming we expected an afterlife at all. Whatever is behind all this rewarded us for being *proactive*, in taking the steps to right what was wrong. It was standing the fuck up for ourselves. Maybe that's an important skill that's in short supply.

"And here's the thing: we get to go back!"

Vincent wasn't sure how he felt. It should have been elation, he knew, and there was definitely something like excitement tethered to trepidation.

"Don't worry, it's not immediate, it'll take some time, get you acquainted with things around here. But we aren't just going back to, you know, resume our normal podunk lives. We get to go back, and I can't believe I get to finally say something like this with a straight face, pardon the expression given we're now currently faceless and all, but we get to go back . . . for revenge.

"Can you believe it? We're being rewarded, finally, after all our suffering, we took the right steps and this is our reward. Who knew? Who knew? Wouldn't life have been different for everyone if people knew that that was the secret to getting an afterlife. Being proactive, standing up for yourself."

To Vincent, this whole conversation felt like being shot out of a cannon. If this was really some inauguration process, it would benefit from being more gradual, but then again, Joel didn't seem like the sort who would stick to an ambassador-approved script.

"Do you really think that's it?" Vincent asked. "Maybe there's something more to it. Maybe we're being afforded this chance, if what you say is true, because of some fundamental, unrecognized goodness about us. Maybe that's it. That expression, 'the meek shall inherit the Earth.' Maybe that's it?"

"Trust me, there are a hell of a lot of meeker people who died and disappeared, sayonara, that's all she wrote. No man, it's the opposite. The proactive inherit the earth, or at least go back there.

"I get it, though, it's hard to get over those thoughts. You'll see, you'll meet the others and see how the system works. But that's still some fundamental search for fairness talking. That's Earth-talk, as we say, that's the stuff you've been indoctrinated into.

"What did everyone say when we were alive? 'Life's not fair?' Well, maybe this system isn't fair, maybe some old guy who dedicated his life to his family and feeding the homeless and taking in stray dogs or something, who led his uneventful but well-meaning life who dies of heart failure or any other everyday reason should be the one who gets to go back, but that ain't the way it is, I'm afraid. But now that unfairness works for us. Saying it's unfair would be just as pointless as complaining about gravity being unfair. It is what it is.

"And isn't it nice to hear someone saying 'it is what it is' and that's not a brush-off, not just some way of telling you to stay in your place, not some friend explaining to you why things aren't going to get any better, but as a rationalization of a system that finally benefits people like us? That's the trick, isn't it? We refused to take it all laying down. We stood up, lost our lives for it, but not for long, my friend. Not for long."

*

Joel had been proven right; or at least everything Vincent was exposed to seemed to confirm Joel's theory. Everyone else he met had a roughly analogous story. Everyone had made some proactive attempt to strike back at an abuser, and either died in the process or died before it had begun.

In time, through training, dedication, and what passed for mentorship, one could cohere, leave this plane of existence. Those who left sometimes came back, emboldened and eager to talk about what they'd done with their chance back on Earth. At peace, their thirst for revenge slaked, they said their goodbyes and allowed themselves to disintegrate, where they went one couldn't yet say.

Maybe, they all speculated, they went to some other greater plane of being, perhaps met the architects of this novel version of the afterlife. There was a comforting irony in being dead yet still entertaining theories about life after death. Although some who cohered chose to come back and stick around, so powerful was the act of giving succor and marinating in the anticipated thrill of another's planned revenge.

"It's my time," Joel told Vincent, after some unknown, unquantifiable amount of "time" had passed, time now a concept that had no meaning. The way Joel made this announcement carried some implicit satisfaction in being in on some secret. Funny, Vincent really had no inkling of how much time passed "down here." (They still used that expression "down here" although for all they knew, they could be "up there" or "in between" or some unfathomable permutation.)

"I'm proud of you," Vincent said. They hadn't spent as much time together as Vincent had expected. Vincent had hoped to learn more about Joel and now was a bit saddened he may never have that chance. Come to think of it, Vincent couldn't be sure how he'd spent his time. All he knew is that he'd hardly ever felt bored anymore, a peace of mind he'd rarely experienced while alive.

"Why thank you, man. I'm proud of you, too." Vincent could tell somehow that Joel was attempting some equivalent of a smile. "You've really matured in the hour or so you've been here, I've seen some real unbelievable growth. You've become a true sage, on Earth they'd have made you a Bodhisattva."

Vincent laughed in amused shock and, while genuinely disbelieving, made a show of it for Joel's benefit. "What, man? An hour?"

"That's right, you died maybe a day ago. You made the transformation and have been down here for about, I don't know, I'd guess an hour of Earth time. What, how else could we get our revenge if we were down here for some equivalent of a hundred years or something? Think whoever designed this system would allow our tormentors to just die of old age? Think we go back on Earth just to, what, badmouth their memories at the local town hall to their distant relatives, write pissy comments on their obituaries on some version of social media? Nah, man, they are alive and kickin'. And here's the kicker. I'm going back, and you're coming with me!"

"Are you serious!"

180

"Yes siree. Call me Willy Wonka, I got your golden ticket."

"Promise not to turn me into a blueberry?"

"Well, you're already dead, so why bother? I only have one person on my shit list, whereas you have a bunch, a few people I mean, so let's get mine out of the way and then strategize on yours. We can have fun with it. Master and pupil, the dream team."

Vincent appreciated that Joel reduced "a bunch" to "a few people." Being reminded that "a bunch" of people bullied him still burned him with shame, the quantity of his tormentors alone raised a suspicion to some hypothetical third-party that his abuse was deserved. How could all those people be wrong? Vincent had somehow been under the misperception that cruelty could be reasoned with or somehow waited out, had not understood that for some cruelty was its own pleasure, and weakness always invited domination.

Vincent wouldn't abide by that anymore.

*

A clear summer, early evening. It was, as Joel suggested, like Vincent had never left. The light was still clear but would soon fade, the fireflies coming out in a few hours' time. He didn't know whether he felt the warming, waning rays or only imagined he did. Whatever it was, it instilled a soft, gliding feeling, those summer nights where the nostalgia and romance seem almost pre-planted, and he expected the crack of a bat hitting a homerun in a nearby park or the jingle of the ice cream man, even though he rarely hung out outside while alive. If this were a weekend and they were near a downtown, the bars and restaurants would be filling up with outgoing, normal people with friends and family, people unlike him.

They were on an ordinary block with large detached homes. This could be a block in his hometown, the block where he lived with his mother and father, the block where one night he decided to unceremoniously and modestly end his life with booze and pills and sleep, disappearing somewhere like a little shrew into some unseen hole, granting his final wish to be overlooked and unseen.

And to think, he'd always thought of himself as so craven, even though he'd made *other* plans, plans that surprised, confused, and then intimidated him by their extravagant elaborateness and didactic subtext, by the obsessive rigidity and imposed importance on the order by which he planned to do what to whom.

But he never went through with it. Partly because his intended victims were all dispersed around the state and even across the country, now that they were in college. And partly because, let's be honest, who was he kidding?

Looking around, Vincent saw some differences between his hometown and wherever they were now. The houses here were closer together and less well-maintained, there was more foot traffic and cars and the roads were narrower. He now noticed a few houses with light blue and white flags.

"So where are we, exactly?" Vincent asked.

"Should be Chapel Hill, North Carolina, and one Alissa Whedon should be living right there." Joel pointed dramatically to a white-paneled, modest two-story house up the block. "And that brand-new Honda CRV, which you think would be outside the price range of a supposedly struggling graduate student unless one has a generous Mommy-and-Daddy who bankrolled her, well, that car should be all hers. I bet it's even in her name, too. Don't worry, I don't plan on us taking long here."

"Okay, okay. I grew up in Pennsylvania and always had UNC on my list, if you remember, before that all went to shit."

"I remember."

"Can people see us, by the way? Like, anyone looking out the windows," Vincent turned back to the corner, seeing the occasional car zip by, "or anyone else?"

"Not yet. And even if they did, what would it matter? But once we get up to her place we'll make ourselves visible. You'll know when it happens, you can follow my lead. I figure now, let's just enjoy the little walk up there. Like two kids out on summer vacation, a summer stroll, right? Makes me nostalgic for childhood even though I always wanted to be an adult, you know what I mean?"

"I know exactly what you mean. You never actually told me what she did to you, by the way?"

Joel shook his head and made a show of stretching dismissively and sighing, as if suggesting, 'don't even get me started.'

"You don't even want to know, trust me, it pisses me off just thinking about it. Trust me, it's too aggravating to even go into."

Ehh, fine. What mattered was the camaraderie, and now wasn't the time to spoil the momentum. Vincent hadn't shared his refined grievances against Paul O'Connor, Gio Terilli, Matt Mayhew, and Matt Manello (known as "the two Matts" or "the M+Ms," some kind of sacrilege that the two most malicious bullies were afforded the bonhomie inherent in a joint nickname). Or how he'd fantasized about the order and execution of making things right, with each and every one of them.

But actually, Vincent wasn't convinced. He didn't want to be kept in the dark anymore, and the only reason he hadn't divulged all his own gory details was because Joel had never really asked. Even at the indulgent pace they were heading up the block, they'd be right at her doorstep in just a few minutes.

"Well, I want to know before we go in there. I'm an open book, and," Vincent changed tact, "it'll help me enjoy this better if I know exactly what went down with her."

"Trust me, I'm trying to just do you a favor, it's so annoying," and out of some desultory instinct Joel slapped at some unseen bug in the air, even though they hadn't yet taken physical form. Joel continued slapping with his fingers, not talking, looked back at Vincent as if not knowing why he was still attentive and waiting, as if Vincent was the one committing the faux paus in not recognizing that bug-hunting had taken precedence and the natural window of explanation had passed.

"Alright, if you really want to know, you wouldn't believe how much I helped this bitch with her coursework, I was always – like no matter what I was doing, or where I was at the time, or anything – I was always there to support her, help her through whatever million different problems she was having, and of course whenever I needed something from her she'd always blow me off. Like, I was an 'as needed' friend. Meanwhile, she'd date or sleep around with every scumbag you could think of, meanwhile never even acknowledging me or just pretending she didn't notice me so she could go on taking advantage of me without addressing the fact that I was obviously interested.

"And I mean, that's fine, whatever, but just, the level of manipulation and deceit from her, it was incredible. She'd lie about getting back together with an ex or something when she needed me, needed me to talk her through things, always 'oh I couldn't get the work done, pleaaaase' and meanwhile she's out getting railed by her ex-boyfriend and I'm being the biggest fucking patsy simp ever.

"So, a couple of other things happened, I wouldn't say anything snapped, but I felt like I didn't have anything to look forward to and may as well take her out with me. I've been a pretty depressed person all my life, surprise surprise, and I just had enough. And I kept coming back to how much I felt scorned by her. So naturally of course I'm doing something about it, got her in my sights, chasing her down Jason-style and of course I get hit by a fucking car."

Vincent waited.

Joel turned toward the house.

Vincent recoiled as if someone had just pegged him unseen with a water balloon. What? Was there more? Was that it?

"Was that – is there anything else? Like, you said 'a couple other things happened,' what was that?"

Vincent hoped for the worst, something like Joel just casually filling in the details that one night in an inexplicable turn of events Alissa tied him up, sodomized him and shared the video with friends, something to possibly justify Joel's rancor. When Vincent got *his* revenge, he imagined himself almost bowled over, weighed down with trembling emotion and terrible relief. He wasn't sure what Joel was feeling now, but it wasn't that. Instead, there was a curiously unencumbered glee.

"Eh, not worth talking about. I was such a fucking idiot to elevate and overvalue this girl. Partly my fault, but mainly hers. Lessons need to be learned. Anyway, here we are.

"Ready? I'm going to blur myself just a little bit so she doesn't recognize me at first, otherwise she'd be smart enough to not even open the door. I trust she'd be smart enough to do that, at least. When she comes to the door, just imagine yourself how you looked, it'll come, don't worry, I heard it's easy-peasy.

"And what's the worst that can happen, we die again? Hah, have fun with it, easy-peasy."

Vincent felt the vacant hollowness that he knew was his condition's equivalent for a stomach roiling with shame and anxiety. If life was unfair and unbalanced, the rules at best arbitrary and capricious and at worst commandeered to be self-serving to those who wielded the power, why'd he expect the afterlife to be any different? Again, always compromised, everything always compromised, nothing just simple and pure and unfettered.

But just think about O'Connor, Terilli, the Two Matts. You know in your heart your mission is pure. This is just a stepping stone; you know what you need to do.

But those appeals weren't working.

*

"Hey, one second." Alissa opened the door, looked back to make sure Stubby, her roommate's cat, wasn't coming close to the front. Stubby was an indoor cat. Alissa was expecting a package and knew she'd need to sign for it.

"Oh," Alissa jolted, confused as to what she'd sworn was an older man in a FedEx uniform, now seeing two men around her age outside her door, the light falling on them weirdly. She flicked the switch for the front-door lights but they were already on. She tilted her head to look up to see if they were working. They were.

"Uhh, sorry," she said, and the man in the lead, his face, it looked like a deflating marshmallow. Alissa blinked hard, her vision was shitty because her contacts were terribly dry and allergies weren't helping, and she couldn't accept entirely what she'd just seen, must be a trick of the light or her contacts. There should be some kind of warning from Amazon to prepare her, like a notice reading 'please be aware that our delivery driver might have a condition that gives him Marshmallow Face or the appearance of a living jawbreaker.'

Neither of these men were holding any packages. The man farther back was, she now realized with unmooring discomfort, was literally indistinct, a darkened outline of a person with a gummy, floaty center.

The man closer to her, she could swear, she could *swear*, he'd been an older man in a purple-and-brown uniform a second ago, where had that thought come from?, and, before she could catch her breath, the face before her, oh God, impossible, no, she recognized him, no, Joel Webber. She recognized that placid moon-face, but now his face was impossibly wide and, as the blurred features now set, jubilant and victorious enough that words weren't needed to get the point across.

Not possible, not possible. Joel became serious and locked eyes with her, made sure she was positive as to what she was witnessing.

Joel looked back at the gloaming sheepish shape behind him, and then back toward Alissa. He screamed soundlessly, teeth pronounced like cliffsides and then rapidly multiplying, his face widening, mouth following suit, until his screaming, voracious face became her entire world.

NOTES

I've always liked "bad values" stories, stories that follow a weirdly sympathetic main character with questionable values and, by presenting the tale through his perspective, gets the reader to unwittingly adopt and even support a warped worldview. I wouldn't say this story is entirely like that, since the ending is supposed to pull the rug out and make the reader re-question allegiances and assumptions, but its hopefully in the spirit of those stories.

I originally envisioned this story as something much longer as part of a planned novella collection, with Joel's sociopathic reasons for seeking his version of "revenge" upon Alissa – which likely just boiled down to rejection – being made obvious to the reader early on, with the reader having more knowledge about Joel's motives than Vincent, with Vincent eventually compromising his ethics to get what he needed from Joel to enact his own revenge. Hopefully, this shortened version works too, with the reveal occurring to Vincent and the reader simultaneously, sickening Vincent at what should be a moment of triumph and weighing him down with the same dreadful compromises of life.

I also always wondered that, if human systems inevitably become skewed, self-serving and corrupt, whether supernatural institutions that serve former humans would likewise end up perverted in the same ways. That Vincent was selected for this after-life initially served as some kind of supernatural vindication or justification for his planned revenge. People often assume that systems select its winners and losers on some kind of moral basis. Being on top, therefore, feels inherently virtuous. Here, the selection process seems to just depend on whether someone chose to take active steps in pursuit of revenge, leaving unanswered whether that motivation was justified. One has to wonder what the ostensible designer of this system is setting up to eventually achieve.

Nights Devour My Days

I wonder if this is what it's like to perceive yourself as old. I'm not old, really, I'm 34. That's not young, although if I were married with a child I'd be a "young mother" in a "young family" and people would look at me and my hypothetical husband and hypothetical child and smile and think forgiving thoughts about the supposedly endearing and precious tribulations of young parenthood.

But I'm single and childless, so 34 makes me old. And I'm 34 in a city where women outnumber men 3:1, so that makes me – in an Einstein-Relativity sort of way – somehow even older. I don't think any differently than when I was younger – I was cautious and deliberating then, I'm cautious and deliberating now – and how I feel day to day while navigating with this "old" body doesn't feel any different than how I've always felt.

But it's when I have moments to reflect. Such as literally when looking in a mirror, and I see how I'm saggier and looser. Or when I'm cycling through the dating apps and realize that the men who respond to my profile are now generally in their 40s. I don't want to date someone in their forties. I know that's prejudicial and uncharitable, but it disgusts me, because forties is middle-aged, the age of middle managers, the age of all of my principals growing up. Middle all the way down. I'm not middle, I'm in my thirties, which is the new twenties, so they say, and as an ambassador of the thirties, I control the borders and decree that the forties cannot encroach upon my territory and slip in through subterfuge by claiming to be the "new" anything.

So, dating. I don't date much, although I should date more. No terrible horror stories, I just find the process agonizing. Men are eager – and I mean that descriptively, not judgmentally – and generally if they feel no connection, they will still try and juggle as many of us women as they can and pursue each of us until attrition takes its toll.

The overwhelming majority of dates won't blossom into anything meaningful. And I wouldn't say I'm picky or selective, just that I don't want to waste anyone's time. And the process of telling someone something like "I don't know if there was a connection, but I'd get together again as friends!" is always dreadful. I just feel bad, I'm empathetic. The men usually understand, shuffle off meekly, on to the next one.

I always wonder to myself if I've made the right decision, if I've should have gone on one more date with person X, even if the date didn't go well because people have off-nights, don't they? Or maybe even worse my entire paradigm is wrong, and I'm doomed to isolation because I have this belief that I should feel, on the first date, some kind of strong emotion. I don't feel strong emotions about much of anything, so why am I holding these prospects to this standard? I don't feel strong emotions about my job, but it pays my bills. I don't feel strong emotions, if I'm being honest, about my parents, but I'm a dutiful daughter. Perhaps love is, realistically, something similar: routine, ritual, obligation, and sacrifice, the dividend being you have someone you trust and care for to share things with.

Maybe I'm wrong about everything.

It was with all these thoughts that I'd met Gerald. There was nothing extraordinary or unusual about our pre-date online banter. (What an unfair standard I'm applying there, isn't it? The same can easily be said about me; perhaps even moreso, since he was proactive enough to reach out and did most of the bantering.) What I liked most was he was 31, and there'd been no strained joke about him liking "older women" that had to be deflected or submerged with a "lol" or eyeroll emoji.

We met at a hip Vietnamese restaurant close to where he worked. I was cautious about going straight into a meal on a first date – I usually just liked meeting for a drink or coffee, way more casual – but he insisted, which I kind of liked for some reason. Even though I was at least five minutes early he was already seated when I got there. I kind of liked that, too.

It seems every place in this city, despite the cuisine, thinks the perfect accoutrement to your meal is some cranked-up song from some neck-tattooed rapper blaring about how he wants to bareback your pussy, and this place was no different. I worried I'd barely be able to hear him, and I've wondered about things like that when I've ended things before: like, if the volume of the restaurant had been lower, would things have been different? But mercifully, just as I joined him the volume quickly subsided to reasonable levels.

What is there to say about a first date? Nothing crazy happened. I used to think there were supposed to be some kind of immediate sparks. Maybe there were, but sparks that were out-of-sight, like a little electrical fire in the sewers. I enjoyed his company. He had great posture and, from what I could tell from the way his sweater clung, broad shoulders and well-developed arms, which was interesting because in his photographs he was fairly ropey and skinny.

"Filled out some since your dating app photo session, eh?" I asked him after the drinks came. I like being cheeky early on, it's like a wave-length check, like making sure our frequencies can align.

"Those were from a few years ago. I should update them, but it weeds out the superficial ladies, I suppose."

"If they are from a few years ago, that means I agreed to go on a date with a man who, when those pictures were taken, was only in his twenties. That means I'm a grave robber."

"Isn't the expression 'cradle robber?'"

Just as I was going to say, "oh right," he added, "Or is it because men in their twenties are basically dead to you."

I gave him that one with a "well played."

He was a few inches shorter than me, which in my mind became the origin story for why this nice-looking, professional, polite, reasonably charming and otherwise perfectly normal man was single. He was also half-Asian, and I know (this is just a sad reality, don't blame me) that Asian men have greater difficulty on these dating apps. I wondered if he was half-Vietnamese, but I didn't ask and he didn't volunteer. I'm a mutt myself, and maybe it's because of this exoticism that I get more online action than I deserve.

We learned about each other but God damned if I could remember much of it. He grew up in Delaware, the blandest state in the country, and moved to the City some years ago and did programming stuff. I am from somewhere else too, and, can you believe this, also do stuff for work. It's not interesting, who cares.

What I remember most from that first date was that his posture was fantastic, there seemed to be some tension or subconsciously recognized discrepancy between his muscular physique and his well-groomed professional image, and I absolutely insisted (as I always do) that we split the bill. I do that on every date, and men always reproach and think it means I'm blowing them off or it's a trick, and then I have to insist upon it and then, ironically, it *does* become a kind of dating litmus test because why is it so crazy to think a woman wants to avoid feeling weirdly indebted for going out? But all he said was "you sure?" and then "alright" and it was as simple as that.

I felt comfortable around him and, while we didn't kiss at the end of the date, my body language was warm toward him and I told him we should definitely do this again sometime, and that next time I'd choose the place.

That night I dreamed of him. For some people that might be romantic, but not for me. I didn't want someone invading my dreams. Here's what a nut I am. Have you ever dreamed of someone you no longer speak to? After you do, doesn't it feel like you're obligated to reach out to them, or like you somehow shared something significant with them? I didn't want to be dreaming of someone I barely knew.

What was the dream? Something stupid. We were at a restaurant and these vampiric servers – I got the feeling that they were actually vampires, but once I awoke I couldn't remember if that'd been literal – kept crowding around us. First it was one, a statuesque blond with angular cheekbones, who stood right on top of us after she took our order. Then there was another, a male, who stood right next to me. Then two others, then another two, all in black. Then they were forming a kind of rectangle around us, giving us space, a bit of a breather, then in an instant they were practically on top of me again. Then I saw myself from above, screaming, as these six servers rotated around me, indifferent to my claustrophobia.

Then Gerald, with his ideal posture, straightened himself and stood upright, and the rotating stopped. The servers all looked at him gravely and then they vanished. He apologized for their behavior, "indecorous," was the word he used, and then "they must not know that you're with me." I made fun of him, asked him if he remembered the date of the dictionary.com email of the day that introduced that word into his vocabulary.

"January 31," he said, his lip pursed one iota to pass for a smile. "My birthday, so of course I had to remember."

I, of course, not wanting to come off as a lunatic, never told him about that dream or asked when was his birthday. We arranged a second date, just cocktails, and something of an opportunistic outing on my part, as it was the Pegasus Club, a bar that recently opened a few blocks from where I worked that looked pretty splashy and fun.

"Classy, I don't know if I'm dressed properly," he said when I met him inside. He said it so dryly and deadpan it went beyond sarcasm into some other realm. At first I thought he was being earnest, as he was wearing jeans after all, but then the sheer dryness double-backed to reveal the irony as he pointed to a giant pink technicolor Pegasus mural behind the bar. "How many winged horses am I going to run into this week?"

It was a type of smirky irony that I usually didn't care for, that making a mockery of everything to protect oneself from feelings. If it had come from some bearded squish, I wouldn't have found it so endearing. You know you like someone when you justify applying different standards.

I'd arrived fifteen minutes early and had been planning on texting him, but he was already there at the bar. Normally, my dating-brain would question, why is he here so early? But I only thought about how I *usually* think about those things, and then let the thought fade.

I had fun with him. Two drinks a piece, me being a bit drunk, him loosening up only in the sense that his top-button came undone and his sleeves got rolled up. I can't remember much of what he said, I just remember the feeling of stability. I don't think I saw him lean over the bar even once – his posture always impeccable – and he seemed to have a knack for getting the bartender to continually refill our waters, which, as a former bartender myself, I know is its own little miracle.

The night ended with a kiss. We left the bar together after our two drinks – it was a weekday, after all – and I told him I had fun again, and made a call-back to something he'd mentioned, which he laughed at, although I can't for the life of me remember what I said. I told him we should do this again sometime soon, and I kissed him, and he kissed me back. I remember when he kissed me that he placed his hand on my back and I don't know if I felt prompted to on my own or whether he guided me but my posture improved.

"You should be a chiropractor, I swear," I said through a smile. A knot of lower back tension was seemingly released with just that light arching of my back.

"It'd be terribly lame if I revealed that I'm actually quite the masseuse, so I won't say anything about that."

"Heavens no." I really said Heavens.

He made no effort to try and go home with me.

I dreamt that night of Gerald's arms emerging through a man's empty eye sockets. In the dream Gerald's wrists were distressingly thin, thin enough to easily pass through eye sockets like floss between two front teeth.

Then came his muscular arms, crisscrossed in victory, expanding in girth, ripping and distending the man's face so quickly and severely that the empathy one naturally extends to another human being was lost, because soon there were no features identifiable, only collapsed gore. My dream-camera silenced all and zoomed into the gaping red hole, discerned the lighter pink of gums, the scattered skeletal corn kernels of teeth, zooming in slowly, slowly, the meat quivering; now the vacant hole was the world that existed where the nose should be, a gurgling suction sound as if that hollowed-out space attempted to inhale breath, like it was calling out to me, a flushing toilet of mucus, begging me to listen and decipher some meaning . . . .

Gerald rose triumphant, the unknown man's body diminished immediately and fell away, literally rolling away as if it was pushed out of a moving vehicle at high speed, and then out of sight, out of mind, was there even a body there at all, and why was I so concerned anyway?

Gerald's gleaming body, confident imposing posture, so distinct from the expression on his face, which was amiable, patient and slightly upturned as if fielding a question. His body was everything a body should be and his face was everything a face should be, understanding and in the midst of conversation, as if unaware of the blood and gore that cascaded off him, or perhaps the gore accentuated the appeal of his sensitive face, as if there was no development that could perturb this equipoise.

Who knows how long dreams last, but there were other scenes of him, always triumphant, always gory, always emerging out of persons whose details were smoothed away just enough for me to always only be on the cusp of identifying them. I felt so close to knowing those bodies, like that burning factoid – that name of an actor you just fucking know – that you beg your friend not to Google before you come up with it yourself.

I didn't wake up in a sweat or anything. But what to do with that? I'd ended things with guys for sillier reasons. I've stopped seeing guys because I've found them too effeminate, which is perhaps hypocritical since I consider myself a mild feminist, or, at the very least, feel myself getting defensive if positions popularly considered "feminist" are being attacked. I don't know if it's something in the water, but a lot of men in this city think being a completely inoffensive, always-agreeable ragdoll is somehow endearing. It's not. I stopped seeing someone because he said he liked this comedian Neal Brennan, so I watched some clips of him and thought he looked like such an untrustworthy, opportunistic kiddie-touching rat that I had to break up with him because I couldn't be with a guy with such awful taste.

But how could I justify stopping seeing Gerald because of a weird dream? A dream where, if viewed generously, he was the hero, vanquishing, albeit bloodily, people I intuited somehow meant me harm.

I avoided reaching out to him for a few days. He texted me three days after our second date. I avoided it and pretended for a day that things would resolve themselves. I don't like confrontation, and after a few days whatever impact that dream had made on me lessened, so I just told him that, sorry, I was just really busy with work but I'd definitely reach out to him in a few days when things cooled down. He understood and told me not to work too hard, and whatever inane response I gave likely involved that laughing emoji that kind of looks like it's laughing so hard it's spitting.

I won't lie, I thought of Gerald quite a bit in those few days where I superficially considered ending things. First time was when a co-worker and colleague on a project, Ben Friedman, cc'ed our supervisor on an email opining about some imagined deficiency in my work, when the tactful thing would have been to email his thoughts to me separately so I could explain to him why I did it the way I did it. Ben is a sycophantic toady who doesn't realize our supervisor sees through what he's doing and would much rather be left out of these things. I always imagined that if Ben Friedman decided to become a rapper, he'd call himself "B. Free" because it's so cringey. I've told a few others that joke and they've howled with laughter. It just makes me madder when I think how accurate that insult is, like he should be aware he's so lame that such an absurdity can reasonably apply to him.

I could swear I saw Ben roll his eyes at me today after I politely emailed him back and requested he send his opinions to me first before including our supervisor. If Gerald were standing next to me, Ben would never fucking do that. I thought of Gerald socking him, and hoped he was one of those ruined faces in my dream; if it was Ben's face deteriorating, I should have woken up cheering.

Next time I thought of Gerald was when my mother called me. I'm too close to my mother, or she's too close to me, in the sense that we talk way too much. At some point I stopped being her daughter and became her combination therapist and grievance counselor, where she feels perfectly normal unloading her troubles upon me, expects me to follow the shifting loyalties and motives of her friends / frenemies, half of whom I've never even met, and demand I provide some workable solutions. While she was correcting me after I confused one old person for another, I noticed the back of my head was bleeding where I'd burrowed in a fingernail and scratched too deeply.

Then I thought of Gerald, with his radiating Zenness. A little blood didn't bother him.

I dreamt of him again. The dream had a lot of commotion, but it felt like I was looking through the wrong end of a telescope or something. There was something significant happening in miniature, a black orb in the background framing little figures throughout their conflict on the stage, the backdrop saturated in deep red cloth, red lights, the greater world around them pulsing, heaving and fleshly-textured in a way not captured by the little figures tussling on the stage.

A translucent, yelling face, eyes closed in effort, dwarfed all and flew toward me, screaming at too high a pitch for me to register, but I could see the thwarted anguish on its face. The miniature action continued, and in the blink of the mind's eye the screaming face was lost behind Gerald's Zen calm, but there were the subtlest movements, something taking place just beyond the ripples of his forehead. It felt like witnessing the existence of some obscure truth recessed behind an obvious one.

A third date. Dinner at a tapas restaurant. I'd found the Basque people fascinating ever since I read a book about them in high school, and really wanted to visit St. Sebastian someday and loved tapas, which the Basque called "pinxtos." Gerald was happy to hear from me. I told him I was pumped for the restaurant, and said it might not be a Basque restaurant but it was the closest we could do.

I dug it. The date went well. I missed him. I learned as much as I could about him and felt connected. I didn't know he was an only child, not that that's super-important, but that's interesting. It made me like him more for some reason. There's this folk belief that "only childs" are spoiled or something, and he was so well-adjusted it was as if he overcame something, and made me trust him even more.

I invited him back to my apartment. I was mildly buzzed from two glasses of wine, but still in complete control of my senses. We held hands in the Uber as we gabbed, neither of us directly acknowledging the intimate contact with words.

We made out in my apartment. I couldn't tell who was taking the lead, or if we were just in perfect lock-step. We undressed in my bedroom with the lights dimmed.

With the lights low I felt at first like I was the victim of a practical joke; first I sensed his midsection was strangely craggly and weirdly shaded, with what seemed like alternating darker lines of skin, and then that swift, barely registered observation disappeared altogether when I realized his penis was frighteningly gigantic, in both length and girth. It added complications to what should have been carefree fun.

I didn't have any condoms at home, and couldn't even think of what size could contain him. I happen to be on birth control, but the issue of protection never came up. I was ambivalent about having sex, and, in other circumstances, would have blown him to completion rather than have sex without a condom. I tried, but blowing him felt like I was demeaning myself somehow, clogging my throat and cutting off my oxygen, subjecting myself to some kind of torture.

I ended that quickly and girded myself for sex, assuming a missionary position because that would be all I could handle, and he was respectful although obviously proud of his distinction. Why I didn't insist upon protection, I don't know. I couldn't say it slipped my mind, but it never matured from a fact observed to a reason for action. Very unlike me.

He was understanding and considerate enough not to attempt to put it all in. It felt, at best, vaguely good, but too bluntly all-encompassing for something as nuanced as pleasure to take root. I was being skewered. I felt like I was somehow suffering permanent internal injury. I grimaced as I imagined him in my stomach, and right as I instinctively put up my hands to temper his thrusting he came inside me.

He seemed to soften instantly and withdrew. When he pulled out, I imagined light becoming visible, the end of an eclipse.

He rolled over on his side, the small of his back to the pillow, arms stretched out, posture good even in the bedroom. As if remembering something, he put a clammy arm around me. I looked up at him and smiled vacantly, thinking it something to do, and excused myself to go to the bathroom and pee.

He was in the same position when I came back. I assumed my previous position slowly. "Do you want any water, or anything to drink?" I asked him, not quite sure why.

"Do you want me to do anything for you?" he asked in a way that seemed incongruous with the obvious sexual implication.

"Not tonight, I had enough. That was a lot to take." I reverted to a kind of slinky, appeasing flattery, perhaps hoping he'd be contented and sleep, and tomorrow, with my privacy restored, I could evaluate my feelings.

"There are a lot of things I can do for you."

"I'm sure."

"I don't think you are."

"Maybe I'll find out next time. We can plan out a little better next time. This was just all so sudden and I'm exhausted. I'm on birth control, by the way, I'm sure that's something I should have said before, sorry if I didn't, I don't want you to worry or anything."

"I'm not worried about anything."

"I envy that."

He turned over, back facing me, making himself at home.

"Be positively indecorous of me not to at least offer. Although the mood's changed, I think. Wouldn't feel right anymore."

"Okay."

He was staring right at me. I blinked excessively, the only flinching I could muster. Paralyzed.

"You won't have to worry anymore." Then he smiled. The first time, I realized, I'd ever seen him unabashedly smile; everything else had been more of a guarded smirk. His lips curled too wide, positively folded back. I saw too much teeth and gums for comfort. "And neither will I, at least for a time."

"Okay."

"A little blood on the back of your head won't bother you so much anymore, either. And you can forget about Ben Friedman, too. And anything else that ever bothered you."

How he said it wasn't reassuring. I just wanted the night to end, I wanted to sleep, to deal with this in the morning, to be alone.

My mind is chattering. There's one voice swelling to be heard about the chaos, but it's not successful, it's all indistinct noise.

I don't want to admit it but I'm having trouble breathing. I'm sweating, and when you're already in bed you can curl up to a pillow and feel like you're somehow treating the problem, like there's nothing more that needs to be done. My face was buried into the pillow, and I felt the presence of something flickering behind my eyes. The blackness behind my shut eyes was invaded by a screaming red, as sudden and violent as opening the door to your bathroom and receiving a shotgun blast to the stomach.

I moved my face from the pillow, head hot, breathing slow to prevent from gasping.

"Gerald," I said, swallowing hard. "Tell me, when's your birthday." I meant to say it confrontationally, but the effect was lost.

His voice had traveled a bit, far enough to inform me he was standing by the light.

"Cute. I think you mean our birthday now. Ahh, is your head hurting? Tense behind the eyes? Best to just go to sleep."

He turned off the light.

<u>NOTES</u>

Some stories develop from images, and here the animating image was the final one: someone in the vulnerable position of being in bed with their partner and realizing that something is deeply, deeply wrong, just as the lights are turned off. I also like this genre, what I'm calling the digressive first-person narrative slow-build. Gerald here is very loosely based off a friend of mine, and hopefully he looks past all of the creepiness and strange scarring and parasitic dream-invading powers and is just flattered I wrote him as having an elephantine penis.

It's Always Time To Go

Aaron's sleepover resulted in a veritable takeover of Grandma Eison's household. Aaron, aged ten, and his three pals and classmates – Anthony, Eric, and Bruce – sat in the kitchen and ate from the smorgasbord of dips, chips and candies. As his friends chowed down, Aaron remembered there was a half-filled bag of York Peppermint Patties in a cupboard and a big carton of Twizzlers in the food pantry. The York Peppermint patties were his dad's; Grandma Ninnie kept them at her house because she knew his dad liked them.

He knew if he called his dad and asked if he could have some, he'd say yes, and he debated, in the ill-formed and solipsistic fashion of ten-year-old inner turmoil, whether he should get the patties and present them for his friends. Maybe his dad would be tired one day and drive over to Ninnie's and want a patty, and he'd feel bad if he took them for himself. But then again, he'd invited his friends over and wanted them to have fun.

Anthony's earlier comment – that the mild salsa had no taste, and then Bruce's addendum that it tasted like moldy marinara sauce – gave Aaron a scare because he thought maybe his friends were let down by the options, but they'd all laughed good-naturedly in a way to let Aaron know that they didn't hold the poor salsa against him. That's why it's good to keep Eric around: he always just seemed appreciative that Aaron included him and never said anything negative. Eric didn't say much at all, really, but he was a reliable and dependable playmate, a new addition to his pantheon ever since he moved to Aaron's block some months ago.

Aaron got the Twizzlers but made no mention of the patties. "We got Twizzlers too!" he announced, though Anthony and Bruce didn't respond as enthusiastically as he'd hoped. Eric, with a mouth full of so many masticated peanut M&Ms that it tasted like he'd licked a scoop of Skippy right off a butter knife, offered the following practical endorsement: "Twizzlers will be good for when we watch the movies later because they last long. You can also drink through them if you bite off their tops." Bruce and Anthony looked at each other as if considering a business proposal, then nodded nonchalantly, evidently satisfied with Eric's conclusion.

After they'd migrated to the living room, Bruce tripped harmlessly, the combined sugar rush and the promise of a night of tomfoolery conspiring to overcome his senses. The boys all laughed, and while he was down Anthony ran over and tagged him, yelling "robbers" and both boys yipped and ran around. Aaron became giddy too, buoyed by his growing confidence that his sleepover would be a success.

"Robbers?" Eric asked, as if annoyed that the boys were conflating "Tag" with "Cops and Robbers," which had different unarticulated rules, and it didn't matter anyway because they were all going to end up running around in circles.

"Whoa, whoa, whoa there guys, calm down, alright?" That was Jacob, Aaron's "uncle," who was in town with his long-time girlfriend Emily, Aaron's aunt. Emily and Jacob were back from grad school and staying with Aaron's parents for a few nights. Aaron's parents were back home, enjoying their rare night alone, with Emily and Jacob earning their keep as back-up security and reinforcement for hosting Aaron's first sleepover at Ninnie's house and shepherding four rowdy boys.

Aaron, Jacob thought, really had grown. Jacob had been with Emily since before Aaron had even been born, and had seen the kid grow from sweet-natured, fat-headed toddler who loved mimicking others and doing funny dances for the affection of his family, to this diffident little boy, still sweet-natured but who kept largely to himself unless pushed into sociability, satisfied in his own world of trucks, trains, cars, video games and YouTube videos. Away at grad school, they didn't see Aaron nearly as much. Now when Jacob saw him the physical changes seemed epochal, as if coming out of nowhere.

Jacob liked Eric. Jacob had met Eric at least once before and liked Eric because he seemed stern and respectful, which at this age could be evidence of early neuroses but appreciated that as a nice feature when you're trying to commandeer four little boys. Even Aaron wasn't listening, which was unlike him, as he was swept away into pandemonium with the other two.

"What, I take you boys to the library, then you ignore me? I'm chopped liver back here? Stop running around, it's getting late."

The boys all stopped. "Hey, I said 'hello,'" claimed Anthony.

"Me too," inserted Bruce. Aaron repeated what Bruce said in a low, wavery baritone – 'me tooooooo' – because repeating stuff is apparently the height of hilarity to ten-year-old boys.

"Liar," Jacob responded, then gave Aaron a jocular bump on the shoulder. "You see Eric here, he's the only one who acknowledged me. Be more like Eric."

Aaron wished Jacob hadn't said that. He'd been worried about having Eric hang out with the other two boys: they'd never all hung out together. Anthony and Bruce played on the same intramural soccer team with Aaron, but unlike Aaron, they hadn't been forced to take up the sport by their parents. Eric didn't play sports and Aaron worried he might not be able to keep up with their energy and general rambunctiousness.

Worse, once in Social Studies Bruce had told Eric he smelled funny, which wasn't true. Aaron has no idea why Bruce said that, other than Aaron suspected that Bruce sometimes felt the need to just say *something*, and usually that something was impulsive and regrettable. Eric never responded and Aaron just hoped he hadn't heard him or just didn't remember. Aaron remembered the vicarious embarrassment he felt for his friend, and told himself next time he'd stick up for him.

Bruce asked earnestly, "What's chopped liver?"

"Chopped liver is when you take out someone's liver, chop it up, and eat it. In the medieval times, like when there were knights and dragons, when the town folk didn't like someone, they used to rip out the person's liver and eat it while the victim was forced to watch." For Jacob, it was fun being alone with the boys. Had Emily been around, she certainly would have said "Jacob..." in that closed-teeth meter she used, just below an exclamation, to let him know he was taking his anarchic tendencies a bit too far.

"Ewww . . ." all the boys expressed in varied laughing permutations. "Why would someone eat chopped liver?" Aaron asked, laughing.

"I'm just joking with you kids," Jacob added automatically, so they wouldn't get him in trouble later. He didn't need one of them repeating that to Emily.

"Uncle Jacob is with my Aunt Emily and they go to school together." This was well-trod territory but Aaron apparently felt the need to repeat it, in case Anthony and Bruce forgot all about the library trip and thought there was a stranger watching over them. If someone was going to give them gruesome fake-history, they may as well know the source.

"I am indeed 'with' her," Jacob said to no audible response. Eric smirked.

"We go to school together but we are back to watch over you rapscallions." He had a line anticipated if one of them asked what a rapscallion was – 'you know those scallions you put on a bagel? Like that, except one that can rap songs' – but none of them registered this unique word or gave two shits. He considered prompting them if they knew what a rapscallion was; he liked the guileless, gamboling question-and-answer sessions.

Tracking the boys' eyes, Jacob realized someone had just come down the stairs behind him.

"That's Aunt Emily," Aaron said dryly.

"Aunt Emily!" Eric ran over to her and hugged around her upper legs as she pretended to strain and fall backward from his onrush. She was wearing a white t-shirt and short-shorts in preparation for bed, and had Eric been a bit older, Jacob thought, he'd have to watch where he was grabbing.

Jacob reminded himself not to stoop to correcting a little boy, especially not when the kid seemed to be coming out of his shell. If Jacob wasn't careful with what he said in front of these kids Eric might be stuck with the moniker "grabby hands" (or something much worse, maybe "rape fingers") until he graduated high school or something.

"It's Eric! Aaron, why does your friend seem happier to see me than you?!"

Aaron shrugged. "He sees you less often."

"Oh geez, thanks."

Anthony and Bruce said hello in the plodding, perfunctory way that little boys interact with older girls.

"How much candy are you guys eating?!" Emily wrapped her lips around each word and exaggerated her interest and surprise, Eric still fastened to her leg.

"You trying to take her to the ground, Eric?" That, Jacob figured, was a casual way of getting Eric to restrain his roving hands.

Eric let go immediately and put his hand behind his back like he'd been caught in something. "No," he said, but didn't smile or laugh away an accusation like the other boys.

"Mean Uncle Jacob is just being mean, you don't mind him. You couldn't take me down anyway," and Emily assumed a wrestling position.

"Nah nah, maybe that's not the best idea Ems, it's late and they're just calming down to go downstairs and get in sleeping bags and watch movies."

Jacob didn't really care about all that. He just didn't want to watch Eric, however innocently, paw over his girlfriend. It was a disconcerting image.

"And ahem, calling me 'mean old Jacob?' I told them what movies to get, and took them to the library to get them!"

"And got candy at the store," Bruce added.

"Thanks for defending me, Bruce."

Bruce appeared surprised that his comment was acknowledged, looked up at Jacob, and nodded formally. If Eric was doing something weird – seemed like he was, as Jacob obviously didn't want him wrestling Emily – Bruce wanted to distinguish himself with civility.

"Okay, guys," and Emily pushed Eric delicately on the shoulders back to the other boys, for which he looked happy solely for the duration he was in physical contact with Emily and not a moment longer. "You all have fun downstairs! I still can't believe how much candy you all have!"

"You boys probably don't know about type two diabetes. You get that when you get older and eat a lot of sugar. You boys are working on, like, type three diabetes right now."

"Ughhh, Uncle Jacob!" Emily pursed her lips, placed her hands on her hips and flexed her eyes, as if each alone wasn't clue enough not to pursue this joke any further.

"Eh, I'm just kidding. They don't know what that all is anyway."

"I think my grandma has diabetes. She can't eat chocolate." Anthony said without affect, and smiled as all the boys laughed as if he'd said something really funny. He wasn't sure why it was funny, maybe because of how outsized Emily's expression became.

"Of course," Jacob dead-panned. Just his luck.

"Enough of all that," Emily added. For a moment Eric thought Emily might embrace him again, maybe in a sudden raucous take down, to distract the group from the awkwardness of morbid topics, but he instantly knew that was only a foolish nothing of a wish.

"Eric's the one who's been eating all the candy! You should see how many peanut M&Ms he ate already! He's the one who's first to get diabetes!" Bruce bellowed, his smile not fooling anyone about his intentions.

"No one likes a rat, Bruce. That's a lesson you gotta learn one day." When Emily wasn't around, Jacob would teach the boys the valuable adage of 'snitches get stitches' and let them guess what it meant.

Emily crouched at the knee to Eric-height. "Is that true, Eric? You? You're the smallest of them all, what's your secret? I wish I could eat like you!"

"I eat anything I want." Eric spoke as if Emily was the only one in the room.

"Enjoy it while it lasts."

"I have."

Jacob figured it would be best to get them all downstairs, out of Emily-range, before he got himself in trouble again.

"Good answer, kid, alright, say good night to Emily. Downstairs, gang. Okay, ramblers, let's get rambling." It was fun making movie references they wouldn't get for years, and the catch phrase – "ramblers, let's get rambling" – was repeated first by Aaron as they gathered up some candies, then Bruce and Anthony chimed in as they were picking up their overnight bags. Eric looked unamused, as if Reservoir Dogs was glib, refashioned hackwork and he was more of a Paul Thomas Anderson man.

*

Jacob had made them a killer list of starter-horror for a sleepover, but the Cloveton Public Library only had two of them: Gremlins and Krampus. Tremors, The Monster Squad, and The Gate would have to wait. Two movies were too much for them in one night anyway, but good to have options. Although, really, there wasn't any option: he'd make sure they damn well watched Gremlins first, and then if they were up for it, could fit in Krampus. He was half-tempted to watch Gremlins alongside them.

Jacob knew the importance of the first sleepover. Shit, even throwing a party *now* gave him anxiety, he could only imagine how he'd feel in Aaron's shoes, having three friends over and making sure everyone stayed entertained. Just from the intimate, carefree way that Bruce and Anthony interacted, he could tell they'd spent a lot of time hanging out, and he could also tell that Aaron and Anthony seemed preoccupied with gauging Bruce's mood before they chimed in. The pecking order of popularity started earlier than he'd remembered, and that was a tragedy. Kids can't even get through elementary school without the machinations of status subtly pulling the sociological strings.

Let's give Eric a leg up in this popularity game. "I just want to officially give it up to Eric, by the way, who found Krampus in the library. Good work, kid." And it was true: there was no Krampus in the "K" section, even though the librarian said it should be there. Eric walked off without a word and found it misplaced, apparently in the "C" section. Smart kid. What, did some library staffer restocking the film section misread it as "Crampus," figure it was a movie about a girl terrorized by a PMS demon?

Jacob even lightly clapped as if to officially coronate Eric as the sleepover MVP, with the other three boys – Bruce begrudgingly – following his lead, Bruce doing really nothing more than just tapping a forefinger against an opposite thumb.

"That being said, do you all promise me: Gremlins first, right?"

They all agreed.

"And please remember: if you don't like this movie, you are never allowed to step foot in this house again. Okay, assemble your chosen candies."

An ensuing riot of movement, all the boys except Eric pouncing, scrambling, and attempting to scoop up as much candy from the floor as their little arms could pin against their chests.

"Chill, chill! More than enough for everyone, don't make me play bread line leader."

"Who would wait on a line for bread!! Bread is so boring and you can get bread everywhere!" Aaron yelled while laughing, Anthony on top of him and both tugging at opposite ends of a box of Milk Duds, as Bruce, unchallenged, threw a few bags of peanut M&Ms up in the air and laughed as they fell wherever gravity dictated.

Jacob snatched the Milk Duds at the middle, the force making Aaron fall back and laugh even more at his thud.

"First, calm down. Second, Milk Duds are disgusting, you should fight over who should be forced to eat these things."

"Bread lines were when there wasn't enough food to go around." Eric explained dispassionately as he assembled a nest of candies. Eric's withdrawal corresponded proportionately with the others' self-absorbed boisterousness. Jacob could sympathize, and hoped it augured well for the kid: one needed to take stock of the company you keep. What further demonstrated that Eric was wise beyond his years was his nest of Reese's Peanut Butter Cups – the most decadent candy – and his Twix and Kit-Kats, the two most sonically and mouthfeel-satisfying candies.

"Eric again speaking straight facts. This is a kid to listen to," said Jacob.

Jacob calmed them down, making a bread line of sorts to distribute candies without everyone causing mayhem, and, as a silent thank you to Eric's composure, allowed the kid to hoard most of his lucre.

"Everyone in positions?" All the kids had assembled their sleeping bags in tight formation around the television.

"Okay, not that close, guys. C'mon, you're gonna burn your eyes out." Aaron put his hands to his face and flopped around as if he'd just had his eyes flash-burned with acid, as the other kids smiled. Before Bruce and Anthony joined in on the squirming, Jacob pushed them all back a few paces. "Chill out, I don't want you smashing your heads against the table. If you cracked your skulls open, I'd really get in trouble with Aunt Emily. So if you kill yourselves, do it on your own watch, alright?"

"Okay," Aaron agreed.

"That seems fair," Anthony nodded without thinking, and Bruce and Anthony seemed to get into a brief competitive nod-off, heads bobbing like hyperactive parakeets as Jacob slid the DVD into the player.

"Remote?" Jacob stated and held his hand back as if ordering a scalpel. When a beat passed and no remote appeared in his hand, he turned around and again asked, "remote?"

"Should be on the table, I think," Aaron turned to the table behind them.

"Dude, clearly it's not on the table. Is it on the arm of the couch? Where's your grandma keep it?"

"Up her butt," offered Bruce, and giggled far in excess of what his witticism reasonably afforded.

Aaron stood over the couch arm. Evidently, it wasn't there either . . . .

"It was kind of under the couch." Eric handed Jacob the remote. "I kind of saw it, like, poking out when we came down."

"My man with the X-ray vision." Kid paid back for his little grabby-hands before. He could speedbag Emily's tits if he made sure these three animals didn't pile-drive each other through the table. But why worry, it wasn't his house; hell, wasn't even his nephew, really, and wasn't a touch of chaos part of the fun of a sleepover anyway?

Rockin' Ricky Rialto and the tune "Christmas (Baby Please Come Home)" kicked off the opening to the sleepover classic, and Jacob left them to their devices.

*

"So which did you think was scarier, Gremlins or Krampus?" Aaron asked, as the four boys huddled in their sleeping bags.

"They weren't scary," Bruce responded.

"Yeah they weren't that scary but they were good, I thought," Anthony offered, ever the conciliatory peacemaker.

"Yeah, they were good to watch." In the obscuring dark, Bruce felt less incentive to take a stark position and see who would follow his lead. It was almost freeing to not feel attention thrust upon him, and he closed his eyes and felt relaxed.

"They were both good movies. I liked Gremlins more. I liked the effects better and the main characters," opined Eric.

Bruce made a grunting noise that could be either a challenge or a concession. It was as if he was too tired or lazy to speak, but couldn't let Eric say something without some notation in the ledger that he'd officially responded.

The Krampus DVD had a big point-of-no-return scratch in the back, and the film had frozen about a quarter of the way into the movie. Eric had taken the DVD to the bathroom and done something with it, rubbed it with a pad maybe, doing a good enough job to make the DVD work again. Bruce let Eric have his crowning moment without comment; he could see why Aaron kept him around, if only for selfish reasons. Eric made up for his lack of personality or interest with administrative efficiency.

A few beats of silence later, as Bruce pondered what to say, and Anthony opened the floor back up with, "Anyone know any scary stories?"

Anthony flurried and squirmed as if electrocuted, a second-wind of excitement for what was to come.

But no one had anything.

Candyman? No one had seen the movie, just knew that you had to say the name three times in the mirror and he'd appear with a hook for a hand. Could be fun to try, but they were riddled with candy, stomachs grossly saddled with junk. All except Eric rolled around in their sleeping bags to find that ideal resting position that didn't put too much pressure on their swollen stomachs.

"One time, a woman went to a gas station and there was a creepy guy who worked there who was trying to tell her something, and she got scared so she drove away but what he was trying to say was 'There's something in your car,' and when she got out of the car she saw there was a hook left in her door handle." That was Aaron's confused contribution, and the closest approximation the boys had to the creaky old urban legends they felt should be shared around imagined campfires, or, more realistically, in darkened basements filled with discarded candy wrappers and fart fumes.

"I know one," said Eric, in a suppressed, husky voice, as he was resting flatly on his chest.

"Is it a good one?" asked Bruce. He wanted to go to sleep. He had hoped that Jacob would come down after Gremlins and do that thing adults do where they say it's time to go to bed for some arbitrary reason, as if all four kids had the same natural bedtime. But no one did. To raise the stakes high enough for Eric to reconsider the propriety of unspooling his no-doubt stupid tale, Bruce continued: "It better be a good one, is all I'm saying."

"No idea if it's good. I never told it to anyone, so probably not."

"Hmm, I don't know about that, then. It's late, only time for good ones." Bruce only sighed again and said "hope it's a good one," as the other two boys whispered, "tell it."

"There's not much to tell." Eric sounded almost short of breath, as if fighting internally about whether to bother. "There was a man about Jacob's age, your Uncle Jacob. He was very smart, and could do very important things, if he thought about it enough. But he was unmotivated," and here Eric struggled a bit for the correct wording. "And fell in with the wrong crowd," he decided upon, as the other boys, not entirely able to parse what that expression meant, nodded in the dark or said "okay" if only to show they were still listening, if not entirely understanding. "Meaning he followed others when he shouldn't."

Bruce rolled onto his back, eyes closed, and was already losing interest in where this was going.

"And he knew better. And he was very smart, smart in a way that others didn't know what to do with him or how to handle him. And it was a problem, and he wanted to get away but he couldn't really figure out a good way to do it. His parents, they cared about him a lot, but they were at a loss, like, they didn't know the best thing to do for him. People were always looking for him. It's hard to explain, it's all a bit different than what we are used to. Some of these people looking for him were really mean, and could do terrible, terrible things."

"What kind of things?" Aaron interjected, goading Eric into filling out the story with the requisite macabre details needed for a stinky-basement yarn.

"Oh, bad things."

"You have to say what kind of bad things, that's how the stories work," Anthony offered helpfully.

"Yeah, that's what's supposed to make the stories good," Bruce said to the ceiling in his back-stroke position.

"Okay. When they'd caught some of the boy's friends, they tried to make them talk."

"I thought he was an old person like Jacob, now he's a boy!" Bruce scolded.

"They went after the boy's friends to find him when he disappeared. They tied up his friends and put them all in a chamber made of a kind of glass that you could see through but never break, and each glass wall in the chamber had all these small holes.

"When they realized the friends really wouldn't talk to reveal the boy's whereabo-, where the boy was, they let out an animal, like a raccoon, that would stick out its nose through the holes, and would stick its nose in their bodies, one at a time, so everyone else could watch. And after someone had their insides sucked out, the people looking for the boy would tell the remaining friends: 'We'll sift through their insides and find out what we need. We'll find out what we need, eventually. Just tell us what we need to know and save yourself.' But they wouldn't do it, they wouldn't tell."

"Whoa," said Aaron. "Cool."

"How could a raccoon do that, though, raccoons don't eat people." Anthony posed it more like a question.

214

"He said it was like a raccoon, not actually a raccoon," Bruce said sternly.

"Yeah, he said it was like a raccoon, maybe it looks like a raccoon but it's like, a raccoon that people experimented on so now it's like, a crazy raccoon that can eat brains," Aaron explained with mounting excitement.

"And there were other things, too." As Eric continued with a distracted sort of sadness the din died down so they could all listen, and they prompted him to articulate each allusion, like the frogs with the nails who didn't know any better but if you left them with a person for long enough, they'd make a nest out of their stomach, or the gasping skinny people, all veins and pointed angles, hanging by their shoulders somewhere in something like a dungeon, the only moisture they retained left in their desperate eyes. When Eric gave a name to one of those skinny people he stopped speaking and curled himself up in his bag, and the boys, all in the same spirit, covered their faces like it was all so gross, and giggled, too, even if they weren't sure entirely what he meant.

Aaron was excited for his friend. He had become the center of attention. But Eric seemed to lose his luster for the tale as he was prodded to continue, and Aaron felt bad that the others pressured him so much because Eric obviously hadn't been able to think of an ending.

"So his family shepherded, I mean got him away from all that. This boy was too special to be caught by the type of people looking for him. It would have been terrible. So his family learned a trick to hide him and themselves, make the man, boy, whatever, look different, not even the same age.

"He was trapped, because he could never go back to his own life. He missed the freedom of what he'd had but he was safe with his disguise. And he sometimes wished he'd just died with everyone else. He could feel the presence of the people looking for him, and sometimes when he got mad, or sad, he almost let down his guard and let himself be found, as terrible as that would be."

It was Anthony who after an extended silence asked, "Is that it?"

"Yes," replied Eric.

Bruce made a loud ripping sound.

Anthony laughed.

"Good try, though," Bruce added as a stinger.

"There's a lot that can be added to it, I thought it was interesting. Good job," Aaron soothed.

"Yeah, it was interesting, we can add to it. It can be the story of our sleepovers. We can add to each time until one day we can write it all down," suggested Anthony.

"Best story of the night," Aaron praised.

"Agreed," said Anthony. "It's the story of the sleepover."

"Thanks," Eric said after a pause, sounding vacant and far away. "I didn't expect Bruce to like it. Funny though, I told it for him. Hoping it would perk his ears a bit."

Bruce considered rolling back on his stomach and confronting him with a righteous "oh really?" but was too tired. The vaguely-fun delirium of fatigue that had made Eric's story exotic had been entirely replaced by deadening enervation.

"I liked it just fine, just fine, don't you worry Eric." Bruce was too tired to get a consistent tone to his reply. "Let's all just go to bed."

They agreed, and to bed they went.

*

"Awake, Aaron?" It was Eric.

"Yeah. I can't sleep for some reason."

"Maybe you are still excited about having such a good sleepover."

"Maybe." Aaron liked to think that he was the guardian of his sleepover and couldn't fall asleep until he made sure all his guests were taken care of.

There was no doubt that the other two were asleep. Aaron was divided, because he wanted to keep talking to Eric but he didn't want to run the risk of waking them up.

"You're a good kid," Eric said plaintively from the dark.

"Thanks. You're my friend, too."

Eric sniffed, a laugh. Aaron thought to say something but didn't as his friend seemed to wrestle himself into a suitable sleeping position.

Some time passed, impossible to tell how long in the deep blackness.

"Hey Aaron."

"How'd you know I was still awake?" Aaron was so tired he wasn't even sure if he was talking.

"Your Aunt seems really cool," Eric said quickly, too quickly for Aaron to at first understand him.

"Yeah, she's cool. She's good at kickball."

"Ever see her changing clothes?"

"What!? Ewww, no that's gross. You're gross," Aaron said giddily.

"I'm sure she looks really good changing clothes. Just, really good. Great legs."

"She plays kickball. She can kick the ball pretty far, farther than I can. Not as far as Uncle Jacob but still pretty far."

"Yeah."

Eric stayed motionless for a few minutes.

"Ever see her naked at all?"

"No."

"That makes sense."

Aaron sensed his friend twisting and tussling in his sleeping back, like someone having a bad dream, but he knew Eric was awake.

"I can't do this, I'm sorry, Aaron. I'm sorry. I shouldn't have even said that stuff, I don't know why I did. I guess maybe you'll understand when you're older, but that's not really an excuse. I just don't have mu-, I don't know."

"It's okay. Go to sleep, we will hang out in the morning."

"No, it's - you won't understand, and that's nothing to do with you as a person. You, you're a good kid. I just can't do this anymore. I need to take my chances. I - I'm sorry. I'm so sorry. It was because of Bruce, he wouldn't shut his fucking mouth and it got me upset. That's no excuse, I should know a lot better.

"I'm sorry, I fucked up. I am getting out of here, and you should come with me. Anthony, too, really, all of you. I, I don't know what–" and Eric stopped speaking.

"Can you not sleep because of your story?" Aaron found Eric's curse words disturbing, because whenever Aaron heard one of his parents say them, the other either laughed uproariously or yelled sharply. Curse words provoked a reaction, and Aaron was too tired for all that.

Eric stayed silent, but leaned up, like he'd completed a sit-up.

"I'm sorry, Aaron. I wish you'd never met me. I don't want to be here. I shouldn't be here. I'm stuck. I need to get out of here. It might be even worse if I stayed."

A moment of silence, and then, "I fucked up."

Eric shook his head. It was hopeless. Despair spread through his chest, but it was a forced anguish, as if ritualized, the meaning behind it lost to time. Eric clenched his midsection, gripped and twisted a curlicue of fat on his stomach to lurch himself down the path of the proper self-abasement and shame he knew he must be compelled to feel. But it wasn't there; just anxiety, the overwhelming urge to flee.

"I'm sorry, Aaron," and realizing that would be his departing coda got him into the realm of self-torment and guilt Eric knew he deserved. How quickly that metastasized into furious self-pity, that sterling companion, and he thrust his mind back to the self-hatred, shame and guilt that was his to bear, but too little, too late, that was the rub, wasn't it? Only so much you can take before the inputs don't register. The wick was too frayed and spent to ignite the eager candle.

Eric fled up out of the basement and out of the house.

*

Jacob leaned against the door that led down to the basement. He closed his eyes, eyeballs reverberating wildly behind his lids, and then opened them up again abruptly and, while not moving, swore he was losing his balance.

It was morning, and he was at a loss as to what he should do. He and Emily had woken up together, and she would be coming down any second after brushing her teeth and throwing on some clothes.

To think about that: she was upstairs, just brushing her teeth, picking out what to wear. She should be there forever, permanently getting ready. His chest caved and ached at the thought of that quotidian world, lost to him forever; he wished to

218

return and hide under it like a dog scurrying under the bed when fireworks blasted nearby.

Emily came springing toward him, unwrapped Tootsie Roll in her mouth.

"I see you judging. Yeah, that's right, I'm eating a Tootsie Roll for breakfast. Got to get rid of all this candy eventually anyway."

He blinked.

"They getting dressed down there?" Emily immediately realized it was a weird question, as little boys wouldn't be dressing and undressing together, until she remembered there was a bathroom down there so maybe they were taking turns.

Jacob shook his head.

Emily shrugged, then shrugged more dramatically as a clue for Jacob to speak. She mentally shrugged as she turned away from him and went into the fridge to scrounge.

"Ooh gawd yeah, there's half an iced coffee from yesterday." She ducked her head into the fridge and came back, slurping from a straw. "Natural sweetener," she tried to say about the rest of the Tootsie Roll she'd stuffed in her mouth.

Jacob had thought it would be fun to wake the boys up. Maybe kick them awake, smash them with a pillow. He expected to go downstairs and have it smell grimy like a turtle tank.

"They awake? You know if they want food or anything?"

Jacob blinked and shook his light slightly, at least now in her general direction. Please stop talking, please remain here with me forever.

Following that thought . . .Oh God . . . it got worse. He was the last one to see them all, wasn't he? And what was he doing now, if not delaying? But no, that's, that's not what he was doing, he was, he had to explain himself to this imaginary but conceivable future interlocutor, there, what, no, what was he expected to do?

Tell someone, but how could he, what could he say to make them understand, to prepare them. The few minutes' span from when he'd gone down to check on them and Emily's arrival wasn't enough time; it would never be enough time, years wouldn't be enough time, from when he went down to check and felt the hot-house humidity–

"Just stay up here with me," he implored before she got the next words out of her mouth. Run away with me, he wanted to say. Run away with me, just let's leave together. I didn't do anything, you have to believe me, he started sweating, thoughts of singeing police lights, the lightheadedness of exhaustion, of being taken away, handcuffed and hungry and alone in a police waiting room.

"What?"

Call 911, that's what he needed to do, call 911 and just tell them something terrible has happened. Professionals will come and see I had nothing to do with this, nothing to do, couldn't possibly have, and he despised himself for succumbing to thoughts of self-preservation, but what else could he do, that was a life raft he understood, and Emily, their relationship was something he must cling to–

Downstairs, that hot-house dankness, the sticky presence in the air, the three, irregularly pyramidical puce-colored heaps of crumbling, powdery flesh, the hardened fragments of what could be bone jutting out like moray eels from coral; get a grip, no it wasn't like that, down there for less than thirty seconds, could be wrong, could be wrong, didn't get a good view, somehow he knew Eric was unaccounted for; find Eric, find Eric, find Eric to find out what happened–

"It's okay," he said to himself, to her, to no one, to the world, to manifest that into truth.

He hugged her and wouldn't let go.

<u>NOTES</u>

After completing this story, I didn't really feel like most people would enjoy it, although I liked it and maybe I'm wrong? This is just a premise I've thought about for a while, a sleepover where there are subtle intimations that one of the children is not what he seems, and in a fit of immature pique (because has donning this disguise made him more childlike, or what's the backstory here, exactly?) he reveals something he's not supposed to, immediately regrets it, and must again deal with the disastrous fallout of this life of (supernatural?) hiding. Not sure what else there is to say about it, except that I hope the story worked for you.

If there's any character that's closest to me here, it would be "uncle" Jacob, because I've always enjoyed feeding kids sarcastic or jokey quasi-bullshit explanations until they realize my answers make no damn sense. Teaching critical thinking skills, right? It's the little things in life.

Beholden To The Past, Impatient To The Present, Cheated Of The Future

Grades in law school came down to one test in each class at the end of the semester, exams made up of a series of ambiguous, borderline scenarios subject to interpretation. The test-taker would be graded on identifying factual scenarios that broached the legal doctrines learned during the semester, and, citing precedent and policy arguments, how persuasively the test-taker argued on behalf of their view while acknowledging, but discounting or distinguishing from, any alternative approach. These were colloquially known as "issue spotter" exams, to see how well the students grasped the one thing that law schools claimed to teach, the one thing apparently worth six figures of debt: the ability to "think like a lawyer."

Now here was an issue-spotter alright, Ethan mused darkly from across the street from his apartment building in San Francisco's Tenderloin District. That stream of excretion that just poured out of that squatting homeless man just beside the entrance to his building, was that shit or urine? Oooh, the test taker here did a good job providing evidence for both interpretations. It was purely liquid, and it's undeniable that urine is a liquid. And it was expelled with a uniform texture, no lumps or disruptions caused by an unexpected, uneven solid. So first you are leaning toward it being urine. You are free to mix in policy analysis and common sense, so it must be noted that the downright casual way with which this homeless man ejected this liquid was further evidence it was urine because, surely, any sane person shitting a jetstream of amber-colored liquid wouldn't be so nonchalant about it, would surely have a panicked, discomfited expression in preparation for his who-knows-what-disease-related imminent death.

But the contrary evidence, always have to consider the contrary interpretation. Here, it was best *not* to consider the contrary evidence – see this was a tough test to really embrace because the implications were so disturbing – but in law school you have to dig deep, don't you? Men don't generally squat to pee, now do they? And the nonchalance could be explained away by the sociopathic tendencies of these Tenderloin homeless, although that's risky to say around here in San Francisco, especially around professors or his sensitive law school classmates, who, while doing everything in their power to live far, far away from these rough neighborhoods, exalted the homeless as holy, oppressed victims and rendered them incapable of moral condemnation. And a purely liquid stream of shit, of course, could easily be the consequence of that hapless man's pharmacological ingestion. There was a reason why San Francisco had municipal employees on designated daily "poop patrols," quite the fitting, if too on the nose metaphor for how this City attempted to sweep away the shitty consequences of its naivete.

What a world. Ethan stared for too long, as if what he witnessed meant something significant, as that accumulating waste of whatever really spoke to him and his condition. He only briefly noted that the way the excretion clumped didn't seem too much like urine. And oooh, one last policy consideration, the cockeyed crazy laugh and pointing of another derelict across the street. Now, experience demonstrates that to get a rise out of that fellow would take more than pure piss.

I think we know what conclusion this balance of factors leads us to.

To think, there was a Hilton hotel not too far from here. Ethan sometimes saw guests, usually Europeans or Australians, making their first tentative steps to "explore" their surroundings, mild concern blooming into bewilderment, or, for the middle-aged men with families, a kind of tight-faced, constricting embarrassment mixed with a need to save face and maintain the patriarch status, as if reconciling themselves to the emasculating conclusion that they'd unwittingly blundered their family into a bad situation.

Tourists got to leave, at least, or realize quickly that they should just stick to North Beach or Fisherman's Wharf. Ethan had no such luck, because this was where UC Hastings College of the Law was, and where the "cheap" apartments were, and hadn't he initially been excited to find such a cheap apartment in the "Theater District" in walking distance to his law school? And he wasn't exactly a hay seed, he'd known the reputation of the Tenderloin and the Mid-Market area, but there was something about taking out those loans, knowing that he was paying for this shithole apartment with borrowed money, in pursuit of a career that looked ever more dim (both in terms of financial and personal reward) that poisoned whatever seedy glamor there'd been in his little adventure.

Fuck it. He avoided the shit-stream, went up to his pre-war apartment ("yeah it's pre-war, the Revolutionary War," the usual joke whenever he'd brought someone over), grabbed his books and laptop and headed to Civil Procedure.

*

"Howdy," Arkady greeted him with his masculinized Dr. Sbaitso's voice as Ethan set up at the adjacent seat. "How goes it with you this fine day." Arkady was twenty-nine, had a PhD in cell biology from UCLA and had lived in America for over a decade, and Ethan wasn't yet sure how much of his labored speech was an intentional Eastern European affectation. Whatever it was, it was always shot through with sarcasm, and Ethan and Arkady took the unavoidable cynicism engendered by the law school life and ran with it, far beyond what their colleagues countenanced. The indignities of law school life were just extra potent feed on already fertile, highly cynical soil.

Arkady was fond of pointing out and laughing about how he was almost thirty with a fucking PhD in cell biology, had prior job opportunities ranging from internships to measly research stipends, and spent his summer before attending law school stocking shelves in a grocery store. Ethan, a California native and twenty-four (which felt old to him but was nothing to Arkady), had spent his two years since graduating with his English degree waiting tables, accomplishing not much of anything other than pedestrian road trips up and down the West Coast, knowingly deluding himself that, in the rudderless sinking ship of his life, his good grades in college would be the escape boat that'd get him ashore to Good Law School Island. Except his LSAT didn't go as well as planned and here he was, not at Stanford (although that was unrealistically expensive) or UC Berkeley or even UCLA but at UC Hastings. More like when he'd gotten off that escape boat into that escape hatch, he couldn't tell which way was up, and he'd been led only down, down, down into this churning vortex of debt and delay.

And regardless, in law school land there was no up.

It was halfway through the second semester of 1L year. Ethan and Arkady liked sitting in the middle of the lecture hall, toward the side. Close enough to listen, far enough away to daydream as needed, and at a fine angle to stare at the comely classmates.

In that regard, Civ Pro was stacked. There was Annie Yee and her best friend Alisha Peirera, their contrasting looks complemented each other quite nicely and who always sat near the front. Plus, there was Jana Stanton, Kate Fujita, Tatiana Anderson, Amber Mosdale, Amy Apricot (could there be a cuter name?) . . . and that was just the cream of the Civ Pro crop. In his two years off in the "real world," Ethan had forgotten the collegiate joy of having a repeat, captive audience of lovely women he got to see day in and day out, outside the strict confines of a work environment.

Ethan turned and watched Jana, and in particular her graceful, muscular legs on display in a spring skirt, as she bounded up the stairs to the seats behind him. He and Arkady nodded at all their not-quite-friends in the class, the module mates (called "mods") they shared every class with. Civ Pro, being a combined class, was a large class made up of three mods, which contributed to the diversity of welcomed visual distractions.

Ethan eyed Annie as she came into the class. She had a lithe, quick-silver intelligence about her, a mind always on, as if always penetrating and exploring the layers of what was being said to her. She always seemed to be actively interested in whatever the other person was saying, as if she truly believed she could learn from others and was not just waiting for her opportunity to talk. Even with whatever Alisha was telling her just now, she looked engaged and interested, and what possibly new interesting stuff could best friends share each and every day? Arkady was Ethan's "best friend" at law school and 90% of what they said to each other was filler and pablum, designed to pass the time, unburden grievances, or just get a rise out of each other.

Whether Annie's visible engagement was an admirable personality trait or the kind of superficial high society and good breeding inculcated by her father, the well-respected, trailblazing Chinese-American Northern District judge Albert Yee, who could say. There was that quality to wealthy, well-bred people; even when they were eminently privileged, their good manners and evident competence made it hard to entirely resent them. Especially not when they were like Annie, who resembled something like a sexy, blonde, high-cheek-boned amber feline.

"No boobs though," Arkady had said at the beginning of the semester, as they'd talked all about the lovely ladies in their classes. Ethan preferred that slim look anyway; better she not have *everything* going for her. Besides, her travel companion Alisha made up for that in spades; expansively busty where Annie was slender and toned; compact where Annie was tall, even brunette to Annie's peroxide whitish blonde, which Ethan hadn't realized wasn't even her natural color until Arkady first pointed out the improbability of a half-Chinese woman having hair the color of muted straw.

"Kuuurrrr-man, what's up." That was Fujita, who always sat in front of them, purring out his last name. She probably noticed him appreciating Annie. Not that he thought she was jealous in any appreciable way or interested in him in any way other than as a friend, but she always seemed to initiate conversation whenever the focus had been on someone else.

In law school, you are usually referred to by your last name, and Ethan had the benefit of a two-syllable name that produced a glottal stop and that ended with "man." Even in his ultra-gunner first semester, he suspected that competitors or other students who found him grating couldn't completely dislike him because of his savory surname. He'd never bothered to point out that it was pronounced "ker-mane."

"Woah, what's your background?" Fujita was referring to the artwork that made up his desktop background. "That's really pretty."

"That's nice, right? It's called 'Ahmi in Egypt,' I think. I don't know why it's called that. It's by this lesser-known female artist who was like a contemporary of Georgia O'Keefe but not really as famous." While the artwork was muddled-up with all the folders on his desktop, one could still make out a blazing wish-upon-a-star within the periwinkle blue, amidst the darkening crepuscular sky. On the left side of the canvass there was an ornate, lacey pattern befitting a royal's bed in an Arab fantasia, shot through with brightly-colored greens, yellows and blues.

"It looks like something out of Disney, it looks like Fantasia. I like the swan in the bottom." The bottom foreground showed a white swan, flecked with yellowish hue, adorned with a regal gold-bond necklace and crown. "Kerman, I had no idea you were such an art person."

"Well, I don't know if I'd go that far, but you know, there's a lot more to me than hand-raising in class."

"Apparently. Well, I'm impressed."

"How've you been? Still living the dream."

"Aren't we all? Maybe you are, I know you love Civ Pro, it's your jam. Maybe not as much as beautiful art, but still."

"I love nothing about the law."

"You love raising your hand and getting answers right, and you can't deny that," Fujita said, face pinched mock-accusingly.

"That certainly cannot be denied," Arkady interjected, tilting his head and smiling, almost as if conceding a point on his friend's behalf.

"Well I mean, who doesn't like answering something correctly, am I right?"

"No experience with the law is ever going to beat the rush you get in raising your hand and giving the right answer."

"Pshh, you mock until you're asking me for my outlines, Fujita."

"Oh I wasn't mocking, not at all. I wish I could care that much about class."

"Be grateful that you have better and wider interests that keep you doing more important things. Class participation is a complete waste of time."

"Amen to that. It is literally worthless; it factors not one iota in your final grades." Arkady pronounced it "eye-oh-da." It didn't take much for Arkady to translate banter of any type into an attack on the law school culture or grading system.

"Better to answer a question you know than risk being called on when you haven't done the reading. See, that's what I'm worried about today, for sure," Fujita said.

"Just tap me on the knee or the foot when you need an answer and I'll whisper it in your ear."

"Hah, will do Kerman."

Fujita turned to face the front of the class, Ethan nodding knowingly while Arkady smiled and looked impressed. Arkady leaned in animatedly as if to say something, but didn't. Ethan knew "the sum and substance" of what he meant to say, sum and substance being another of those artificial legalese phrases that invaded their everyday world. Arkady had a theory that proper flirting required a sensual, tactile element, such as the talk of a touch, the use of a whisper, and should also reference future actions and promises, a subconscious anchor to reel the receiver back in. Ethan was skeptical, but indicated that he'd least listened and made a show of it in front of his friend. In a sense, he thought, I'm friend-flirting with Arkady; what else could be said about demonstrating subtly to a friend that you paid attention to their previous advice?

Fujita's lower back tattoo crested above the rim of her pants as she leaned forward. Ethan could never tell exactly what it was and never asked, piecing it together and visualizing the whole of it with each glimpse. Something like a rather-complicated combination of a red star or tribal shape that must have held some meaning to her, although the amount of meaning that could be attached to a tattoo that was best appreciated when bent over, who knew. Ethan and Arkady met eyes about that too, giving each other the molasses-slow nod of 'that's what I'm talking about' commiseration.

Ethan kept his eye on the teacher and the notes on his computer, with only scant glances at the lovely female forms and other students' computers. A fair amount of people appeared to be drifting off, indicated by a bright-colored or garish website logo popping up on someone's computer before being quickly minimized.

This attention he paid in class was purely vestigial, some misplaced loyalty or uncorrected instinct from his college days, where participation actually mattered. Here, it really all came down to that one final fucking test at the end of the year. He'd done fine his first semester, he guessed, B's, one A-, although one B-, too. But that's all: just fine. There was no hope of getting a Big Firm summer position with B's at Hastings; there was no hope of transferring to a top 14 law school with B's, either. There was some feeling of pride, perhaps, in preparing his own notes, relying only on commercial outlines as back-ups, at paying attention in class, but that was thin gruel, like being proud of trying. His focus on classroom participation was a sign of inertia, of failing to adapt, of doing what you know rather than doing something – like relying exclusively on outlines or joining study groups or networking around for copies of past exams – that would be more efficient and effective.

Ethan volunteered to answer a question about Gray. v. American Radiator. He explained the ruling – that the Illinois Supreme Court held an out-of-state company could be sued in-state because the company presumed there was a substantial chance its products would be incorporated into water heaters sold in the state – and referenced the policy considerations of International Shoe, the whole "sufficient minimum contacts" that did not "offend traditional notions of fair play and substantial justice" stuff, and the words came out as a means to an end, passcodes unthinkingly recited to get access to the teacher's approval.

Just as when he was a child and he knew but never could actually imagine what it must be like to eventually work for a living, he could never imagine circumstances where he might have to actually grapple substantively with the type of material he'd just been spouting. He definitely knew that there'd never be a time when he'd crave doing so.

*

How'd Ethan and Arkady become friends, exactly? Orientation day, and at the first orientation mixer it seemed like people already knew each other, how that was Ethan wasn't sure. Ethan had listened in on others' conversations, made small talk, but couldn't help ignoring the fact that these were literally his academic competitors. Law school operated on a strict grading curve: there had to be 20% of people getting As, 40% getting Bs, 40% getting Cs, something like that, meaning if everyone submitted flawless exams there'd need to be some pretextual frivolousness to get that required distribution. Maybe in those situations it'd come down to hunting for the exams submitted without hanging commas, or the A's would go to the students who properly used semicolons rather than a colon, or en dashes instead of the em dashes for their long pauses.

And the closer a classmate was in age, the more they felt like a rival. The older folks, perhaps realizing the inherently petty nature of academia by dint of their wider experience, had a more relaxed view on things. Arkady, with his distinct accent, impressive science credentials, and vague resemblance to a young, bulkier, non-union Eastern European Harrison Ford stand-in, was an inviting, interesting reprieve from the pressure and combativeness he felt simmer inside him around the other prospective classmates his age. And, while everyone else had talked about what they wanted to do with their law degree, Arkady was the only one who laughed at Ethan's admission that he just hoped he didn't end up homeless and penniless near the Golden Gate Bridge, giving hand jobs to Mexican day laborers for wooden nickels. (Having never gone to a graduate program in a large city, Ethan didn't yet realize that no jokes were allowed about poverty; or, as a Caucasian, he was not permitted to make mention of a person of color – no matter what the context – unless such person was being championed and a white person's ignorance or unhappiness served as the punchline).

A typical Ethan joke. There was a false modesty there, true; he'd been confident that he'd do well in law school. He figured he was only a few years out of college and could get back in the habit of academia.

And awkward formality invited irreverence, didn't it, someone to ease tensions, get a few laughs, point out that hey, this is all pretty weird, right?

Apparently not, based on everyone else's reactions.

When no one else responded, other than looking momentarily flustered or askance, he'd followed up with, "well, I hope by graduation I'd be at least earning real nickels. I mean, with that amount of practice I should be able to show something for my efforts."

"Once you do, put in a good word for me! The legal career is all about networking," Arkady had responded excitedly.

And a friendship had been born.

*

"Oh yes, thank you Jesus," was how Arkady greeted the beers that arrived in advance of their dinners. He took a hearty quaff of his Brew Free or Die IPA, a beer from 21st Amendment Brewing Company, which was native to San Francisco. "That is good, very good. As much as I hate to credit anything that comes from San Francisco, I must acknowledge this is good. Although IPAs were taken from the British so who can say, it's not like the idea of an IPA came from this shithole city."

"Too bold a taste for these types."

"Exactly."

Ethan took a smaller drink of his cider.

"How can you drink that, it's so sweet. It's like drinking candy. Ciders are for dates. You need a man's drink, to strengthen your resolve." Arkady made a fist as he spoke. He was a weird one, because he was both kidding and not, which, Ethan supposed, could characterize much of their banter.

"You gotta get with the times, old man. I don't think alcohol is the thing that's going to strengthen any resolve here. I'm drinking it for the exact opposite reason."

"Drinking a cider, that's one thing I will never do. Actually, did you know ciders predate beer, so it is in fact I who am the trailblazer, drinking a newer form of alcohol. But you are definitely right, my friend, about that last part, cheers to that." They clinked glasses. "Must drink so I can pay the bill without screaming."

"Drink enough so we are only screaming on the inside."

"Well, that's always the case."

They descended upon their burgers as if they were famished.

"And this is nothing, burgers and a few drinks, and still my heart drops with each bill, more borrowed money down the shitter. It'd be nice to be out eating at, what is it, Chez Panisse like some of our more blessed classmates, but that is not the lot for us," Arkady said, surveying the emptying plate as if lamenting the decadent expense of it all.

"In a few years after we graduate and the interest starts accruing and we are working slave hours for slave wages at some shitty dump solo shop we'll be reminiscing about the days when we had the time and money to eat burgers."

"Kill me now sweet Jesus."

"I don't know what I expected, what was I thinking, fucking Hastings, coming to the most expensive fucking city in the country for the honor of going to this podunk shit school, and I did alright I guess last semester, but not big firm good-"

"In this legal economy now, you think fucking Latham and Watkins gives two shits about us losers at Hastings when they have Stanford and Berkeley next door, and even those rich kids are worried about paying off their loans? Where does that leave the rest of us? Not like even if I did really well I would get hired at those white shoe firms, think they want an immigrant like me there? I don't help their diversity numbers and I have an accent."

"Well don't worry, right, weren't we told by Hastings' administration that ninety-five percent of us get jobs after graduation?" Ethan asked mockingly.

"Yeah please, they count jobs at fucking Burger King as employed for their purposes. Fucking snakes. It's so interesting, we all knew this was bullshit coming in, yet we still all did it, didn't we? I mean, your sweetheart Annie Yee did great last semester, or so I've heard, and can get a good job, and she could get that job anyway because of her daddy, but for the rest of us? There should have been a warning that this school was just for connected kids who needed a law license stamped before they could make use of Daddy's connections. No one else cares about this shithole."

"Well, at least the women at our school are hotter than at the good schools. And at least we aren't Golden Gate University."

"True. I mean we are screwed, but at least not literally retarded like the people who end up at Golden Gate. I mean, good God those people just needed to spell their names correctly on the LSAT to get into Golden Gate.

"By that logic, why don't we just transfer to, what is it, University of Arizona, where the girls are supposed to be the hottest? Maybe that's not a bad idea, if we are going down the tubes, might as well enjoy it. I wonder why it is that the women in our class seem better looking than I imagined. I have a few theories." Arkady always had theories. "The most beautiful girls from California end up at USC, of course, The University of Spoiled Children."

"Better schools call it the University of Second Choice, but what would that make us?"

"Good point. The really high-achieving girls went to Stanford or, for those with the mousy, hippyish bent, Berkeley. The girls from respectable families who were pretty enough to get pulled away from their studies and invited to parties in college and didn't do as well their first couple of semesters came here. They had good enough upper middle class breeding and sense to be good-looking, and enough social instincts to not be complete workaholic losers like the Stanford people. A depressing but true fact is that people from wealthy families are generally better looking, because, traditionally, a high-achieving male would attract a good-looking female and then have reasonably good-looking offspring. That's what we have here: good-looking, upper middle class offspring, but not superbly smart, not the cream-of-the-crop, not Berkeley or Stanford material."

"That gives us a fighting chance."

"Maybe you. No one wants a foreigner like me."

"Well, find out for yourself, come out to Bar Review tonight." That's what the weekly organized drinking night was called: Bar Review, har dee har har. Ethan already knew Arkady wouldn't go. To his discredit, Arkady liked socializing early and didn't like staying out too late. When the crowds came, he wanted to leave, which didn't serve him well in such a densely-populated city like San Francisco. Ethan had pled his case earlier in their friendship as to why Arkady should go out to Bar Review, but to no avail. Ethan hated going to social events by himself – it was like he was branded a loser upon entry, wasn't everyone wondering 'what, he couldn't bring a single friend?' – and he didn't necessarily like drinking, even, but he'd drink as long as someone else was willing. Better than going back home alone, to his dingy apartment, to studying this shit, and for what?

The prospect of collecting those wooden nickels per hand job loomed larger and larger, not so much of a joke these days.

"No, I'm good. You should go, though, I bet your girl Annie will be there. You take Annie, I wouldn't mind, what do you call it, wing-manning with Alisha, not mind that at all."

"Then come out then."

"Nahhhhh, you know."

"Figure I'd try."

"You should go try and see if something might happen with Annie. You gunners stick together, I think she recognized a bit of herself in your go-get-'em attitude first semester."

"Yeah, except without the grades to rationalize it, my gunner days are over, fucking waste that was. But you think so?"

"Ehhhh, I saw her glance back at you a few times."

"Really?"

"Ehhhh." Arkady smiled. "I'm not in the business of giving good news, it doesn't come naturally to me, as you can tell, not to any of us ex-Soviets. But, maybe."

"Ever hear anything?"

"Please, you think I talk to people?"

Ethan rocked back and forth a bit in his chair, a warm glow inside that made him slightly delirious, one of those fleeting feelings that seem to firmly bolt the skewed universe into a steady position where one can understand, finally, why it is that everyone else seems optimistic about life. Potentiality, that's what it is.

"You know what I'd be worried about, for real?" Ethan began. "You know that phenomenon when people are near a steep edge and some part of their psyche can't deal with the anxiety and responsibility of not-falling, so they just want to jump to end the tension?"

"High Place Phenomenon, it's called. Remember, I'm a former scientist."

"Unimaginative name. Anyway, I always think about Annie Yee's name. I mean, Annie Yee? God she's lucky she grew up pretty and smart and everything to dodge that bullet."

"What do you mean, her Dad is Chinese, there are a lot of Yees there, you know."

"Annie Yee? It sounds too close to Anally. I'm always so afraid of calling her Anally by accident, part of me just wants to do it to end the tension."

Arkady closed his eyes and shook his head in a bubble of laughter.

"I mean it, if I had that name growing up, I'd be so terrified of people calling me Anally, that could so easily could have been a nickname she could have gotten stuck with."

"You have some serious problems, my friend, I don't think I can help you. Maybe she was called that, and she overcame that nickname and that's why she's so smart and hard-working and pleasant, because she suffered, you know, it built character."

"Well, that's maybe a 'deep into a relationship' type of conversation."

"Well, get working on that and get us an answer."

By this point, they'd gotten another round of drinks, a cooling-off interregnum.

"You have yet to make a date with that, what was her name, Zip, Zippy or something?" Arkady asked, his parched throat sated.

"Tzipora."

"Zee-pora, these American names," Arkady shook his head. "Let me see her picture again."

Ethan told him to give him a second and pulled up Tzipora's dating profile.

"Not bad, not bad," Arkady formed the words around the fries he'd just popped in his mouth. "Not bad at all, a fine specimen right there. Good teeth."

"That what they cared about the most in your country, good teeth?"

"Hey, I miss my country more and more these days. Never thought I'd say that but when the Fannie Mae debt collectors come to break my knees I can escape back, Soviet flight in reverse. You can have Annie and Tzipora as girlfriends, I only have Fannie Mae. Why'd you not set up a date with her already?"

"I don't know, I have no excuse, really." Other than that things are always better in the expectation, and he was wittier online than in the flesh. Online flirtations could be returned to at your leisure, the comments timed and well-curated, he didn't have to compete with other distractions, worry about his breath or his posture or what he was doing or whether hairs were out of place, either atop his head or a nose hair sticking out.

"Well, I suggest you do, as I'm sure other guys are plotting for this Tzipora as we speak. Good teeth like that, after all."

"I'll have to get a date with her before some aspiring dentist cuts in line. Hey, I'll make you a deal, you come out tonight and I'll set up a date with her."

Arkady guffawed into his beer. "Are you crazy, I don't care that much. Think I'm going to sacrifice my quiet, dignified night at home for that."

"You mean jerking off?"

"Well, that's part of it. Tzipora, that's a Jewish name. You know Ethan, I'm technically Jewish. My grandmother on my mother's side was Jewish, and since it's matrilineal, which I think was done to increase their numbers on a technicality, very shrewd, these Jews, I mean, us Jews. So, I'm technically Jewish. Think that will help me get a Big Law job?"

"You can try to put that on your resume. You can put that in your skills section: 'Can Be A Jew when Needed.'"

"I'll take what I can get."

They finished their food and brews and eventually got the check. Arkady's shifting discomfort with the growing crowds and boisterousness was rubbing off on Ethan, best to get out of here.

"So now that we're done eating dude, you'll love this, let me tell you about this shit that I witnessed outside my apartment before Civ Pro today."

*

That night's Bar Review was down in the Mission District, the largely Mexican neighborhood engaged in a tug of war with a kind of party-forward gentrification. This resulted in, Ethan sensed, a kind of covert warfare between the well-off and the old-timers. Raucousness generally made him uncomfortable, especially raucousness amidst resentment, although he had to admit that, if he ever wanted to impress someone with an actual City-like atmosphere, the Mission would do, crowded as it was with bars, restaurants, and late-night vendors. There were homeless and vagrants here, like everywhere else in San Francisco, but unlike the Tenderloin it wasn't a neighborhood that seemed composed exclusively, like some experiment gone terribly awry, of the homeless and drug addicts. (Chinatown for the Chinese, Castro for the queer community, Fisherman's Wharf for the tourists, the Tenderloin for the crackheads). Rather, the seedy element in the Mission felt more like the expected byproduct of the street traffic and excitement, perhaps exacerbated somewhat by the increasing rents and the drunk kids with disposable incomes.

It was pretty packed tonight at Doc's Clock, a cash-only beer bar with shuffleboard that appealed to the post-collegiate crowd. Ethan hadn't been to a Bar Review for the longest time, and he was pleasantly surprised how many "Ker-mans" he got while waiting in the unvariegated line-mass for a drink. Each such utterance was tinged with the friendly subtext of, 'surprised to see you here!' He saw Karla Melendez, who he hadn't spoken to since last semester, who gave him an interestingly warm greeting, which he made note of. That, and how nicely she filled out her shirt.

The reputation he'd earned last semester, as a hard-working, no-nonsense 'gunner," focused on his grades to the exclusion of all else, might have given him an unexpected allure. Perhaps people thought his gunnerism had naturally resulted in good grades, that he was going somewhere, and he'd be a good person to know. Maybe they figured his grades had been so damn good that he could now afford to lighten up this semester, or maybe people just liked seeing a new face. Or maybe, it occurred to him as both self-evident and depressing, that in a school training students for a career that was notoriously cut-throat and aggressive, being perceived as cut-throat and aggressive was considered attractive.

With drinks in hand, Ethan joined in conversation with Jaime, a charming fellow 1L who'd always been pleasant. Jaime was a gay Cuban-raised, Florida-bred man in his thirties who had worked in public health in DC and then moved to San Francisco before deciding to go to law school. Jaime was regaling a group of students with some stories about past relationships, including a few where he'd agreed to sleep with some of his lonely straight female friends from time-to-time.

"Really?" Ethan was fascinated. "They'd sleep with you knowing you weren't straight? Was that weird for you?"

"Kinda," Jaime responded with his heavy Cuban accent, sultry enough to serve as empirical evidence supporting his story. "But sometimes when you are horny sex is just sex, sex with a friend, it was good times."

"Wow. That's amazing dude, I'm jealous."

A few beers into the evening, on top of the drinks he'd had earlier with Arkady, and here came Annie, with Alisha in tow.

"Kerman!" Annie bellowed as she navigated her way through the morass of familiar faces. "I didn't know you were coming out."

"You know, figured it's the second semester, time to try and change things up."

"Nice!" Annie seemed to really mean that; she seemed actually happy to see him, a prospect which dizzied and somehow rattled him, as if he'd realized there'd been some fatal error in computing and these results couldn't possibly be right. He had liked the security of the classroom interactions, where the banter had its natural constraints in the ebb-and-flow. Here, he was unrestrained, and that wasn't good: structure suited him.

Annie looked and smelled nice, a spritzy, floral scent, which complemented her uplifting feline grace and intelligence. He wondered what had first compelled her to dye her hair blonde. It was a shame that all the interesting questions were considered impolite to lead with.

"You come to these Bar Reviews often?" He settled for cliche.

"Yeah we come out like every week." The obvious "we" meant her and Alisha.

"No way, really, you are able to balance that and all your on-point studying and journals and, I don't know, being on the real Bar Review?"

"Hah, no, I make it work. After this semester I'm going to really chill it out. If I'm lucky enough to get a firm job this summer I'm absolutely going to coast on through the rest of these two years, hah, cherish the time, get an easy schedule and explore as much as I can before having to work 24/7 for the rest of my life."

"Sounds like a plan." Ethan took a conspicuous swig of his beer, biding time on what to say. He needed to keep the conversation flowing.

"Hey, what are you drinking?" Ethan took the beer from his lips, tipping the drink toward her as if just struck with a brilliant insight.

"Nothing yet."

"What do you want, I'm going back to the bar." He took a larger-than-usual gulp of his beer to finish it off.

"I'll go up with you. I'm not letting you get me a drink, but I'll go up with you."

"Ahh."

"In another context I'd let you get me the drink, but not at Bar Review. From one broke 1L to another, no way."

"Ahhh, okay, so at another time, if I asked you out, you'd let me get you the drink, right?"

"Maybe," and the sideways glance, the development of that unexpected smile, the symmetrical beauty of those defined cheek-bones . . . there was an image he wished he could freeze-frame and hang up on the interior wall of his mind, for whenever he was anxious or stressed and needed something soothing and lovely to distract himself with.

"Ahh, let me get you a drink now, when you're a big high-powered corporate lawyer you can repay the favor. Here, stand in front of me, your feminine wiles and . . . feminineness will get the bartender's attention way before me." Ugh, that was a confusing jumble of words.

"The bartender's a woman," she laughed. "I think whatever feminine benefits I get aren't going to work now."

"Everyone's attracted to beauty."

There was some combination of a snicker, a non-disparaging eye-roll, and a smile.

They didn't get to talk much more that night. Alisha returned and consumed Annie's attention, and then others did, too, as everyone seemed to love Annie. Eventually some more raucous, attention-seeking members of the Bar Review tilted the natural orbit of the evening toward themselves, people pulled this way and that. Ethan left relatively early, and it seemed everyone else was still there when he left; he didn't want to pay for an Uber and getting back too late in his neighborhood was never a great idea.

Annie was the only person he tracked down to say good-bye to. The way she pivoted to focus her attention upon him, the way she said "ohh, you're leaving so soon?," the way she pulled him in for a hug, the way she said "will definitely see you soon": it was unbelievable to him that she really seemed to mean it.

*

Back home, and the good tiding evaporated, in the sense that someone can recall pleasure but can never bring readily to mind whatever made the experience so vivid. He should still feel happy about how the night went, and he supposed he did, theoretically. Hard to think of that when back home, his depressing five hundred square foot studio, his clumped up sheets on his unmade Murphy bed, the pre-war bucket-of-a-kitchen-sink that took a few seconds to spurt out water, the two options being boiling hot or freezing cold; and, perhaps worse, finding what must unmistakingly be mouse droppings in the drawer that housed his utensils.

He'd pretended for a while that he was his apartment's only occupant, even though he'd even seen the little fucker once before. About a month ago, Ethan had been watching TV, sitting in his all-purpose rolling desk chair, which leaned up against the foot of his Murphy bed. He had one other chair in his living room, an old wicker chair which he never used. While eating pretzels,

YOU KNOW IT'S TRUE

he'd glanced over to his left and saw the round, larger-than-expected mouse, white as snow and completely stationary, at the foot of his wicker chair. He'd looked back immediately to make sure he wasn't imagining things, but there it was, snout pointed in the direction of the television, one paw up, almost, Ethan imagined, like they were watching TV together and the little guy was requesting that he pass the pretzels.

Then Ethan moved, and the mouse darted forward, toward the clutter of wires near the television stand. Ethan didn't pursue him, what was he going to do, try and squish him? Ethan hadn't seen the mouse since, at least not directly, and knowingly pretended to be convinced that his habit of throwing out his garbage each day had gotten the mouse to begrudgingly seek more fruitful opportunities elsewhere.

There were probably mice all over this dump. Now that the mouse was using his utensils drawer as a toilet (why? There was no food there, unless it was just a convenient restroom as the mouse made passage throughout the walls), Ethan would have to bite the bullet and get traps from his landlord.

Glass broke loudly somewhere down below on the street. Someone yelled something in sum and substance which sounded like "now dat's some shit!" while a chorus of street denizens made their insensible contributions.

There could be a sundry romance to all this, this mouse-infested ghetto dump hole apartment, the struggle before the success, if there was any expectation of any actual success. The real terror lurked behind the scenes: the electronic loan deposits, the interest that silently grew and grew, the voracious, uncontrollable maw that Ethan knew he could only placate with crumbs until this beast of his own creation burst free and financially devoured him.

Until this debt decided to mercifully kill him, it tormented him by occupying most of his mental real estate. Wouldn't any man condemned to death feel the same? Annie's poise, intelligence, and, most of all, her known academic success made Ethan's stomach feel burny and bloaty, as he thought about his own LSAT score. It wasn't fair. (What wasn't fair? That she did well? How does that make any sense?)

J.R. HAMANTASCHEN

Stupid, he knew, why torture himself, why? They say "you can't think like that" or "you can't think about the past like that," but you know what? You can, and he did. Why, he was living proof, and doing so just now! His LSAT score was like a metaphysical gunshot wound: it healed, but he never forgot the scar and was prone to picking at it. Any tertiary failure always brought him back to thinking about that chief failure.

A 158. He'd gotten a 158 out of 180, even though he'd tested in the mid-160s, got as high as 168 on one sample test, which was in the 98% percentile. A 168, combined with his college grades, could conceivably have gotten him into Berkeley, or at least UCLA; or at least one Top 14 school, a Cornell or Duke or University of Virginia (such an arbitrary number: top 14, but that just whets the appetite for the arbitrariness that was the name of the law school game).

But nope, a 158, and here he was at Hastings.

He had to move his bowels. He did so, in his cold bathroom with the ugly greenish-tinged tiles, always drafty even though the windows were closed, sitting on his skewed, rusty toilet seat, and noticed that the metal rod in his shower that held up the curtain had once again fallen down (it had to be angled just so between the wall and the shower door). It was always a balancing act trying to get that to stay up – what, why was this the only rod that fit in here, like the architects had all sat around, carefully calculating the dimensions of the exclusive metal rod that fit just so between the wall and the shower entrance? Was this shower built before normal shower dimensions had been determined?

Who was he fooling?

He knew what he was going to do tonight.

It was nice pretending otherwise for a while, when he'd come home and rooted around his kitchen for a while, imagining that getting rid of that mouse was the first thing on his mind. Then he'd surfed the Internet, going to the usual sites, Above the Law and other stupid legal blogs and some movie websites, SF Daily, blah blah blah, circling around from where he knew he was going to end up. The reason his bowels needed a release, a kind of weird, diverting self-preservation system, like his body was trying to prevent himself from succumbing to the digital

243

temptations by working to disgust himself with his own dirty effluence.

Porn. He was stressed, depressed, and irritable from a lack of stimulation, and he knew what he would end up doing. First to MyFreeCams, to see if his "friend" "Gamay" was online, who went under the moniker Book_Whore. He'd been chatting with her online for months, visiting her cam room, "privating" with her and getting to know her, or at least the portions of herself she was willing to share.

She was an art student at a college somewhere in New Mexico and a reader, intelligent and well-read: (Ahh, see, he'd think sarcastically, by giving her tips during her live shows I'm serving as a patron of the arts!) It was deeply pathetic in a sense, but again, not really; he did legitimately consider her a friend, albeit a friend who he gratuitously paid money he didn't have to see her naked. He didn't like to take without giving, so unlike the other grifters and bums on the website he gave contributions even after he finished up.

He'd also "privated" with her a few times – where it was just a one-on-one video chat which got saved automatically in his MFC Private folder – and he'd watch those, witnessing the happiness and pleasure of his friend, so carefree and unencumbered (and gloriously naked and moaning) and hear her lusciously repeat kind words in her rapture, and it'd make him feel better, if only temporarily.

But now she wasn't online, and he weirdly sometimes didn't like watching her videos without her also being online, so she could say "yay!" or "woo!" and give her stamp of approval. One time he'd jerked off to one of her saved private sessions and the come-down was so alienating and pathetic that it always stayed with him. When he'd started jerking off that time, his mind had swelled with fantasies of the two of them sharing a wonderful, event-filled day in San Francisco together, him showing this intelligent, modest rural girl from New Mexico all the sights she wanted to see in the "Big City," then they'd come home together (she'd forgive and excuse his Murphy Bed and apartment, joke that, "hey, it's still in San Francisco,") end the night together in bliss . . . then he came, both literally and then out of his stupor, saw himself as he truly was, huddled hunchbacked by his computer, clutching his wilting penis and a crusting-over towel, boxers suctioned-sucked to his thigh with his "homemade glue," and cleaned himself off in shame.

No fawning, impressed Gamay, no shared bliss: just his apartment in disrepair, plates in the sink, notes needing to be outlined, hobos screaming at each other outside. One of those days he's going to hear one of them yell "that motherfucker jerking himself off in there!" and he's going to explode in shame.

So, no MFC tonight. But there was a universe of porn out there, and he could be very, very picky. The amount of work and searching that went into finding just the right porn was enough to qualify it as a hobby. He knew he'd be wasting his night, like it was a foregone conclusion, and as some type of penance he texted Tzipora.

"Hey Tzipora, how about we finally meet this weekend! Free Saturday night?" And about ten minutes later when she said "Yes! This Saturday works for me!," while his cock was in one hand and his phone in the other, he proposed a midday drink in the Haight Ashbury. Midday was good for a first date, shorter and less pressure. She said that was perfect and he felt, somehow, that now his hours-long self-abasement would be a kind of reward for his initiative.

And during the tail-end of this hours-long process, as his penis began to get sore and a grayish-dirt stain appeared on the tip from all the spit-lubed friction, he'd think of certain women he fancied and wanted to be with.

It started with Tzipora, who he had the luxury of never having met yet, although that made it hard because he couldn't attach a voice to the fantasy; then Fujita and her full lips, her chatty face curled in a smile; Jana and her long legs sashaying up the stairs in class (but she could be a bit cold so she was quickly filtered out); Karla and her huge chest, and he kind of enjoyed that she wasn't classically pretty; Charlotte, a short, somewhat out of shape classmate with a weak chin, but who was smart, good at math, and who he suspected had some interest in him and might prove to be extremely happy and grateful to roll around in bed; and then of course Annie, her sharp feline grace, a smirk as she watched him masturbating, a bit too-cool-for-school and measured, displaying her interest with an expression, a chuckle, a "so what do you got there?" but even in his fantasy he somehow felt unworthy of her, harboring this secret that despite his gunner pretensions he hadn't lived up to academic expectations his first semester so he didn't have clearance to seduce her, and he grimaced a bit, trying to clear the image or introduce some other novel aspect, maybe Alisha was there, cleavage-out, daring Annie to blow him, why not, it was Bar Review (no that was stupid) and then he erupted into a towel as a shot of nerves rang out in his back.

Oww, fuck, it was like when you smash your funny bone, except this was in the small of his back. He heard that MDMA could fuck up your spine ("So we walk around lookin' like some windup dolls, Shit stickin' out of our backs like a dinosaur," went that Eminem song), but could intense masturbation do the same? That actually hurt. Maybe his body's self-defenses against excessive masturbation graduated from having to shit himself to self-inflicted mystery back pain.

The trance of masturbation lifted and he was exhausted; or more likely, he'd already been tired when he got home, and now three hours of masturbation later he realized just how tired he'd been. It was about 2 a.m., and he had Friday class tomorrow, although fortunately not until 10 a.m. How would he ever live a normal life, with a normal schedule, when he jerked off well into the wee hours just to have something to do, when that something to do should obviously have been working or sleeping?

How many nights would this continue? He constrained himself when absolutely necessary, when something had to get done. But the looseness of student life didn't serve him well, and neither did living alone. He needed some mediating force, someone to check up on him, to take care of him. If excessive masturbation was akin to drug addiction, he thought, a drug that you could self-generate had to be, in a sense, the most addictive.

He dreamt of nothing, or at least nothing memorable, his imaginative faculties run dry.

*

The next morning around 9 a.m. and Ethan had gotten himself a seat at Philz coffee shop on Golden Gate Avenue. There weren't too many people inside, most were other students, and he got himself a choice mini-couch seat, all to himself, with the miniature table before him. He was rarely one of those people who took out his laptop at a coffee shop and made a mini-bunker like some of his classmates. First, it was rude and obtrusive; second, he was very picky about his study environment and generally needed silence; and third, in the Tenderloin especially, there was a discomfiting showiness and naivete to studying while hooked up to a laptop in a rough neighborhood. He wasn't really working, just incorporating some notes into a master outline for Constitutional Law and listening to a podcast – well, a snippet from a podcast – on YouTube called "Stoicism in the Age of Pornography."

Ethan was dimly aware that someone had said his name and was pointing in his direction. He looked up and saw Arkady near the counter, computer-bag slung over his back, with two of their classmates. Arkady was with Jason, a classmate in his forties who'd gotten a Masters in English, gotten tired of the low pay in private school teaching, and thought (erroneously, as they all had) that law school was safe route for improving the prospects for his wife and young child; and Charlotte, who Ethan had last seen cameoing briefly in last night's masturbatory fantasia.

Arkady left Jason and Charlotte in line and hurried over, the two of them still in quiet conversation.

"Hey what's up man, surprised to see you here," Ethan gave as greeting. Arkady usually preferred the Peet's coffee on Van Ness, arguing that there was a reason Peets was a national, if not global chain (the coffee shop that Starbucks ripped off, he was proud to point out), and Ethan's fetishism for these small or regional chains with their inconsistent service and products was a kind of Western-liberal softness. Ethan took out his earbuds as Arkady spoke, making sure to close his browser. Ugh, the ear buds looked like they'd just been smooshed inside of a Reese's Peanut Butter Cup. He hoped Arkady didn't notice all the collected ear wax.

"Ewww, clean your ears man, put that away before any ladies come nearby."

Ethan made a grumbly noise as he wiped them clean.

"Anyway, you know my position on these types of places, but different times call for different places. I knew our classmates like these types of places, everyone will be congregating at these crappy-type of places and Peet's will be lonely."

"What do you mean?" And before he could let Arkady respond, he said in a low, quickened voice, "hey, I set up a date with our lady Tzipora last night, seeing her this weekend."

"Ehh, good for you. Making the most of these strange times, I see."

"What do you mean?" Did he just ask that?

"Did you hear?" Arkady turned back, as if to beckon the other two, who were now approaching with their orders in hand. Coincidentally, Ethan noticed a different group of classmates in ambulatory conversation while entering the store. He distinctly saw, as if framed just for him, a classmate Sheila's look of concern and disbelief, topped off with a mournful shake of the head.

"Dude, did you hear about what happened?"

"How many times are you going to say that-"

"Annie died last night."

"What!" Ethan screeched. His voice cracked embarrassingly and, in normal circumstances, Arkady would immediately call him out for it. In these trying times, Arkady waited at least a few seconds before deciding it was appropriate to mock his friend's reaction and laugh.

"Geez, calm down, you just sounded like a little girl. But yes, seriously."

"Kerman, you really didn't hear?" That was Charlotte. She said it with an air of assumed familiarity that Ethan didn't mind, as if saying 'typical Kerman.' For a beat, Ethan and Arkady looked at the iced frilly drink she held, with its shredded lacy chocolate and swirly pattern, and both thought privately that there was something comically incongruous about this news and the presence of that drink. "I guess that means you don't check our mod's email list."

"I don't even think I'm signed up for it."

"Did you unsubscribe from our own mod's list?!" Charlotte said, shaking her head and smiling. "Taking this antisocial thing a bit far."

"I guess. But what happened to Annie?"

"I don't think they know yet." That was Jason. With his brow-beaten, weathered face, black San Francisco Giants cap, and more-situation-appropriate hot coffee, which he took a tentative sip from as he spoke, he looked like an old school detective. "I heard someone say it might be an aneurism. I think her roommate Alisha found her."

"Alisha? Jesus. How does a twenty-two-year-old, healthy girl like Annie have a freak aneurysm?" Ethan asked. He wondered if he should have said "woman" for Charlotte's sake. Something about Jason's appearance made Ethan wonder if police officers were going to visit him and perhaps everyone else at Bar Review and take statements.

No one had any answers, because how could they? Arkady only differed in surmising that no one is as healthy as they seem, and maybe she over-exerted herself studying so hard last semester, which everyone rejected out of hand. Annie never broke a sweat, her academic outgoingness was just who she was, as natural and perhaps even as unnoticed to her as getting dressed and showering. Classes were cancelled for the day, and might even be for all of next week, apparently, which Arkady thought a bit much. Charlotte just gave a friendly roll of her eyes.

"This is terrible. I can't believe it," Ethan said. He had the paranoid, strange feeling that, as much as, say, Charlotte and everyone liked Annie, they all saw the upside in having the potential valedictorian out of the picture. Charlotte, who'd previously been an accountant and kept talking about how much the law sucked and she'd probably end up going back to accounting or finance, was surreptitiously competitive and judgmental, and, Ethan suspected, quietly displeased at how easily good things seemed to come Annie's way. Ethan knew he was just projecting and mounting theoretical defenses on behalf of Annie's honor and let the thought drop.

He thought of the version of Annie from last night. She'd become, in a way, a glorified vision immediately after he'd left the bar and gone home – isn't that how all people become, a vision, a memory of a person, a mental projection – and it wrenched something inside to know that's all she'd now ever be. When he'd be old and gray he'd think of beautiful Annie, the star of his class, forced to repeat the blanketing, obscuring bromides like "what a shame" and "terrible, just terrible," the type of things people say as covers and sympathetic fill-ins when they've lost the ability or the memory to say something meaningful or particular.

Jason and Charlotte left separately, might as well go back and begin their commutes, Jason down in the South Bay, Charlotte out in Russian Hill. Notably, Charlotte seemed to only give Ethan eye contact as she left, looking straight at him when she said "see ya." Arkady and Ethan, bums as they were, had no other plans and Ethan just lived a few blocks away anyway.

"Now you will never get to ask Annie about her nickname growing up."

"True," Ethan said, finally remembering that he had gotten coffee of his own, now gone lukewarm. Arkady helped himself to Ethan's commandeered section of the couch.

"This is fucking terrible, man." Ethan always fancied himself sullen, low-energy, always on the ground floor within the architecture of happiness, but had just now discovered the basement.

"I know, I know, no doubt it is. I liked Annie, you know that, and I don't like many people, but she was one of the good ones. Sharp girl, she was. That is going to do a number on Alisha, that's for sure, not be surprised if she disappears for a while." Arkady paused, and Ethan, knowing Arkady well, suspected Arkady was weighing whether to joke about the misfortune in not seeing Alisha and her cleavage in class for the foreseeable future. Apparently, he declined.

"At least you have that date to look forward to this weekend."

"Should I cancel it?"

"What?! Why, and sit around and be sad about Annie? She doesn't know Annie, it's not like she cares. What good would that do?"

"I guess."

"We have gallows humor, we ex-Soviets. Life goes on, you have to keep moving. Keep moving, can't let this death distract us from the conveyor belt that is the law school assembly line."

"Were you even born during the Soviet Union, dude, that ended like in 1989?"

"The humor and sentiment are inheritable."

"I guess. Any idea on when her funeral is?"

"No idea."

It dawned on Ethan that he'd likely not be invited, as he didn't know Annie all that well, and certainly no one in her family would have any idea who he was. That thought felt like a kind of nail in the coffin into ever really learning all he wanted to about Annie.

Ethan wondered how much longer he'd make small talk at the coffeeshop and noodle around on the Internet until he ceased pretending that, since the moment he'd learned of the school cancellation, his pressing itinerary became anything other than 'go home and jerk off.'

*

Entering his building, he figured that he'd do something to redeem himself, however slightly, by doing something productive. The super's office was on the main floor, just to the left of the lobby entrance, and he noticed that the door was slightly open, as if the super planned on closing it but didn't bother forcing it all the way shut. The super was "the super" because Ethan couldn't remember his name.

He knocked and was invited in, the super sitting back in his chair, busying himself with paperwork.

"Hello." Ethan scanned the room, saw the super's name on the door in gold-plate, "Abdul" (something about saying that name aloud sounded racist, as if that would be the name some television yahoo would invent and assign to this guy during the course of yelling racial invective), "how's it going?"

251

"Good, good, as good as it can be, I suppose," Abdul responded. It was difficult to gauge Abdul's age, likely in his forties, bald-headed, had a crumpled air about him that made him relatable and approachable, as if he was always harried yet persevering in good humor. Ethan wondered how much of that was an act, a way of obviating the allegations of angry tenants coming in pissed about roaches, rats, water problems or whatever other godforsaken stuff went on in this apartment, by adapting this 'tell me about it' attitude. Then again, Abdul likely had spent the last few days cleaning up splattered human feces and was often picking up needles around the building so this beaten-down persona was likely well-earned.

Ethan decided he liked the guy. "You're from Lebanon, right?"

"Yes, sir."

"That's cool. Just wondering, ever miss it?"

"Ahh well, I don't really have family there anymore, everyone moved to the States. I been here now, hmmm, let me see, over thirty years now, most of my life spent here now. Why we had to move to San Francisco area instead of something like New York or Chicago or something, I do not know and cannot say." Abdul shrugged. "Or Las Vegas."

"Vegas? I've never been, if you can believe it."

"Really? Flights cheap, not as cheap as from Los Angeles or San Diego, but still cheap. You should go, see a show, gamble, drink, have fun, you know what they say. It's quite something."

"I already gambled all my money away on law school."

Abdul gave the same slow-roll feint, a kind of shrug with his face, as if acknowledging and temporarily unbalanced by the burdens of others. "That is the way of the world, unfortunately. Debt, debt everywhere, always so quick to sign us up for debt. School, school is supposed to be the safe investment, no longer, everything so expensive. This city, unlivable. My daughter went through college, can't afford to live here, lives in South Carolina, if you can believe it, so much cheaper. Not much to do, but cheap. Debt, so much debt she has. My son, never went to college, works helping to build bridges, doing electrical work, barely any debt. One does the right thing with college and ends up in debt in South

Carolina; another does not apply himself in school and ends up fine. Who knows anymore?"

"I know, right." Ethan breathed in and sighed. Abdul, he'd remember his name for next time. Sometimes when he unloaded grievances, for the splittest-of-seconds he imagined that his burdens had actually been unloaded, as if by sharing the nature of his burdens and obligations they had been fulfilled.

"So I think I may have a mouse in my apartment."

"Ethan, check your lease, no pets allowed."

It perhaps was not the most comforting of signs when a complaint of a rodent infestation was met with a stored bon mot.

"I've tried leaving an eviction notice but I don't think he can read."

Abdul did his shrug and routed through a drawer. "Just one? Consider yourself lucky. It's these homeless people all over the place, throwing food and garbage all over, doing foul things, well what do I need to tell you for, you see it with your own eyes." He pulled out a few cartons. "These are glue traps, ever use these before?"

Ethan made a wishy-washy face. "You have any other types? I kinda feel bad about those."

"For the mouse? You think he feel bad for you when he eating your food and crapping all over the building? Sorry, these are only ones we have." Abdul went back into the drawer and pulled out two more, Ethan's lagniappe for his prefatory chitter-chatter.

"Alright, I guess. Hope this little fucker knows what's good for him and leaves. Okay, thanks man, see you around."

"Good luck."

Ethan went up the rickety-elevator – the type you could easily imagine detaching, plummeting, and being reduced to timber – and into his apartment. He opened his utensils drawer, looked around, pretended for a moment the few little brown flecks might be something other than new poop. He took out his utensils, put them above his fridge for the time being and sanitized the drawer. On the very top of one of the traps he smeared some peanut butter and placed it in the utensils drawer.

He likely should have put it closer to the center of the trap so the little beast could get good and properly stuck but, Ethan told himself, this should be fine and he didn't want to get that gunk all over his hands anyway, he had work to do later. It should be fine. He pictured a cute scene where the crafty little mouse, the protagonist of his own private adventure, stuck his furry little face into the butter and came away frolicking with a nut the size of his head, a big score to show off to his mouse family. He wondered if he should put the tray back in which held his utensils: would the mouse notice its absence, think something was suspicious? No, the lure of peanut butter should be enough. Hell, the peanut butter was working on him, and he made himself a PB&J.

Then he jerked off.

*

"Tzipora," Ethan said as he gave a single-finger point to the tall, fuller-figured woman with long blonde hair, dressed in a black and white button-down shirt and form-fitting jeans, standing outside Zam Zam Bar on Haight Street. Blonde hair, he immediately wondered if it was natural – aren't Jews not usually blonde? – and so came thoughts of Annie, which he pushed aside.

"Ethan," she said, a broad smile on her face. She did have nice teeth, structurally, although her teeth were prominent and her smile a bit gummy. Not that Ethan cared at all, but he noticed these little things, just as she undoubtedly noticed a million little things about him, perhaps like what she perceived as the unnaturalness of his dress, although he actually always dressed like this: black sacks, black dress shoes, a button-down shirt, this one a fiery red and black, bold colors that hopefully excused his own lack of said boldness.

She smiled as she spoke his name. "My friends call me Zip."

"Well, give me ten minutes or so and let's see if I get to call you that."

"Okay," she said with a nervous laugh, and then she looped her arm around his as they walked to the door, which quelled his self-reproach at his stupid comment. His heart was skipping beats – Lord, you would think he was a virgin or something, what's gotten into him? – but no, he just hadn't been with anyone since he and his college girlfriend Becky broke up in senior year, what was that, three years ago now? Only time someone had since

254

looped an arm around his own was when he'd been walking around late in the Castro District last semester after spending a night solo drinking, and a rather attractive young man looked at him for a few beats too long, Ethan gave a desultory nod and a polite finger-salute, and all of a sudden the young man had sidled up to him and looped his right arm around Ethan's left as Ethan crossed at the light. Ethan mumbled, "sorry, I'm not, sorry," heart pounding from the unexpectedness of misreading the encounter, felt bad about letting the guy down and also a bit prideful that he'd attracted a looker, and as the man almost immediately separated and went his own way. Ethan's body missed the electricity of the physical connection, the space where chest met chest, found the loneliness incredibly sobering.

No bums at the corner, that was good. Haight Ashbury might not have been the best choice, it was a neighborhood that mostly coasted on the goodwill of the 1960s and 70s, where goodhearted if naive young people came to "tune out, drop out," whatever that Timothy Leary expression was. That childish optimism had since curdled into a bunch of meanspirited sociopaths and rich kids from Marin County coming in on the weekends to get high and LARP as crust punks and tell everyone who didn't give them cash to fuck off and die. He saw a group of them a block away yelling and harassing people by the Ben and Jerry's, a good visual metaphor for the hippies of old dishonored and pushed to the side by the rancor and nihilism of the disaffected new generation, and made a note not to take her in that direction.

Seems like he wouldn't need to worry. They spent the whole date in the bar. There were seats at the bar, and she liked the interior: atmospheric and dark, red-backlit bar, colorful yet relaxing pastel mural of, what was that, indigenous people on horseback riding around a bucolic garden? She made it quickly apparent that she loved San Francisco, said how amazing it was that she'd grown up here and there were still so many places she'd never been. He'd save his contempt for this city for a later time.

Kismet graced him. Got a seat early, menus immediately, the bartender with the walrus-looking facial hair gave thoughtful suggestions, she liked her whiskey-based drink – that was something to note, a San Franciscan who likes whiskey – and he liked his whatever-the-fuck it was he got, and the date was going well enough that a few minutes in they were trying each other's drinks.

"Ooh that's good, even if it's a girl drink," Tziporah told him.

"Hah! Well, what can I say, this is San Francisco, an open-minded place, and I'm in touch with all sides of myself?"

"That's a good attitude to have."

"And I must say, we San Franciscans don't really like that close-minded attitude."

"Judging me already? You've truly become a San Franciscan; I'll give you the keys to the City."

"Excuse me, those keys better be in the form of those heart sculptures all around town. The keys to this City take the form of those hearts. I like that heart with the cows on it in Cow Hollow. I like animal things, make sure it's that one." Why he was explaining this he didn't know.

"Noted."

One topic that either fascinated her, or she pretended it fascinated her to lubricate conversation, was the fact that he grew up in a town small enough that he had to use Chico, California as a reference point, a city she never heard of, about three hours outside San Francisco.

"No wonder you like cows so much, sounds like Farmville," she said when they were on their second drink. He'd no doubt have a later bout of staircase wit, but he had nothing in response to that jibe now and drinking wasn't helping.

Another area of fascination for her was that he lived in the Tenderloin.

"Seriously? Why?"

"I just loved that song 'I left my heart in San Francisco.' I wanted that to come true for me, as well as my teeth and my wallet." That'd been a prepared joke he finally got to use, which came across with mixed results. She took her drink, made a jostling movement with her shoulders that was a bit like 'hur-hur-hur,' and said "but seriously, why? I mean, there's some cool nightlife there, around like Polk Gulch it's called, but why live there?"

Ethan explained that it was right by his school, he didn't have to own a car, and all the other reasons one gives when they don't feel like explaining the obvious: that there wasn't much of a choice in the matter as it's one of the only "cheap" neighborhoods in a city full of conceited, oblivious yuppies that refused to allow more housing to be built, so the two options were being confined to a dangerous ghetto or commuting hours and hours away from the boonies. Hey, if she was offering her parents' place up in Noe Valley or her own in Inner Sunset Park, he was down.

Tzipora didn't talk much about herself, really, saying she went to Boston University and missed that city, felt like it was the San Francisco of the East Coast and wouldn't mind going back someday, to which she prompted him to answer whether he planned on staying on the West Coast. He said he'd initially be barred only in California but would be interested in traveling wherever, as if he was already trying to prevent her from breaking up with him due to future life plans on the first date. She asked him what kind of law he wanted to do, and he hesitated, indicated he was undecided, but said he was leaning toward corporate litigation.

"Like, courtrooms and suing each other?'

"Yeah, but corporations suing each other, like corporation A alleging corporation B broke a contract, so not like hurting small businesses or normal people, you know."

"Sounds exciting."

"I like writing and researching, I was an English major, so it's a good use of my skills, I guess. I'm not sure, but that's where I'm leaning. I find the whole civil procedure stuff fascinating." Why, right now he was testing his skills of persuasion to see if she believed – and maybe if he believed – the bullshit he was spouting. God, corporate litigation, duking it out over pharmaceutical shipments or whatever, what could be more fucking boring and draining, 'your honor, on March blah blah, my client entered into and executed a contract, including the following indemnification provision of Section 9(f), which reads-'

"As long as you're passionate about it, that's what's important." She was suitably convinced, apparently.

"I love helping people rent and buy apartments, I really do," Tzipora continued, granting him a reprieve from peddling his bullshit. "It's rewarding, it's fun, I get to learn about neighborhoods and, like, all this design and architecture and moulding, and all this other stuff, and when you are done, people have a new place to live. It's great, I love it."

His immediate reference point was the PropertySex series, where comely female real estate agents used their wiles and physical charms to get skeptical male customers to buy properties.

He brushed that aside. "How's your inventory in the Tenderloin?"

"Oh dear, we will work on that. Once you are doing your corporate law, we'll get you somewhere nice."

"Have to wait that long?"

"We can work on that," she gave him a sleepy, mirthful smile. "Whoa, has that been two drinks already? Time flies, as they say. I should be getting back."

"Okay, me too. The Tenderloin beckons." He was making too many call-backs, a pedestrian rhetorical tic, conversation filler.

She tsk tsk'ed. He paid the bill on his credit card, and once that was settled, they went outside.

It was still light out, late afternoon. He checked his cell, 4:08 p.m.

Ethan turned around and Tzipora put her arms around his neck, and he put his around her waist, which was tighter and smoother than he'd imagined. She closed her eyes, leaned in and kissed him, open-mouth making out so he had to adjust his mouth-game mid-kiss to keep up. She pulled back and looked at him, pleasantly vacant, that reconciled to your time and place countenance of the moderately intoxicated.

"So, I'll see you again?" she asked lazily, looking directly at him. "By the way, that's Pilates you are feeling right there, it paid off."

"Indeed it has."

"It's the middle of the day otherwise I'd put your hands lower. I've been told I have a pretty juicy ass."

"Mhmm," Ethan responded blearily. "Well then." Was that meant to be sexy? A juicy ass? He knew what she was trying to get across, but who'd she think he was, fucking Flavor Flav? Does anyone want to hear that? What does that even mean? What would make an ass juicy, that would necessarily have to be ass-juice, wouldn't it, who would want to deal with something like that?

"It's been great finally getting to meet you. I guess some things are worth the wait," she said as she disembarked.

"Absolutely." Okay he had run out of things to say, time to end this.

"Okay, good bye," she said with reaching lustiness, took a few steps back, turned back and looked at him over her shoulder. He waved in a way he intended to be seductive and suggestive, and she smiled and blushed.

He was drunk and hungry, so he walked far enough to make sure he didn't accidentally run into her. He wasn't a big fan of this area, Haight Ashbury was like JV-hobo squad, Tenderloin being where the hardcore pros ended up. It was a nice day, crisp and clear, the bustle of the City, the sloping greens of Buena Vista Park and the N-Judah streetcar, tethered to the electrical power source above, jangling through the park to pick up outbound travelers, navigating charmingly and mechanically like a little boy's train set: at this moment, San Francisco could actually pass as enjoyable.

He treated himself to a burrito and then figured he should get home. Catch up on work, send out emails and research about potential summer jobs, do that bullshit where you ask to set up an "exploratory lunch" to ingratiate yourself into the offices of some plaintiff's side chop-shop for a summer of indentured servitude, or whatever other bullshit the career services recommended for the students with grades too low to get into the corporate recruitment process.

Well, at least he was alive, right? Fannie Mae was counting on him!

*

Later that night and Contracts could wait because Gamay was online, wearing a threadbare white-T with a visible purple bra beneath. Her hair was now braided, a new look for her.

"Hola chica,' he typed into her chatroom.

"Heyyyy you!" she said aloud, to Ethan and the twenty-seven others in her chatroom. Then, Ethan got a private message, "Hola chico." That's right, he got clearance to send and receive private messages, he was big time.

"Been a busy little art student recently? Haven't seen you online," he typed into her group chat.

"Yeah, it's been crazy here, been working a lot at the day job, and had a big project due, like, this layered mirror thing I've been working on." The peanut gallery chimed in about how camming should be her full-time job, some asked what her day job was, others asked elementary questions about what she was going to school for, etcetera.

These newbies.

"I like the hippie braids, you'd fit in perfectly here in SF," he typed. He liked reminding her he lived in San Francisco, assumed it had some cache with an art student.

She laughed. "Hah, I'm doing the white girl art school braids. Where I live I'm a rebel, I bet in San Francisco, I'm one in a million."

"San Francisco doesn't even have a million people, actually, people think it's a lot bigger than it is," he typed, as other users wrote "SF Sucks LOL," while KINGTITFUCKER4LIFE explained why Gamay should instead visit him in New Orleans.

"I'll keep that in mind, uhhh, Kingtitfucker," she said aloud while laughing. "I've never been to New Orleans. I've never been anywhere, actually, although I once visited Colorado." Then a bunch of people jumped in to opine about how great Colorado was.

Someone contributed 10 tokens "to make her smile," which, Ethan knew, came out to about 50 cents.

"Thanks CottonMouthKing!" she said in response to the tip, giving a big smile. "How's that? Big enough for you?"

"I can think of why it'd need to be bigger," CottonMouth typed in the chat.

"Hey G, want to do a private session," Ethan privately messaged her.

"Sure!" she typed back. Ethan didn't have any tokens left and knew that the models could see how many tokens each customer had. "Gimme a sec," he typed back. Seventy-five bucks got him about fifteen hundred tokens. In a private session, every second was worth about 1.5 tokens, which would buy him about twenty minutes of private time, and the session would be automatically saved in his video catalog.

"Yayyy!" she exclaimed as the session started. "Put your camera on, love," she asked, and he did. "Mhmm, I missed that dick," she purred, as Ethan worked on himself. She eagerly got completely naked, lovely and shorn, and immediately started working on herself, putting her right leg over her back. "See how flexible I am, babe?"

"I see." He didn't want his own voice captured in the video stream, so he stuck to single-handed typing. Nothing ruined the allure of watching the recap then hearing his own pathetic bleating.

"Mhmm yeah baby. What do you want me to do for you?"

"Just be happy, loving, and enjoy yourself with me," he typed back.

"Oh you are so sweet!" Gamay said with enthusiasm, fingering herself with zeal. "See how wet I am for you." She rubbed her wetness across her sizable bust; Ethan liked how the right was obviously bigger than the left, one of those perfect imperfections.

He asked her how she was doing, how work was going (he knew she worked at a T-shirt manufacturing company; he liked "knowing" things about her), how school was going, and he asked to slow things down, which he often did. The primary appeal was getting to share a moment with a lovely woman that he knew and cared about. He liked the idea that she might use these tokens for, who knows, art supplies or her tuition or her rent or the coffee habit she'd told him about or any other thing she wanted.

"Tell me you love me," he typed.

"Mhmm baby, I do, you are so sweet, I love you, and I love that cock of yours. It looks so sweet, just like you."

"Tell me you love me again, and please say my name as you do."

"I love you Ethan, I do, you are just, so, so sweet, you are the sweetest friend by far I've ever met on here."

"I may not be on here that much longer, to be honest. I mean MFC. School and everything. Can we communicate via email?"

"Of course.' And she gave him an email address that had "Gamay" in it, which he knew wasn't her real name. He wanted her real email, he wanted a real relationship with her, but he didn't press it and instead asked Gamay again to tell him why she loved him.

Time was running out, and he told her he wanted to watch her cum. She obliged, and he relished the happiness in her face, the tight-eyed release, imagined the tickling in her spine and unclenching of her toes that she'd previously described as little tics and sensations she felt when she came.

"Cum for me too, babe," she said, catching her breath. "How can I make you cum, love."

He had about twenty seconds left before the tokens ran out and they automatically went back to group chat. She'd be naked when she returned, and in a sense the gaggle of commoners would reap the benefit of his generosity in unrobing and exciting her.

"I'll think of you when I cum, I promise," he typed, ever the gentleman. "Have a good night."

"Good night Ethan!" she exclaimed, and bounced and waved her boobs at him. "Think of these!"

He closed her chat before it officially went back to the group; he didn't want to watch her back to plying her trade with strangers.

His dick was sore and battered, red like a Hebrew National. He was alone again, still hard but softening, his balls aching, and he needed to finish up quick. For some unknown reason, he felt there was something either deeply pathetic about thinking of Gamay while alone – he should think of a real woman he knew –

or maybe some chivalrous impulse let poor Gamay off-duty in his imagination.

Instead, he thought of Jana from Civ Pro, who often came off as callous and distant, but he'd seen her smile and laugh at certain times, knew there was a warm heart in there. He imagined Jana atop the stairs in Civ Pro, her long, slinky bare legs as she swayed awkwardly; awkwardly because this type of seduction didn't come naturally to her, and she was trying her best to be both sexy and goofily charming, as Ethan watched her, jerked off, waved his cock around and offered her a chance to ride.

She shook her head and rolled her eyes, smiling, but gave an extra thrust to her sways, and he leaned forward to see she wasn't wearing underwear. And in the fantasy's conclusion she couldn't help but look back and gape, breathing heavily, as he shot his load all over the Civ Pro steps.

Back to reality, this dingy apartment, his Murphy bed beckoning, sheets begging to be changed, and, why not?, a police siren now going off outside.

Even in his fantasies he was reduced to jerking off.

*

This didn't stop him, of course, from jerking off the following morning. Laziness begets laziness, and it was Sunday, the Lord's lazy day, and he woke up naturally around 10:45 a.m. He should shower but didn't feel like it; it was too late in the day to waste on showering, and, if he did go out to a coffee shop or something, it would be in a neighborhood where being disheveled was tolerated, whether it be artful, twee and cultivated (the Mission, Dogpatch, Potrero Hill), unavoidable (Tenderloin, South of Market), or indulgent or tourist-related (North Beach, Haight-Ashbury). More likely, he would just pop out for a quick bite and come back and … well, he was actually pretty well caught up with his studies. But what else would he have to do?

He checked his phone, no message yet from Tzipora (he'd never actually called her Zip, he realized, perhaps for the best). But then again, hadn't even been a full day yet. He pondered whether he should message her today, strike while the iron was hot and see if she was around tonight, or wait mid-week, allow things to simmer until the following weekend. That was the superficial level of pondering. The deeper level would have been him reflecting upon whether he even wanted or cared to pursue a relationship: given the time, effort, financial expenditure, and strong statistical likelihood of failure and disappointment.

There was a reason why the world was gravitating inward, tending toward isolation. He could satisfy his needs by himself. No partner could exceed the pleasures he took the time and care to carve out for himself. Tzipora would need super-human patience and understanding to even attempt to dedicate the time and approximate the regimen he applied to himself. He was like a crack addict being invited to rejoin the wider world with promises of yoga and vape pens. Limitations on his time and finances, and the growth and availability of porn-based technologies, increasingly made his version of self-care more and more appealing. If only these porn purveyors could provide some way to quell the post-porn time-waste hangover of grief and shame, then there'd be really nothing stopping him.

Ethan bartered with himself. What better way to get himself to get up and shower then to foul himself with his own semen? Further, a bed-based self-flagellation could deplete him for later, which made it less likely he'd waste hours on the internet. That was something: force himself into about three ten-minute imagination-only jerk-off sessions, just as a way to force him to make better use of his time. But without spending hours on the Internet, where would his focus turn to? His disappointing first-semester grades and how he parried around his father's well-meaning inquiries, or his mounting debt, or the blasted hope of transferring to a better school, or how he had absolutely no desire whatsoever to either apply for or obtain the middling summer positions jobs available to him?

Addictions were addicting because they were fantastic, strangely satisfying and rewarding, and better than the available alternatives.

He thought about Amber Mosdale, tall, thin but busty, brassy-voiced, straight-haired, a bit of get-to-the-point sass about her, from what he could tell. She'd make a nice visual counterpoint to lithe Jana with her dancer-quality legs. He didn't know her that well, which made it better. Before coming to law school, Amber had bit parts in some garbage sub-independent movies, and he'd found a trailer for one that featured a quick scene of her walking toward the camera in a negligee. He conjured that image, thought of her raising her eyebrows in approval as he worked himself, slowly pulling up her shirt, promising only to unveil them in all their weighty glory at the moment he came.

Somehow, memories of him skirting around the issue of his grades with his dad started interfering and he physically grimaced and moved his head, as if the memory was an unsavory item someone was trying to push into his mouth. He came weakly, shooting in the sheets, his poor, poor sheets, and there was enough on his hands and legs to get him to get up and shower.

"Hang out later," he texted Arkady as he was getting up, semen still on his left hand. He couldn't say "brunch" because Arkady hated brunch, but a bite or coffee or drinks during the day was something he could do.

After his shower he saw that Arkady was down for lunch a bit later, and offered something to the effect of why not go to Japantown or Chinatown and at least get some good food for a change?

Reaching for a spoon from atop the fridge and biding himself with yogurt and some fruit, Ethan checked the utensils drawer. Nothing. All for the best, he figured.

*

Waiting in the shadow of the Peace Pagoda, the five-tiered concrete stupa within Peace Plaza, Ethan kept his attention on his phone, the tourists and a sprouting tree that was somewhere in the latter sapling stages. This would make a nice photograph, having the firm sapling in the lower-left of the frame, with the multi-layered Peace Pagoda towering in the background, the bright blue inviting sky beyond. The nine-ringed bronze spire on top of the Pagoda, which ended in a structure meant to resemble flames, with what appeared to be a tiny ball meant to represent Earth pinned to the top, gave the pagoda a vaguely threatening vibe, in that neo-Futurist Terminator way.

Arkady was nearby, based on the text Ethan just got. Ethan uncomprehendingly noticed another email from the Hastings administration, thought he should search his emails later to see if there was anything mentioned about Annie, either a memorial service or a GoFundMe or a funeral. They wouldn't do that on a weekend, probably, and those arrangements might take some time, clear things with the family first.

"Hey!" Arkady was waving at him, somewhere between excitedly and furiously, and sounded a bit out-of-breath. "Why do we have to meet in the middle of the park, why not in the mall or something?"

Japan Center Mall was nearby and had a good range of food options.

"Eh, I don't know, it's a nice day out."

"True, true, good to see our fellow San Franciscans, or even better, the much better-looking tourists, and always good to get some vitamin D, make sure we don't add rickets to our list of problems. You hear about that in Middle Eastern countries, it's not uncommon for women wearing those shawls or whatever they are called all day to have vitamin D deficiency, what do they expect for not letting women out of the house?"

Two women eating vanilla ice cream walked past them, both attractive in their one right, one in particular having a gigantic bust, her two-buttons-unbuttoned shirt straining to keep herself fastened within. She had what appeared to be a purplish birthmark on the left side of her face.

"Quite the interesting specimens on display here, for sure."

"You seem pretty hyped up today."

"Well, crazy times. I also did just have a double-espresso at my beloved Peet's while I am still alive, Lord have mercy. Dude, did you see these emails? Fucking absolutely crazy time? What is going on?"

Ethan's look signified that he wasn't shocked by Arkady's conclusion, but not entirely sure about everything that led to it.

"Don't tell me you didn't see these last two emails? Another girl in our school died this weekend, the email said she died instantly, as if that is supposed to make anyone feel better. And then Amber died today, first they said she went into a coma, and then was pronounced dead an hour later. Do you not check your emails?"

"Not really, I guess," Ethan said remotely, as if the information was floating around his brain, awaiting permission to dock and be processed. "Amber died?"

"Yes, Amber. It's like all attractive girls in our class are dying. What the fuck is going on, there must be some contagion going on? I can't think what it is, could it be something they all ate? Why did Annie and this other girl appear to die instantly, but Amber first went into a coma and *then* died?"

"Who - was the other person?" Ethan asked, as they walked in the direction of the Japan Center Mall. He had originally thought to propose just ambling around Japantown but was fine with, and if anything preferred, being within some kind of enclosed space.

"Look it up yourself, make sure you are getting these emails. They are coming from the school administration directly, and then as you can imagine everyone follows-up, saying how terrible this all is, making grand plans to do something about it though knowing no one will realistically do anything, you know."

"Gimme a second, let me check."

"Fine, fine." Arkady walked a few paces, canvassed the park, looked up at the Peace Pagoda. "I should become Buddhist, I like 'life is suffering.' Their first premise is correct so I'm halfway convinced," he said, with his back still facing Ethan.

"Jana Stanton," Ethan said somberly. The school regretted informing the student body of the recent passing of Jana Stanton. The email did specify that she is believed to have died instantaneously.

"Yes, Jana, that was her name. I did not know her at all, don't think I ever talked to her, but she was in Civ Pro with us, I believe. All in Civ Pro with us, very odd, don't you think? She was a fine, healthy specimen as well."

"If you go around referring to the deceased as specimens, people might look at you as a suspect," Ethan said in auto-pilot, pitter-patter banter reflexes kicking in.

"Yes, Americans are a suspicious lot, that is true, and they dislike technical language."

"I can't believe this."

"I just hope this is not some kind of new normal. Do you think we should get tested?"

"Tested for what? And you're the scientist, not me."

"Former scientist. I've sold my soul in an attempt to grovel and earn a living to fight about patents, Lord help me."

*

Ethan popped edamame in his mouth through a mental haze, suddenly exhausted, the cause and effect between the edamame in his hand and then in his mouth being lost a few times as he pondered off into space. Arkady ate the appetizer with his usual wolfishness.

"It feels kind of weird being out knowing that three of our classmates just died in like less than a week."

Arkady looked up at him and did something between a nod and shrug. "It is certainly alarming. I wonder if they might actually close the school down for the semester? Definitely I bet the next week of classes will be cancelled. Law students are a particularly sensitive bunch."

"Three classmates in like four days, I wonder if anything like this has happened before? I also wonder if I should get a drink when the dumplings come?" Ethan asked.

"Now you are thinking like a true law student. I don't think they'll have any of your weak ciders, though. Sapporo is okay. I do like sake, too."

"Would you want any?"

"Nah, I'm on a budget."

"So am I."

"We may need drinks, in these times."

"If we get sake, it's on me." Ethan needed the torpor of alcohol.

"Sold." Arkady, of course, immediately had suggestions about which bottle to order and they settled on something dry and moderately priced.

Arkady questioned whether they should be clinking their sake glasses to toast, who knew what viruses were going around now, so they refrained and went straight to drinking.

"The date with Tzipora went pretty well."

"Oh yeah?"

"Yeah, she was cool. We met in the Haight and I took her to some cocktail bar."

"Nice, nice, professional women want you to seek out the opportunities for them and spend money to demonstrate your interest. Did she look like her pictures?"

"Yeah. And we had a few drinks and talked, made out a bit at the end, and kind of made tentative plans to see each other again. Was wondering whether I should text her today."

"That's good. Hey if she looked like her pictures there's nothing to complain about. I say give it a day or two. Text her Monday. You saw her Saturday, right, so that will be two days. Women know to expect the three-day thing, this shows you are your own man."

"Yeah, I was planning on it."

"You don't seem too enthused, my friend."

"Eh, I don't know. Maybe all this shit going on?" Ethan suspected that even in normal times his enthusiasm would be similarly muted.

"Need distractions, though."

"I feel kind of guilty about it, actually."

Arkady poured himself another glass. Ethan felt comforted by the gesture and his alcohol-induced drowsiness, both indicating that the wider world could cool its jets in waiting for him to re-engage with his responsibilities.

"There's no reason to feel guilty. That's just something, like, an abstract negative feeling that you are unnecessarily fixating upon yourself. Like, negative things have happened so you feel bad, and when you feel bad, you assume you feel bad because you have done something to deserve it. That is this entire Western culture. While I don't like Russians, it could serve you well to read the Russian masters, they spent years and years and pages and pages writing about this stuff, trust me, I had to read all that shit growing up. At least you can say you saw Annie the day before she died, hung out with her and everything."

Ethan leaned in. "Want to know why I feel guilty?"

Arkady joined in the faux conspiratorial lean-in. "Always."

"For literally all three of them, I jerked off thinking about them the day before they died."

Arkady laughed aloud, gagged on his sake, continued laughing and slapped the table, loud enough for the table across from them to beam a cross look their way.

"Fucking sake burning my nose here!" Arkady said, red-faced. "Trust me, I doubt you are the only man who jerked off thinking about them recently. If that was a reason to feel guilty, I'd be atoning for the rest of my life like Sisyphus."

"Instead of rolling up a boulder you'd be cleaning up your cum."

"Exactly. Although I do it in the sink."

"Really?"

"Yes, much more hygienic."

"Smart."

"But, my friend, as long as you were jerking off to the thoughts of them while they were alive, you have nothing to feel guilty about. If otherwise-"

"But, I mean, joking aside, I'm being literal. I think the day before each of them died, I jerked off to them. Annie on Thursday night-"

"Right after you saw her?"

"Yeah. I mean, while the iron is hot, you know?"

Arkady nodded sagaciously. "I got ya, I got ya, while the image is still fresh, the details can be recalled."

"And then she passed sometime Thursday night or Friday morning, right? Then, let's see, thought of Jana Friday night, appears she passed Saturday, and-"

"Amber again Saturday night? And didn't you see that Tzipora that day, too? How do you get the time to do your work also, impressive."

"No, Amber this morning, actually."

Arkady returned to laughing and table-slapping, although the slaps were lighter this time, to the welcome reprieve of other guests.

"Perhaps because you had exhausted your reserves from the previous nights, that explains why Amber didn't die instantly like the others."

"Or actually, I got distracted at the very end so the fantasy, as it were, got kind of muddled, maybe that had something to do with it."

"Who can say my friend, who can say. You are like the Jerkoff Whisperer."

"Yeah." Ethan took a sullen sip from the sake. His growing withdrawal and discomfort with the topic seemed to have the reverse effect on Arkady, who Ethan couldn't remember seeing so zippy.

"You can't really feel that way. It's of course just a coincidence. Think about it, you also messaged or spoke to Tzipora on each day, too? By that logic, maybe that's the connection, eh?"

"I mean, I obviously don't think there's any causal relation."

"Or even correlative."

"Or even correlative. Just, I mean, well not to get too personal-"

"I think we've trampled over those boundaries, my friend."

"Well, I guess the Annie one was a big one, I was excited since she'd seemed kind of interested in me at Bar Review, and, you know, it was a major event and I did it for either so long or so much that my back hurt immediately after, like my spine."

"Whoa." Arkady seemed impressed, the smile plastered on his face seemed to widen a bit. "Even though we all need escape, and self-gratification might be one of the few pleasures left to us that doesn't sink us further and further into debt, when you are physically disabling yourself from it, it may be time to ease it back. And it gets better the longer you hold out." Arkady had this way of winking without winking, or like winking with his mouth, little eager fluctuations of overeager talk. He had a particular fondness for what must still be relatively new English terms for him, like "edging," that American men had known about since their early teens.

"Easier said than done," Ethan said, to which Arkady heartily agreed. "And I know deep-down it can only be a coincidence, but, what a coincidence. What are the statistical odds, that of all the attractive women in the world? Maybe it should serve as a

wake-up call. It's not the worst thing on Earth to do the whole
No Faps thing, at least for a while. Take it easy."

"Especially now that you have this Tzipora to look forward
to," Arkady said with gusto, with Ethan somehow detecting the
aftertaste of sarcasm and jealousy just beyond the top-layer of
support.

"We shall see, I guess. Speaking of which, I think I'll take
your advice and shoot her a text tomorrow. Will have a lot of free
time this week, anyway."

Arkady thought to suggest that, if Ethan were concerned
about this whole theory of his, he should jerk off to each one of
the deceased again, as perhaps that would bring them back to life.
He smiled, imagined saying it, gauged how it would go over,
concluded the joke would actually go over well but decided
against it, knowing that Ethan, despite his jocularity and
irreverence, would have a longstanding sore spot, especially as
regarding Annie.

"Well, let me know how it goes," Arkady said after they paid
their bill, with Ethan making good on his sake promise. Ethan
thanked Arkady for coming out, as going out wasn't always
Arkady's thing – if it weren't for law school, he'd never leave
home, he often said – and, truth be told, Ethan wasn't too far
removed from that position himself. But that would change. Best
to make use of this time off, take BART out to the East Bay or
something, hang out in Berkeley or a nice part of Oakland.

Before they departed, Ethan asked, "hey, with our free time,
on the next nice day want to check out Mountain View Cemetery
in Oakland? It's supposed to be nice, designed by the guy who
did Central Park."

"Eh, Oakland, that's so far from me. Hang out in Oakland
enough and you'll end up in a cemetery."

"Eh, alright, your loss dude." There were limits to Arkady's
generosity, it seemed. Know what, he'd plan some little outing
for him and Tzipora. Though proposing a cemetery, no matter
how harmonious and lovely, might not be the best second date
outing.

*

North Bay, he'd decided. That's where he'd take her, some nice weekend, up to Sausalito. Maybe that was too ambitious for a second date, especially since he didn't have a car and that would be a bitch of an Uber, unless she drove, although he didn't like the optics of being ferried around by her on their second date.

And that would have to wait, because he texted Monday night and she offered Wednesday night, and he said sure, that works, and he would have said so even if classes hadn't been cancelled for the week.

Sure, he was supposed to keep up with this week's previously assigned reading and assignments, as each professor vowed to make up the lost time somehow. Not having to go to class gave him an excess of free time, which he knew could be dangerous. He didn't want to let her know he'd had more free time than usual. Why was that? Why did her receptive enthusiasm for their next date stir up this anxiety?

She'd said she just had to take him to her favorite neighborhood spot in the Inner Sunset, The Social Kitchen and Brewery, which had this confit duck leg that inspired a series of lust and heart emojis, to which he reduced himself to responding in kind. She emailed him confirmation for their reservation for Wednesday at 7.

Her neighborhood. That should be a good sign, but why didn't it feel that way? He looked the place up online and saw it had a large tap list, bet she likes to drink, perhaps too much. No, that wasn't fair to conclude, he was just doing that thing where he looked for reasons to be negative.

Ethan felt compelled by both an inborn and fraternal masculine obligation to see her again, see if she would take him home. It was as if he strained his ears he could hear the tender cry of fellow men issuing orders, 'of course go for it, what are you doing!?' Wasn't that what he wanted, to be accepted by a woman, wasn't that self-evidently better than jerking off for hours on end (in the privacy of his own home, a curated experience on his own schedule, without pressure or obligation . .).

Why yes, yes of course, he was sure every man would tell him so, if he could take an official survey of other young men, why of course, a night out with an attractive young woman, with the dangling prospect of her apartment nearby, sounded greatly preferable; however, if one could make that a secret survey, those numbers might fall precipitously.

Self-discipline. He was disciplined by nature, at least for most things. This masturbation habit wasn't even seen as a vice, that might be the problem, just more like an essential component of who he was and what he did. Fond memories as a teen, sequestered alone in his room, crawling through chat rooms for hours on end, the dopamine rush of novelty, simultaneously desirous of affection and resentful of how much he wanted their approval, how he wished to be the one on the receiving end of someone's romantic efforts. Then, hours in, or days in, or weeks in, or months in, of repeated conversation with someone, to have his personality and efforts unequivocally rewarded, to be shown that he was loved, in the form of NSFW selfies or cyber-sex. The thrill, the feeling of accomplishment, the prospect of this enduring relationship, this confidante in love, communication immediate enough to be intimate, far removed enough not to cramp or impose upon him. For them it was probably just a lark, a way to kill time when they were bored, but for him, it was something more, each new online relationship a new possibility, a potential entryway into another life, a new direction, someone to take his pain away.

Back to self-discipline, focus. No masturbation, none at all. Store up his reserves. Get his energy up. Do push-ups. Cut his fingernails. He showered and cut his pubes, nice and trimmed, couldn't shake the nagging feeling that he hoped, for some woebegone reason, he wouldn't need to show them off.

*

'Hey there," Tzipora greeted him outside the restaurant. "You waited, how sweet of you," she gave a big smile. He noticed again despite himself how gummy her smile was.

"Hah, of course I did." The reservation was under her name, after all, but he took the compliment.

Ethan opened the door for her and followed close behind. She wore a white-and-light-blue vertically-lined shirt dress with an ornamental thin brown belt above her stomach, with sharp blue heels. Her outfit was a bit flip, spritzy and fun, and he wondered if that was how she presented herself to her Bay Area real estate clients. He wore black slacks, matching laceless black work shoes, and a button-down dark blue and white shirt from J. Crew, which, in a sense, looked like the masculine counterpart to her softer-colored shirt dress.

The restaurant was fairly crowded, although not terribly as it was a Wednesday night. Tzipora made slight, intimate contact with him as she slipped past to take the lead at the host stand and he imagined how they looked together, this attractive, professional young couple, out for the night.

"So, how'd work treat you today," he started off after they were seated at their table. Why, he wasn't sure, he just wanted something to say. "Your hair looks really nice, I like what you've done with it, it's so straight." He was making an educated guess, her hair looked fuller and straighter than last time, signs of being feted over. Her straight blonde hair made him think of Annie again. No, that wasn't accurate. It was like he forced himself to think of Annie, conjuring guilt because that was a standard emotion that, however unpleasant, he was well acquainted with, as if trying to obscure the other emergent anxieties with this handy excuse if things didn't work out.

"Aww thanks," she made an appreciative face, though he wondered if it was bad form to let her know that he knew she had her hair worked on. "It's nothing, just a dry bar, they just wash it and blow dry it, but I like it," and she lifted her shoulders and smiled, like a little girl imagining herself a twinkling princess. Her appreciation of such a simple pleasure and her lack of guile battened down his defenses.

"Got to appreciate the simple things," he said, true advice which sounded idiotically meaningless when expressed aloud. She was busying herself with the extensive tap list menu, and Ethan bought time by doing the same.

The date went well. He kept up, made eye-contact, got her laughing, and slipped in that he had this week off from classes. That fact was introduced a bit artificially, shoehorned into his discussions about law school generally, and he didn't tell her why, let her think it was something like Spring Break. He had to let her know that, right, let her know he had nothing to wake up for early tomorrow, right guys, am I doing this right, making you proud, nudge nudge, wink wink, she knows the score, that's what I'm supposed to do, this is what I'm supposed to do, date and be out and be a real person....

Tzipora spoke passionately about her job, widened her eyes in a face that read "oh yes I just did" when she helped herself to a forkful of his plate in response to his faux-protectiveness. He let her have two of the three melty chocolate chip cookies that comprised dessert.

For drinks, she'd ordered two different hop-forward IPAs from niche breweries he'd never heard of. Even her beer choices were respectable. He got two beers that had also sounded good to her, and they drank freely from each other's glasses.

She still, however, made no effort to even pretend to reach for the bill when it came, or attempt that gambit where she insists that they split it, even though they both knew that wasn't going to fly. Tzipora, he felt, liked what it represented when her dates plunked down for the bill: that she was worth the expenditure and the effort, that the date was, in a sense, a courting process by which the male was the unabashed wooer and she the woo-ee.

The thought came to him disruptively: he hated dating. He wanted the heady, all-or-nothing exhilaration of someone who was all-in, committed one hundred percent, an unabashed loyal companion: this tip-toeing and skirting and tentativeness and feeling things out wasn't for him. Although he knew in reality that this was a necessary process, and what he wanted was frankly unrealistic, an expectation no one could meet, something more akin to the quest for the unalloyed, perfect love from God than one could expect from a flawed human with her own personality and set of needs.

Bill paid, and no mention yet of any further plans or date spots. As they headed to the door, Ethan noticed a flabby white guy around his age, if not a bit older, navigating through the crowd and approaching them in such a way to show he meant to get their attention.

"Tziporah?" the flabby man said with the mildest twinge of uncertainty, as he caught up with them just as Ethan reached the door.

"Hi," she responded before processing, and then, "oh hey! Cliff!"

"I thought it was you but then I thought, is she in San Francisco? I remember you were from here but I didn't-"

"Oh yeah! I moved back here a few years ago, after college! Do you live here, what are you doing in the Sunset of all places?"

"Yeah, I moved here like three months ago, I'm down in the Mission, was just grabbing drinks with a friend who lives out here." This Cliff character turned quickly in the direction of another chubby white guy, this one with a beard, who gave an upraised hand-acknowledgement from his table.

"Oh I'm sorry, by the way, I didn't mean to interrupt anything," Cliff said placatingly, again some sacrifice to the masculine edict not to disrupt another man's date. Ethan made a face to show that of course it was nothing, and, between the way Tziporah introduced Ethan and Cliff's limp handshake, Ethan knew he wasn't a threat.

"Cliff, I - think - we are Facebook friends? I'm on Insta also, under Zip underscore Segal."

"Sounds like a good band name," Ethan said, one of the easiest comments to make, although it got a chuckle.

"Reach out to me sometime! Also, actually, hold on," and she took out a card from her purse. "I'm a real estate agent here, too! So also of course reach out to me for any apartment purposes, or if you know anyone looking, and shoot me a line sometime and we can catch up!"

"Will do," Cliff said with good humor, headed back toward his friend, and waved goodbye without actually waving, just a hand-up.

Ethan held the door open for her and they left, walking very slowly. He checked his phone subtly, 8:47 p.m.

"So funny. Small world. I hadn't seen Cliff since, like, junior year. We had a ton of classes together; I think he was a business major."

It wasn't like they ran into each other at some backyard wrestling match in rural Arkansas, a truly what-are-the-odds-we'd-both-be-here event. It was San Francisco, a pretty big city where people ended up.

"Smart to give him your business card."

"Hah, I know, I felt bad about it, sort of, but a girl's gotta keep selling, build that brand! And," she leaned into him, a bit of a playful push, as if thinking he was jokingly teasing her, "I'm good at my job so it's mutually beneficial." She was play-acting sassy, as when conversation petered and people didn't know each other too well they assumed roles and attitudes as a way of keeping the momentum going.

"So," she turned in front of him. "My place is only a few blocks away, it's a nice night out, if you want to walk with me? Since you don't have any classes this week and everything, I was wondering if you wanted to come up and see my place? It's early."

*

She had a real person's apartment, a mat to wipe your feet and an umbrella stand by the front door, modern furniture, a smart-looking, well-groomed tan couch with throw pillows, a geometric glass coffee table with brightly-colored monochrome coasters, artwork that was a mix of the silly (a grinning monkey face atop a cartoon ballerina in mid-pirouette) and geographical (a black and white photo of a fog-ensconced Golden Gate Bridge). While it was dark now, he could tell that during the day the wraparound windows that stretched from the couch to the adjacent wall provided ample natural light. The recess lights made him feel he'd been spending his days at home in dim, janky low-resolution, and now this was high-def. No matter what she claimed or promised, she'd never be able to tolerate his apartment, not for a moment, and he'd need to refuse her entreaties. He'd never seen the show, but he knew the premise of The Beverly Hillbillies and felt himself in a similar scenario.

Tzipora was well-mannered, well-provided-for, happy, and seemingly untroubled by neuroses, which naturally left Ethan unhappy and uncomfortable. A part of him wanted to rebel in some way, as if this well-kept apartment represented some oppressive staid authority that needed undermining. Of course, that was idiotic, and he knew it. What was he doing, why was he psyching himself out, just relax –

"Would you like a drink? Let me show you the place." He debated whether to have a drink. The first stop on the tour was the bar rack in the kitchen, which featured about two representatives of each type of alcohol, one modest, one upscale. For gin, she had Tanqueray and Monkey 47. He could go for a gin and tonic, and never had Monkey 47.

But he shouldn't. He'd already had at least two drinks, probably closer to two-and-a-half. A gin and tonic now, one he bet she would make with a strong pour, would get him drunk for sure. Still, the urge to ask was strong, to reproof his chattering mind, but no, don't, resist these intruding compromises, don't intentionally sabotage yourself. Just relax, focus.

"I'm good for now, let me see the rest of your place. You real estate agents know how to pick them."

"How could I help clients pick out a place to live if I couldn't do it for myself?" she said over her shoulder, in a showroom mood and clearly heading for the bedroom. She knew about the sexual allure of being a young, female real estate agent, knew about the whole porn subgenre, he bet, and was playing off that now.

"So, this is my bedroom, whereas the rest of the apartment is supposed to be a bit light and" – she took a deep breath and stirred her hands, as if ventilating the air around her – "airy and make you feel at home and alive. For the bedroom, I like the dark color, the dark wood dresser, the black cool sheets" – she ran a swift hand across them – "the goal is to make the temperature a bit lower in here, nice and cool and relaxing to get that good night's sleep."

"Mhmm," he said.

"So did you want that drink? We can see what's on Netflix, do you like - comedy."

"I like this bedroom of yours."

"You do?" She said, with too much false-innocence.

"Yeah," and, pushing past his doubts and the awkwardness of the whole charade, he slowly put his left arm around the small of her back.

Tzipora made a noise that was either "oh" or "oooh," leaned back and smiled as their lips closed the distance. His hands went to the expected places, and she pulled them to her ass, which he squeezed out of etiquette and then brought his hands back up to the small of her back, repelled by thoughts of what a "juicy ass" would literally entail, something caving in completely in his hand like soft cheese or leaving stains on his fingers like a mushy raspberry.

She pulled him in the direction of the bed by the middle of his shirt.

On their back, and he was again pleasantly surprised and impressed by how smooth her stomach was. She pushed herself back to more of a sitting position. "You can unwrap me," she said. He wondered how she imagined herself; a femme fatale, a classic movie siren, there was no devilish purr or bit lip but there didn't need to be.

So much pageantry for the base act of fluid swapping.

No, that wasn't true, that wasn't fair, this was fun, dramatic, exciting, the pleasure that makes life worth living…. if this was truly it, he was truly fucked indeed.

"I'd love to," he forced himself to say, singularly aware of his beating heart, his off-pace breathing. Ethan bet she thought he was just overcome with lust.

He pulled her belt, and she dramatically played the part, even if the belt wasn't what undressed her as the buttons still needed to be undone. Tzipora undid the top buttons herself as part of her dramatic unraveling, and slid in close to him, voracious.

Her hands went to his crotch, and her lips came forward, mouthing the outline of his penis through his pants. A mouthful of slacks couldn't have tasted too good. His heart rate increased.

What normal man wishes he had to suddenly take a shit? That would be a good excuse, wouldn't it, to put a stop to this? A flight to the bathroom, the tumbling energy leading inexorably toward sex disrupted by a reminder of the disreputable, shameful side of the human body. But he didn't even have the urgent filling of his bowels that usually, and strangely, accompanied his lust, his body's way of slamming the brakes. So nuanced were his bowels that they somehow knew that this upcoming sexual exchange was a normal, desirable one, rather than his usual hours-long waste of abasement that his bowels attempted to sabotage.

"You first," he said, and soon she was bottomless, and Ethan was doing everything in his power with his fingers and mouth to sexually fulfill her to the point of exhaustion. She smelled and tasted fresh, and was, for this very occasion, neatly trimmed to the point of hairlessness.

He did good work, if her sounds and gyrations could be believed.

She wanted more. And he wanted more too, didn't he?

"I want your cock inside me," Tzipora whispered after pulling away from his ear to make sure her panting plea was articulated, something which would fill most men with satisfied glee but only served to expedite his looming panic. She pulled down his pants, pulled down his boxers, his barely-hard penis flopped out, and did she find that surprising, that he wasn't hard yet? No, not from her zeal, from the way she closed her eyes, devoured it, reflected his own gracious giving spirit right back at him, acted like she needed some essential salt to survive that could be obtained only from consuming his cock.

He wasn't getting hard. He should be, his balls were aching, but he wasn't getting hard, other than the autonomic semi-erection that comes from the application of any lubrication to the tip and shaft of his cock.

He closed his eyes and pretended to enjoy this. Crazy thing was he *did* enjoy it, there was nothing wrong with the physical sensation. He could be hard as a rock if only he was at home, jerking off thinking about her sights and sounds. In fact, if he could replicate this precise physical experience while looking at porn and masturbating, that would be out-of-this-world. It was the expectation, it was the lack of control, it was the presence of another person, it was having to perform, it was someone else's hand – poor girl, she was applying her hand now, which was great, except it wasn't his own hand, applied at the angles he was used to – and he had to continue closing his eyes and thrusting slightly and pretending to be in heaven while his penis stayed obstinately limp.

Enough time had passed that she must have known something was wrong.

"Let me sit down here baby," he said, flopping onto the bed, spreading his legs wide. That helped blood flow into the major arteries in his legs, he knew. Ethan even put his arms behind his head, like he was still readying himself for some decadent pleasure.

Such a trooper, she played along, came at him from an angle, riding her tongue up from his balls up the shaft of his penis, swirling the tip around her mouth, one hand under his testicles, slowly rubbing and stroking his shaft. His softness, he realized with a mix of relief and horror, was being interpreted as a referendum on her skills. Up to a point, of course, because shockingly soon the first dread words came, the words that punctured any equipoise he was trying to maintain:

"It's not working," Tzipora said, with evident dismay, disappointment, maybe even repulsive condemnation.

"Sorry, I'm just, maybe a bit nervous and a bit drunk," he said weakly, started tugging on himself with his left hand. He needed to be seated at a chair to get that angle he really liked; the wetness of her saliva extant enough to get a good lather but soon dried out.

He'd made some progress, maybe at a solid-half erection. He got on top of her, pushed his mouth onto hers, kissed her, began to finger her again, distract her with pleasure and surreptitiously smuggle her wetness onto himself, fingering her with his right hand, rubbing himself with his left.

"I'm just really nervous for some reason." He didn't go so far as to humiliate himself with a line like "because I just really like you," but her harshness had softened in league with his renewed fingering and impassioned kisses.

"I have an IUD," she told him. Great, so he wouldn't even have a constricting condom to blame for his downfall. He realized he somehow hadn't even thought about condoms up until she mentioned it. That could have been his way out: well, sorry, I just don't feel comfortable having sex without a condom, but no, no. That was fucking bullshit, this should be glorious, he needed to get it up, get it up, overcome whatever this is and get it up.

"I just sometimes get nervous if I feel like I'm being waited on. Can, I, do you mind-" and by the end of his blubbering, so accommodating was she that she had consented to him covering her fucking face with a mixture of the blanket and a pillow, because the best and most intimate lovemaking comes when your partner isn't entitled to lay eyes upon you. The rank absurdity of it just deepened his shame – look at him, a healthy twenty-four-year-old man with a lovely woman so eager to make love to him, and here he was, at best semihard, dick still pointing down toward his knees. He rubbed it against her pussy to test whether he was hard enough to enter and, as he attempted, she gasped prematurely, perhaps as a sign of encouragement, and no, no luck.

He thought about that flabby fucker Cliff, Ethan bet Cliff would give anything to trade places with Ethan right now. Cliff would make the best of this situation, wouldn't he, he'd have no troubles, soon Tzipora would be so disheartened and upset about wasting her time with such a limp dick loser that she'd be lowering her standards to let Cliff rail her, screaming, moaning, so alive and grateful to have a real man plowing her, slapping that "juicy" ass that Cliff pines for, maybe even yelling "pound me you flabby fucker, never stop pounding me."

Succumbing to his self-debasement actually worked, and he was suddenly hard. This was a shameful boner, but he needed to capitalize on it. He thrusted and she gasped with pleasure, and he felt from the shifting weight that the pillow no longer concealed her face. He kept his eyes tight, imagining Cliff pounding her, imagining what it'd look like if he were watching her getting fucked on video, the best angle to highlight her form, her face right up to the camera, the gradations of mounting pleasure . . . but it wasn't working and he slipped out of her, and his cock seemed to shrivel in shame. He thought damningly and outrageously of a raisin under a hairdryer.

"I'm really sorry. This is terrible, I'm so embarrassed." He rolled over, eyes closed but knowing wet tears would smear his vision if he opened them.

"It's okay, Ethan. Really, it is. It's okay."

Of course it wasn't, he knew, and things were irredeemably destroyed between them.

"I, I've just been really stressed recently." (Would he debase himself by telling her about his dead colleagues, pretending it had anything to do with them? No, no he couldn't.) "I've been really depressed recently," (recently, as if this were a new phenomenon), "and I think I've become addicted to masturbation and porn, honestly." Just what every woman wants to hear from their partner on their second date.

"It's been going on for a little while," he added as a compromise with the truth. "I had a big break-up a while back and it's kind of gotten worse, the porn and masturbation, I mean, since then, but I'm working on it, it's just, sometimes I get really nervous, you know it's like when it doesn't go well once, then you just get so nervous for the next time?"

"I understand Ethan, I do. I haven't told almost anyone this, but back in college I actually had, I guess, what you could call a cocaine problem."

"Really?" He opened his bleary eyes and smiled. "I can't imagine that." It was relieving to focus on someone else's failings.

"I don't want to oversell it," she said, making an exaggerated, extended face, like jokingly backpedaling or talking around an uncomfortable subject. "But yes, I thought it was a problem and it made me act in ways that weren't helpful to me or my family."

"Thanks for sharing that, I appreciate it. I just feel really, really, really embarrassed. It has nothing to do with you, I swear." He knew he could dedicate his life to swearing to this fact, but it would do no good. "I just need to work on this, I need to. Well, how about this, we can try again soon. How does that sound?"

"Sounds good."

"I hope it was still fun for you."

"You made me cum twice Ethan, I would call that a good night."

284

"Really?"

"Yes, really. Do you want me to make you a drink?"

He didn't deserve a drink. He was emotionally and physically exhausted.

"No, that's okay."

"I'm actually really tired myself, if that's okay. I have a showing early tomorrow. Here, I can show you the rest of the apartment and the bathroom while I get ready."

Nothing she said lessened the shame. Not as they brushed their teeth and went to sleep, or the minor cuddling, or the next morning when they only spoke briefly as she got ready for work, her urgent early-morning routines having eroded last night's consoling gestures.

*

The N-Judah streetcar to Civic Center station and a walk home, a day in isolation in his apartment, and his resolve stayed strong during the day, no porn, no masturbation. The foggy, alien hangover from a night of emotional exhaustion. What he feared had come to pass, and it'd been terrible. He checked his peanut butter mouse trap, not sure of what he wanted to find, maybe a creature suffering worse than he; no, he didn't really want that, and he luckily found only dried peanut butter. He wondered if he should replace it with fresh butter, but didn't want to, rationalized it because how picky could mice be? They ate garbage, think they'd really abstain because the peanut butter wasn't creamy enough?

He viewed masturbation as a disease, with the last time he'd done it being his recovery day, like the day a fever broke. Just as someone ceases to be a communicable disease vector sometime after the symptoms cease, some day after his masturbation habit ceased would his penis, rid of the disease of excess masturbation, respond normally to female stimulation?

He spent time scanning online forums about masturbation addiction, cringing at the resemblances to his own plight, kept reading the extreme outlier cases and comforting himself that he'd never lost his job from getting caught jerking off at work, although, of course, he didn't have a job currently to get fired from. With long nights at a law firm in his future, could he be so confident?

And the exhortations and reminders that ended several of the posts, this mantra, that you are not alone; could there be a support group without a mantra? You are not alone. That repelled him, only because he knew he'd never be able to convince himself it was true, even if he so desperately wished it were. You Are Not Alone? Why, because he shared the same disabling, humiliating addiction? He was alone with his lonely nights, he was alone as he went to sleep, he was alone with his history, he was alone with his thoughts, when his credit card bill needed to be paid, he was alone, when his rent needed to be paid, he was alone, in his reactions to reading 'remember, you are not alone,' he was alone, his thoughts were his, and his alone, and how he longed for someone to take over for him, to right the things he knew were wrong.

At night, he received a text from Tzipora. She said she enjoyed meeting him and had a fun time, but it was better to be friends. Apparently, she thought harder (such a cruel word to use given the circumstances) about the night before, and she'd been uncomfortable with how he'd covered her face with the blanket and the pillows.

Last night's anguish bloomed afresh, and the fiery pinprick in his stomach, the way he shook his head to himself, as if the news were a bug on his head that could be shaken off: his individual reaction, that was his alone, too.

At night, the only illumination from his laptop and his desk lamp.

Gamay was online, "Gamay," better known as Book_Whore, and he poured tokens into his account to take her into a private session. Presented as an act of charity, that made him feel better. Now she could buy groceries, he told himself, get herself some art supplies, although the healthy number of tippers in her chat room before he whisked her away to private let him know that she wasn't exactly hurting. And as absolutely pathetic and shameful he knew it'd be to view this from afar, it made him feel better to tell her he'd just broken up with someone who didn't understand that he wanted to take things slow in relationships, because he was unusually sensitive and needed to trust someone before doing something as sacred as the sexual act. Gamay played along, expressed disbelief at what an idiot that woman must have been and lamented how insensitive people were these days, thanked him for sharing, told him she loved his cock, and that things will be okay, baby.

He felt his heart beating healthily, his pleasure in having a healthy, functioning, circulating body, and looked down at this throbbing, beet-red cock and couldn't imagine how this was the same flaccid, uncooperative embarrassment of the night before.

"Can you tell me you love me, Gamay?" Ethan said with his eyes closed. It was intended to be a moment of triumph, because, of course, this yielding, moaning woman loved him, but the yearning that slinked through in his request brought him back to Earth.

"Aww Ethan, of course I love you. You're so sweet to me. I love how hard you get for me. How long have we been chatting?"

"Over a year."

"That means a lot to me. Of course I love you. And this time I want to watch you cum. I want to watch you forget your troubles, stay here with me and share your orgasm with me."

"Because you love me?"

"Of course, I love you," Gamay said with rising enthusiasm, the way she'd respond to any submissive request, and he imagined the goonish voices of the other lowlifes who cammed with her.

He closed his eyes and shook the thoughts away, concentrated on the feeling, on her love, yes, she did love him, in her way, they were friends, he knew all about her, where she lived, her job, her schooling, her –

Who loves someone as long as they are getting paid? It's her job. Who loves someone so much they won't tell them their real name, their real email address, agree to visit –

He shook his head again, shook the thoughts away.

"Mhmmm that cock is so big it's ready to burst," he heard her exult in his headphones. "Look at me baby, open your eyes I want to see how much I love you."

He opened his eyes as he came, spurting everywhere, more than he'd cum in a while; his laptop, his desk, his lamp, nowhere spared. A few breaths, back to Earth, thinking, God, how disgusting was his laptop keyboard, no wonder certain keys stuck when he typed, it was filthy, horrifying.

"Mhmm baby, you came so much for me."

Now naked and vulnerable, unblinded by lust, the anxieties and failings he'd blanketed now finding their footing and coming back to roost, wishing he could stay put forever, not having to assess the damage around him. "I did," he admitted to her, "that was all for you," the words both true and sounding hollow simultaneously. "I'm spent." He wanted to be offline, alone with himself, although needed to be courteous and grateful.

"Have a good night," he typed out, and, in the briefest of glimpses between when he clicked on the "X" to close MyFreeCams and when he released his mouse he saw, out of the indistinct corner of his eye, her midsection flopping back and forth and her arms arcing, as if caught in an invisible and repeating crash test demonstration.

Ethan blinked rapidly, and it was as if the vision had been washed out. Cum was pooling on his leg, soaking his threadbare boxers. He folded them a bit, made sure none spilled out, used wet paper towels to clean himself off, and then went to work on the laptop, the cover of his lamp, around his desk. The one pencil he had in his nest of pens was capped with a white crown, and he thought of the white nighttime caps Donald Duck wore in the cartoons.

Reviewing what he'd just seen: her naked in her chair, face to the ceiling, violently spasming, thighs lunging toward the camera, completely without control of her body, couldn't see her face but imagining her eyes vacant and unseeing, mouth wide open, emitting a ragged clicking, the sound of a throat gasping for breath.

What had he just seen? No, that couldn't be, she'd just said something about how much he'd cum? That's what she last said, right? Interrogating his actions, and he wondered if he did nothing because the longer he did nothing the less there was he could do. He went back to his computer and logged back into MFC.

This user is no longer online, he saw under her profile. She must have signed off. If she'd died or had a seizure (why are you thinking these things, had a seizure, what?) then her camera would still be on, wouldn't it, as if transfixed, unrelentingly capturing her lifeless body in her chair. He saw Gamay in his mind's eye, now slumped over, her naked body still on display. He fumed at the wretched comments he imagined other losers would leave in her chatroom ("A shame! But this view! No complaints!"), and then wondered to himself why such imagined ghastly comments came so readily to him.

What could he do, call 911? "I have an emergency, a cam girl, that's, that's a woman who performs on webcams for money, they don't always have to be naked but usually are, this one was, look, anyway, that's not the important part, I was watching her and then she started spasming, no, I don't know exactly where she lives, I know she said New Mexico, but these cam girls usually don't entirely tell the truth because they need to keep their identities secret, oh, yeah in that regard I don't know her name. She told me it's 'Gamay' but that's not her real name, she went by Book_Whore, so canvass the nearest libraries and used book stores for an enthusiastic blonde with braids and a giddy smile, early twenties, green eyes I think, not sure, definitely at least a C-cup, unshaved down there."

No, that wasn't going to work. He spent the next hour signing in and out of MFC, hoping that he'd see her online, checking her profile to see if there was some update in case he'd missed some blink-and-you-miss-it login. But he was already exhausted, and the more tired he became the more he felt the onrush of last night's tidal wave of shame and humiliation cresting toward him. He limped to the bathroom, brushed his teeth, who cares about washing his face, and then slumped into a restless sleep, aberrant, fragmentary dreams about being exhausted, sweating in boiling temperatures and sliding off every chair and bed he took refuge upon.

That'd be the last time he masturbated, for sure, a promise he renewed the following morning, literally formed the words in his head: that is the last time I will ever masturbate.

*

Classes began that following week. Naturally, the mood was hushed and sullen, as if even the most trifling hint of fun would be somehow disrespectful. Bar Reviews had been cancelled for the rest of the month, although very quickly some suggested it would be best to keep the weekly tradition to assist in the healing process, and soon enough, Ethan knew, things would be back to some semblance of normal.

That Monday morning a thought came to him: sure, his performance with Tziporah had been dreadful, barely qualifying as "sex," but his penis had still made contact with her vagina. Could he have infected her with whatever contaminant, whatever he had that was causing all these deaths? (Yes, he told himself, this was all connected to him, it had to be. These couldn't all be coincidences.) Tziporah had texted him the day after their encounter, however, hadn't she? Gamay's reaction seemed to occur about a minute after he came.

What did he have to lose, his conscience could be assuaged with a quick text, which he pounded out and sent that Monday morning between class, before he could think too hard about it. "Hey Tziporah, I know things didn't work well with us, that's fine, may sound weird but just sending text to make sure you are feeling okay?"

By that afternoon she'd gotten back to him. "Yes, thanks for asking. Y?" So quickly had he lost the courtesy of having full words spelled out for him in text messages. Okay, she was fine, conscience assuaged. She dumped him because of a performance issue after he'd confided in her, thrown him away, she didn't deserve an explanatory text back. This little victory blotted out, just for a moment, the panic, unease, and physical dislocation he felt, a feeling of almost losing his balance, that he experienced when he again thought about this predicament.

"So how'd it go with our Tzipora," Arkady asked as they sat in the cafeteria. It took Ethan a moment to comprehend, as he was staring at Fujita in conversation with some other classmates, hoping she'd notice him and give him a confirmatory head nod or, even better, that little 'catch you in a second' head nod and then come on over to their table and chat. And after he heard the question, he wanted to keep staring, occupying himself in some way as to avoid answering.

"That well, huh?" Arkady laughed.

Ethan leaned in with furtive intensity, a clue to the assumed confidentiality of what he was going to reveal. "Let's just leave it at not well. Arkady-"

"Ethan," Arkady intoned. He loved a conspiratorial reveal, and was responding in the type of hushed tones this conversation required.

"I'm not even going to preface this all with the 'I know this will sound crazy' stuff. I just have to ask you because you know about science."

"In these crazy times, nothing is totally off limits from legitimate inquiry. Ask away."

Ethan just remembered that Arkady had once told him about some book he'd read that argued that AIDS was not caused by HIV. Arkady hadn't gone so far as to say the book was persuasive or correct, just that it'd been "very interesting, very interesting indeed," in that way he did when he wanted to say something could be true but not be stuck definitely to a position. Maybe Arkady wasn't the best person to ask, but he did have a PhD in cell biology from a top school, and they just didn't hand those out.

"I know this is absolutely impossible, I know. But I - look, do you know about a website called MyFreeCams?"

"Of course. I go on all the time. I never tip," and he started laughing in embarrassment at this admission of his stinginess. "If I get a good job, I will, though. But why buy the cow, as they say."

"Well, so, okay so I was camming with this girl."

"You private cammed? You are spending money on this stuff! Have you not heard, the Internet has more free pornography than you will ever need in a lifetime?"

"Well, not if you're a connoisseur like me. But anyway, I'll just say I cammed with her, you know, finished, and then I swear to fucking god seconds later I saw her have a seizure or something even worse."

"Jesus."

"And then, you know, with the deaths of our three classmates, Annie, Jana, Amber."

"Yeah?" Arkady said, an expectant tone that showed he was not following. It dawned on Ethan that leading Arkady down this path of lunatic-logic was far easier and more enjoyable than revealing his emasculating tale of reality-induced impotence.

"I know with hundred percent certainty that I thought specifically of Annie, Jana, and Amber each time, doing, ya know-"

"I got it."

"And then they immediately had their incidents, and then this cam girl thing-"

"Not possible."

"I know it's not possible, but still-"

"You just want me to confirm for you, on a scientific level, that your habit of," and here he remembered the need to lower his voice, "that your habit of jerking off to women who seem to have unfortunate ends, assuming what you are recollecting is true, is entirely coincidental."

"I know it is, but still-"

"It's just probably for the best if you stopped doing all that for a while. You'd feel better, spend that time doing that going to the gym, get your heart pumping and feel better! Be like Arnold! And if I'm wrong, by stopping you will be saving lives!"

"The gym, dude," Ethan gave him a light-hearted point of the finger, to reaffirm what he just said, "the gym. How often do you go?"

"I go every day."

"Every day?"

"What, do you think this body is an accident?" Arkady said, shifting his body as if flexing, without being so unaware as to actually flex in the cafeteria. "I told you, I want to be like Arnold, he is my hero, another Central European from a shit village who came to this country and did great things."

"A stretch to call yourself Central European since you're from Bulgaria."

"Central-Southeastern European. To Americans we are all from the same place anyway. Did I ever show you those pictures when I was in my prime?" Yes, Ethan remembered when Arkady brought up something about when he first started his PhD program, knew nobody and spent all his time at the gym, to pretextually show a cornered Ethan and Charlotte his locked-jaw, topless selfie flex photos.

"Kur-mannnnn, what's up." It was Fujita, her usual mix of being both friendly and distant, as if en route to doing something else.

"Hey Fuji," (he resolved to not use that attempted nickname again) –

"Uhh Kerman, not that, I heard that all the time growing up."

"A good apple," Arkady consoled. "The best, maybe."

"Sorry Fujita. How are you holding up with all this craziness?"

"I mean, what can I say. Just awful, just the craziest thing that I bet has ever happened to a law school class."

Ethan saw Arkady move his head slightly in concentration, as if evaluating the veracity of what she just said and imagining counterfactuals.

"It's just so strange, back to all this, three of our classmates, I don't know, just try and keep going, I guess, wait to see if the school does anything, or the families reach out to the school, not sure, but we keep going." She raised a coffee mug to her lips, as if to emphasize that she usually drinks coffee and is keepin' on by doing the same.

Ethan hadn't even noticed she'd been carrying anything. Something about her plump, luscious lips pursing and separating slightly as they pushed against the coffee cup made his heart start pumping. He was impressed, if that was the right word, how equanimous she was about all this, although he didn't know why he'd expect otherwise, and realizing this made him feel deeply ashamed, like he was harboring a guilty conscience, that she wouldn't be so even-keeled if he admitted the truth, the truth that this was all his fault, that he was a walking virus; no, even worse, a walking, communicable pervert-virus.

"So no Bar Reviews for the foreseeable future I take it?" Ethan asked for something to say.

"No, no there's not," she said as if saying 'well you can say that again.' "Although I'm sure there's going to be a couple unofficial outings around the City, some were talking about even going out to Berkeley or Oakland for some, see some new sights."

"Oh, that sounds pretty awesome," Ethan said, looking at Arkady like that was something Arkady would be remotely interested in. "Let me know about those. We should swap numbers, I think."

"We should, huh?"

"Yeah, you know with everything going on, and I want to go to Berkeley to drink, and, you're pretty smart, right?"

"Am I? Lemme think and get back to you about that."

At first he thought she was referring to thinking about whether to reveal her number and not self-deprecatingly evaluating her intelligence; it wasn't like him to misunderstand self-deprecation. In fact, when he'd first moved to San Francisco, he marveled at how his classmates seemed unable to comprehend self-deprecation and other varieties of potentially uncomfortable humor.

"Well, I think you're pretty smart, or at least you convincingly present yourself as smart, so it'd be good if we exchanged numbers to study in the future. And with everything going on, you know?"

"Better to be safe than sorry. Asking for my number directly in front of a friend, I'm impressed, Kerman."

"Oh Fujita, c'mon."

"I'm just kidding. But here, let me take yours and I'll text you." And she did, in fact she stood right at the table as she texted him her number.

"Is there a particularly good picture of you I should put in for you for your profile on my phone?"

"Oh, you do that for all your friends, I'm sure? Let me see the ones you put in for your other friends and then I'll send you a good one."

"Okay, I mean, expect to see a lot of cock shots but sure, take a look."

"Oh God, Kerman, you're nuts. Okay, I'm outta here, keep in touch though I feel you will."

"Peace Fujita."

Arkady looked at her as she cleared the room – she was wearing particularly flattering dark jeans – and respectfully bobbed his head. "Look at you, man, you seemed to have bounced back. A bit too cavalier, maybe, but that was good when she said she'd send you a good picture, keep the sexual tension flowing there, and you did get her number there."

"I mean, when I'm in your presence I gotta impress, right?"

"All the more reason to go to the gym. You have her interested, now build up those pecs and seal the deal."

"I'll build up pecs that can't be denied."

Why bother, he wondered? So he could prance around and make a show of things, so he could flame out again in humiliation? God, never with someone he went to school with, never, he couldn't live with that fallout. It was as if he overcompensated for his inability to execute by making a show of his glib pursuits, a dog constantly chasing cars, terrified of what to do when he caught one.

*

The gym helped, Ethan found. He went every day, whenever Arkady did, and it was amazing how a workout focused the brain. Struggling to lift weights shunted other issues to the netherworld, at least for a time. And the continued bullshitting with Arkady was always fun, and there were some other law student-regulars at the gym they'd bullshit with between sessions. And afterward, the exertion would bolster his mood to some degree and fatigue him sufficiently for sleep.

It wasn't all great, though. Undergraduates at other SF public colleges were allowed to use the gym, and particular pulchritudinous images of certain undergrads in work-out pants and tight tops had a way of lodging in the brain. Arkady confirming the obvious attractiveness of each didn't help. On some nights, he wondered if his masturbation-hex could affect a woman whose name and identity he didn't actually know, but still, he resisted. He kept half-wishing, half-fearing that Fujita might show up at the gym, lower-back tattoo in full display, in whatever inherently revealing outfit that was apparently required for the gym.

And working out gave him more energy, which meant more random, unaccounted-for erections. That was good, of course, because the better condition he was in, the easier it'd be to have sex, "be a real boy," so to speak, rather than a porn-obsessed simp. But it'd be a tricky balance: how would he know when his mind was purged completely of porn's insidious influence or his dependence on his hand's touch for arousal? He couldn't risk another humiliating wipe-out like last time, but nothing good could come from waiting and waiting, from the pressure mounting. He could tell the next girl he dated that he was waiting for marriage, he half-joked to himself. That wouldn't fly in godless San Francisco, where the relatively rare, professional and desirable sex-starved heterosexual women were under-pursued by the even rarer professional and desirable heterosexual men.

Getting hard and feeling pleasure wasn't the cause of the incidents, he told himself (already, they were obscured into "incidents"), it was cumming, that's what it was, so he could touch himself but not allow himself to cum. But then he thought of Gamay: affixed helplessly, as if pinioned to her chair, her whole body shivering, spasming violently, choking on the frothy spittle that dripped from her unseen face, desperately facing starward.

Ethan habitually signed into MFC to check her profile, and again, she was never on, and her last broadcast date stayed the same.

Ethan had watched her die, and he had killed her.

He was convinced, he realized, that he was to blame. It didn't matter that it was, by every sane account, physically impossible. He was spiritually guilty, morally condemned. No, he told himself, he hadn't known, how was he to know?

No, don't look back. He couldn't do that. He couldn't bring Annie, Amber, or Jana back, and for Gamay, he was only speculating.

It was lonely in his apartment at night. Law school was horseshit: this wasn't a full-time job, this wasn't all-consuming. He could coast, do his outlines, get his mediocre grades.

He could study more, but that was depressing and likely pointless. He had a little text rapport going with Fujita, and he wondered if she was wondering whether he was going to ask her out. But he needed to purify himself first, strengthen himself, physically and morally, before he would ever attempt to.

There were movies, and reading, and little travels, and cooking healthy food. And it was one night after he'd made dinner, cleaning up his dishes and checking his inventories for his next planned meal when he indistinctly thought about his old utensils pantry, opened it up and immediately smashed it closed.

He smelled and breathed it in before he oriented his thoughts to realize what he'd seen. Oh God. Oh God. A poor little white mouse, snout smothered in glue, body contorted at an unnatural angle, unable to pivot away from its own shit. He didn't want to look, but he swore he saw pink threads of what could only be intestines peeking out the side, whether the poor animal's intentional, frightened doing or a result of its continued efforts to escape, he couldn't know.

God. He opened the drawer and his sin was laid before him. The trap quivered and shook gently, the mouse was still alive. He slammed his eyes shut, they burned hot, and again he imagined Gamay, spasming and shivering to death with nothing but the indignity of her nudity, and all the pent-up shame, guilt and confusion compounded to where he fell down to his knees and wept. Weeping for a mouse for falling into a trap that worked as intended, that he'd set up. He never wanted it to work, he just wanted to console himself by "doing something" for a nuisance he didn't really mind, and positioned the peanut butter at the far end of the trap, thinking the little guy might just have a snack. How childish and stupid.

Ethan couldn't just keep the drawer shut. That's not how he could spend his life: slamming the drawer shut. Problem? Slam the drawer shut, go about his life.

Sinuses clogged from crying, he filled a large mixing bowl with water. Fucking old apartment, only options were burning hot or ice cold, so he balanced the two to something slightly warm, maybe soothing. With a gloved hand he took out the trap – saw just how much stringy shit spooled out of the insensible beast – and held the trap under the water, face averted the whole time. Whether it was truly seen or not, in his mind's eye he fixated on the last image: the water pressure extending the mouse's eyes out of their sockets, little white protruding nubs.

He held the trap under for minutes, long enough to make sure the mouse had to be dead. Ethan drained the water, threw the trap-and-mouse into a plastic bag, and, before going outside to the dumpster, decided to throw out the mixing bowl, too, even though he was sure he could clean it properly. He deserved to lose something of his own as penance, even if just this cheap mixing bowl.

His head felt clammy for the rest of the night. He showered but that didn't help. There was a way to seek solace, he knew, that had always been there, an endless ensorcelling sea of it, an avenue that had never yet failed to quell doubts and quiet his mind.

But no, no. He refused. He refused. He thought of Annie, even though he meant nothing to her; he thought of Jana, even though he barely knew her; he thought of Fujita, what could but would, he knew, never be.

Sleep, just go to sleep. But how long the night stretches, the night stretched on practically forever, and he knew he would touch himself to distract from the anguish. In darkness, physicality left behind, he allowed himself to become convinced of his evident overreaction: it was only a mouse, right? A nuisance, right? What, allow it to shit around his apartment forever? He'd never use a glue trap again, he'd stay firm on that, that was compromise.

Only with going to the gym had he found any sense of joy in just being alive, blood flowing, heart pumping, muscles flexing.

This was part of it, physical pleasure, wasn't it? Before he was even convinced, he was touching himself again, but he dissolved any discrete thoughts of any distinct people or scenarios. Somehow some images slipped through the murk, suddenly there was a glowing, full-lipped Fujita – and how excited he felt, his porn-starved imagination so good at its own realistic renderings, he could see her fully-nude, tattoo included, bent over and looking back at him, beckoning – and he was about to cum and he stamped the image out, stamped it out again when it recrudesced. It kept flaring back, and he was cumming and made himself think something else to protect her, hide her, let some other image pop in and blot her out, anything, something cataclysmic and dramatic she could hide behind, so when he woke from this fugue state, semen covering his hands, he had a mind full of a spasming, desperate woman and a feces-covered, disemboweled and drowned mouse.

*

This anxiety-hangover, he assured himself, must greatly outweigh whatever pleasure that last night's masturbation brought him. It must always be the case, yet still, he did it, didn't he? If that were true, why'd he continue down this path; unless, there remained the obvious answer, that compulsive masturbation was far more exciting, comforting, welcoming, and pleasurable than reality.

This time, he didn't need Arkady to tell him the breaking news. He was checking his Hastings email compulsively. Since there was no email at 9 a.m., which is the official start of the business day, he deluded himself that nothing happened. 9:47 begged to differ.

The terse email: fellow student Kate Fujita had been rushed in the early morning to St. Mary's Medical Center for a "medical issue" but was in "stable condition," and given the recent events, classes were again cancelled for the week. Three deaths and this sudden "medical issue" must have the University brass terrified of some kind of undiagnosed new contagion, and they wouldn't be taking any chances.

It was one thing to announce the death of a fellow student; but a hospitalization, for a medical issue. Did she give permission? She had to have, right, which meant she truly must be in a "stable condition."

Ethan was the first person to visit her in her hospital bed.

She closed her eyes and, crying without tears or even noise, hugged him graciously upon entry. He hugged her tightly, trying to squeeze out the poison her appreciation dredged up inside him, the burning wish to transport the scars upon her face to his own organs, punish himself for his insolence, for his insolence in even insisting upon being alive.

He was sure he wasn't making her feel any better with the way he instinctively looked down, looked away, cried profusely. It almost became that she was consoling him, perhaps taken aback by this depth of sentiment and feeling she had never imagined he possessed. It wasn't that bad, objectively, she told him, and he told her the same, although how could he know, as he couldn't entirely see her face, the left side bandaged up quite extensively. The bandages, she assured him, covered much more than the actually affected area.

And she took it with amazing stoicism, or perhaps Fujita was just still shellshocked by the whirlwind of events. Or, perhaps, it wasn't that bad for her right now, because right now she was isolated from the judging world, laid up in a hospital bed, being attended to and mollycoddled by staff and the expected parade of friends and well-wishers. Here she wouldn't need to strive, or work, or fear about her well-being, her perception, her status. How would she feel when the context changed, and she found herself dragooned inside this new life, a life where strangers gave her sideways glances, when people desired less to be in her presence, when society's doors wouldn't open so easily, when the mottled and warped flesh under those bandages caused children to gape and shudder?

How did this happen, Ethan insisted, which perhaps wasn't such an unusual question: surely, wouldn't everyone be asking that? How could this happen to a healthy young woman with no pre-existing conditions? And who would be next? She described how she woke up in the middle of the night, the left side of her face on fire, reached up to find a sliver of her left cheek melted away, as if a spurt of rogue acid just happened to make its way on her sleeping face.

Was it one heavy spurt, followed by a slightly softer one, followed by a few goopy dribbles and drabs, the sociopathic comedian inside of him wanted to ask. He thought of himself last night, doing his best to obscure her face in his mind's eye, frantically clipping the spectral strings that tethered her image to his roiling fantasies.

Fujita would survive, of course. There was reconstructive surgery, and he was surprised, at least for now, at the steeliness of her resolve. He'd never imagined anyone – let alone an attractive young woman with a well-formed face – not coming entirely to pieces at the news that she'd awoken with a fizzing, bubbling scar of unknown origin. Ethan freaked out sometimes when he woke up from sleep and found his eyes a bit dry and his vision blurry, always afraid maybe this was some permanent condition; he couldn't in a million years imagine the terror of being awoken from what felt like a phantom razor slash to his face. Maybe Fujita felt some kind of gratitude that it wasn't actually some midnight invader.

Fujita thanked him so much for her visit, and he told her that after this, they were definitely going out for drinks. She seemed to fade for a moment, and that was the first time he'd ever seen her look embarrassed or not in control, as perhaps the thought of a social outing with obvious undertones of a planned date served to remind her of the real world, the other patrons of the bar who'd double-take, not have the insider information on what they were seeing.

"I mean it," Ethan insisted, trying to conjure the irreverent playfulness of times past, "you aren't getting out of a date with me, Fujita! Not this time!" He babbled. And she smiled and said "okay Kerman."

*

And Ethan was back home and beside himself, a flurry inside him, this is what a nervous breakdown must be. He felt an uncontrolled, manic energy, but not anything that could be translated into actual physical movement: rather, his mind was racing a mile a minute, a raging rapid, and all other aspects of himself drowned, unable to control the geysers flowing within him. It was like downing ten cups of coffee while being anaesthetized and immobilized, the only evidence of this mania these frantic rambling thoughts.

He had to kill himself, didn't he? Isn't that what it had to be? On this otherwise normal, crummy day, where there was laundry to do and meals to make and reading to catch up on, and, oh, by the way, a mandate to end himself. How could that be?

To think, his family had no idea what was going on, and what could he explain, what explanation could he ever give? They'd live the rest of their devastated lives utterly baffled. He couldn't do that to them? He deserved to die, but there would be fallout, the old collateral damage, as they said. Fujita, even, would be devastated; maybe some part of her would darkly wonder if he was just desperate to get out of that promised date.

Ethan looked at his sharpest blade. It was a bit funny he still had to climb up to the top of his fridge to grab it. To die, like how he killed Jana, Annie, Amber, that mouse.... was it disrespectful to include that mouse in there, not really comparable, but it was evidence of his depravity so it stayed in the equation.

He knew he could never stop touching himself. What, would he never masturbate again, was that realistic, really?

And if he overcame all this, whatever this was, what was the reality he'd be saving himself for: a life of mediocrity. Mediocre grades at a mediocre school to flail and struggle into an industry he wanted no part of, an industry of strife and stress and pressure, to toss dollars in vain against an ever-expanding, insurmountable beast that was his debt. The high-drama of being a plague contagion seemed downright appealing in contrast; at least there was something novel in that. For now, he was just another statistic, a pinpoint on a downward trending graph.

It was funny, come to think of it: what a putz he'd become, yet still, it was he who had this "power," if that's what you could call it. Orgasmic explosions so powerful they maimed faces and ended lives. Were there others like him, promising but arrogant young people who'd, through avoidance or timidity or just blind inertia squandered whatever they had and made a wreckage of their life, only to have something like this – this nonsense power

– as their reward? Was there some overconfident business student in a third tier toilet program somewhere out there, humbled by reality, drowning in debt and self-doubt, whose reward was, what, maybe the ability to make a single stair disappear at will from a staircase; or cause birds of different species to fight one another; or something else that could match the sheer stupidity of his own secret power?

Because his power was, after all, a power. In a sense, he killed people with his thoughts; or at least thoughts manifested in some type of simple, self-contained action. That wasn't nothing.

The rationalization process had begun, he knew. The excuse-making. He wasn't going to kill himself. To put that blade to his wrists, to experience the searing, burning pain, the panic that must have felt like no other, the hopeless, gasping-brain pangs of disbelief, of regret. No, he couldn't do that.

Perhaps this was his reward, of sorts. Mired in debt, dissatisfied with his life choices, disappointed with himself . . . but wasn't that just that old arrogance talking again, that quiet belief that sustained him his whole life that, without evidence, he was just somehow better than others?

That wasn't fair, he reminded himself. He worked hard in college, he worked hard in law school, too – even if the results didn't speak for themselves, he had that gunner reputation last semester for a reason, didn't he? – he made mistakes, true, but he'd always been precocious and responsible, hadn't he, where his colleagues had squandered, took the easy way out, made excuses, whereas he'd always been reliable and goal-oriented, hadn't he? He never caused Mom and Dad distress, never overindulged, never truly idled, didn't still live at home like many people he knew still did....

And Ethan could feel the gears shifting, the outlook changing, under the guise of reevaluating things and thinking things through. Perhaps this was a gift, perhaps this was a reward, and why shouldn't he take whatever rewards he could from this gaping maw of a life. Was the student-loan industry scam his fault? No, but he was one of its inextricable victims. Was this law school curve his fault? No, and he worked harder than most and still fell victim to it. Had he known the inner-workings and reality of law school status before he enrolled in this middling law school? No, and you know these schools do everything in their power to hide the truth. All these societal systems to which he'd been sacrificed to, and no one lifted a finger, no one gave two shits, and now he's the one bestowed with a remarkable gift and this is his response, to relent and panic and beg forgiveness? How could he have known. How could he have known?!

Well, now he knew. He would try and stop, and do the best he can, but he must learn to forgive himself if he failed.

Yes, the excuse making had begun. The greatest thing about being rational is it allowed you to rationalize anything, didn't it? He hadn't asked for this gift, but to destroy himself over it did no one any good.

(Well, maybe it would have done Jana, and Amber, and–)

And then he thought, why question it, why question this, why torment himself, just let the rationalizing happen, let his brain molt in that direction, how glorious that would be, how glorious it would be to feel proud about something, something unique and powerful and mine alone, something this corrupt, unequal society couldn't take from me. Let that self-hatred and self-doubt just wither away, and what would he be left with except something truly fantastic, his own little secret, his own little magic. Life couldn't grind this out of him, the world wouldn't take this from him, this something all his own, his power, that somehow made him – no, proved – that he was separate and distinct, just as he'd always suspected.

<u>NOTES</u>

This is probably the most J.R. Hamantaschen-y story of all time, don't you think? The title was taken from a line in Albert Camus' *The Plague*. I thought of this story as a J.R. Hamantaschen version of *Crime and Punishment*. All the J.R. trademarks are there: self-loathing, depression, delusions of grandeur, a granular focus on a small-scale twist, weird mental and sexual hang-ups, revulsion of bodily functions, all on display in one of my more unsavory premises. It's a fitting potential last short story in my most likely last collection, and truly a "for me" type of tale. I mean that was the kind of story that someone writes when they've come to terms with not writing short stories anymore, amirite?

There's a lot culled from real life here. Let us count the ways:

(1) Like Ethan, I lived in Northern California for a few years while attending a graduate program (not Hastings School of Law), and obsessed and catastrophized over my levels of debt. My sardonic, cynical-yet-well-meaning New Yorky humor didn't go over well.

(2) The incident in the beginning of the novella – a homeless person shitting outside my apartment building – is ripped from the headlines of my life, and a moment I obviously did not forget. Whereas it seemed all my classmates lived in some gilded neighborhood, I lived in a fairly rough area where stuff like . . . well, where stuff like homeless people diarrheaing in front of your apartment and throwing batteries at you or your friends when you don't give them money occasionally happened. (We ducked.) Ethan's feelings of resentment toward his classmates weren't hard to tap into, let's just say that.

(3) Given (1) and (2), I devolved into a sad little self-reflective universe of ceaseless pontificating and squalid semi-hermitage. The efficiency apartment I described matches the one I lived in, and the whole building actually burned to the ground not long after I moved out.

(4) I too had mice in my apartment, set up a glue trap that was given to me by my landlord while hoping it would never work and tried to assuage myself that I was "doing something" while trying to sabotage it, and was terrified when it worked and still feel quite guilty about the poor little guy, who met the same end as the mouse in the novella.

(5) The relationship between Ethan and his friend Arkady was very similar to my main friendship during my graduate school years. Like them, our foolhardy decision to enroll in graduate school and doom-and-glooming about what the future held was a constant source of conversation. I've fallen out of contact with my "Arkady," unfortunately, as he stopped responding to emails. That's a shame because I hope he's doing alright, and I really nailed his manner of speech. I mean, it's pitch perfect. I'm not sure what happened to him, although I would not be surprised if he decided to go back to his native county to avoid the Sallie Mae mafia.

But that was all the past, in my early twenties (when I was working on several of the stories that would later appear in *You Shall Never Know Security*, my first collection). I'm obviously all fine now, problems solved.

Well, we're wrapping up here. Now you know so much about me whereas I know nothing about you! All I can say here is that hopefully one day in the likely very distant future you will see a J.R. Hamantaschen novel, and I'm still doing my weekly podcast titled "The Horror of Nachos and Hamantaschen," and you can still reach out to me at jrtaschen@gmail.com with whatever you have to say.

I appreciate your readership, even if you since regret it.

Your pal,

J.R.

Printed in Great Britain
by Amazon